IVY SMOAK

To all the girls out there who think their voices are too small to be heard.

You're braver than you know.

Don't give anyone the satisfaction of silencing you.

CHAPTER 1

Thursday

No.
Never.
Nunca.

The words rolled around in my head as I stared at Isabella's father. *My father. This isn't happening.*

I turned in my seat and watched Mrs. Alcaraz and Matt getting smaller and smaller through the back window of the car. There was no way in hell I was going anywhere with this man. Whether he was blood or not, he'd never be my father. I'd never be a Pruitt. And this was kidnapping. I grabbed the door handle and pulled, but the door didn't budge.

"Calm down and put your seatbelt on," Mr. Pruitt said.

Screw you. "Let me out." My voice came out shakier than I hoped it would.

He ignored me.

I tried the handle again and then banged on the glass. "Let me out!" I couldn't even see Mrs. Alcaraz and Matt now. *Let me out of here.* I slammed my palms against the glass.

Mr. Pruitt put his phone down. But instead of saying anything, he just stared at me. His eyes felt like ice on my skin. The trail they made down my body made me shiver. "You look like her."

I swallowed hard. "My mom?" For just a second, I didn't want to flee. I wanted to ask him a million questions about my mom.

He frowned. "But you don't look at all like me." He squinted his eyes. "There's a doctor waiting at the apartment. He'll run a paternity test just to make sure. And other tests to ensure that you're…clean." He said *clean* the same way he'd said *ethnic* when referring to Mrs. Alcaraz being my guardian.

I didn't even want to know what he meant by that. And it didn't matter. I'd refuse any tests he wanted to perform. Mrs. Alcaraz was my legal guardian, not him. "What apartment?" I asked. Would Matt know where he was taking me? Matt knew the Pruitts. He could help sort this out. He would come get me. *I hope.*

Mr. Pruitt ignored my question, his eyes still scanning my face like I was a puzzle he couldn't solve.

"Where you live?" I asked. It was a stupid question. Of course he was referring to his home. Some people in New York referred to their homes as apartments. Which didn't sound at all homey to me. Despite the fact that it was a stupid question, I asked another equally stupid one. "With…Isabella?" Something constricted in my throat. This couldn't be real. I couldn't be related to her. Did he have a wife that was just as hateful as his daughter? Were there any more demon siblings I didn't know about?

He eyed me coolly.

No, his home would most definitely not be homey. It couldn't possibly be if someone who lived there had such a cold, hard stare. And he already had a perfectly hateful daughter to go home to, so he didn't need me. "Look, I'm glad that you decided you wanted to get to know me," I lied. He was sixteen years too late. "But…this isn't the best time. It's actually the worst possible time." Mr. Pruitt knew that already. He'd taken me from my uncle's funeral and didn't seem to feel any remorse. I blinked away the tears threatening to escape my eyes. "I'd appreciate it if you'd let me out."

He looked back down at his phone like the conversation was over. But then added, "My family doesn't know about you. I need time to sort out this mess. So you'll stay put until I say otherwise."

So that's what I was to him? A mess? That was fine, I didn't want to be his anything. But if that was the case, why the hell wasn't he letting me go? There was really only one logical reason. "I'll save you the trouble," I said. "I don't want anything from you. I don't need your money. Or your help. I swear I won't even tell anyone that you're my father, if that's what you're worried about. I just want to go home." I tried to think of something else I could add so he'd get the point.

"Home to that dingy apartment with a woman who barely speaks English? I'm saving you."

"I don't need you to save me."

The car pulled to a stop in front of a high rise that looked like any other newer building in the city. Tons of glass. Cold hard lines. If that was where Isabella lived, I didn't want to touch it with a ten-foot pole, let alone go inside. He couldn't make me. He couldn't do this.

"Your mother is dead," Mr. Pruitt said. "So is your uncle. You have no money. No prospects. Nothing. You'll thank me later. And in the meantime, you'll stay here. I'll be in touch shortly."

One of the bodyguards opened my door.

I looked back at Mr. Pruitt who was focused on his phone again. "You're not coming with me?" The thought of entering Isabella's apartment without her father was more terrifying than entering it with him.

He ignored me as the bodyguard gripped my arm.

"You can't just leave me here," I said.

Before Mr. Pruitt could respond, the bodyguard hauled me out of the car. He slammed the door shut and the town car pulled back onto the busy city street.

I tried to yank my arm away from the bodyguard, but his grip tightened on my bicep.

"Let me go or I'll scream at the top of my lungs," I said.

He pulled me toward the building.

"Help!" I yelled.

A few passersby looked my way but then kept going.

Are you serious? I was being kidnapped and people were just looking the other way? What the hell was wrong with New Yorkers? If screaming didn't work, maybe pleading with the enemy would. "Please, just take me back to the church. It's my uncle's funeral."

No emotion crossed the bodyguard's face at all. I might as well have been talking to a brick wall.

"There's still a reception being held in the hall. I need to go back."

He looked over his shoulder where Mr. Pruitt's car had just disappeared. "I'm sorry about the funeral. But I can't take you back."

"Please." I felt myself breaking again. I couldn't handle this right now. I needed to be back at the church. I needed to say goodbye to my uncle. I needed to put the yellow rose down on his coffin, just like I had with my mother's. I needed to be there. I had to be there.

"One thing you should learn fast. The Pruitts get whatever they want. So if you don't willingly go inside right now, I'm going to have to force you to go in. I don't want to have to do that. I don't think you do either."

I didn't move.

"Look at it this way, kid. The sooner you come with me, the sooner this will all be over."

That finally sounded like something I could get behind. And him calling me kid reminded me of my uncle calling me kiddo. Maybe the testing wouldn't take that long. Maybe I could get back in time for the burial. Maybe, maybe, maybe. But the longer I waited, the longer it would take. I let the bodyguard guide me into the building. A chill ran down my back as I stepped onto the shiny marble floors. The air was colder inside than it was outside. But I didn't think it had anything to do with the temperature. I was in Isabella's territory now.

The Pruitts get whatever they want. I was hoping this bodyguard was right. Because there was no way in hell Isabella wanted me as a sister. As soon as she knew I was in her home, she'd demand that I leave. It wouldn't take long at all. I could already picture the scene in my head. She'd scream and throw a fit. Probably make fun of my outfit and threaten to make me disappear. And then I'd be able to go home to the Alcaraz's. Everything would go back to normal.

I ignored the tears pooling in the corners of my eyes. Normal? Normal would be back in Delaware with my mom. Normal would be watching a movie with my uncle. There was no more normal.

The bodyguard escorted me through the lobby. The man at the concierge desk smiled at us like it was normal for a huge man to be pulling a teenager through the building. It was tempting to tell him I was being kidnapped. But his smile and general air of not caring about my obvious kidnapping weren't leaning in my favor. I just needed to get into Isabella's apartment and make sure she knew I was there. It would all be over soon.

The elevator doors dinged open. I stepped on and tried to ignore the feeling that I was entering the gates of hell.

CHAPTER 2

Thursday

The elevator doors opened to an apartment that was as cold as I expected. For just a second I held my breath, as if breathing the same air as Isabella would turn me into a monster like her. Or maybe I was just scared that she'd appear out of thin air and spit on me. Or worse. I didn't want to be here. I couldn't be here. Before I could beg to be taken back down to the lobby, the bodyguard ushered me forward.

Shit. But I didn't fight him. I was resigned to my choice. Because as much as I didn't want to ever interact with Isabella, I needed her to throw a hissy fit and throw me out of her apartment. And that involved finding her. I glanced into the living room we were passing. It didn't look like anyone lived there. There wasn't even a snuggly blanket on the untouched couch. Yet, I knew she was here. I could feel her presence. She was the reason why a chill had just run down my spine. She was the reason why I kept glancing over my shoulder. "Where's Isabella?" I asked.

The bodyguard ignored me as he steered me past the kitchen and down a hall.

Everything was white and pristine and...impersonal. There wasn't a single picture of Mr. or Mrs. Pruitt or Isabella on any of the walls. *Maybe he hates Isabella as much as I do.*

We stopped outside a bedroom. There was a man in a white lab coat in the room. He turned toward me. "You must be Brooklyn Pruitt," he said. "I'm Dr. Wilson. If you could please take a seat." He gestured toward the edge of the bed he was standing beside.

There was a lot wrong with this situation. But one thing stuck out the most. "Sanders," I said.

The doctor raised his eyebrows.

"My last name is Sanders, not Pruitt."

"Ah." He made a note on the file he was holding. "This won't take very long, Brooklyn. I just need to run a few tests." He set down the file and lifted a needle.

There was no way I was entering that room and sitting on a bed while a stranger either gave me a shot or took my blood. "No, that's okay. Actually this is all a big misunderstanding. I don't want anything from Mr. Pruitt."

Dr. Wilson cocked his head to the side. "You don't want to know if he's your father?"

I hesitated. I was pretty sure he saw it too. But then I shook my head. "No." I took a step back and ran straight into the bodyguard.

He looked down at me with a hard gaze.

What was my plan here? Run past him to the elevators? There was no way I'd be able to escape this buffalo of a man. And even though the bodyguard didn't say a word, I had a pretty good idea that his hard stare involved some kind of threat. I didn't want to find out what it was.

Honestly, I hadn't been to the doctor in ages. My mother didn't have insurance. I couldn't remember when my last checkup was. Maybe in middle school. What could it hurt to let Dr. Wilson run a few tests? My mother died too young from heart disease. My uncle too young from lung cancer. Wasn't it better if I knew I was healthy?

I looked up at the bodyguard like he could read my thoughts. But I'd only known him a few minutes longer than I'd known this doctor with a needle. It wasn't like I had a lot of options on who to trust.

The only encouragement he gave me was a nod of his head toward the doctor.

I pressed my lips together and turned around.

The doctor smiled. "Really. It'll only take a few minutes."

I slowly nodded my head. "I don't mind making an appointment and coming in at a more convenient time," I said. I was stalling, even though I couldn't think of a single way out of this.

"I'm a family doctor. Your father pays me good money to be on call. Trust me, I don't mind." He chuckled and the sound made me feel a little more at ease. "When was your last period?" he asked and looked back down at his file.

Okay, not at ease anymore. Who just randomly asked such a personal question with zero segue? I could feel my cheeks turning red and I looked over my shoulder at the bodyguard. He didn't make eye contact, but he also didn't move. Apparently he was going to be here for this too.

I swallowed hard. "A few weeks ago."

"It started or ended a few weeks ago?"

"Started." What kind of doctor's visit was this?

"Wonderful." He wrote it down while still balancing the needle precariously in his other hand. "Come in, come in, don't be shy."

My feet guided me into the room even though my head was screaming no. The sooner I did this, the sooner it would be over. I answered the rest of his invasive questions. I tried to slow my rapid heartbeat when he scolded me for my heart racing. And I grimaced when he drew blood.

"I should have your results by tomorrow morning," he said. "I know your father wants them as quickly as possible, and I'm not one to keep him waiting."

"Alleged father." I was still holding out hope that I wasn't related to this demonic family. I touched my arm where the doctor had left the cotton swab and strip of tape.

"All will be clear soon," Dr. Wilson said. "Did you have any questions you wanted to ask me before I head out?"

How could I be related to someone so cruel? How could my mother have fallen for a monster? Would I become one too? I shook my head.

"Very well." He finished packing up his things, gave me one last smile, and disappeared out of the bedroom.

I went to stand, but my head started to spin. I immediately sat back down on the bed.

"Whoa, take it easy," the bodyguard said. He took a step forward like he actually cared if I fainted. "You need something to eat. What would you like?"

I just stared at him.

"I can go grab whatever you want. Just pick something."

"Anything?"

He nodded.

"My legal guardian makes great empanadas. Can we go there to eat? I can show you the way."

"There's a great Mexican place down the street. I'll be back in a few minutes." He turned and disappeared down the hall.

For just a second I sat there in silence. And then I heard the ding of the elevators opening and closing. He'd left me all alone in the Pruitt's apartment. Which basically meant he'd given me my freedom. *Oh thank God.* I needed to get the hell out of here.

I stood up and my head spun again. *How much blood did that weird doctor take?* I pressed my hand against the doorjamb as I made my way out into the hall. My fingers trailed the pictureless walls while I kept myself upright.

I hit the elevator button and waited. And waited. I hit it again and realized that there was a keypad.

The little hairs on the back of my neck rose and I turned around. I could have sworn someone had been watching me. But the apartment was empty and lifeless.

I slammed my fist against the button again. How could they leave me in here without the code to get out? What if there was a fire? I swallowed hard, knowing it probably wouldn't bother my alleged father if I died. Wouldn't that be convenient? He wouldn't have to tell his wife or real daughter about me. I'd just be…gone.

A chill ran down my spine and I turned around again. "Isabella?" I hated how much my voice shook.

No one responded.

There were three ways out of here. My Isabella freak out plan, cracking the elevator code, or finding a phone and calling for help. All of them involved exploring the apartment. If there was an office somewhere, I might be able to find Mrs. Pruitt's and Isabella's birthdays or something. One of them could be the code. There also might be a phone in there. I liked both of those options better than actually running into Isabella herself.

I made my way back down the hall and past the bedroom I'd been in earlier. There was a hallway bathroom that was bigger than my bedroom at my Uncle's apartment. Another empty bedroom. A master bedroom that was just as unlived in as the other two rooms. I walked up to the last door and turned the knob. It was locked. I'd checked every other possible room. There had to be something in this one. Or…someone.

I knocked on the door.

Nothing.

"Isabella?" I called.

No response came.

I tried the door handle again and then pressed my ear against the door. It was completely silent on the other side.

"You're not allowed to go in there."

I jumped. I hadn't even heard the bodyguard come in. He was holding a few brown paper bags and I could smell the cheesy, fried goodness from where I was standing. I couldn't remember the last time I'd eaten. It was hard to make yourself eat when all you wanted to do was cry. I ignored the audible growl of my stomach.

"Where are Mrs. Pruitt and Isabella?" I asked.

He just stared at me.

"Is Mr. Pruitt even married? Does he have other children?"

He squinted his eyes at me like I was some kind of puzzle he didn't understand.

This wasn't working. "I need to make a phone call. My friends will want to know that I'm safe." My stomach growled again.

"We'll discuss it after we eat."

After *we* eat? My curiosity made me follow him. He started to unpack takeout container after container.

"They didn't have any empanadas," he said. "I wasn't sure what else you liked."

I sat down and lifted the lid off the closest container. It was filled with a bean burrito and rice that were both still steaming. Bean burritos were one of my favorites. *He bought me all this food because he didn't know what I preferred?* I stared at him as he grabbed a second bean burrito and started eating it. Was it one of his favorites too? He was significantly younger than Mr. Pruitt. He couldn't be more than mid-twenties. His hair was dark like Mr. Pruitt's and Isabella's. "Are you his son?" I asked.

He started choking. "What? No." The way he said it made it seem like the thought truly disgusted him.

Being related to the Pruitts disgusted me too. I pushed some of the rice around with my fork. I wasn't hungry anymore.

"He's not that bad."

I looked back up at the bodyguard. "Isabella is."

He finished chewing his bite. "I'm not supposed to talk about his family with you."

For some reason that was better than him denying that Isabella was horrid. "What's your name?"

"You can call me Miller."

"Is that your first or last name?"

"It's just what you should call me."

That was vague. But Miller sounded like a last name to me. "What's your first name?"

I could have sworn he was trying to hide a smile. "Eat your food, kid."

Kid. I felt that stab in my heart as I remembered my uncle. Would that feeling ever go away? I got it when things reminded me of my mother too. It was like someone was following me around with a knife, constantly jabbing at my heart. I wasn't sure it would ever stop.

"Fine. Make your call. Two minutes. Then you eat." Miller slid his cell phone across the table. "But you're staying here tonight. So there's no point in asking someone to come get you."

"Okay." I grabbed his phone and slid out of my seat. I wasn't allowed to ask someone to come get me. But that was fine. Because the only person I wanted to talk to right now was someone that would just show up anyway. Because that was what he always did. He'd figure out a way to get me out of here. He'd fix this. He had just as many resources as Mr. Pruitt. I dialed the number and put the phone up to my ear.

"Hello?" His voice was rigid and cold like he was in the middle of an argument. For a second I wasn't even sure if it was him. But I'd memorized his number by heart.

"Matt?"

"Brooklyn? Is that you?" The anger in his tone was gone. It was just that familiar warmth I'd grown used to. Hearing him say my name like that made my tears start again. I turned away from Miller so he wouldn't see.

"It's me." I tried to stop my tears so I could have a coherent conversation. Recently Matt's arms around me were the only thing that could calm me down. He'd held me as I fell asleep every night after my uncle's death. I couldn't be here tonight without him. I couldn't do it. I needed him.

"Where are you?"

"I'm at the Pruitt's apartment." Technically I didn't ask him to come. But I could still feel Miller staring at me.

"I'll be right there."

I gripped the phone tighter in my hand. "Thank you." *Please hurry.*

"Are you okay? He hasn't hurt you?"

Was Mr. Pruitt violent? I gripped the phone even tighter. I wouldn't put it past him. He was certainly uncaring. "I'm okay." I looked over at Miller and my untouched food. *I'm not. I'm really not.* "He had a doctor run a few tests to make sure I'm his."

I heard a car door slam. I'd never seen Matt drive before. He was always riding with James. I couldn't imagine James assisting him in this, even though Matt swore James was sorry about what he'd done. Humiliating me in front of the whole school and then coming to my rescue? It didn't seem like a realistic jump.

Matt's parents had been at the funeral. Would they help? Would they even think this was an issue?

I heard Matt tell someone where to head.

"Are you with someone?" I asked.

"Rob. He borrowed James' car."

Something about the way he said *borrowed* sounded a lot more like *stole*.

"Don't worry, Sanders!" Rob yelled. A car honked. "We're coming to save you!"

Matt and Rob were coming to save me from being trapped in Isabella's home. It was such a preposterous thought that I almost laughed. But instead "I love you," tumbled out of my mouth.

There was a long awkward silence.

So long that my eyes burned. And my throat felt parched. And I couldn't breathe.

"We'll be there in ten minutes," Matt said.

"Okay." Maybe we could just pretend I never said it. I could take it back. I could...

"Brooklyn?"

"Yeah?" I closed my eyes tight, wishing I could rewind time.

"I love you too."

I could already hear Rob making fun of him. The call ended, but I kept the phone pressed against my ear. Matthew Caldwell loved me. For just a second, my heart didn't feel so broken.

CHAPTER 3

Thursday

I waited for Matt to come. And waited. And waited. Ten minutes turned to an hour. An hour to two. Two hours to three.

Miller showed me back to the room that the doctor had been in. I didn't bother getting ready for bed. I just laid down and stared at the ceiling as three hours became four. And four became five. I stared at the ceiling waiting for Matt to come. But he never did. And my already broken heart broke a little more.

***

There was a knock on my door and I turned my head to see Miller walk in.

"Did you sleep okay?" he asked.

No. But there was no point in telling him how pathetic I was. That I didn't know how to fall asleep without Matt's arms around me. That somehow sadness gave me insomnia. Matt had an uncanny way of lifting my spirits just to crap all over them. It wasn't the first time that he'd let me down. It was just the first time he'd let me down immediately after dropping the L word. "Yeah," I lied.

"Mr. Pruitt will be here in about 30 minutes. There's some things for you in the bathroom so you can shower and freshen up." He left before I could respond.

I slowly sat up and made my way to the huge bathroom. The water pressure in the shower was amazing. The shampoo smelled like a million bucks. And I hated all of it. I just wanted to be able to go back to Kennedy's house. I quickly dried off, ran my fingers through my hair, and pulled on the same clothes I'd worn to my uncle's funeral.

As much as I wished Matt would appear last night, I also wished that I wasn't a Pruitt. The first wish didn't come true. So the second one had to. The universe owed me this. Just this one tiny thing. After everything that had happened in the last few months? Yeah, it definitely owed me. I made my way out into the hall.

But the universe hated me. Mr. Pruitt was standing in the living room holding a freshly pressed Empire High uniform. That couldn't be a good sign. I didn't think I'd be allowed to go back after my uncle died. He was the only reason I was a student there. So if Mr. Pruitt was holding that uniform, it either meant he was really nice and somehow persuaded the board to let me keep attending through the end of the semester. Or I was allowed to attend because... I swallowed hard. *No. Please God, no.*

He smiled, but it seemed forced. "Did you sleep well?"

I liked him less than I liked Miller. So I didn't bother sugarcoating it. "No. I didn't sleep at all."

"Me either."

We both just stared at each other. I tried to ignore the fact that he may have said that to imply that we were more similar than I thought. I didn't want to inherit anything from him, including insomnia. Including a ticket to Empire High. Including half my freaking genes. But instead of saying any of that, I just kept staring. *Don't say it. Please don't say it.*

"Good news," he said with that same fake smile. "You are in fact my daughter."

I was pretty sure I was grimacing.

"So…" he cleared his throat. "Classes start in half an hour. I'll have someone stop by this afternoon to take your measurements. But in the meantime, Isabella said you could borrow this one." He draped the uniform on the back of the couch.

He wanted me to wear a uniform that belonged to Isabella? Was he kidding? There was no way that his daughter was okay with that.

He smiled again. It almost seemed like it was a new action for him, it looked so forced. But he was trying. I could tell he was trying. He wasn't nearly as cold toward me as he was yesterday. And yet…I still didn't like him. Not even a little bit.

"Miller will escort you to and from school," he said. "I'll officially present you to my family tonight at dinner. So make sure the stylist gives you something to wear for that."

"I…no." I shook my head. "I don't want measurements. I don't want dinner. I don't want any of this. Please just let me go back to Kennedy's place."

"I'm afraid that's not possible. But Miller will also grab all your old things this afternoon and set them up in your new room so you'll feel more at home. Speaking of which…what's your favorite color?"

"My favorite…what? No, I'm not moving in here."

"I know. You're moving in with us."

I just stared at him. "Right. Moving in here." I pointed to the bedroom down the hall that I had no intention of ever calling mine.

"This isn't my home." He laughed.

Then what the heck was it?

"I'll see you tonight. You'll have a busy afternoon, so don't make Miller wait long for you after school. And Isabella said to make sure you sit with her at lunch. She's excited to get to know you better. She's always wanted a sister."

I was pretty sure I vomited a little in my mouth. There was no way that anything Mr. Pruitt had just said about his daughter was true.

He turned to leave.

"Wait."

He stopped but didn't turn around.

"Why are you doing this? Why can't I just go back to the Alcaraz's place? Please. We can have dinner once a week or something to get to know each other. Just…not…not this. Please, Mr. Pruitt."

"You're my daughter." That was his only reply before he stepped onto the elevator. He didn't even look back at me.

That one fact alone wasn't enough. Not when I knew the truth. He didn't want me. He told my mom to get rid of me. I wasn't the daughter that he wanted.

"We need to get you to school before you're late," Miller said and lifted up the uniform.

"I'm not wearing that. We need to swing by Kennedy's place so I can grab…"

"There's no time." He shoved it into my hands. I looked down and the tag was still on it. Isabella had so many uniforms that she didn't even need to wear all of them? I only had one Empire High uniform. And it was second-hand. I'd never even touched a new one before.

I shook my head. "I can't do this. I can't be related to him. Can't we run another test? Maybe they mixed something up at the lab?" I tried to hand the uniform back to Miller.

"He's not that bad," he said, just like he had last night.

But I didn't believe him then. And I didn't believe him now. When I'd asked him if he was related to Mr. Pruitt, he'd almost choked on his bean burrito. I'd seen his face. I'd seen the truth. Mr. Pruitt was horrible. He was just like his daughter.

I could refuse to go to school. Throw a fit. But even thinking about it made me feel like I was already becoming Isabella. I didn't want to be anything like her. And if that meant not getting what I wanted right now…then so be it. "Just give me one second," I said.

Besides, there was a silver lining in all of this. I'd get to see Kennedy. And Matt. At least I didn't have to worry about Matt suddenly hating me. I'd told him I was at the Pruitt's house. And…I wasn't. Apparently. So him not showing up was because of that. Not because he flaked.

I was in Isabella's uniform and in the car before I could change my mind. *It's going to be fine. It's going to be fine. It's going to be fine.* I said it over and over again until we pulled up outside of Empire High.

"Have a good day at school, kid," Miller said.

"You too." I cringed.

But his laugh made me smile for the first time all morning. I climbed out of the black sedan. I wasn't sure if it was my imagination, but it felt like everyone was staring at me as I stepped out onto the sidewalk.

My smile quickly evaporated. No, I wasn't imagining it. Heads were literally turning in my direction. I looked down at the ground and hurried up the stairs. Before I even reached my locker, Kennedy threw her arms around me.

"Are you okay? I can't believe Uncle Jim didn't tell you that you were related to Isabella. Does everyone already know? It seems like everyone already knows." She gave someone an evil glare before pulling me into her arms again. Instead of demanding answers to her onslaught of questions, she just let me rest my head against her shoulder. "It'll be alright," she said and squeezed me harder.

She didn't need an answer. She'd always been able to read me.

"My mom will figure it out," Kennedy said. "She has a meeting with the lawyer that filed the paperwork for her to be your guardian this afternoon. It's going to be fine."

"I'm related to Isabella," I mumbled into her shoulder. "Nothing is fine."

Kennedy laughed. "And you are truly the better sister in every sense of the word. Sweeter. Smarter. Prettier."

God. "I'm a Pruitt." I shook my head. "I can't believe I'm a Pruitt."

"No." She held me at arm's length. "Your mom raised you. You're a freaking Sanders. Always have been. Always will be."

I felt my bottom lip start to tremble. "How was the rest of the funeral?" I couldn't believe I'd been forced to miss it. That wasn't something Mr. Pruitt could ever heal. He'd taken saying goodbye away from me. All the fake smiles in the world wouldn't make me forget.

"I was a little distracted trying to figure out what happened to you. But it was beautiful. Uncle Jim was really loved." Now it looked like she was going to cry too. "I miss him so much."

"Stop it. You're supposed to be holding me together."

"I know." She wiped away any tears before they could even fall. "It's just been a really hard week."

"I know. I miss him so much."

"Ahem," someone said from behind us.

I closed my eyes and prayed that it wasn't Isabella. Even though I already knew it was. It took every ounce of energy I had left to unwind my arms from around Kennedy.

Isabella was standing there, surrounded by her minions, with a smile as fake as her father's. "Hey, Sissy."

Sissy? So…fake friendly was how she was going to approach this? Great. "Hey. I should get to class."

"Not so fast." She flipped her hair over her shoulder. "I wanted to invite you to sit with me at lunch. You can both come, I guess," she said and smiled at Kennedy too.

I knew the friendliness behind the lunch invite was fake. She knew it was fake. But she was still doing it. And I was beyond shocked. Apparently the only person Isabella listened to and respected was her father.

"Um…" I didn't really know what to say.

"Come on," Charlotte said. "It's going to be so much fun getting to know you better."

This was the same minion who always got me in trouble in class. The same one that said she'd make me *disappear*. She was almost as bad as Isabella. Almost.

"Maybe another day," I said.

Isabella flashed that smile at me again. "Daddy wants us to get to know each other better." She reached out and grabbed my hand. "Pretty please? I've always wanted a sister. And that new blazer looks so cute on you. I'm so glad it fits. Oh my goodness, I just realized we're going to get to share all our clothes!"

Ew. Just…ew. "Yeah, sure." All I wanted was for her icy fingers to release me.

"Great. Later, babes." She blew us each a kiss and then clicked away in her high heels.

"Daddy?" Kennedy said and pretended to gag. "Gross."

"Yeah." I opened up my locker and pulled out a few things. Most of my books were at Kennedy's place.

"We're not really going to sit with her at lunch, right?" Kennedy asked. "Because all that was over the top fake. And if I hear her say Daddy again I will actually hurl. Especially if I'm eating."

"I was thinking the same thing."

"Okay, good. I just wanted to make sure you weren't buying it."

"Definitely not."

She pulled a folded-up piece of paper out of her blazer pocket and handed it to me. "Before I forget…Matt summoned you."

I laughed. "How do you know that?"

"I accidentally read it."

"Accidentally?"

She shrugged. "He wants you to meet him outside."

"But class is about to start."

She winked at me. "Looks like you're not going to your first class today. Later, babes." She blew me a kiss just like Isabella, pretended to gag again, and disappeared into the crowded hallway.

The bell was going to ring any minute. I opened up the note.

I think we have something more important to do than first period. Don't leave me hanging. I can only steal James' car one more time before he completely loses it.

I folded the note and slid it into my blazer pocket. He didn't have to ask me twice. I thought being back at Empire High would be comforting. But it just made me miss my uncle even more. I kept thinking I'd see him like it was a regular day. Just thinking it made it hard to breathe.

Matt was the only person who could make me feel better. Missing a class or two was worth it if I could spend the morning in his arms. Or whatever he had planned. It would certainly be better than this.

CHAPTER 4

Friday

Matt was leaning against the side of James' Benz, staring down at his phone. Him showing up each night after my uncle died was the only thing that had held me together. And if I was being truly honest with myself, just seeing him in the hallways when I first moved to the city had held me together too. Without him I'd still be in pieces.

I ran down the front steps. He looked up from his phone just in time to catch me as I launched myself into his arms.

He held me tight, not letting me put my feet back to the ground. "I'm sorry about last night," he whispered into my hair. "I went to their apartment and Mr. Pruitt just kept saying you weren't there. He wouldn't tell me where you were. He wouldn't even let me up. And then this morning when he left, he said you'd be at school."

"Wait." I unwrapped my arms from around his neck so I could look at him. "You stayed outside the Pruitt's apartment all night?" I stared at the dark circles under his eyes.

"I thought he was lying," Matt said. "I didn't want to leave just in case you were up there. I wanted to make sure you knew you weren't alone. And I called that number you called me from about a million times, but no one answered."

Miller probably wasn't thrilled about all those calls. But I didn't care about Miller. Or Mr. Pruitt being annoyed. Or any of that. Matt had camped out on a city sidewalk because he was worried about me. He wanted to be there for me even though he couldn't hold me in his arms. It was the sweetest thing I'd ever heard of. And that was all I cared about.

He reached out and traced the circles under my eyes with his thumb. "Where were you?"

"I thought I was at his place. But this morning he mentioned that I'd be moving into his actual apartment with the rest of his family. So maybe it was like…his spare apartment?" I didn't know what sorts of weird stuff rich people were into.

Matt frowned. "Why would he have a second apartment?"

"I don't know. Maybe a place to hide his illegitimate children?"

Matt winced.

"I'm kidding. He probably just rented it for the night or something." I didn't want to talk about this anymore. I wanted Matt to distract me like only he could. But I could see the question in his eyes before he even spoke.

"Did he…" Matt's voice trailed off. "Did he get the results from the paternity test back yet?"

Everyone in the whole school was acting like they already knew. But it was probably just rumors circulating from the scene Mr. Pruitt created at the funeral. Matt was the only one that knew about the paternity test. He was the only person left that thought I was still just…me. I didn't want that to change. Especially because I knew what he thought of the Pruitts. He told me Isabella was a disease. Toxic. And that it wasn't just her. Her whole family was the same. Did that make me toxic too?

I took a deep breath and remembered what Kennedy had just told me. "I'm a Sanders. I'll always be a Sanders. But yeah…he's my biological father." I shrugged like it meant nothing. But we both knew that wasn't true. It changed everything. I swore it even changed the way Matt was looking at me. Or maybe it was just my own disappointment that I felt.

He reached out and ran his fingers through my hair.

His touch was so comforting. It helped give me the courage to ask him all the questions that I knew he had answers too. "Is he married? Does he have any other kids?"

"It's just his wife and Isabella."

"Do you know how long they've been married?"

Matt shook his head.

Isabella was older than me. So the odds that Mr. Pruitt was married to Isabella's mom when my mom got pregnant with me were pretty high. Which meant he was a cheater. Did my mom know? I swallowed hard. None of it mattered. I didn't want anything to do with his family. He didn't want me. He'd told my mom so. "I don't want to live with them, Matt."

"And you won't. My mom agreed to meet with your uncle's lawyer along with Mrs. Alcaraz this afternoon. We have a great family lawyer that she's bringing. They'll figure it out. You won't have to spend one night at their place."

I heard it in his voice. What he'd told me about the Pruitts was true. He hated them. And it felt like maybe he hated a tiny piece of me too now. I didn't want to think about any of that. "Thank you for asking your mom to help. I want to hear all about how that conversation went, but right now I just really want to get the hell away from here. Are you sure James doesn't mind that you're borrowing his car again?" Not that I really cared. Hopefully Matt would scratch the paint on his car or leave a ding. As far as I was concerned, James was an asshole. One of my uncle's last days had been spent hearing insults thrown at him from Isabella. And it was James' fault.

"He wouldn't care. But my note was a joke. We're not actually taking his car." He threw his arm around my shoulders and directed me through the small parking lot. "Where we're going, we can just walk."

"So where are we going?" I was actually glad that we weren't driving. Fresh air always made me feel better. If you could even describe any air in Manhattan as fresh.

He smiled over at me as he steered me toward Central Park. "One of my favorite places."

It was like he could read my mind.

For a while we just walked in silence. Eventually his arm fell from my shoulders and he grabbed my hand. I was happy to be walking around Central Park with him and not hiding our relationship to the world. But just thinking about it made me sick to my stomach. I didn't want to go back to school and pretend we weren't together. Not today when it still felt like my world was falling apart. I gripped his hand a little tighter.

"Close your eyes," he said.

I laughed when I looked up at him. The smile on his face was contagious. Any negative thoughts I had were easy to dismiss when I was staring at him.

He reached out and covered my eyes with his hand. "Now keep them closed." His lips lightly brushed against mine. "I'll be right back."

"Wait, what?"

His hand fell from my face.

I reached out for him, but my fingers came up empty. "Matt?"

There was no response. I squeezed my eyes closed, despite the fact that I really wanted to open them. I trusted him. He'd be back. But as the seconds turned to minutes, doubt started to creep in. I remembered that day with him in the auditorium. I'd thought it was some terrible prank. He'd scared me half to death. Today felt exactly the same. My heart was racing and I could feel panic setting in. He'd left me alone in the middle of a path in Central Park. Wasn't that dangerous?

I started counting in my head. Trying to focus on something besides the random footsteps I kept hearing. *Where are you, Matt?*

I screamed when he swooped me into his arms. My eyes flew open.

"You're terrible at keeping your eyes closed," he said.

"You left me."

"I didn't leave you. I just needed to grab something real quick. Now close your eyes."

I followed his directions as he started to carry me somewhere. The farther we walked the better it smelled. I'd barely touched my food last night and I'd been in too much of a hurry to eat breakfast. I prayed my stomach wouldn't make that same embarrassing rumble that it had last night.

Matt stopped walking and set me down on my feet. He put his hand over my eyes and turned me just so. "Here it is," he said. "The best view in the city." He pulled his hand away from my face.

I opened my eyes and smiled. We were standing on a little bridge with water stretched out in front of us.

"I used to come here with my family and feed the ducks when I was little. Sometimes we'd stay in the park so late that we'd eat at that restaurant over there." He pointed across the water at a cute little place. "My favorite part of those days was walking through Central Park after the sun set. Because at night that restaurant turns on tons of fairy lights on their outdoor patio. It lights up the water and looks like the stars. Seeing it makes the city feel more like home."

Matt's house was anything but homey. But he lived in the suburbs right outside the city. So I understood what he meant. No matter where you were, if you could see the stars, there was some sense of familiarity. I'd felt it on the fire escape at my uncle's apartment. Back then I wished I could go home back to Delaware when I stared at the stars. And now? I didn't even really know where home was anymore. Just thinking about the word made me want to cry. My uncle's home had become my home. And now he was gone too.

"I know you lost your family," Matt said. "But it doesn't mean you don't have one."

I could feel my eyes watering.

"Brooklyn Sanders," he said and dropped to one knee.

My heart started racing. "Matt, what are you doing?"

A smile stretched across his perfect face. "Will you…" He reached behind his back.

Was he seriously about to propose to me? Had he lost his mind? We were sixteen. We couldn't be engaged!

"…be my girlfriend?" he asked.

"What is wrong with you?" I said with a laugh. "You scared me half to death." I put my hands on his shoulders when he didn't get up off one knee.

"That isn't an answer." He stared up at me. "I know we've been together for a while now, but I realized we never actually made it official. Will you? Be my girlfriend?"

He was the sweetest person I had ever met. "Yes." I was smiling so hard it hurt. But as I stared down at him, I knew I needed more from him. Because I was barely holding on as it was. And he'd hurt me before. I didn't want him to do it again. "As long as you promise not to break my heart. Because it already feels broken and I can't…" I took a deep breath. I didn't want to cry. He was being wonderful and I refused to ruin this moment. "I can't handle you breaking it too."

"I'll never hurt your heart. You're my forever, Brooklyn." He smiled up at me.

I was pretty sure he looked as happy as me. "Get up," I said with a laugh. I wanted his arms around me.

Instead of standing, he pulled out what he'd been hiding behind his back. And I was relieved it wasn't a jewelry box. "And since you're now part of my family, I thought maybe you could adopt some of my family's traditions." He handed me one of the foil packets he was holding as he stood up. "I know you like to eat healthy. Sometimes you need a little comfort food though. And whatever you don't eat you can feed to the birds."

I pulled back one of the layers of foil and laughed. "I don't think ducks like hotdogs."

"But they do like bread." He tore a piece of bread off his hotdog bun and tossed it in the water. Sure enough, one of the ducks swam over and grabbed the bread in his beak.

I smiled as I watched the water ripple where the bread had been. The duck slowly swam away to find more food.

"You need to eat something," Matt said. "Please."

I looked up at him. And for the first time I could see how worried he was about me. I could feel him staring at the dark circles under my eyes. I wouldn't be surprised if I had lost some weight. The last few days had been terrible. I smiled to help reassure him, and then took a bite of the hotdog. "Oh my God, this is so freaking good."

He laughed. "I thought you might like it."

"Where did you even get this?" I looked over my shoulder at the empty path.

"The best hotdog vendor is just right over there." He pointed down a path in the opposite direction, but I couldn't see any farther because of the trees. "There's so many things about this city that I can't wait to show you. Stick with me and this will feel like home in no time."

I tried to hide my smile as I took another bite. I had no problem sticking with him. The issue was that it was hard to stick to someone who wasn't allowed to be seen with you in public. "So you told your mom about me, huh?"

He nodded.

"How did that go?"

He smiled. "Good. She saw you at the funeral. She said you were pretty."

I wasn't sure why, but I was expecting a bigger reaction than that. I couldn't be someone that his parents approved of. But then something hit me. He'd told her after the news broke. He told her after everyone believed I was related to the Pruitts. I suddenly wasn't hungry anymore.

"But we mostly talked about how we can get you out of staying with the Pruitts," he continued.

"Wait. Aren't your parents friends with them?"

"No, not really. They used to be in business together, but then they had a falling out."

Interesting. "Is your mom the only person that knows about us?" I was happy he finally told someone. But it made me a little sick to my stomach that he only fessed up after he realized I was related to a monster. A rich monster, but still. And I was happy that Matt wanted to ditch class with me this morning. But I wasn't an idiot. He'd given Kennedy the note to give to me so we wouldn't be seen together. And we were in the middle of central park because no one at school was allowed to know I was seeing him. All of it was twisted. And it resulted in my stomach twisting into knots. I was his girlfriend right here right now, but I wouldn't be at school later today. He'd keep his love for me hidden.

"I told Rob too. Technically *he* borrowed James' car yesterday so we could find you. And that combined with the fact that he overheard our conversation on the phone...I didn't have much of a choice."

He didn't sound mad. But he also seemed to purposefully avoid the word love again. I was worried I knew why. It felt like my heart was beating too fast. I didn't want him to take it back just because I was a Pruitt. I didn't want anything to change. But everything already had. I'd given him a condition for being my boyfriend – to not break my heart. Maybe he had a condition too – we'd be in a relationship only if I could get away from the Pruitts. "Did you tell Rob why you're keeping our relationship a secret?"

He lowered his eyebrows as he looked down at me. "You know I can't."

Honestly, I didn't. That was the whole problem. I knew there was some secret that Isabella was holding over his head. I knew it would hurt James if it came out. But that was all I knew. "Didn't Rob ask why?"

"I think he just assumed it was because of...you know. Our economic differences."

Economic differences? Something about the way he tried to make it sound fancy pissed me off. It was almost as if he was confirming why he finally told his mother about me. Because maybe we weren't so economically different now. "You mean because I'm poor and you're rich?" I took a step back from him. "You let him think that you're embarrassed to be with me?"

"That's not..."

"That is what you did. And that is what he thinks. Of course that's what he thinks."

"Hey." He grabbed my hand and pulled me into his chest. "I just need a bit more time. But I promise I'll figure it out, okay?" He cupped the side of my face with his hand. "I could never be embarrassed of you. I love you."

I couldn't exactly stay mad at him when he said that. I had worried he wasn't going to say it ever again. But there it was. "I love this hotdog," I said and took another bite to stall. He'd told his mom so he could get me out of this mess with Mr. Pruitt. And he'd already told me our relationship had to be a secret for now. Nothing had changed really. *Except my living arrangements and possibly my last name.*

He laughed. "Anything else you love?"

"This view." I gestured to the water. His stupid perfect face and perfect smile were tipping the scales back in his favor.

"Is that all?"

I smiled up at him. "No." I bit my lower lip, pretending to think. But there was nothing to think about. I'd still love him even if we had to hide from the world for a few more days. Or weeks. God, hopefully not months. I stared into his chocolaty brown eyes. "Oh right. I'm pretty sure I love you too."

He leaned down and kissed me.

And I knew I could never stay mad at him when I craved his lips this much. I was pretty sure the taste of cinnamon on his lips somehow soothed my soul. And I needed more. I gripped the back of his neck.

He groaned into my mouth and pulled away far too soon. "As much as I want to keep doing that right now, I have one more stop on our adventure before we need to go back to school. I have a test third period that I can't miss." He grabbed my hand before I could respond and we started running through Central Park.

***

We did need a car to get to our second destination. So he hailed a taxi. He didn't ask me to close my eyes this time. And as we made one turn after the next, I knew exactly where we were going.

When the taxi pulled up in front of the cemetery, I was already having a hard time keeping a straight face.

He knew how important it was for me to say goodbye. He knew how much missing the second half of the funeral weighed on me. He was already fixing everything.

I tried to hold it together as Matt opened the taxi door for me. And as he held my hand, winding me through the tombstones until we got to a patch of fresh dirt. And as I forced myself to not fall to my knees.

If Matt wasn't here, I knew what I'd probably do. I'd cry big ugly tears. I'd sit on my uncle's grave and have a conversation with him, like I so often did at my mom's gravesite. I'd cry some more. I'd pray to go back in time. And most importantly, I'd tell him I was sorry that he gave up his last several weeks on earth to take care of me. I owed him everything.

But Matt was here. So I didn't do any of those things. Instead, I just stared. I stared at the gravestone and tried to tell myself to hold it together. But in the end the grief won. I wasn't strong enough to hold it in. I missed my uncle. I missed him so fucking much. And I regretted that the whole time my uncle was here with me, I'd been missing my mom instead of appreciating him. He'd never know how grateful I was that he'd taken me in when I didn't have anyone else. He'd never know.

Instead of saying a word, Matt just held me so I wouldn't fall. He let me cry all over his school blazer. I was pretty sure some snot got on there too, but he didn't even flinch. When I'd sat on my mother's grave, I had never felt so alone in my life. I expected the same thing to happen right now. But it didn't. Because I wasn't alone. I had Matt.

I closed my eyes hard and tried to stop the tears from falling. And my thoughts latched on to the first distraction, even though it wasn't a great one. My mother didn't want me to know who my father was. My uncle wanted to keep me from it too. Even Mrs. Alcaraz wanted to protect me from whatever went on under the Pruitts' roof. Standing there on top of the dirt I was devastated. I couldn't even stop the tears streaming down my cheeks. But mostly? I was terrified. Because I didn't know why I needed protection from my own father. I knew his daughter was cold and cruel. It was likely Mr. Pruitt was those things too. But what if it was something worse?

Right now the only thing that felt worse, though, was knowing what moving in with the Pruitts would mean. It would force me to see Matt even less. There would be no late-night sneaking into my bedroom. Or coming over for dinner. I'd be living with Isabella…the one person that wouldn't allow our relationship. She'd take Matt away from me for good. And he was the only thing holding me together.

But there was nothing to say. Matt knew it too. He was doing everything he could to fix it. So I just had to wait. But I'd never been good at that. I'd never been good at wasting time. Because time was the only thing that was limited.

I started to cry harder. I cried for my uncle. I cried for my mother. And I cried for myself too. Because it was then that I realized that I had been wasting time. I'd been taking life for granted. The one thing I knew for sure I couldn't. I'd wasted away the time I had with my uncle. My last real home. My last real semblance of normal. It was gone before I ever really got a chance to appreciate it. And now I had to spend all my foreseeable time with a family I hated. A family who might have secrets worse than their cruelty. A family everyone who loved me tried to protect me from.

"He knew that you loved him," Matt said and kissed the top of my head. "He knew."

I was too embarrassed to tell him that I was mostly crying because I was scared.

CHAPTER 5
Friday

Felix was great at making me laugh. But the thought of going to gym and running when all I wanted to do was curl up in a ball and cry made me actually feel ill. Besides, I didn't need anyone else staring at me with concern. Kennedy kept poking me during English and asking if I was okay. And I was tired of putting on a smile and lying. I wasn't okay. I wasn't even a little bit okay. I couldn't focus in class. I couldn't stop thinking about what would happen after school today. I felt paralyzed.

The nurse smiled at me when I made my way into her office. "Oh my, your face is so pale. Tell me what hurts."

"It's just cramps," I said and sat down on one of the beds. It was the second time I'd come in here with the lie. Eventually she'd have to catch on. But I just hoped she wouldn't today. I made a show of lying down as I clutched my stomach. *Please let me stay here for the rest of the day.* Scratch that. The rest of the year would be preferable. Maybe I could just sleep here too. It would be better than living with the Pruitts.

She nodded at me, but this time she didn't hand me a Midol or a glass of water. "Cramps *again*?" she asked.

Apparently the gig of fake periods was up. I didn't even know what to say. I didn't have enough energy to continue with the lie or make up a new one. So I just lay there and tried not to cry. Maybe she'd think I was depressed and just leave me alone. But I had no such luck.

She sat down on the bed next to me. "Your uncle was a great man."

Did she think this was going to help me? I closed my eyes tight, trying to keep the tears at bay.

"I think that maybe a visit to the counselor might be better than camping out here. I can write you a note if you want."

I kept my eyes closed. "I just need a few minutes," I said. "Then I'll go back to class, I promise."

She patted my shin. "Okay, dear. A nap always makes me feel better too."

The mattress shifted when she stood up. And I waited until I heard her typing on her computer before I let myself cry as silently as I could.

***

When she patted my shin again, I jolted awake. A few minutes had definitely turned into a lot more. My stomach growled and she smiled.

"Lunch is about to start," she said. "How about you go get some food. If you want you can even bring it back here."

I wiped the sleepy out of my eyes as I sat up. "No, that's okay." A normal lunch actually sounded really great right now. Felix could make me laugh without the run. And Kennedy and I could talk without having to whisper. It was exactly what I needed.

Before I could leave she handed me a slip of paper. It was an appointment with the school counselor.

"If you can't make that time work, just stop by her office and she'll reschedule you."

"Yeah." I shoved it into my blazer pocket without even looking at the time on the sheet. I didn't need a school counselor. I wasn't worried about grades or getting into the right college. I was worried about sleeping in enemy territory and not having any family left. "Thanks." I hurried out of her office before she had a chance to reply.

The cafeteria was already buzzing when I walked in. I was glad Matt had left me a salad in my locker like always because the lines were still long. I sat down in my usual spot across from Kennedy. She was laughing at something her boyfriend, Cupcake, had just whispered in her ear. It was tempting to grab her camera and snap a photo of the two of them. They looked so happy. And I was happy for her. I really was. But that didn't mean that I wasn't horribly sad right now. I sniffed and hoped they hadn't heard.

"You made me run all alone," Felix said as he plopped his tray down next to me.

I laughed, but it sounded forced with the counselor note burning a hole in my pocket and the sadness stabbing at my heart. "You really expect me to believe you ran without me instead of sitting on the bleachers?"

"I kinda like running now. What, you think I did it every day just to hang out with you?" He winked at me. "Please, that would be desperate."

My smile felt genuine now. "Quite desperate."

He laughed. "Well, I will admit that running is better with a partner. Where were you?"

I didn't want to talk about my tearful slumber at the nurse's office. And it was like Kennedy could feel the awkwardness in the air because she jumped in to save me.

"Dessert is always better than running." She held out her latest box of treats from Cupcake.

Felix grabbed one of the pastries and took a big bite. "Can't disagree with that."

I pushed my salad around with my fork instead of starting with dessert. Just seeing the name *Dickson and Son's Sugarcakes* made me want to cry. My uncle had loved them, but I'd been forcing him to eat healthier. I'd been ruining his last few weeks without even knowing it. If I'd been dying, I would have wanted all the dessert I could get too. My stomach twisted into knots.

"Sissy, aren't you going to sit with me?" Isabella asked from behind me. The words themselves were friendly. But the way she said it wasn't.

The knots in my stomach grew tighter. I turned around and looked up at her smiling face. "Maybe Monday?" I said. "I really just need a normal day."

She rolled her eyes. "Why be normal when you can be elite?"

Was that a serious question? I didn't want to be elite or however else she described herself. Besides, Cupcake and Felix were just as elite as her. And Kennedy's personality was a thousand times more elite than Isabella's.

"Come, come," she said like there was no possible excuse to what she'd said. "And I'm sorry, Kennedy. I forgot to tell everyone and I was only able to save one seat."

"Really, Isabella," I said. "Monday would be better…"

"But Daddy insisted." She stuck out her lower lip, like that would somehow affect my decision.

Ew. I heard Kennedy pretend to gag and tried not to laugh.

Isabella cleared her throat. "Trust me, Sissy. You don't want to upset Daddy. If I tell him that I invited you to sit with me and you refused…well…you don't want to see what happens when he gets mad."

My heartbeat kicked up a notch. No, I really didn't want to know what her father was like when he was mad. *My father.* Yeah, I was definitely going to be sick.

"You could sit with us," Kennedy said. "There's a seat right there." She pointed to the one on the other side of me.

"No. I sit at *that* table." She pointed to the Untouchables' table. And for the first time I looked over too. Matt was staring at me so intensely. The two seats across from him were empty. Which meant…I'd be sitting with Matt at lunch for the first time since we started secretly dating. And now that we were officially boyfriend and girlfriend? That didn't seem like such a bad thing. I wouldn't be alone over there. I'd have him.

"It's just a table," Kennedy said.

Isabella ignored her and looked back at me. "Last chance, Sissy. Or Daddy will be hearing all about this."

I lifted my salad off the table. "Okay."

"You don't have to sit with her," Felix said and grabbed my arm.

It wasn't that I wanted to sit there. I didn't. Not even if it got me closer to Matt. But I had to go. Because I was already scared of Mr. Pruitt. "It's just for today," I said. I

- 44 -

looked at Kennedy and hoped she could read my mind. I didn't want her to think I was ditching her. I'd figure a way out of this from here on out. But today? I might have to spend all weekend with the Pruitts. I didn't want to start that off on bad terms.

I followed Isabella over to her table. She sat down across from Matt, and I sat down next to her.

Matt was staring at Isabella now. But not the way he stared at me. He looked beyond pissed off. I hoped he never looked at me like that. No one said a word to me when I sat down. And I felt myself shrinking. I focused my gaze on my salad and hoped the next twenty minutes would hurry up already.

The person next to me cleared his throat up. I looked up. I hadn't even realized that Isabella had made me sit right next to James.

He gave me a sheepish smile.

I looked back down at my salad.

"Brooklyn." He nudged me with his shoulder. "I'm really sorry about your uncle."

"Thanks." *I'm sorry, I'm sorry, I'm sorry.* I hated those words. And he wasn't sorry. Because if he was, he'd apologize for what he did to my uncle. Not apologize for his untimely death. *I'm sorry? Screw you.*

"And I'm sorry about what happened in the cafeteria before. I didn't know about your mom. I swear."

That sounded a little more sincere. But I knew the only reason he was apologizing was because Matt probably made him. And I didn't want to play games with any of these people. I just wanted to go back to my normal seat.

"Why else would I live with my uncle? Did that thought really not cross your mind?"

He ran his fingers through his perfect hair. "Honestly?" he asked, lowering his voice. "I wasn't thinking at all. That was the whole problem." He stared down at his food like I had been doing a moment ago.

Something about the action pulled at my heart. He was actually sorry. I could feel it. And ultimately, he was Matt's friend. Which meant...wasn't he going to be mine too? And maybe, just maybe, a little bit of the reason I was angry at him was because he was part of the reason keeping Matt away from me. But that was Isabella's fault, not his. And I couldn't put that blame on him. I needed to stop blaming him for something he knew nothing about.

"It's okay," I said and nudged him with my shoulder like he'd done to me when I first sat down. "Maybe we can just start over? I'm Brooklyn." I awkwardly held out my hand.

He looked back up at me with a smile on his face. "Deal." He shook my hand.

"Sissy, you're not making a good first impression," Isabella said. "Introduce yourself to everyone, not just James."

I let my hand fall out of James'. "Oh. Um. Hi, I'm Brooklyn." But I was pretty sure everyone already knew me. Isabella and her minions had been trying to make my life hell ever since I started going here. Matt obviously knew me. Rob knew me. James knew me. I'd even met Mason once at a party.

"Sup, Sanders?" Rob asked as he shoveled some pasta into his mouth. "Are you really related to Isabella? That's...wild."

"Yeah." I wasn't sure why it came out as more of a question.

"Sucks to suck," Mason said with a laugh. "Just kidding. So you're friends with Felix and Cupcake?" He nodded at the table behind me.

I didn't turn around. I knew they were probably staring over here. And I was worried if I turned around I'd run back over to them. "Mhm." I took a bite of salad and prayed that no one else would speak to me.

"So now that we're friends, does that mean I get a discount?" asked Mason.

I stared at him. First of all, he'd only ever spoken a few sentences to me. The only things I knew about Mason were that he was the Empire High quarterback and he liked to smoke pot on the weekends. That didn't make us friends. And second of all...what was he even talking about? A discount on drugs? Because Felix stopped selling. *Mason must realize that.* "I don't know what you're talking about." I took another bite of lettuce.

Mason put his elbows on the table and leaned forward. I couldn't help but think that somewhere out there, someone would have fainted at the sight of such a brash disregard for etiquette. "Of course you do," he said. "Everyone knows that you and Felix are...close."

The word "close" was laced in innuendo. It felt like my lettuce went down the wrong pipe and I started coughing. I swallowed a huge gulp of water and tried to ignore

Matt's angry gaze. "We're not that close," I said as soon as I could speak again.

"Great, you met Mason," Isabella said.

For a second I thought she was saving me from the awkward conversation. But then she opened her mouth again.

"And speaking of close, this is Matt," she said. "We're super *close*." She said the word the same way Mason had. "And I think you two have a class together, right?"

I looked up at Matt. The intensity from his gaze was gone. He nodded. "Yup." He didn't offer anything else.

Everyone at the table was quiet.

James was kind to me. Rob was his usual funny self. Mason was...at least interested in talking to me. But that one simple *yup* hurt more than I wanted to admit. A few hours ago he'd asked me to be his girlfriend. And now he couldn't even look at me? I wasn't sure if I was cut out for a secret relationship.

"The other night when Matt and I were hanging out...he told me that you two and Rob have a group project together," said Isabella. "It'll be so fun now that we can all just hang out and work on it at my place. Sorry...*our* place." She smiled at me with all her sweet insincerity.

They were hanging out together the other night? As in one of the nights he'd come over to my uncle's apartment to hold me while I cried myself to sleep? Had he held her too? Right before he held me? I tried to take a deep breath. "Yup," I said, mimicking my brooding silent boyfriend who was a fantastic actor. So fantastic that it stung. So fantastic that I wanted to cry. So fantastic that I hated him in that moment.

"Sorry, I shouldn't have said hang out. Because you're not friends with any of them. It's just a group project that you were forced to do together. That's what Matt told me the other night when we were hanging out just the two of us alone in my room. Right, Matt?"

He didn't respond. He just sat there and stared at her. *Her.* Not me. I tried to swallow down the hurt.

"What the hell, Matt?" Rob asked. "We both know that's not…"

"Rob, no one cares what sarcastic thing you have to say," Isabella said. "So keep it to yourself, yes?"

"Fuck off, troll," he said.

She ignored him and turned to me. "Speaking of things that don't belong to you."

"No one was speaking of that," Mason said with a laugh.

She glared at him and then back at me. "Speaking of things that don't belong to you," she repeated. "I need my blazer back. Right now," she added when I didn't respond.

"What?" I didn't have a spare. Her dad said I could wear this one today. "The only other one I have is back at Kennedy's house. And I'll get in trouble if I'm not wearing it."

"Yeah, but I got a spot on mine." She pointed to absolutely nothing on one of her lapels. "You can't expect me to walk around like this all day."

I shook my head. "I don't see anything."

"Oh." She laughed. "That's right. I'm sorry. It was actually on yours." She lifted the milk off her tray and poured it down the front of my blazer before I even realized what she was about to do.

"What the hell?" James yelled as he shifted me out of the way. But he was too late. The front of my blazer was soaked. I was too shocked to say a word. But I heard Matt's silence loud and clear. And I felt James' arms around me when it should have been Matt's. Matt was the one that was supposed to defend me. He was supposed to be on my side. I was supposed to be able to rely on him.

I stood up, letting James' arms fall from my waist. I looked down at my borrowed blazer. The one her father said it was okay to wear. Tears stung the corners of my eyes, but I refused to cry in front of her.

"Oops." Isabella smiled at me. "Accidents happen. And that's exactly what I'll tell Daddy if you're stupid enough to bring it up. And he'll believe me, because he actually wanted me. Unlike you. And just so I'm perfectly clear. You're unwanted *here* too." She tapped the seat I'd just jumped out of. "So don't ever sit with me again. And stop being so utterly naïve, it's embarrassing. Clearly I was just messing with you by asking you to eat with me. We'll never. Ever. Be sisters. Because you're a garbage person just like your uncle. And I'm a Pruitt. Later." She blew me a kiss and turned back to her friends who were all laughing.

I didn't look at any of the Untouchables. I just turned and ran as fast as I could out of the cafeteria.

"Brooklyn!" I heard Kennedy yell from behind me.

But I kept running.

CHAPTER 6

Friday

The tears streamed down my face as soon as I pushed out of the cafeteria doors. I ran down the hall and into the restroom. I threw my soaked blazer onto the bathroom floor before the milk could get on my collared shirt. And I broke. I leaned against the cold sink and let all the tears I'd been holding in all day come out. I cried and cried so hard that I was gasping for air.

I wasn't at all surprised when I heard the bathroom door open. Kennedy had already been running after me.

"I'm so stupid," I said, moving my hands to cover my face. "I didn't see that coming at all. I'm just as naïve as she said. I can't stay at her house. I can't live with the Pruitts." I wasn't even sure she could hear me through my sobs. "My uncle didn't want me to. He wanted me to stay with your mom. She said she signed all the forms. I don't understand why he's doing this to me."

I jumped when someone's hand that was absolutely not Kennedy's touched my back.

I looked up at Felix. I was surprised at how relieved I was. Because if it had been Matt, I was pretty sure I'd punch him in his perfect face. He was the real reason I felt stupid. He'd just…sat there. He sat there and did nothing.

And I wasn't even sure I was surprised. It wasn't like it was the first time Matt had let me down.

"You're not stupid. You're perfect, newb."

Perfect? I was a freaking mess. But I loved that he saw me that way. Because I'd lost everyone in my life that thought I was perfect. I threw myself into his arms before I had a chance to second guess anything.

He held me tight, like he was the only thing holding me together. And maybe he was.

Being in his arms felt so safe. So warm. So loving. I closed my eyes tight and tried to hold on to this moment. Because I knew I'd need it. If I had to go to the Pruitts' tonight, I needed any happiness I could hold on to.

He ran his hand up and down my back. "And I know you probably thought I was Kennedy, but you know you can stay at my house any time you want. My mom wouldn't care. My parents are never around."

"I may have to take you up on that offer," I mumbled into his chest.

He continued to rub his hand up and down my back. "Stay with me tonight then."

I pulled back from him so I could see his face. Before my life turned upside down, I'd told him I wanted to be friends. He'd agreed, but he said he'd wait for me. For whenever I was ready to be more than friends again. He didn't know about Matt. And I couldn't correct him because Matt said our relationship needed to be a secret. Hell, I'd even said yes to going to homecoming with Felix. But I'd also said I'd go with Matt. And I hadn't sorted any of it out because I could barely breathe, let alone think about any of that.

I thought my heart couldn't hurt anymore. But I was wrong. My life was a mess. Everything was a mess. And I was too worn out to fix anything right now. "I'll call you if I can," I said. I wasn't sure where the Pruitts' home was. I wasn't sure if I'd have access to a phone. But if I was able to leave, I'd go to Felix. I didn't care whether we were dating or not. I just cared that he cared. And I needed him right now. I needed him so badly.

He wasn't my best friend. Or my boyfriend. He was somewhere stuck in between, and maybe that was why it was so easy to share my darkest fears with him. "I lost my mom. And my uncle. I don't have anyone anymore. I'm alone. I'm all alone."

He pulled me back into his arms and rested his chin on the top of my head. "You have me."

I felt my body start to shake with my tears. Felix's words just made me miss my uncle more. *You have me.* It's exactly what my uncle had told me when I'd needed him.

"Is that really so bad?" he asked.

I laughed through my tears.

"And you have Kennedy. If there's one thing I know about Kennedy, it's how fiercely she loves. You have her."

"I wasn't crying because you're one of the only people I can rely on. I'm crying because you offering to be that person is really overwhelmingly sweet. And I don't deserve it. All I do is cry recently."

"Well maybe if you didn't skip gym class I could get you to smile again. Me making you laugh is kinda our thing."

"I'm sorry. I was hiding out in the nurse's office. I wasn't ready to come back here. Everything reminds me of him."

He held me as my tears started to subside. "I know." He ran his hand up and down my back again until I was finally breathing normally.

"Thank you," I mumbled into his chest. "For coming after me."

"I had to race Kennedy, but because of you I'm pretty fast now."

I laughed and looked up at him. "I guess you're welcome?"

He smiled down at me. "It also helped that you ran into the boy's restroom."

"I what?" I pulled out of his arms and spotted the urinals for the first time. "Oh my God, what is wrong with me?"

"Not a single thing."

The way he said it made my cheeks flush.

The bell rang and Felix shrugged out of his blazer. "Here." He held it out to me. "I know you don't want to be any later for class."

"I can't take your blazer. And you're late too," I said with a laugh. I wiped away the rest of my tears.

"I'm always late for class." He shrugged. "Take it."

"You'll get in trouble."

"And I'm always in trouble." He pushed his blazer into my hands. "Call me tonight and I'll come get you from wherever you are, okay?"

"Okay." Matt had promised me I wouldn't have to spend the night at the Pruitts'. But I knew Matt's promises weren't guaranteed. He promised me all sorts of things in the darkness of night. But in the light of day? I wasn't sure he meant a word of it.

I pulled on Felix's blazer. It was way too big, but at least it didn't smell like spoiled milk.

"That looks better on you than it does on me."

I smiled at him.

"I'll see you tonight." He winked at me and disappeared out the restroom door.

If only I was as confident that I'd see him. There was a pretty slim chance I'd be allowed to leave or call him. But I hoped I'd be able to.

I grabbed Isabella's blazer off the bathroom floor. All I wanted to do was throw it in the trash. But I knew how expensive these things were. There was a reason I only had one. Despite the fact that I was already late for class, I scrubbed the milk stain out of the front, hung it up in my locker to dry, and then just stood there in the empty hallway. If I closed my eyes really tight, I could almost picture my uncle standing there too.

***

I was glad it was finally time for my last class of the day. But I was also terrified about what would happen after school. I pictured the Pruitts living in a big haunting mansion like Matt's. *Matt.* I wasn't thrilled to see him either.

He'd been so sweet this morning. But he was able to turn off his affection for me so easily. Like it was just a switch. It wasn't an easy switch to me. And he wasn't just ignoring me in front of Isabella. Matt sitting there and letting her pour milk all over me and call me a garbage person? That was just cruel. And I'd never thought Matt was cruel.

"Hey," Matt whispered.

I didn't look up from the blank page in my notebook. "Hey." How was it possible that I already felt like crying again? I should have been out of tears after this week.

"I'm really sorry about what happened at lunch."

That was a lame apology. "Yeah?" *Because it certainly didn't seem like it at the time.* I wanted to tell him that, but it was easier to stare at my notebook. I wanted to ask him if he was really hanging out with Isabella every night before sneaking into my bedroom. I wanted to ask him if he realized he was being cruel. I wanted...more from him.

"What are you wearing?"

I was surprised that his tone was suddenly harsh. Couldn't he see that I was barely holding it together? I lifted my gaze to him. Yeah, he looked pissed. But he wasn't allowed to be angry with me for borrowing a blazer. I was the one that was pissed with him. "I'm wearing a different blazer. Because Isabella poured milk down the front of mine. While you sat there and did nothing."

"Whose blazer is it?"

Of course he ignored the last thing I said. "Felix's." There was no point in lying. Felix had been the one to come comfort me. Felix was the one that kept showing up. Felix never made me feel alone.

"Take it off."

What? "I can't. I'll get in trouble."

"Take it off, Brooklyn."

ELITE

"And put on what? Your varsity jacket? Oh right…I can't. Because no one's allowed to know about us." For some reason it was really easy to turn my sadness into anger. And it felt good to feel something besides despair.

"Look, I know this whole relationship is supposed to be a secret," Rob said. "But…"

"Would you lower your voice?" Matt said.

Charlotte wasn't even in the room yet. I thought about how Matt just let Rob assume that our relationship was a secret because I was poor. This didn't feel like a secret tryst. This felt like he was embarrassed of me. Honestly, I was embarrassed of myself. What would my mother think of the fact that I agreed to be Matt's dirty little secret? What would my uncle think?

How had I let myself become this person? This wasn't me. My mom had raised me better than this. I was a Sanders. And Sanders women were good at walking away from assholes.

"It's okay, Rob," I said. "No need to worry about keeping it a secret." I shoved my notebook into my backpack. "Because Matt and I are done."

"Brooklyn!" Matt hissed as I stood up.

I didn't turn around as I rushed out of the classroom. No one else said a word. Not a funny comment from Rob. Or an insult from Charlotte when I almost ran into her in the doorway. Mr. Hill didn't even scold me for leaving. I was invisible again at Empire High. I mean, who wanted to talk to the girl that lost her whole family? The girl who was hated by the queen bee, Isabella Pruitt? The girl who cried more than smiled? I didn't even want to talk to that girl. And it sucked that I was her.

It wasn't until I got onto the busy city sidewalk that I realized I had nowhere to go.

CHAPTER 7

Friday

The black sedan pulled up next to me on the sidewalk. I quickened my pace, but Miller was out of the car and blocking my path in a matter of seconds.

"You have an appointment with the stylist in twenty minutes," he said.

I had no idea how he'd found me. Did Mr. Pruitt put a tracking device on me like I was a dog or something? I wouldn't put it past him. I'd been roaming around the city aimlessly for the last hour and his minion had still found me.

The whole time I'd been taking turns crying and seething. Mostly crying. Because I kept reminding myself that a broken heart from a stupid boy wasn't at all comparable to losing the two people I loved most in the world. And the fact that I was even thinking about Matt made my stomach turn with guilt. He wasn't important. He didn't matter. I kept saying those two sentences over and over again like I could convince myself they were true if I heard them enough times. But it was hard to convince my heart that it was fine when it felt like Matt had driven over it with James' Benz.

I tried to sidestep Miller but he blocked my path again.

"What happened to the blazer you were wearing this morning?" he asked.

I stopped moving and just stood in the middle of the sidewalk. "It doesn't matter." *Nothing matters anymore.*

"It does matter. The stylist has a whole list of things you're going to need. And if you lost it, we need to add a new one to the list."

I clenched my jaw. *Lost it?* I didn't just lose items of clothing randomly during the day. I could barely afford this stupid uniform. I'd never lose it. And just the thought made me actually lose my mind. "I don't need any more blazers! Or clothes! Just let me go back to Kennedy's!" Yeah, I'd lost it, screaming at a practical stranger.

"You know I can't do that, kid."

Today the nickname wasn't reassuring at all. Only my uncle was allowed to call me kiddo and make everything better. Not this random security guard. "Don't call me that." I tried to sidestep him again, but he put his hand on my shoulder.

"What happened today?" he asked. "Why didn't you meet me outside the school like you were supposed to?"

"I didn't meet you outside because I have no intention of going anywhere with you!"

"What happened?" he asked again in such a calm voice that my bottom lip started to tremble.

I wiped my angry tears away, hopefully before he could see them. It wasn't like I could tell him about the lunch incident. Isabella's threat had been heard loud and clear. She'd have some alternate story about what happened today. And no one would believe me over her. "Nothing. It's not important," I said.

He pressed his lips together. "I think it is important."

"You're really not going to let me go back to Kennedy's place, are you?" I asked, ignoring what he'd said.

"I grabbed your belongings this morning. It's all in your new room. It'll be just like you're there."

Was he kidding? The Alcaraz's apartment was warm and homey. There wasn't a chance in hell that Isabella lived in a place like that. But there was no point in arguing more with Miller. He was just following orders from the devil himself. I might as well get this over with. One weird stylist meeting. And one awkward dinner. There was no way Isabella would let me stay at her house longer than that. I'd be back at the Alcaraz's in no time. Or at Felix's. I'd go anywhere as long as it was far away from the Pruitts.

I sighed. "Okay. Let's get this over with."

"That's the spirit," he said with a small smile.

We were both quiet as we got in the car. But as the minutes ticked by, I was getting more and more anxious. I leaned forward in the back seat. "What's Mrs. Pruitt like?" I asked.

"Um. Like Isabella."

"And what do you mean by that exactly?" I asked, even though I had a good guess.

He cleared his throat. "You know. A lot like Mr. Pruitt."

Great. I leaned back in my seat. He didn't need to elaborate. I did know. The whole family was toxic, just like Matt had said. I refused to let myself think of Matt as the tall buildings flew past in the window. He didn't deserve to occupy any space in my head. But when I glimpsed one of the entrances to Central Park I wanted to cry all over again. This morning he'd been so sweet. *This morning when no one was watching.*

I was surprised when the car suddenly came to a stop. I'd just assumed we'd leave the city and drive into mansion territory. "This is it?" I asked as I stared out the window.

"Home sweet home," Miller said.

It was an older building, so much different than the modern monstrosity Mr. Pruitt had locked me up in last night. It reminded me more of the outside of Felix's place. I opened up the door before Miller had a chance to. I squinted at the building. Wait…was this Felix's apartment complex? It certainly looked the same. But I didn't re-member his address. Kennedy was the one that knew it.

"Aren't you coming?" Miller asked.

I realized I'd been awkwardly standing on the sidewalk staring at the front doors. "Mhm." I wasn't sure why he'd asked. He'd made it pretty clear that I didn't have a choice in the matter.

The doorman greeted us as I walked into the lobby. The whole building screamed old money. And even though it was definitely restored at some point, it still pos-sessed its old charm. It was the same thing I'd thought when I walked into Felix's apartment building. And I was positive it was the same one. I thought about the way he winked after saying he'd see me tonight. He must have known. I mean of course he knew. You couldn't live that close to evil and not know it.

Why didn't he tell me? Knowing he was close by made me feel so much better. I breathed a sigh of relief while I listened to the elevator music. Yup, it was definitely the same building. Now if I could just remember what number his apartment was. I knew it felt like it took forever to reach his floor. So he had to be pretty high up.

I was barely paying attention when the elevator came to a stop. I followed Miller down the hall, one with the same plush carpet that had been in Felix's apartment's hallway. And when we reached a door that had an uncanny resemblance to the ornate front doors of Empire High, I was 100 percent certain I was in Felix's building. It made me significantly less scared to enter the Pruitts' evil lair.

I was expecting it to look completely modern like Felix's apartment, but the Pruitts had gone in a different direction with their interior decorating. Everything inside looked like it was an antique. There was art in gold frames, fancy vases on display, and even a statue in the middle of the foyer. I just stood there, afraid to move in case I broke something. It reminded me more of the decorating in Matt's huge mansion. Is that why he came over here to hang out with her? Because it felt like his creepy vampire-esque home? I swallowed hard. I didn't want to live here. I already knew I'd have nightmares and never be able to sleep. Even if it had been homey and quaint, I'd still have nightmares living down the hall from Isabella.

"The stylist is upstairs," Miller said. "I'll give you a tour after your fitting."

"Okay." My voice echoed around me. The thought of being alone in the foyer was enough to pull me out of my thoughts. I hurried after him up the stairs. We passed a few rooms and the smell of fresh paint hit my nose. He guided me to the room all the way at the end of the hall. I peered inside. There was a woman with thick glasses and wiry hair standing in the middle of the room with a long rack of clothes. It was an odd sight, but I was more shocked by the room itself.

The room didn't match the aesthetic of the rest of the house at all. Everything inside was light and airy. There was a white fourposter bed with pristine white sheets and a poofy white comforter. There was a matching nightstand and dresser. A huge window was on the far wall with a view of the city. But the most shocking thing of all was that the whole room was painted bright yellow. Almost the exact shade that my mom's kitchen had been.

"Sorry about the smell," Miller said. "The painters just left."

"It's yellow," I said.

"You didn't choose a color when Mr. Pruitt asked your favorite, so he chose for you."

"He chose this color?"

Miller nodded. "If you don't like it, you can just choose a new one and I'll call the painters back tomorrow."

"No. No, I like it." Actually, I loved it. The yellow hue couldn't be a coincidence. Yellow wasn't exactly a safe choice for a teenager's bedroom. Mr. Pruitt knew my mom's favorite color. He chose it because he wanted me to feel like this was home. *Right?* The thought made my chest ache. What else did he know about my mom? What else did he know about me?

"We don't have much time," the stylist said. "I have another appointment in three hours."

Three hours? What was she planning on doing with me for three hours?

"Miller gave me a guess on your measurements so you'd have a few things to wear this weekend. But come, come, so I can get you fitted perfectly." I swore it looked like she pulled a measuring tape out of thin air.

I looked up at Miller. He'd guessed my measurements?

"I'll be back in a bit," he said without looking at me and closed the door.

I turned back to the stylist. Her eyes were magnified by her glasses and it seemed like they were about to bug out of her head. She hurried over to me and started measuring every inch of my body. She rapid fired questions at me about styles I knew nothing about. I wasn't even sure how she was talking because there was a handful of pins sticking out of her mouth.

She forced me to try on every single item on the garment rack she'd brought in, even though I insisted I didn't need anything. And the whole time all I could think about was how did she get this rack of clothes up the stairs? It looked like the metal beam holding all the hangers was about to snap from the weight of all the clothes. She said it was just for stuff to wear this weekend. How often did the Pruitts change in one day?

She tightened a skirt around my waist and put a pin in it. "Perfect, perfect," she mumbled. "I'll alter that one but the next one should fit fine." She handed me a dress to change into.

I stared around at the comforting yellow of the walls as I pulled what felt like the hundredth garment over my head. I stared at my reflection in the floor length mirror. I'd never worn anything so beautiful in my life. My fingers traced the sequins on the shoulder.

"A perfect fit," the stylist said.

I smiled. For just a second, it felt like this random woman was my fairy godmother. And that maybe, just maybe, everything would be okay.

"Wear that one tonight," she said. "Mrs. Pruitt loves red."

The idea that this was my fairy godmother quickly disappeared. Because all I could think about was that Mrs. Pruitt loved red. A shiver ran down my spine. Red was the color of blood. No matter how hard I tried to shake away the image, I couldn't.

CHAPTER 8
Friday

I sat down on the edge of the bed and practically sank into the cushiony mattress. My butt had never touched something so soft before. I sighed. Half my closet and a few of the dresser drawers were already filled with the most expensive clothes I had ever touched. I should have been grateful. But all I felt was…empty.

I ran my fingers across the white down comforter. I didn't need a soft mattress or nice things. All I needed was a home where I was loved. And this would never be it.

I pulled over one of the boxes that had been stuffed in the closet. There were a few school books, some pictures that had been on my walls, and… It felt like something was caught in my throat as I pulled out Matt's varsity jacket. I'd never even gotten a chance to wear it. I'd never even gotten a chance to go to any of his games.

There was a knock on the door and I shoved the jacket back into the box. "Yes?" I said. I didn't know who was on the other side of the door. The last thing I needed was an impromptu torture session from Isabella. Wasn't eating all our meals together enough? And I didn't even want to think about what she'd do if she saw this jacket. I closed the flap of the box.

"Dinner starts in a few minutes," Miller said from the other side of the door. "Do you still want that tour real quick?"

Not really. But walking around the house with him was better than sitting here alone. I smoothed down my dress and opened the door.

A smile stretched across his face. "That dress looks great on you."

I wasn't even sure why I blushed. It was probably part of his job description to be nice to the ladies in this apartment. "Um. Thanks." I tucked a loose strand of hair behind my ear and waited for him to start the tour. But he didn't move. "You mentioned a tour?"

"Yeah. It's just…you need shoes."

I looked down at my bare feet. I could see that maybe it seemed a little silly to be wearing such a fancy dress and no shoes. But I had my reasons. One being the fact that my black flats I'd worn to the funeral pinched my heels and I'd been enduring their wrath for the past two days. I also hadn't unpacked my Keds yet, but I had a feeling that Isabella's parents would appreciate them about as much as she did. And my uncle wasn't here to fix them if they threw food on them. Oh, and then there was the most obvious reason. "But we're inside." The only other thing I'd consider wearing were slippers. And I had a feeling the Pruitts would frown upon that too.

"Right. I'm just letting you know that they usually wear shoes to dinner."

Who wears shoes to dinner? The first answer that popped into my head was Nazis. I'd bet the zero dollars I had that Nazis did in fact wear shoes to dinner. "I think I'll take my chances," I said. I wasn't a Nazi or a Pruitt, and I wanted to keep it that way.

"As you wish," he said and stepped to the side.

I padded across the plush carpet as Miller pointed out a hall bath.

"Is this the one I'm supposed to use?" I figured humoring this arrangement was better than letting anyone know I'd be fleeing to Felix's tonight.

Miller gave me a weird look. "No, you have your own bathroom. In your room," he added when I didn't respond. "Didn't you see it?"

There was another door in my room. It looked just like the one for the closet and I just assumed it was more room for all the garments the stylist was shipping me. "Oh," I said. "Yeah, right. Sorry."

He smiled and continued down the upstairs hallway. He pointed out a few guest rooms. An office. Some locked door that he skipped entirely. He frowned when I tried to open it.

"Just ignore that room," he said.

Okay. Why was Mr. Pruitt obsessed with creepy locked rooms? There was even one in his other apartment. Or rented apartment. Or whatever it was. We'd reached the top of the stairs.

"Isabella's suite and the master suite are on the other side of the hall." He gestured toward the hall that stretched out to the right of the staircase.

It was fitting that I was on the side of the hall with the guestrooms. And not just on that side, but at the very end of it. Like if I was far enough away maybe they could forget I existed.

I realized Miller was already walking down the stairs. I quickly followed and tried to remember every turn that took me from the dining room, kitchen, and the staff kitchen where a few people were busy preparing dinner. And then we made another turn into some kind of sunroom, a small library, a living room, a family room, a second more grand office, a room that just had a piano in it, and a few rooms that I'm pretty sure were just to show off more antiques? Even though the interior design was the opposite of Mr. Pruitt's other apartment, it was the same in that it looked like no one ever touched anything. Did they all just stay in their bedrooms when they were home? Or maybe there was a separate family room reserved for purebred Pruitts or something.

"And that leads to the lower floor where the staff stays," Miller said and nodded to a door.

"Wait, you live here?"

"I'm on duty 24 hours a day. So if anyone ever needs something in the middle of the night, I'm around."

"Don't you…have a family or something?"

He shoved his hands into his suit pockets. "I'm not supposed to discuss that kind of stuff with you."

"Just like you're not supposed to tell me your first name?"

"Yeah." He gave me a small smile. "Like that."

"You know I'm not one of them, right? You can tell me your first name."

He shook his head even though that smile remained on his face.

A bell sounded from somewhere behind me. I was so turned around that I had no idea where we were.

"Dinner is ready," Miller said. "Do you need me to show you the way back?"

I laughed. "Yeah, I have no idea where the dining room is."

"Follow me."

"Do you eat with us too?" I asked as we made our way backward through the tour. This time I didn't try to pay attention. It wasn't like I was going to actually have to stay here.

"No."

"Where do you eat?"

"In the staff kitchen with the rest of the staff."

"How many staff members are there?"

"Well, you met the chef and his assistant in the kitchen. And you know one of the other security guards from yesterday."

Mhm. How could I forget? He was the one that had knocked Matt down on the steps of the church. Although I wouldn't say I *knew* him.

"There's one more guard. One for each family member, but sometimes we have different assignments. And then there's…"

"Wait, so who are you usually assigned to?"

"Mr. Pruitt."

"Oh, I'm sorry."

He laughed.

I hadn't even realized I'd said the words out loud. And he didn't get the chance to tell me about the rest of the staff because we'd wound our way right back to the entrance of the dining room.

I was pretty sure I was wearing the most expensive dress I'd ever worn in my entire life, but the whole family was staring at me like I was a barbarian. I looked down at my bare feet. *I should have just worn the stupid shoes.* The way they were staring, I might as well have been butt naked.

Isabella smiled at me the same way she had right before she poured milk down the front of my blazer. I forced myself not to wince as I let my gaze wander to her mother. Mrs. Pruitt was a spitting image of her daughter. Unnaturally so. The skin on her face looked oddly stretched out. Botox maybe? Or some kind of face-lift? Either way, she was still beautiful. But the way she was staring at me wasn't.

She cleared her throat and set down her wine glass. "If you'd like to eat with us, you'll need the proper attire. Miller, take her back upstairs for a pair of shoes."

"It's fine, Patricia," Mr. Pruitt said to his wife and then looked back at me. "Brooklyn, sit."

I stood frozen on the hardwood floors. What had I been thinking? This wasn't a home. Only homes were for bare feet. I mean, Mr. Pruitt had instructed me to wear a dress. Of course that meant I was supposed to wear shoes. I swallowed hard as I looked back and forth between them. This was an awful way to start this already awkward dinner.

"No," Mrs. Pruitt said. "Just because we let in a stray doesn't mean we have to lower our standards."

Ouch. "I don't mind," I said and took a step back from the dining room. "It's no trouble at all. I'll be right back."

"Brooklyn, sit," Mr. Pruitt said before I could flee. "Miller, get her seat. Now." He snapped his fingers like Miller was a dog.

Miller stepped forward and pulled out my chair for me.

Who treated people that way? I wanted to run. I wanted to be anywhere in the world but here. But wasn't this all kind of going according to plan? Mrs. Pruitt clearly hated me as much as Isabella did. I'd be kicked out in no time.

"Thank you," I said to Miller and sat down in the chair.

"That'll be all, Miller," Mr. Pruitt said. "I'll let you know if we need anything else."

Miller nodded and retreated into the kitchen. I would have done anything to be allowed to run away with him.

Mrs. Pruitt took a huge gulp of her wine and glared at her husband. "So this is how it's going to be now? Utter chaos? Darling, we have standards."

"It's a pair of shoes," he said and gave me a smile that he probably thought was kind. But it looked like a grimace. "She probably just didn't have any that looked good with the dress. Right, Brooklyn?"

"Actually, I just thought…" I let my voice trail off as I eyed the salad in front of me. Were they going to serve a three-course meal during a family dinner? This was not the place to tell him my opinions of what a home should be like. Because I wasn't even staying. "Yeah," I said. "It's that."

"See." He took a sip of his wine. "All will be remedied by tomorrow when her order arrives. Now let's try to enjoy this delicious salad."

Mrs. Pruitt rolled her eyes so hard I thought they'd pop out of her head. "I think we should get a second opinion."

"On what? The salad?" He popped some lettuce in his mouth. "It's delicious."

"No, not the salad. On whether or not this child is actually yours."

"Dr. Wilson ran the test twice," he said.

"I mean a second opinion from another doctor. Obviously."

"Dr. Wilson has been our primary care physician for years. Are you saying you don't trust him now?"

"I trusted you too."

"It was years ago, Patricia. And we've already had this conversation. Several times. You've exhausted it to death. The last thing we need is to hash it out again at dinner in front of our daughter."

I wasn't sure why I did it, but I braved a glance at Isabella. She was smiling like this was the most entertaining thing she'd ever seen. I looked back down at my salad. I wasn't hurt by the fact that he'd said daughter instead of daughters. I didn't want him as my family either.

Mr. Pruitt cleared his throat. "Where are my manners? Brooklyn, this is my wife, Patricia. And you already know Isabella."

"Mhm." My voice sounded so small. "It's nice to meet you, Mrs. Pruitt."

She just glared at me. I was pretty sure if I was smaller she'd flick me away like the nuisance she saw me as. "I'd like to say the feeling is mutual. But it is most definitely not." She finished her wine in one big gulp. She snapped her fingers and someone came out and refilled her glass.

"How was your day, Isabella?" Mr. Pruitt asked, ignoring his wife's comment.

"Fantastic, Daddy. I got an A on my physics test. James told me about his early acceptance to Harvard. He's so excited and I'm so proud of him. We're all supposed to meet up after that game tonight to celebrate his news and what I'm sure will be another Empire High victory. Oh, and I almost forgot! I had a lovely lunch with Brooklyn. We had so much fun we almost didn't hear the bell for class. She's just the sweetest. And we have so much in common. It's like we've been sisters this whole time. Isn't that right, Brooklyn?"

I was lucky there was no food in my mouth because I probably would have spit it out. But this was my chance. Even though the dinner was already tumultuous, I wanted the mayhem. I wanted to be kicked out. Disowned. Whatever it took to get out of this mess. "That's one way to put it. The other would be that you poured milk down the front of my blazer and told me to never sit with you again."

Someone's fork clattered against their plate. And then for just a second, everyone at the table was completely silent.

Isabella's laugh pierced through the silence. "Sissy, that's too funny. She's kidding. She's always been a little bit of a prankster. Everyone at school says it. Tell Daddy that you're kidding. Tell him."

I wanted to run away or hide. But I'd already been strong once today when I told Matt off. I could do it again.

And I'd already had to sit here listening to Mr. and Mrs. Pruitt talking about me like I wasn't here. I tried not to think about what the repercussions at school would be if I went through with this. My life was already hell. What did it even matter? I swallowed down the lump in my throat. "I'm not joking. She said I was unwanted. She called me a garbage person like my uncle. And said that I'd never be her sister."

More silence.

Mr. Pruitt pushed aside his salad. "Isabella, is that true?"

"Of course not, Daddy. She's lying."

He looked over at me.

"She's been torturing me ever since I first stepped foot in Empire High," I said. "And today, if anything, was worse."

"What?" She laughed. "That's not…Brooklyn." She laughed again but the strain was evident. "We're friends. Tell Daddy that we're the best of friends. Sisters."

I was tired of being her punching bag. I kept my mouth closed.

"I'm going to ask you one more time, Isabella," he said. "Is what Brooklyn said true?"

She rolled her eyes like her mother had. "Technically it was *my* blazer, so…"

"Apologize to her."

Isabella folded her arms across her chest. "No."

"Now."

Isabella's lips pressed together in a harsh line.

"She didn't do anything wrong," said Mrs. Pruitt.

I was pretty sure I wasn't the only one that jumped when the wine glass collided with the wall.

"Both of you get out!" he screamed at his wife and daughter. It looked like he was about to throw more food.

"You have to be kidding me, Richard," Mrs. Pruitt said as she calmly sipped her wine. Like this was an every-day occurrence. "Can we please have a civil conversation about your illegitimate child without the theatrics? As far as I can tell, Isabella didn't say anything untrue to the girl. No harm no foul."

The muscles in his neck twitched. "Spend the weekend in the Hamptons. Clearly you both need more time to adjust to her presence. And don't come back until you're ready to act more appropriately."

"But, Daddy!" Isabella protested. "I need to be at the game tonight! And I just told you about my plans after-ward."

I doubted that the cheerleading team actually needed her. Or that James wanted to celebrate his acceptance to Harvard with her rather than with his actual girlfriend.

"Then leave town after the game," he said.

Isabella huffed and stood up. "Does that mean you aren't coming?"

"I'm no longer in the mood," he said.

"Richard." Mrs. Pruitt stood up. "You're taking the word of that little trollop over our own daughter."

Trollop? I felt myself sinking into my seat.

"No. Isabella admitted it. Now go. Both of you." He waved his hand to gesture them out of the dining room.

Isabella gave me a look of pure fury before stomping after her mother.

The awkward silence stretched between us as doors slammed upstairs. Mr. Pruitt finished his salad right before the main course came out. And then he held up his hand before the plate could be placed down. He looked at me. But it felt a lot more like he was looking through me. "Is there anything else you need tonight? Anything at all?"

I shook my head.

Isabella was right. His wrath was terrifying. Even though it wasn't directed at me, I still felt my accelerated pulse. Mr. Pruitt was scarier than Isabella and her mom put together. I wanted to tell him that all I needed was to leave. I didn't want to be here. But no words escaped my throat.

"I'm going to finish my meal in my bedroom. I'll see you in the morning. And don't worry about shoes," he said with a wave of his hand. "Please just come to breakfast however you wish." He walked out of the room without another word and the chef's assistant dropped a plate in front of me before rushing after him.

Instead of getting up, I just sat there and I watched the red wine drip down the paint. I was too scared to move. My plan had failed. Isabella hadn't gotten me kicked out. She'd gotten herself kicked out. I cringed as I heard another door slam upstairs. All I'd done was make Isabella hate me a thousand times more.

CHAPTER 9

Friday

I wanted to crawl under the table and cry. I'd been brave all day. Or at least, I'd tried to be. I'd alienated myself from all the Pruitts by standing up for myself. Matt had treated me poorly, so I'd pushed him away. And now? Now I was all alone in a place that could only be described as a haunted mansion in apartment form. I looked at the creepy portrait of the Pruitt family above the fireplace. It felt like all of them were staring at me. And I couldn't shake the feeling that the two females in the picture wished I was dead.

I couldn't stay here. If I did, I'd probably never wake up. I looked behind me at the door to the kitchen. No one was watching me. If I was going to escape, now was my chance. Felix was somewhere in this apartment building. All I needed to do was sneak out.

I stood up and looked down at my feet. *I guess it would have been a good idea to wear shoes so I could flee.* But I didn't necessarily need shoes to roam the halls of this apartment building. I was sure the fancy carpets in the halls were regularly cleaned. And even if they weren't? I'd risk the cleanliness of my feet to stay alive.

A floorboard creaked as I tiptoed out of the dining room. I cringed even though I was pretty sure Isabella and her mother had left. Running into them without Mr. Pruitt there to protect me was my worst nightmare. And why had he protected me? It didn't make any sense. He'd kicked out his legitimate family and taken my side. To someone else, it may have been reassuring. But it wasn't when I knew for a fact that he'd never wanted me. It was just odd.

I took a left down the hall past the room with the piano. The way to the front door was the only thing I'd remembered about this whole stupid place. I was relieved when I reached it without running into anyone. I grabbed the handle, but it didn't turn. I turned the lock and pulled again, but it didn't budge. *What the...* I stared at the keypad to the side of the door. *Oh no.* It was just like the one by the elevator in the other apartment. What kind of maniac made it impossible to leave? This was a fire hazard. The apartment complex shouldn't allow it. I tried the handle again to no avail. *Damn it.* Freedom was just on the other side of that door. I hadn't come this close only to be stopped by a stupid code. *Come on.* I pulled again.

"Mr. Pruitt insists on locking everything down once he retires for the night."

I almost screamed. I hadn't heard Miller sneak up behind me. "Miller, you scared me half to death."

He smiled. "I'm sorry. I was trying to find you, but you left the dining room before dessert."

I just stared at him for a moment. Had he heard the argument? He must have. Or he must have at least seen the red wine on the wall and the shattered glass.

He cleared his throat. "A young man stopped by while you were eating dinner. Felix Green. Here's the message he left." He handed me a folded piece of paper.

I opened it and read the short note.

I was hoping to surprise you. But apparently the Pruitts don't do surprises. Pretty lame if you ask me. And the guy that answered the door said I needed to be on the approved visitor's list? I requested to be put on it, but then he said it would take a few days to run the necessary background checks. What the hell is that all about? I'm pretty sure he just didn't like me. Call me. Or better yet, get the hell out of there and come over. I live in 24C.

-Felix

"Boyfriend?" Miller asked

I didn't even realize I was smiling until the corners of my mouth fell. "What? Oh. No. Just a friend. Why didn't you let him in?" It couldn't have been the background check that Felix had mentioned. That was clearly a joke.

"Mr. Pruitt has rules about these things."

Or maybe it wasn't a joke. "Background checks for visitors? Really?"

He shrugged but didn't offer any details.

"So…instead of letting Felix in, can you let me out?" I gestured to the keypad behind me. "Or give me the code?"

"Locking everything down when Mr. Pruitt retires extends to everyone in the household."

Okay. "But Felix invited me over." I waved the note in the air. "He lives in this building. I'll be back in just a few hours," I lied. I was never. Ever. Coming back to this place.

"I'm sorry, but I can't let you out."

"You're…that's…isn't this kidnapping?"

The corner of his mouth lifted ever so slightly. "If I was allowed to let you out or give you the code, I would. But I can't. And I almost forgot, I have about ten missed calls and a voicemail for you on my phone from...Matt?"

Oh God. "I'm sorry about that."

"Is he your boyfriend?"

Why was he so interested in whether or not I had a boyfriend? "No." My voice came out harsher than I meant for it to. But I didn't want to have this conversation with him. I wanted to be on the other side of the door.

"Pretty sure he thinks otherwise. Mr. Pruitt will want a full disclosure on all your relationships."

Ew. No. I stared at Miller. "What did Matt say in his voicemail?"

"Something about needing to talk. And that his lawyer is having trouble finding a loophole. He said he was sorry like ten times."

I knew I'd asked him what Matt had said in the message. But the fact that he'd listened to it was a little invasive. I was too defeated to care though. A part of me had been holding out hope that Matt's lawyer would come through, even though Matt never seemed to. Matt had promised I wouldn't have to stay here. But another broken promise added to the list was no surprise. And honestly, he probably didn't even care anymore. If the rumors about him were true, he was probably getting over me by working his way through the cheerleading team a second time.

"Are you okay?" asked Miller.

I nodded even though I was anything but okay.

"I'll mention to Mr. Pruitt that you need a phone."

"No, that's…" I let my voice trail off. Honestly, getting a phone would be really nice. Especially if I was trapped here. "That would be great actually. Speaking of which, is there a phone I can use in the house?"

"You can use mine again if you'd like." He pulled it out of his pocket.

I wasn't sure why, but this felt like a trap. Was someone going to jump out from behind that antique vase and punish me for accepting the cell phone? "Am I allowed to use your phone?"

"No, not really."

"I don't want to get you in trouble." That was the last thing I wanted to do. Miller was the only one in this house that seemed capable of a genuine smile. I didn't want to lose that.

The smile that I'd just been thinking about spread across his face. "It's fine. Really." He held it out to me.

I wasn't going to fight with him over this. He was handing me a lifeline and I was going to take it. I called Felix first and let him know I wasn't allowed to leave. I was very aware of the fact that Miller was staring at me. And because of it, I ended the call sooner than I wanted. "Can I make one more call?" I asked.

Miller nodded.

I dialed the number and held the phone back up to my ear. Kennedy picked up after only one ring.

"Please tell me this is my best friend and she hasn't been murdered by Isabella yet?"

I laughed. "It's me. And I'm alive…for now."

"Oh thank God. I've been so worried. I looked all over for you after school ended and you were nowhere to be found. I've been answering the phone all day like this by the way. I really freaked out the pizza delivery guy."

I laughed again. "I miss you."

"I miss you too. What's it like there?" asked Kennedy. "Oh wait, let me guess. Creepy as hell?"

"Pretty much."

"Do you think you'll come to work tomorrow? I know you had called out sick today, but I thought you were still planning on coming tomorrow. I think it'll feel normal, you know?"

Normal. I doubted that. But a night of work sounded a lot better than a night of whatever the hell this was. "Yeah, if I'm allowed out, I'll be there. I'll talk to Mr. Pruitt about it in the morning."

"If you're allowed out? What does that mean?" Kennedy asked.

"It means there's a keypad and I don't have the code."

"Weird."

I stared at the keypad. "I know."

"Maybe the code is Isabella's birthday," Kennedy said. "Do you have any idea when that is?"

"Nope."

"Hmm. You really should know your sister's birthday, Brooklyn."

"She's not my sister."

Kennedy laughed. "I know, I was just kidding. Maybe the code is 666. You know…the universal code for Isabella."

"That's not a bad guess." I didn't try it though. Just because I thought the Pruitts were evil didn't mean they personally identified as evil. Or did they?

"So you're really stuck there?"

"Yeah. Nobody is allowed in and I'm not allowed out."

"Are you going to be okay tonight?"

"It's the same apartment building that Felix lives in. It's nice knowing he's nearby even though I can't see him."

"Well, that's not so bad then. His apartment isn't exactly homey, but it's nice. Not even a little creepy."

"The Pruitt's place isn't decorated like Felix's. It's more haunted mansion-esque in here."

Miller laughed from behind me.

I turned around and smiled at him. "I should probably go. I'm borrowing a phone."

"Okay, but you should call Matt when you get a chance. He's kind of...losing it. He stopped by about an hour ago and he looked awful."

I swallowed hard. He'd been a jerk. Countless times. But it still hurt me to know that he was hurting. Or...hurt me more. I was already hurting. "So I guess he told you what happened in class?"

"No. What happened?"

I gripped the phone a little tighter in my hand. He hadn't told her that I broke up with him? He just showed up at my best friend's place to try to get her to make me call him back? That wasn't him being hurt. That was him being manipulative. "We broke up."

The line was silent for a few beats. "Because of what Isabella did?"

"No. Because of what he didn't do."

Another stretch of silence. Kennedy knew about Isabella blackmailing Matt. I'd spilled everything to her on the

steps of Empire High the morning before Matt was supposed to announce to everyone that we were dating, but
didn't. The same day that my uncle died. We hadn't talked
about it since. I hadn't talked about it with Matt either.
None of it seemed important after that. But for some reason I expected today to be different. Especially since Matt
had just asked me to be his girlfriend officially. Today was
my first day back at school and I'd needed him. I'd needed
him and he hadn't stepped up. I'd lost my whole family. I
just needed one person to rely on to have my back. And it
wasn't him. I sniffled, remembering how sweet he'd been
in the park this morning. Secret rendezvous weren't
enough. "I'll explain it all at work tomorrow. I just can't be
with someone who…"

"I'm proud of you," she said, cutting me off. "God, I
was so freaking mad at him for just watching when Isabella
poured milk on you."

I should have known she'd have my back. I didn't
need Matt. I had her.

"Screw Matthew Caldwell," she said.

Yeah. Screw Matthew Caldwell. I said goodbye and gave
Miller's phone back. For just a second, my fingers brushed
against his palm.

He cleared his throat and shoved his phone back in his
pocket. "Do you want me to have some ice cream sent up
to your room?"

He got me. A recent breakup meant eating a huge
bowl of ice cream in your room and crying. But that wasn't
what I wanted. I didn't want to be alone. But I also knew
how inappropriate it would be to ask if I could eat ice

cream with him. He'd already let me borrow his phone. So instead of saying anything at all, I just nodded.

"Have a good night, Brooklyn." He gave me one last smile and walked back toward the kitchen.

I hugged my arms around myself to help prevent the chill in the air. A good night? That wasn't possible. I watched him disappear down the hall. I was pretty sure I was already going mad in this house. Because all I could think about was how Miller's arms looked just as strong as Matt's. I didn't know how to sleep alone anymore. I'd quickly grown used to falling asleep in Matt's arms. But running to Miller wasn't the answer. He worked here. He wasn't my friend. And I was sure he didn't want to hang out with a high schooler on a Friday night.

I knew all that. I knew it, and yet…I hurried after him.

CHAPTER 10

Friday

The kitchen was empty, so I pushed into the staff kitchen. Miller was leaning against the counter laughing at something the chef had just said. But his laughter faded away when he saw me. The chef turned around to see what he was staring at.

"I'll be right up with some options, sweetie," she said.

"Actually, is it okay if I just eat it in here?"

She looked at Miller and then back at me. "I guess that would be alright. What do you prefer, mint chocolate chip or..." she tugged open the freezer and pulled out two containers "...there's also raspberry with chocolate chips."

I wasn't paying attention to the options because I was focused on the fact that each ice cream container had a little label with Miller's name. "Oh, I don't want to steal anyone's ice cream. Don't the Pruitts have some?"

She laughed. "No. The Pruitts don't eat ice cream."

"Are they lactose intolerant or something?" I was glad I didn't inherit that. I wasn't sure which was worse...never eating cheese or inheriting the evil gene. Probably the evil thing. But it was close.

"More of a vanity thing," she said. "So, which flavor will it be?"

I looked over at Miller. "That's okay. I'll just…" I looked over my shoulder at the door. I really, really didn't want to leave.

"It's fine," Miller said. "I got this, Barbara." He grabbed the containers from her.

"Very well." She untied her apron and hung it on a hook. "There was a show I wanted to catch so I'm going to scurry off. Have a great rest of your night, you two."

"Which flavor?" he asked once Barbara disappeared out of the kitchen.

I tucked a loose strand of hair behind my ear. "You didn't have to offer me your ice cream."

"I could tell you needed it." He pulled out two bowls and I couldn't even try to hide my smile. "So…mint chocolate chip or raspberry chocolate chip?"

"Mint. Thanks for sharing." He didn't reply, he just got to work scooping out two bowlfuls. I sat down at the table in the middle of the room and watched him. I could add the fact that he liked ice cream with chocolate chips to the few things I knew about him. He was also generous. And kind for letting me use his phone. He could have been doing a million other things tonight, but he was giving that all up to hang out with a practical stranger just because he'd overheard a conversation about my breakup. It was really sweet.

He placed a heaping bowl of ice cream down in front of me and sat down across from me. The look of pure indulgence on his face when he took a bite was kind of adorable. I remembered when a bowl of ice cream could make me that happy too. I took a bite and smiled. Maybe it still could. I just needed to remember how to embrace that feeling. Seeing his smiling face made it seem possible.

"How old are you?" The words tumbled out of my mouth before I could stop them.

"Older than you." He resumed eating, like that was a suitable answer. But before I could question it, he beat me with a question of his own. "So what didn't he do?" Miller asked.

I swallowed down my bite of ice cream. "What?"

"You said you broke up because of what he didn't do." He lifted up a huge spoonful of ice cream. "Your ex," he added when I didn't respond.

"Oh. Um…"

"I figured since you came in here that you needed someone to talk to. But we don't have to talk about it if you don't want to."

I shook my head. "I just didn't want to be alone."

His jaw tensed. "Look, Brooklyn…I'm not even supposed to be talking to you. Let alone sitting here with you. I should probably go." But he made no movement to get up.

"Just tell me something about you. Anything."

He pressed his lips together.

"Please, distract me from whatever hell I'm currently living in. Like how you ended up working for the Pruitts of all people?"

"It's good money. And I'm saving up for college."

College. So that made him what? Eighteen? It was older than me, but only by two years. He acted like we were a whole lifetime apart. "Surely there are other high paying security jobs in the city."

"Not this good."

"Why?"

He took another bite of his ice cream as he thought about the question. "Because it's the Pruitts."

"Yeah. But this city is full of wealthy families. Like the Hunters and the Caldwells. The Greens and the Dicksons." I wasn't sure if Felix and Cupcake's parents were as wealthy as the other families I'd mentioned, but surely they could afford the best security. Hell, most of the kids at my school were from families as wealthy as the Pruitts. "What's so special about this gig?"

Miller finished his ice cream and put his elbows on the table. "Higher risk means higher salaries."

"Higher risk?"

"Because of Mr. Pruitt's line of work."

I just stared at him. "What's his line of work?" I didn't know anything about the man I was living with. I hadn't had an opportunity to ask. The only hint I could even think of was that when I first met him, he'd asked if I'd ever picked up a newspaper.

"I also get paid to keep his secrets." He smiled.

"Really, what does Mr. Pruitt do?" If he was in the paper, that made him…what? A writer? Or maybe someone that graced the pages of the local paper. A politician?

"I've already said too much. Now back to you. Are you sure you don't want to call Matthew Caldwell back? He keeps lighting up my phone."

"No."

"No you aren't sure? Or no you don't want to?"

"Both." I took a bite of my ice cream. I didn't want to talk about me. I wanted to talk about Mr. Pruitt's secrets.

"The whole staff heard the argument at dinner. Did Isabella really pour milk all over you at lunch?"

I nodded. But I couldn't tell if he believed it or not. He was just staring at me like I was a puzzle he couldn't solve.

"Why didn't you tell me when I asked you what happened to your blazer?"

"Because I wasn't sure if I was going to tell anyone. But then I thought it was the perfect opportunity to get Isabella to explode and get me kicked out of the house. My plan kind of backfired though. Now her mom hates me as much as she does."

"Yeah, you really don't want to be on Mrs. Pruitt's bad side."

"Now you tell me?" I said with a laugh.

He smiled.

"It doesn't seem like she was really open to getting to know me regardless."

"The circumstances are pretty uncomfortable. Besides, did you really expect for it to be an easy transition with people like this?"

People like this. I smiled. He didn't think I was one of them.

"Just a little tip for you when it comes to Mrs. Pruitt. Don't back down from her. It'll make it worse."

I nodded, even though I didn't really know what he meant. It was her house. Her rules. What was I supposed to do?

Miller let his spoon fall into his empty bowl and then stood up. He grabbed my bowl too and I watched him silently do the dishes.

"Thank you for letting me have some of your ice cream," I said as he placed the last dish in the dishrack.

He folded his arms and leaned back against the counter behind him. "No problem at all. I hope it helped."

"It did." Just knowing that there was one nice person in this apartment meant a lot to me. More than he probably knew.

"Tomorrow will be better," Miller said.

"Will it?" I wasn't so sure.

"At least Isabella and Mrs. Pruitt won't be here. You'll have some time to get to know your father."

That wasn't time that I wanted. But instead of saying that, I just nodded.

"It's getting late. I should head to bed."

"Okay." My voice sounded so small. I was about to be alone in this horrible house. A shiver ran down my spine.

He walked over to the door but then stopped and turned around. "For the record, a guy who doesn't stick up for you isn't someone who's worth your time."

I felt frozen under his gaze.

"Goodnight, Brooklyn."

"Goodnight, Miller." His last name felt weird on my tongue. Even though it seemed like he was on my side, the use of his last name was like a line in the sand. He was hired to keep Mr. Pruitt's secrets. And I knew that meant he'd keep them from me too.

For a while I just sat there. Going to my room meant another sleepless night staring at the ceiling. But when the clock ticked closer to midnight, I finally got up. I made my way through the creepy house and up the stairs. I looked right at the top of the stairs, down the hallway where the real family slept. Was Mr. Pruitt awake right now? Was he wondering how the hell he wound up in this situation too?

He'd taken my side at dinner. I should have felt something. He'd protected me like a father should. But I just felt confused. He had a wife and daughter that loved him. Why would he defend a girl who didn't?

I retreated down my hall and stopped at the locked door. I looked over my shoulder to make sure no one was watching, and then tried to open it. But it was locked just like the front door. I turned my head and pressed my ear up against the wood. I don't know what I was expecting to hear. But only silence greeted me, just like the locked room at Mr. Pruitt's other apartment. I took a step back and stared at the handle. There were secrets in there. Secrets that Miller was keeping for Mr. Pruitt. Secrets that Isabella and Mrs. Pruitt probably knew. What horrible things did he do that made him pay his staff exorbitant salaries?

I heard the creak of a door and threw my hand over my mouth before I could scream. Instead of looking behind me to see where the noise was coming from, I ran toward my bedroom. I threw the door closed and turned the lock on the doorknob. My heart was racing so quickly that for a second I thought the noise outside my bedroom was my heart thudding against my chest. But then there was a very audible squeak of a floorboard right outside my door.

I took a step back and stared at the crack between the bottom of the door and the hardwoods. There was definitely a shadow in the middle of it, blocking the light. For a few seconds everything was still. I couldn't even hear any breathing besides my own.

And then there was another squeak of the floorboards, and the shadow beneath the door disappeared.

I knew it was a person. Every logical conclusion pointed to that. Someone had heard me upstairs and come to see what I was up to. And then they'd walked away when they realized everything was fine.

But if that was true…why did it feel like someone was watching me right now? I turned around and looked at my room. Empty except for me. But I felt it. I folded my arms across my chest to help stop the chill running through my bones. It was almost as if the shadow had come under the door and into my room. Which made no sense. Neither did the fact that it seriously felt like it just dropped ten degrees. I swallowed hard.

Earlier tonight I'd been scared to be all alone. Now I was worried that I wasn't.

CHAPTER 11

Saturday

I didn't sleep at all. I'd tossed and turned and dreamed of ghosts for the first time since I was a child. I kept my eyes closed shut all night, wishing that sleep would come. But all I could see was the shadow under the door as it seeped into my room.

A loud bang made my eyes fly open. I screamed at the top of my lungs when I saw a man hunched over in my closet.

He turned around, holding a dress in his hand. "Calm yourself."

"What? Who…what are you doing in my room?" I'd locked the door. I was sure of it because I was so freaked out last night. I pulled the comforter up to my chest even though I wasn't wearing anything even remotely revealing.

"You're going to give yourself premature wrinkles," he said as he slipped the dress on a hanger.

"Who the hell are you?"

He smiled, not at all alarmed by my tone. "Justin. I'm Diane's assistant."

"And who's Diane?"

"Your stylist. You met her yesterday. You know…big glasses, crazy hair, about yay tall." He held his hand out to the side to show her height.

I just stared at him. "How did you even get in?"

"The door was unlocked."

"No it wasn't."

"Um…yes it was." He slid another dress on a hanger. "Would you prefer if I organize by color or are you more of a hang-all-the-pants-together kind of girl?"

"I've never even hung up a pair of pants."

"Interesting. It's best if we just do it my way then." He turned back to the closet.

For a few seconds I just stared at the back of his head. The morning had just started and I already felt completely out of my element. I climbed out of bed and opened one of my moving boxes. Before I could pull on some of my old clothes, Justin stopped me.

"Absolutely not. Try this." He tossed me a pair of dark washed jeans and a sweater that would definitely show off my midriff.

"I don't think this is very…me."

"Nonsense. Diane wouldn't have picked it out for you if it wouldn't look good on your figure. Trust me. Some of the celebs she dresses would die for that outfit, but if they can't pull it off, Diane won't send it to them."

"She dresses celebrities?"

"She's Diane Cartwright. The head stylist for Odegaard. What kind of depressing hole have you been living in?"

The kind in Delaware, I guess. I didn't want to fight with this weird man. So I took the clothes to the bathroom and quickly changed. I stared at my reflection in the floor length mirror. The cut of the waistline of the jeans and the length of the sweater only left about an inch of skin showing. I smiled at my reflection. It actually looked really good. And unlike the itchy sweaters I was used to, this one was crazy soft. When I walked back into the room, Justin whistled.

"Get it girl. Spin for me."

I wasn't sure why, but I twirled in a circle for him. It should have made me feel ridiculous, but it actually had the opposite effect.

"It's even better with your smile. Perfection. Before you get me too distracted, some delicious man just stopped by and said breakfast was ready. Aren't you a lucky little thing to ogle that eye candy all day?"

Every word out of his mouth was confusing. But I was pretty sure he meant Miller had stopped by and announced breakfast. "Is it okay if I leave you here?" I asked. "Or did you need my help?"

"It's my job to get everything organized. Until I can realize my true potential, that is."

"What's your true potential?"

He looked up from his work. He seemed surprised by my question. "I was born to be an event planner."

"All events or something in particular?"

He was staring at me like I was an alien. "Weddings specifically."

"That sounds like a fun job."

He smiled. "Fun. Flirty. And fabulous. The trifecta of "F's. It's the best job in the world. The only one for me."

I smiled back. I really didn't know what he was talking about, but he seemed excited. "So is being Diane's assistant a stepping stone toward wedding planning?"

"Absolutely. Diane has all the connections." He gestured around the room. "Remember me when you're planning the wedding of your dreams."

I laughed. "Not any time soon I'm afraid. But I'll certainly remember you."

He stared at me for a moment. "I guess I can fold your pants and put them in a drawer for you. But only because I like you."

I laughed. "Thank you. That will actually be a lot easier for me." Especially since I had no intention of ever hanging them up again.

"You're so welcome. What a breath of fresh air you are." He started humming and turned back to his work.

I left him to it and wandered out of my room. For just a second I let myself think of Matt. He'd made a joke a few nights ago, about how he'd be my first husband, like he'd take all my firsts. It didn't feel like a joke at the time. But now it did. How could he ever marry someone he refused to be seen with in public? Matt and I were done. We were. So why did I miss him so much?

I tried to push the thought aside as I walked down the stairs and made my way to the dining room. The house seemed less creepy during the day. But before I reached the dining room, I glanced over my shoulder. It really felt like someone was watching me. I ignored the shiver down my spine and walked into the room.

Mr. Pruitt was sipping a cup of coffee. He stopped mid-sip and looked up at me, a smile stretching across his face. It was the most genuine smile I'd seen on him. "Good morning, Brooklyn."

Was it a good morning? He'd kidnapped me. He'd kicked his family out of the apartment last night. Nothing about this situation was good. "Um…good morning." It came out as more of a question.

He gestured to the buffet spread out on the table. "Help yourself. I wasn't sure what you liked, so I had the chef make quite a bit. I hope you're hungry."

I was starving. All I'd eaten last night was ice cream. And before that? I hadn't had an appetite. So there was no way I could turn down this feast. I sat down and piled my plate full of fresh fruit, bacon, scrambled eggs, fluffy waffles, and syrup. I pushed the eggs into the syrup.

"Your mom liked syrup on her eggs too."

I looked up at him. "Yeah. She did." I wasn't sure why it surprised me that he knew that. Clearly he did know her. My mom never made it sound like a one-night stand or anything. I was pretty sure she'd been in love with him. Had he felt that too? "You painted my room yellow."

"You never told me what color you preferred. And it was your mother's favorite. I took a gamble. If you want to change it…"

"No. I love it." I tried not to wince. Loving my new jail cell wasn't exactly the right thing to say. I still wanted to leave. But I did have a million questions for him. And right now seemed like the perfect opportunity. There was only one that really mattered though. "You could have reached out to me my whole life. Why'd you wait until now?"

"Your existence only just came to my attention."

What? That was a lie. "My mom told me that you didn't stick around after you found out that she was pregnant. I know that you knew about me."

"Yes, but I gave her money to take care of it. And then I never heard from her again."

It? I wasn't an *it*. Of course he never heard from her again. She wanted me. I was never an *it* to her. "You never thought of following up? To make sure you didn't have another kid out there?"

"I was married. It was complicated. And I had no reason to assume she didn't go through with the abortion when I gave her the proper funds."

How could he talk about it so nonchalantly? He'd tried his best to get rid of me. Didn't he see how fucked up this situation was? Why would he think I'd want to be here with him? I tried to focus so I could get the rest of the answers I needed from him. "Did she know that you were married?"

He shook his head. "No. Not until the last time I saw her."

When you told her to get rid of me. I took a deep breath. I'd never think differently of my mother, but it was nice to know that she didn't know he was married. If she had known…that would have been a lot harder to swallow. She was the only role model I ever had. And I didn't want my memories of her to be tainted by…him. God, how had she loved him? I couldn't see it. My mom had been so full of life. And Mr. Pruitt was…cold and cruel. "So if you didn't want me, why am I here?"

"Because you're mine."

"I'm not yours. That's the whole point. You didn't want me. And even if you've changed your mind, you can learn about me over dinner once a week or something. I don't need to live here."

"I'm trying to protect you."

"I don't need to be protected. Please just let me go back to the Alcaraz's place."

He shook his head. "I can't let you live there. Ah. Here, your presents have arrived."

One of the bodyguards I didn't know came out with a big wrapped package complete with a huge bow on top. He placed it down in front of me on the table.

Did he seriously think he could buy my love? "I really don't need anything else. Honestly, you can return all those clothes upstairs. I already have everything I need."

"Nonsense. You like your new clothes. Or else you wouldn't be wearing them. Besides, you need these things. Just open it."

I stared at the gift like it was toxic. *I shouldn't have put on this stupid outfit.* It didn't matter how soft the sweater was or how good it looked. Putting it on made him think I wanted something from him. I didn't. "Really, it's…"

"You look lovely this morning by the way. That color suits you."

His compliment threw me off guard.

"And your mother would have wanted you to have nice things. Go on. Open it."

I was wrong before. He didn't know my mother at all. She cared about quality time, not quality items. The only expensive thing she owned was a floor-length cobalt blue dress that she wore on special occasions. Like when I pretended to open a bakery in the middle of our kitchen and she came to my opening night. Mr. Pruitt didn't know me or my mom. He wasn't my family. But I also didn't want to fight him. I'd be gone soon enough.

I pulled the bow and lifted the lid off the box. There was a laptop and a cell phone staring back at me. And a black Amex card with my name on it.

"This should make you feel more at home," he said. "You'll still be able to converse with the Alcaraz girl over the phone without actually seeing her in person."

Throwing expensive things at me wasn't the way to make me want to stay. And talking about my best friend like that? It made me want to run in the opposite direction of him. "Her name's Kennedy."

"This will be better for everyone. You'll stay nice and safe here instead of ever being in that dingy building you came from."

Wait. "Am I not allowed to leave?"

He laughed. "Of course you are. I have a whole list of approved visitors and of people you can visit as well. Miller will accompany you for all outings. And itineraries for the upcoming week must be submitted to me on Sunday mornings so I have time to approve them. If you'd like to give a list of friends to Miller, he'll do the proper background checks."

He had to be kidding. I waited, but he didn't laugh. "There's a code on the front door. What is it?"

"You don't need to worry about that, since Miller will be accompanying you."

"But…"

"It's for your safety."

It was a fire hazard. Not a safety precaution. But I didn't care. I'd already gotten a plan in my head. I wouldn't be coming back. I just needed to get out of here once and I'd be all set. "My friend Felix Green lives in the building. Can I go see him today?"

"The Greens?" He took a sip of his coffee. "They're art dealers, right?"

"Yes." Although, Felix had implied that was just a front for something much more sinister. The less Mr. Pruitt knew about that, the better.

"Very well. Miller can take you over to their place after our round of golf."

"*Our* round of golf?"

"Yes. I thought it would be nice to show you around the club and introduce you to some of my associates."

That sounded worse than my nightmares last night. I didn't want him to parade me around to his associates. Whatever that meant. "Unless you count mini-golf, I don't know how to golf."

"Really?"

Where the hell would I have learned how to golf? "Really."

"Then I'm afraid today won't work. Bill is a real stickler for speed-of-play. I'll have to teach you another day. As it is, I have a tee time." He placed his napkin down on top of his plate. "Enjoy the rest of your day. And please don't hesitate to ask the staff for anything at all that you need. Their numbers are already programmed into your phone."

"Wait." He'd sidetracked the conversation so much I'd completely forgotten my most important question. "I have work tonight." It seemed like telling him was better than asking. "So I won't be here for dinner."

He laughed. "No. Absolutely not."

"No?" I purposely didn't ask his permission. He didn't get to tell me no. Despite what he thought, he wasn't my parent. He wasn't even my legal guardian. He was a kidnapping psychopath.

"You won't be working anymore," he said.

"But I have to work."

He tilted his head to the side as he stared at me. "I can give you everything you need." He gestured to the presents still sitting on the table.

I don't want anything from you. "I'm saving up for college. I…"

"You get decent grades. I looked at your transcript. Pick any school you please and I'll make it happen."

I opened my mouth and closed it again. "I don't want to get into a good school because of your name."

"Of course you do. You're already reaping the benefits. Why do you think you didn't have detention yesterday after you started that food fight last week? I got you a clean slate at the school. Have fun with Mr. Green. And expense whatever you want to your card." He strolled out of the dining room.

I honestly hadn't thought about my detention at all. I'd been a little too preoccupied with my grief and being taken from my uncle's funeral. And a food fight was stretching it. I'd thrown one green bean at Isabella after she'd berated me and my uncle. I didn't even deserve detention. Isabella did. And it twisted my stomach into knots knowing that it was Isabella's last name that had gotten me out of it.

CHAPTER 12

Saturday

"You really don't have to come with me," I told Miller when we reached the front door.

"Actually I do."

"But you could just give me the code…"

"You know I can't."

I felt bad dragging him into this. But I couldn't think about what would happen to him when I ran off. All I could focus on right now was myself and getting as far away from here as possible. My backpack was stuffed with everything I needed. I'd even snagged a few bottles of water and some granola bars from the kitchen. I wasn't coming back.

Miller typed in the code, being careful not to let me see. And then we walked in silence down the hall and into the elevator. The elevator music played through the speaker system. For some reason it was really soothing.

"So what are the two of you doing today?" Miller asked as he shoved his hands into his pockets.

"Just hanging out." Felix didn't even know I was coming. But hopefully he was home. If I didn't see a familiar face right now I was pretty sure I'd lose it. I knew Mr. Pruitt was trying to be nice this morning. Gifting me a phone, inviting me to his tee time, complimenting my outfit. But at the same time, he was also controlling and rude. I didn't want to be here. I couldn't do this.

"Sounds like fun," Miller said.

"Mhm." The doors opened on the 24th floor. "Are you sure you want to be an awkward third wheel?" I asked as we stepped off. I wasn't sure anything about Miller was awkward. Which made me think I'd somehow wind up being the awkward third wheel with him and Felix. This was going to be a disaster.

"You won't even notice that I'm there. That's the whole point."

"I'm pretty sure I'll notice that you're there."

The corner of his mouth ticked up.

I wasn't giving him a compliment. I just meant that if he was staring at me and Felix it was going to be weird. But his smile made me smile. We stopped outside of apartment C and I knocked on the door that looked exactly like the Pruitt's apartment door. After a few seconds I knocked again. *Please, Felix. Please, please, please.* If he wasn't home I wasn't sure what I would do. The thought of being dragged back to the Pruitts place was horrifying. Felix was my ticket to freedom. But first he had to show up.

"Can I use your phone?" I asked.

"Didn't Mr. Pruitt give you one this morning?"

Oh right. I pulled it out of one of the pouches in my backpack and tapped out a text to Felix.

The door opened a few seconds later. "Sorry about that, newb," he said with a laugh. "I don't usually get many visitors. How are you doing…"

I launched myself into his arms before he could finish his thought. God it was so nice to be hugged after walking around the Pruitts haunted house for the last day. I'd started to believe in ghosts for goodness' sake. And the chill that wouldn't leave my skin dissipated in his arms.

"Uh…hey, man," Felix said, his arms wrapping more securely around me. "Can I help you?"

I pulled myself out of Felix's embrace. "This is Miller. I believe you met him last night when you stopped by?"

"Yeah." When no one said anything for a beat, Felix added, "but that doesn't explain why he's here now."

"Miller has to follow me around all day because Mr. Pruitt is insane."

Felix looked back and forth between us when Miller didn't even offer a hello. "What do you mean follow you around?"

"He's my bodyguard or something like that."

Miller nodded.

"Well thanks for dropping her off," Felix said.

Miller shook his head. "If she's coming in, so am I."

"Oooookay. Well, come in then I guess."

Miller walked past him and looked around the foyer like he thought there were explosives and guns about to go off. He peered behind a few pieces of framed art and looked under a console table.

"What the hell is this?" Felix whispered.

"I'm sorry. I only just found out that he'd be accompanying me during all my outings." I watched Miller look behind another painting. He'd been so normal last night. And now he was acting like a guard dog. Was he sniffing that vase for a bomb?

"All your outings?" Felix asked.

"There's a whole list of rules about who I'm allowed to hang out with. Luckily you made the cut, because it doesn't seem like Mr. Pruitt is ever going to let me hang out with Kennedy again. He has some grudge against people that aren't in his zip code or something. Which is why I need to ask you a favor," I said, lowering my voice.

"What do you need?"

"Can you distract Miller for me for a few minutes so I can make a run for it?" Actually, I wasn't sure if I'd need Felix for this. Miller seemed plenty distracted all by himself. Seriously, what was he looking for?

Felix looked over at Miller and then back at me. "Where are you going to go? Why don't you just stay here?"

"I'm supposed to be back for dinner with Mr. Pruitt tonight. Miller wouldn't let me stay here, he'd drag me out of here when the time came. He already dragged me away from the funeral. I have to get away from him in order to pull this off. I'm going to go to Kennedy's. I'm pretty sure Mr. Pruitt would never follow me there. He's repulsed by it."

"Doesn't mean he won't send Miller."

Good point. "Then I'll just…go somewhere else. Please, Felix, you have to help me. I can't spend another night there."

"Well you don't have to make a run for it just yet. Come in and relax for a bit and we can strategize."

He was right. I didn't have to flee this second. Mr. Pruitt would be gone for hours. At least, I thought golf took hours. Whenever I saw it on TV, it certainly felt like I'd been watching for hours.

"I'll let Kennedy know you're here too." Felix pulled out his phone and shot her a text. "Wait, you texted me." He looked up at me. "Does that mean you got a phone?"

"Yeah. And a laptop. And a new wardrobe. And an Amex card for…something. I don't know."

He laughed. "I like your outfit." He put his hand on my shoulder and gently ran it down to my elbow. "Your sweater is really soft."

Miller cleared his throat. "Everything looks good here. Can we maybe choose one room to hang out in so I don't have to do this all day?" His voice practically echoed. The last time I'd been to Felix's there were students everywhere dancing and drinking. It was weird seeing it so empty. But empty was a lot better than haunted.

"Sure," Felix said as he threw his arm around my shoulders. "Right this way."

I was pretty sure Miller was glaring at us as Felix pulled me to the family room. Yeah, I could definitely feel Miller's eyes burning a hole in the back of my head. *I knew this was going to be awkward.* Miller had insisted it wouldn't be, but he was the one being weird. And I hadn't even run away yet. At least he was the third wheel instead of me.

"Is this okay?" Felix asked.

"Yeah it's…"

"It'll take me a few minutes to make sure," Miller said, cutting me off. "Just stand there for a second." He lifted a couch cushion and inspected the zipper.

"Welcome to your new life," Felix whispered.

I laughed. My life for the next few hours maybe. Because this? The weird precautions. The security detail. The clothes. None of it was me. "Is this normal?" I asked. "Do you have a security guard that goes into people's houses and acts like this?"

"No, I have a driver. And a chef. And a maid. No security. But even if I did…this would be a bit extreme."

Miller picked up a lamp and looked under it.

"Scratch that," Felix said. "This is very extreme."

It really was. "Do they have this many precautions with Isabella too?" I asked Miller.

He looked up from the magazines he was overturning on the coffee table. "I don't know. I'm not on her security detail."

"Does Mr. Pruitt have you do this with every room he walks in?"

"No."

What? "So why are you doing it now?"

"Because he asked me to."

"What does he think is going to happen to me?" I laughed.

Miller didn't respond. He just kept examining pieces of furniture.

This was ridiculous. "You can stop securing the premises or whatever you're doing," I said. "No one's trying to hurt me. Felix's apartment is safe. I've been here before. What are you even looking for?"

"Mr. Pruitt gave me strict instructions about this," he said, ignoring my question. "Just give me a few more minutes."

"Why? Am I in danger or something?" I said it as a joke, but as soon as the words left my mouth, they freaked me out. "Wait, am I in danger?"

He paused for way too long. "No, of course not."

That was not convincing at all. "So if I'm not in danger, why are you doing all this?"

"Because he asked me to."

Well this conversation had gone in a perfect circle. I sighed and sat down on the arm of the couch. Mr. Pruitt had said something about wanting to keep me safe. That was why he didn't want me staying with Kennedy. But what could possibly happen to me there? Or here? It didn't make any sense. I was surrounded by good people. The only person I could even think of that wanted to hurt me was Isabella.

"Okay, you're good to go," Miller said. He walked over to the entrance to the room, folded his arms, and stared at me.

"You said this wouldn't be awkward."

He ignored me.

"It's fine," Felix said and sat down on the couch. "Just ignore him."

I didn't know how to ignore him. And I wasn't even sure that I wanted to. Miller was the only person at the Pruitts that was nice to me. I didn't want...whatever this was. I wasn't cut out for a security guard following me around. It was too uncomfortable.

"This is weird," I whispered to Felix. "I'm sorry."

"It's fine. I'm just glad you're here. How bad was last night?"

I moved to sit next to him and let myself sink into the soft couch cushions. God, I was so tired. I was pretty sure I hadn't slept at all. "Awful. I told Mr. Pruitt about the lunch incident and he threw Isabella and her mom out of the house."

"Whoa. I didn't expect that to be the end of that story."

"Me either. I don't get it. Why did he take my side? He was supposed to throw me out of the house for slandering his daughter. Not this."

"That was your plan?" He smiled. "Well I could have told you that would backfire. He sought you out, newb. He clearly wants to get to know you."

"But why? He didn't want me. Why now? It doesn't make any sense. Why can't he just leave me alone?"

"Is it really so bad that he cares? You lost your whole family. Why are you fighting off someone trying to take care of you?"

Why am I fighting off Mr. Pruitt's affection? I knew he was trying. In his own way. I looked down at my hands. My fingers were clasped so firmly together that my knuckles were turning white. I pulled my hands apart. "He left my mom to take care of me all on her own." It didn't matter if he thought she got an abortion. He still left her. I know what it felt like to be left. My mom left me. My uncle left me.

"Maybe he's sorry."

"Whose side are you on here?"

He laughed. "Yours. Always yours. And I'll help you get away if that's what you want. You know that."

I smiled.

He reached out and tucked a loose strand of hair behind my ear. "But I really don't mind having you in my building."

"You being close by is the only positive, trust me. But I can't stay there, Felix. I couldn't sleep at all. I'm pretty sure a…" I stopped talking before I could embarrass my-self. I'd almost said there was a ghost in my room. He'd think I was nuts. *Oh God, am I nuts?* One night in that place and I'd officially lost my mind.

"Pretty sure what?"

"Nothing."

He moved closer. "No, what were you going to say?"

I was saved by a knock on the door.

"Both of you stay there," Miller said. His voice was so firm I actually froze in place. "I'll be right back."

"What's going on?" I asked, but Miller had already dis-appeared.

The banging on the door grew louder and I grabbed Felix's hand. For just a second, I thought the ghost had followed me here. That it was trying to get in and terrorize Felix too.

"It's okay," Felix said. "You're safe here. If it's Mr. Pruitt, I won't let him take you. You can stay with me."

Right. It was a lot more likely that it was Mr. Pruitt than a ghost. But I squeezed Felix's hand tighter still. Or maybe it wasn't either of those things. Maybe it was what-ever Miller was supposed to be protecting me from.

"I have every right to be here." Kennedy's familiar voice flitted into the room. "So get out of my way."

Kennedy! I stood up and ran toward the foyer.

"Move it, buddy," she said.

"I can't let you in," Miller said. "You aren't on the list."

"What list? Brooklyn!" she screamed. "Brooklyn, are you here?"

I ducked under Miller's arm that was blocking the door and threw my arms around Kennedy. And I immediately burst into tears. Felix's hugs were great. But Kennedy smelled like her mother's cooking and home. She smelled like everything I was missing.

"Brooklyn," Miller said from behind me. "You need to let go and come back inside. Right now."

Fuck you.

"Neither of them are on the list," he said.

Neither? I opened my eyes and looked over Kennedy's shoulder at Cupcake. He was holding a box that I was sure was filled with high calorie, sugary treats.

"Hey, Brooklyn," he said. "I brought dessert. Thought it might make you feel better."

It was the first time I'd ever been happy to see him. Another familiar face, even if it was one that had thrown a dodgeball at my nose. "Thanks for coming, guys. And for bringing snacks."

"Where else would we be?" Kennedy said. "Felix said you were here and I knew you needed me."

I had the best friends in the world.

"That's enough," Miller said more firmly. "Brooklyn, get back inside this apartment right now or…"

I turned around. "Or what? They're not going to hurt me if that's what you're worried about."

He frowned.

"They're my friends. I don't care if they're on Mr. Pruitt's approved list, because they're on mine."

"Brooklyn…"

"Miller, please." My voice cracked. "Please."

He sighed.

"Come on man," Cupcake said from behind me. "I brought cupcakes."

"Yeah, we brought dessert," Kennedy said. "And we absolutely won't hurt her. That's not really what you're worried about, is it?" There was an awkward silence. "Wait, that is what you're worried about?" She lifted up her camera. "The worst I could do is sell pictures to the paparazzi, and I'm not even going to do that."

I laughed. "See? Please, Miller." I blinked up at him. We'd shared some kind of moment last night. Maybe it was one-sided. Maybe it wasn't. But it felt like he was at least my friend. "Please."

"Fine. But don't tell Mr. Pruitt."

That was a promise I could easily keep. Because I was never going to see Mr. Pruitt again.

CHAPTER 13

Saturday

Kennedy pulled me into the bathroom with her before Miller had a chance to demand to search it for…whatever it was he was looking for.

"Are you okay?" she asked and put her hands on my shoulders. "Tell me everything. What was it like at their place? Were they as awful at home as they are in public?"

"I messed up." I tried to blink away the tears that had started the moment she'd hugged me.

"What do you mean?"

"I told Mr. Pruitt the truth about what happened at lunch and got Isabella and her mom kicked out of the apartment for the weekend. Isabella's going to be worse than ever to me. What was I thinking?"

"You were thinking that the truth is better than lies."

"Not when it comes to the Pruitts apparently."

Kennedy's hands fell from my shoulders. She was staring at me with so much concern on her face. I didn't know if she was waiting for me to say more or if she had more to say. But it was easy for me to fill the silence.

"I don't know what to do," I said. "I can't stay there another night. And I was hoping Felix would help cause a distraction and then I'd be able to sneak away to your place. But he brought up the point earlier that Miller would easily find me. And I don't have anywhere else to go. What am I supposed to do? They'll always find me. Won't they?" I'd already answered my own question

Kennedy nodded. "Here's what you're going to do. You're going to be brave. And you can tell me all about how horrible they are when we hang out every day. And you're going to get through this. Before you know it, we'll be off to college and you never have to see them again."

That wasn't what I was expecting her to say. At all. What was she talking about? "College?" That was two and a half years away. "Your mom told me she was going to fix it. She's…"

Kennedy shook her head. "Matt even had his fancy lawyer go with my mom. There isn't anything they can do."

"But Mr. Pruitt isn't my legal guardian. Of course they can do something. He freaking kidnapped me."

"Trust me, they brought up that point. But no one's budging. Matt's fancy pants lawyer thinks Mr. Pruitt bribed someone. Everyone my mom goes to just looks the other way. Maybe he bribed a whole lot of somebodies."

"So you're telling me that there's no way out?" I tried to take a deep breath, but it didn't feel like my lungs were expanding anymore. "I'm stuck here?"

"Brooklyn, you're the strongest person I know. You got through your mom's death and…"

"I'm not through it." I couldn't breathe. "My heart is still broken."

"That doesn't mean you're not strong. You're still standing here, fighting the next battle."

I was barely standing.

"And I'll be there for you the whole time."

"Kennedy, he's not going to let me see you. He barely let me leave the apartment today. I'm...I'm..." I let my voice trail off. *I'm trapped.* I'd known it all along. I'd held on to hope when I tried to sneak out last night. And hope that today I'd be able to run away. But I'd known the truth all along. I was trapped in this hell.

"He has to let you see me," she said with a smile. "We go to school together."

She didn't get it. Mr. Pruitt had made it very clear about what he thought of Kennedy and her mom. Yes, I'd get to see her at school. But never after. Not on the weekends. Not at work. But all the fight was out of me once the truth sunk in. *I'm trapped.*

"Let's just try to forget about it for a day."

That was easy for her to say. She wasn't living with the Pruitts. She hadn't lost her whole family. But instead of saying anything at all, I just nodded.

Kennedy smiled. "Come on. It'll be fun. It's kind of like we're having a double date."

Oh God. That's exactly the way it looked. But she had to realize that I couldn't possibly be on a date right now. My heart had broken when my mom died. It had shattered when my uncle died. And it got tossed into oncoming traffic when I broke up with Matt. I didn't have a heart left for anyone.

Kennedy pulled me out of the bathroom and we practically ran into Miller.

His arms were folded across his strong chest and he looked...pissed. Or was it amused? I didn't really know him at all.

But then I realized that amused and pissed were probably exactly right if he'd just been listening to our conversation. "How much of that did you hear?" I asked.

"Just about all of it," he said.

So…my plans to run away and the double date bit. *Great.* As if my day couldn't get any more terrible, now he had to be mad at me too. But why was he mad? Really, I should be the one who was mad. Was it actually in his job description to eavesdrop?

"Awkward," Kennedy said a little too high-pitched and pulled me past him.

Felix and Cupcake had already cracked open the box of sweets. I usually didn't eat much dessert. It was easy to be hyper-aware of the food I put into my body when my mom and my uncle had both died so young. But today, I really didn't give a shit.

I picked up what I figured was the infamous sugarcake and took a huge bite. It practically melted in my mouth. *No wonder these things are so popular.* I took another bite. And another. I grabbed a second sugarcake and pretty much shoved half of it into my mouth like a barbarian.

"You should probably slow down, you don't need all that," Cupcake said and grabbed my arm.

Excuse me? I was pretty sure that offhand comment about my weight was worse than him literally throwing a dodgeball in my face.

"What's your problem, man?" Felix said, breaking the awkward silence that followed Cupcake's comment.

"Nothing," Cupcake said. "I just really think one's plenty for her."

There was no other way to look at it. Cupcake thought I was fat. I looked down at my sweater that showed off my midriff. I tried to pull it down a little. I knew wearing these stupid clothes was a mistake. Justin was wrong about Diane Cartwright knowing how to dress people because I clearly wasn't pulling this off.

"Don't be rude," Kennedy said and lifted up her own sugarcake. "She's had kind of a rough few days if you haven't noticed."

"Right." Cupcake nodded, but he still looked weirdly concerned about me downing a second dessert.

Screw you too, Cupcake. I picked up a third just to annoy him.

"Ignore him," Felix said. "You look amazing."

It was sweet of him to say when his friend had just called me fat. But all I could think about was that it was also very awkward. Because I could feel Miller staring at me.

I turned toward his piercing gaze. "Miller, don't you want any?" I asked. I hated that he just stood there watching us. Couldn't he just sit down and join us instead?

He didn't budge from his spot on the wall, so I brought one over to him.

"They're really good," I said and handed it to him.

"Thanks." He took it from me. "Who's that little jackass?"

I didn't need him to clarify who he was talking about. "Cupcake. He's Kennedy's boyfriend."

"Want me to take care of him?"

"What does that even mean?"

Miller brushed a crumb off the lapel of his suit jacket. "You don't need to know the specifics."

Was this the kind of stuff that the Pruitts paid their security detail extra for? I didn't need to hear anything else. I could tell by Miller's tone that it was something sinister. "That's definitely not necessary."

"Let me know if you change your mind."

I could take care of myself. I didn't need him to do whatever it was he was referring to. And why was that Miller's first reaction? Seriously, what line of work was Mr. Pruitt in?

I retreated back to the couch. Miller was the only person in the Pruitt's apartment that I thought was nice. But nice people didn't offer to "take care" of things in that tone.

"Are you feeling okay?" Cupcake asked. "You look a little pale."

"So now I'm fat and sickly?" The words just spilled out of me like I had no filter.

"What? No. That's not…" his voice trailed off. "I was just asking," he said a little quieter.

And for some reason I started laughing. Once I started, I couldn't stop. My stomach, which as far as I was concerned was very flat, hurt with laughter.

Cupcake started laughing too, probably just relieved that Miller wasn't going to kick his ass, and then everyone started laughing.

"I feel like I haven't eaten in a week," I said and grabbed another sugarcake. "Cupcake, these really are great."

"Thanks," he said when he finally caught his breath. "I made them myself. It's a new recipe with a secret ingredient."

"What's the secret?" Kennedy asked. "Love?"

He smiled and nudged her with his shoulder.

It was the first time that I actually thought they were cute together. I polished off my third sugarcake and sunk into the couch. I'd had that kind of love with Matt. And I threw it all away because he was being blackmailed by Isabella and refused to acknowledge my presence in public. *That was oddly specific and conclusive.* And despite that, all I wanted to do was text him. I looked down at my new phone. It was a bad idea. But I did know his number by heart…

What was I even doing texting Matt? I shook my head. *Thinking about Matt.* I was most definitely not texting him. Which was good because there was a guy that actually cared about me sitting next to me. He had my back. He cared about me. And he wasn't embarrassed of me. Even when I did stuff my face with three sugarcakes.

"Have you thought about what you're going to wear to homecoming?" Felix asked. "I want to make sure my tie matches your dress."

Homecoming. Crap balls. I'd told both Felix and Matt that I'd go with them. But seeing as Matt and I were over and he was never allowed to be with me in public in the first place…he was out of the race. Which was good. Because telling one of them that I overbooked would have been very uncomfortable. So really, the breakup saved me. *Yup.* "I don't know yet. As soon as I do, I'll make sure to tell you."

"I've found a few dresses online that I thought you might want to see," Kennedy said. "But I guess you can kind of buy whatever dress you want now, right?"

I didn't want to talk about this. I wanted to forget about the Pruitts, not picture myself in one of the stupid dresses Diane Cartwright had fitted me for. They probably all showed my midriff and Cupcake would just make fun of me all night. "Do you guys want to watch a movie or something?" I asked. It was a lame segue, but I prayed that it would work.

"Sounds good to me." Felix put his arm behind me on the couch, being careful not to touch me.

I breathed a sigh of relief. Apparently my segue was perfection.

Kennedy abruptly stood up. "Better idea. Let's play never have I ever."

"Oh, good idea, babe," Cupcake said.

Felix looked at me like he was waiting for me to make the decision for both of us.

"Yeah, let's do it." I was actually feeling a little too wired to sit and watch a movie anyway. All the sugar had made me forget about the fact that I hadn't slept at all. I'd just be careful not to bring up homecoming during the game. "Miller, you're up first," I said with laugh.

He just stared at me, but I swore I saw a hint of a smile.

"I can go first," said Cupcake. "I always forget, do I say I haven't done something, and if you guys have done it you raise your hands?"

"Yup," Kennedy said as she settled herself into his lap.

He nodded. "Got it. Never have I ever…used a public restroom."

I laughed. He clearly didn't understand the game. That was just a flat out lie. I was about to correct him, but Kennedy beat me to it.

"Wait," Kennedy said. "Your thing is supposed to be something you *haven't* done."

"Right. I've never used a public restroom. That's what I just said."

"Wait," Kennedy said again. "Are you seriously telling me that you've never used a public restroom?"

"Never."

Her jaw dropped. "How is that humanly possible?"

"I always just go home."

"So if you had to pee right now…"

He shrugged. "I'd go home."

No freaking way. That was the weirdest thing I'd ever heard in my life. Had he never had a bathroom emergency? Oh, no, what if he had? That meant he'd probably wet his pants in his fancy town car.

"But you'd have to drive like 20 minutes," she said.

"You're supposed to raise your hand if you have done that thing," Cupcake said. "You're not supposed to question it."

"I'm sorry, babe. It's just…you're serious?"

"Of course I'm serious. Public restrooms are gross."

So is peeing your pants. I giggled to myself even though Cupcake hadn't admitted to such an incident.

He finally corralled us into finishing our side of the game. We all raised our hands. Because we weren't psychopaths like him.

"Okay that was…interesting," Kennedy said. "Well, it finally all makes sense. Now I understand that thing you told me. You know…that tidbit of information would be really great for this game."

Cupcake looked horrified. "Don't…"

"Never have I ever sharted my pants at school," Kennedy said before Cupcake could stop her.

I almost spit out the sugarcake I was eating when I saw Cupcake's eyes bug out of his head.

"I told you that in confidence," Cupcake hissed at her.

She held back her laugh as only Cupcake raised his hand.

"It was one time," Cupcake said.

Felix laughed. "Man, maybe you should start using a public restroom."

"One time," he grumbled.

Suddenly Cupcake nailing me in the face with a dodgeball or calling me fat didn't seem so bad. The poor guy hard sharted in school. It was hard to come back from that. And yet…he was one of the most popular kids at Empire High. With the name Cupcake. He was basically a genie for pulling that one off.

"Okay." I rubbed my hands together while I tried to think of something fun and witty too. "Never have I ever had a real boyfriend or girlfriend. You know…one that takes you on dates in public and holds your hand in the hallways of school." *God, that wasn't fun and witty.* It was pathetic.

Kennedy, Cupcake, and Felix all raised their hands.

"So you've only had a fake one?" Felix asked with a laugh.

Something like that.

"That's not part of the game," Kennedy said, saving me from answering. "It's your turn," she said to him.

"Coming from someone who forced Cupcake to clarify about a thousand times," Felix said.

Kennedy threw a pillow at him.

Felix easily caught it before it hit him in the face. "Never have I ever wanted pizza more than I do right this second."

I let the sentence roll around in my mind. "Wait, does that mean you do want pizza?"

"I think it means he doesn't?" Kennedy said. "Because he said I never." She put her hand up in the air but she looked really confused.

Cupcake shook his head. "No it means he definitely wants it right now?"

"My head hurts. I have no idea whether or not I'm supposed to raise my hand," I said. "But all I can think about is eating pizza right now."

"Same!" Kennedy yelled and waved her hand in the air. "Pizza please!"

Felix started laughing. "I was trying to be clever but I have no idea if that made any sense. I'm starving. Who else wants pizza?"

I shoved Felix's shoulder. "Cheater. You're supposed to confess something like the rest of us."

"I'll make it up to all of you by ordering pizza."

"Oh, you should use my Amex card. I think it's for stuff like this."

"It's fine, I got it," he said with a wink and started talking on the phone.

"Amex card?" Kennedy asked.

"One of the perks of being a Pruitt. Mr. Pruitt gave me a credit card and told me to expense whatever I wanted on it. Pretty irresponsible of him if you ask me."

Kennedy shrugged. "I guess he trusts you."

That was it! I'd just had an epiphany. "What if he didn't trust me?"

She just stared at me.

"I should just go crazy and buy a ton of stuff. Then he'll hate me and disown me."

"How much stuff do you think you'll have to buy to make him mad?"

"I don't know. Like…a thousand dollars' worth?" I looked down at the couch I was sitting on. "I should buy a couch! That would really show him."

Kennedy nodded. "Those are expensive. We got ours second-hand and it was still a few hundred bucks."

This is genius. "Miller, can we go furniture shopping?"

It wasn't just a small corner of his mouth to lift up this time. He was full on smiling. He even laughed. "It'll have to be more than a couch. You're thinking too small."

"So like…the matching love seat and chair too?"

"He won't even bat an eye at that. He'll just think you're decorating your room."

"Well what do you suggest I do?"

"I don't know." He walked over to us, his air of seriousness completely gone. "But I'm going to have another one of these." He picked up a sugarcake. "They're great."

"Thanks," Cupcake said.

"What if I bought a thousand sugarcakes?" I asked. "That would be…a lot." I couldn't mentally get over the number one thousand. Anything more seemed so extreme.

"Why don't you just tell him how you feel?" Felix asked. His arm was still stretched out behind me on the couch and I let my head fall on his shoulder.

"I already tried that. It didn't work." I left off the fact that Mr. Pruitt swore he didn't know about me. It didn't change anything. It was my mom and me against the world. As soon as I thought it, I closed my eyes. *My mom and me against the world.* For a few minutes there, I had forgotten that my mom was dead. I'd forgotten everything that hurt. I took a deep breath and breathed in Felix's familiar cologne. It was him. He'd taken away the pain.

God, I was such an idiot. I thought Matt was the one for me. Hell, for a few minutes there I even thought Miller could be it. But it was Felix. Clearly it was Felix. He was literally my shoulder to cry on. And he'd made me forget. My whole body felt weird and light, like the realization had put me on a cloud. I'd let myself forget about Matt for an hour and it had given me all the clarity I needed.

"I love you, Felix," I thought to myself. I did. I loved him. It had always been him.

Everyone around me stopped laughing and talking. A hush fell over the room. I lifted my head off Felix's shoulder and stared at them staring at me.

"What did you say?" Felix asked.

Holy hell in a handbasket. Had I just said that I loved him out loud? Like…the words came out of my actual mouth? I reached up to touch my lips and was weirdly surprised that they were even there.

"What?" I croaked.

"You said you loved me." Felix's voice was soft. Like butter. *God, butter was so good.* I wanted some right now. I wanted *him* right now.

"I did say those words out loud, yes."

The doorbell rang, but Felix didn't break eye contact with me.

Miller cleared his throat. "The pizza's here. I'll get it."

Felix reached out and ran his fingers down my jaw.

The action made me shiver.

"You love me." He touched me like he was scared I'd disappear.

And I realized it wasn't just me that didn't have any love left in my life. I lost everyone who put me first. But Felix had said his parents never put him first either. They were always gone. He was all alone. Just like me. And when I'd told him I was all alone at school the other day, he told me that I wasn't. That I had him. *I had him.* But that wasn't why he was looking at me like that. He was staring at me because he had me. And he needed love just as badly as I did.

I tilted my head up to his. I didn't care that Kennedy or Cupcake were watching. Or that Miller and a pizza delivery guy could probably see too. I was much too curious to find out if two broken souls could make one perfectly whole one. Because I really needed them to. I didn't want to feel like I was drowning anymore.

Just before our lips touched, I heard the one person that could break me out of my trance. The person who had thrown my broken, shattered heart into oncoming traffic. *Matthew. Freaking. Caldwell.*

ELITE

"Get your fucking hands off my girlfriend."

CHAPTER 14

Saturday

Nunca.

I was imagining Matt standing there, right? Like I'd imagined him kissing me a million times before he'd ever even spoken to me? He was just ingrained in my brain and wouldn't go away no matter how much I tried to force him out.

But then Felix's face morphed from a smile to a frown. "Girlfriend? What is he talking about, newb?"

Oh no. No, no, no. Felix wasn't supposed to find out about this until I figured out a great way to tell him. Definitely not like this. *Shit.*

"I'm not going to say it again," Matt said. And then he appeared before me. His chest rising and falling like he'd just sprinted here. I was definitely not imagining him. Or imagining the way it felt like there was a knife twisting in my heart. I wanted to run into his arms. I wanted to scream at him. I wanted to cry because I didn't have any idea what I wanted.

"Brooklyn?" Felix asked. His hands were still on my face, trying to get me to look at him. Trying to get me to answer his very simple question. But it wasn't simple to me. Nothing was simple anymore.

And then Matt's hands were on Felix, ripping him away from me. I wasn't sure who landed the first punch, but before I even realized what was happening, they'd toppled onto the coffee table, snapping its legs with a crunch that echoed around the room.

Kennedy and I both screamed.

The snapped wood cracked even more as they rolled on top of it. And the sound of broken wood was quickly replaced with bone slamming against bone as they broke out into a full out brawl.

"Stop it!" I screamed and tried to grab Matt's arm before he could land another punch. But his fists were too quick. "Stop it! Miller! Miller, do something!"

For some reason Miller was laughing as he got between the two boys. He was bigger and older, but not that much bigger and older. The weird laughing confidence was alarming. He could easily get hurt.

"Miller!" I yelled as Felix's fist hit him before it hit its final destination of Matt's face.

Miller immediately stopped laughing.

"Oh my God," Kennedy said. "Cupcake, help him break it up."

"There's no way I'm getting into that," Cupcake said as he helped himself to another sugarcake.

"What are you doing?" she shrieked and slapped the sugarcake out of his hand.

I tried not to pay attention to them as Matt slammed another punch across Felix's jaw.

"Don't you ever fucking touch my girl again," Matt yelled.

"She doesn't belong to you," Felix said and elbowed Matt in the throat.

"Stop! Please stop!" I yelled. But they didn't listen. Someone needed to stop them. I stepped forward, but Miller blocked my path.

"Just give me a second," he said. He was able to pretty easily separate the two of them when he finally tried. Miller pushed them apart with a grunt. "That's enough. Cut it out you two."

Matt wiped the blood from the side of his mouth. "Why was he touching you?" He sounded so pained.

"Matt." My voice cracked when I said his name. "You and me…we broke up."

He shook his head. "Like hell we did. We had a disagreement. That doesn't mean you go running into someone else's arms without talking to me."

I felt so small. And that was the whole problem. Something about being with Matt always made me feel small. At least when we were around other people. I didn't want to have this conversation in front of everyone. Not now. Especially when he was kind of right. We broke up yesterday and I was already telling someone else that I loved them. There was seriously something wrong with me. It was like all my thoughts were colliding. I didn't have an explanation for him. "Matt…"

"Come on. We're leaving."

"What? No." I wasn't going anywhere with him. I wasn't even allowed to. "What are you even doing here?"

"You invited me," he said.

"No I didn't. And I think you should leave." What was he talking about? I looked over at Felix and grimaced at the blood on the side of his jaw and his eye that was already swelling shut.

"You texted me asking me to come here," Matt said.

I absolutely did not. Sure I had thought about it. But I didn't actually do it.

He was staring at me like I'd lost my mind.

I grabbed my phone and looked down at the text message thread. I had indeed texted him. It was right there in front of me. But I had no recollection of doing it. "No." I shook my head. "I didn't write that."

Matt looked over at Felix like he was about to attack him again.

"It wasn't Felix either. I don't…I don't remember." It felt like my head was spinning. And for some reason, I really wanted to laugh. Because Matt's face was so serious. Everyone's faces were so serious.

"What do you mean you don't remember?" Matt said. "It was less than half an hour ago."

"I…" I didn't know what else to say. Maybe someone had stolen my phone. But I didn't think Felix would do something like that. I looked over at Cupcake. If I had to guess one person who would steal my phone and text Matt randomly, I'd guess him. We were barely even friends.

"Matt, she asked you to leave," Felix said. "So I'm not going to ask you again. Get out of my house."

"Are you kidding me?" Matt sounded more pissed than ever. But he wasn't looking at Felix. His eyes were trained on me.

I tried to take a step back as he took a step closer, but the back of my legs collided with the couch. What, was he mad that I was staring at Cupcake? I was trying to figure out what the hell was happening, not checking him out.

"Your pupils are huge," Matt said. "What have you been taking?"

"Nothing." What was his problem? First Cupcake implied that I looked huge. And now my pupils were big too? All men were jerks.

Matt drew even closer. "Have you been drinking?"

"No. You sound insane right now. I think you need to go home and chill out."

Kennedy giggled. "Chill out, bruh." She laughed again as she lifted up a sugarcake. "Do you want one? They make me happy. They'll probably make you happy too." She held it out to him.

Matt looked at the sugarcake in her hand and then down at the almost empty box of desserts. He grabbed it out of her hand. "Did you put something in these?"

"Um no, psycho," said Kennedy. "What would I have put in them?"

Matt turned toward Felix. "What the hell did you do?"

"I didn't do anything," Felix said.

"You expect me to believe that? You're a drug dealer." He tried to step around Miller, but Miller blocked his path. "You wanted to get with my girl and the only way you could do it was to get her high off her mind? You laced these with something, you dirtbag." He threw the sugarcake at Felix.

Felix ducked, but not quite quickly enough. The sugarcake smooshed into the side of his face, smearing the blood along his jawline. Felix lunged at Matt, but Miller stopped him.

"Enough!" Miller said. And then he laughed. And then he stopped. And then he laughed again. "Shit. There is definitely something in those."

Everyone turned toward Cupcake, who was sitting there happily on the couch munching on a sugarcake.

"What?" he said. "I told Brooklyn not to have any more and everyone made it seem like I was a monster. I was trying to get her to pace herself. She didn't listen."

"Pace myself?" I asked. "What the hell is in those sugarcakes?"

"Pot, obviously. I was trying out a new recipe so it would be easier to get away with selling them at school. It was Felix's idea. He's a freaking genius. We're all about to make so much money."

"Fuck," Felix said and ran his hand down his face. "We were supposed to work on the recipe together, you dick."

"I thought you'd be happy that I did it so fast. Surprise."

"Happy? You freaking drugged us, Cupcake. What the hell is your problem?"

"Wait," Kennedy said. "You're selling drugs?" She looked upset. Furious even. But her face looked so calm, like she was about to fall asleep.

"Yeah, Felix gave me a stake in his business when he had to stop selling himself. I thought everyone already knew this? Kennedy, you tried out my first batch last night."

Her face went ghostly pale. "I can't believe you," Kennedy said. Instead of falling asleep like I thought she was about to, she stood up. "I trusted you, Cupcake."

That sentence was ridiculous. She did realize that, right? Trusting a cupcake? I held back my laughter because I could tell it wasn't the right time. But I swore the smile on my face probably looked like the Cheshire Cat from *Alice in Wonderland.*

"Why do I always fall in love with drug dealers?" she said and put her face in her hands.

Always? I looked at Felix. He was the only other drug dealer I knew. Kennedy had told me she didn't like Felix when I'd confronted her about it. But then I thought about how weird Kennedy had been when I'd first started hanging out with Felix. How she'd tried to get me to stay away from him. How she'd kept saying she thought Felix was probably related to me. *God.* Rob had even tried to warn me about this, but I hadn't listened to him. Kennedy really was in love with Felix?

But Felix didn't react to what she said at all. No one did. The only person that knew what she meant was me.

I put my hand on her back. I didn't even care about the fist fight that had just happened right in front of me. I was solely focused on my friend's pain. "Kennedy, I'm so sorry. You told me you didn't…I didn't…" I let my voice trail off. My best friend was in love with the guy I just told I was in love with. And I couldn't say any more in front of all these people who were still clueless.

"What?" she said and pulled her face out of her hands. Her eyes grew round as what she'd just said dawned on her. "I didn't mean that. I'm just upset that my boyfriend is selling drugs without telling me and tricking me into being his guinea pig!" Her throat made a weird squeaking noise when she swallowed.

For a second everyone just stared at her.

"I have to go." She sprinted so fast I would have sworn she was on the track team.

"Shit." Cupcake ran after her.

I tried to move around Miller to run after her too, but he stopped me.

"You were only given permission to come here," Miller said. "You can't follow them wherever they're going."

"So now we're following the rules again?"

"I only didn't follow them one time by letting those two in in the first place. And look at what happened." He gestured toward the broken coffee table.

"No, this happened because you just let Matt waltz in here and he's not on my approved acquaintance list. Or whatever the hell it's called."

"Actually he is," Miller said. "All the Caldwells are."

"Of course. The one person I don't want on it already is."

"Pizza delivery," some stranger said as he entered the family room. "Whoa, what happened here?"

Miller cursed under his breath and grabbed the pizza delivery guy by the arm, hauling him back toward the hallway.

Felix, Matt, and I were left standing there in an increasingly awkward silence.

I wanted to make a joke about how good the pizza smelled, but it didn't seem like it would be well received.

"So he's the one you kissed?" Felix asked. "When you promised I could be your first?"

I wasn't sure if his words were just harsh against the silence, or harsh because he was angry.

I swallowed hard. "Matt stole my first kiss. I didn't give it to him."

Felix shook his head. "Were you seeing him that whole time? Or just after you told me you wanted to be friends until you were ready for more?"

"Felix…"

"I'm just your backup plan." He ran his fingers through his hair. "I feel like a fucking idiot."

"Felix, that's not…"

"Then how else would you put it?"

"That I really like you. And I'm confused."

"A few minutes ago you looked me right in the eyes and told me that you loved me. So that I'd keep crawling back to you like an idiot. You're not confused, newb. You played me."

"Felix, please…" I reached out to him, but he side-stepped my hands and walked away without another word.

I looked at the broken table and the drops of blood on the plush carpet. What the hell had I just done? I didn't realize there were tears streaming down my face until I tasted the salt on my lips.

"Brooklyn." Matt's voice was gentler than it should have been. Wasn't he going to tell me I was a terrible person and run off too? But he didn't run. He just stared at me with so much concern on his stupid perfect features.

"Matt." *My Matt.* The one that held me while I cried every night after my uncle died. The one who took me to his favorite spot in NYC so I wouldn't feel like I didn't have a family. The one that got down on one knee to ask me to be his girlfriend, just to make me smile. I took a deep breath. The one who did nothing when Isabella poured milk on me. The one who let his best friend believe he was keeping me a secret because I was poor. The one that made me lie and sneak around and hurt the people that I loved. "I don't have anything left to say to you."

"Well, tough luck. Because I have a lot to say to you."

God, he was exasperating. "Matt, I told you that I couldn't date you because my heart couldn't take it. I told you that. And you kept pushing it anyway. So I gave it to you and…" I couldn't keep going. "I trusted you. And I feel…nothing. I'm not even sad anymore. I can't feel anything. I'm numb."

"That's the drugs," he said.

"No, it's you."

"Brooklyn…"

"You just sat there and watched at lunch. All those terrible things Isabella said to me and you did nothing. Your friends actually stood up for me. But you…you were silent. I get that you didn't want Isabella to know we were dating. But even strangers can be kind. And I don't want to be with someone who isn't."

I walked away from him without looking back. But I was very aware of his footsteps following me.

CHAPTER 15

Saturday

I ran to the elevator and pressed the button to close the doors. But they stayed open for an agonizingly long time. *Come on.* I slammed my fist against the button again. I just needed a few minutes alone to clear my head. *Come on.* I pushed on the button again. Just as the doors started to close, Matt slid into the elevator.

Damn it.

I didn't say a word as Matt hit the button for the Pruitts' floor. I tried to focus on the elevator music, but it was hard to pretend Matt wasn't there. We were alone. When we were alone, we were always kissing or holding hands or I'd be wrapped in his arms. But he didn't touch me now. And I could feel the distance between us.

"Did you kiss him?" Matt asked.

The elevator music wasn't loud enough to drown him out. "No." I shook my head. "I mean, not today. Not recently."

"Not recently?"

"Not since you left me your varsity jacket." Even though Matt and I hadn't made our relationship official that night, that's when I was all in. That's why everything he did hurt so freaking much.

"Do you still have feelings for him?"

Why weren't these doors opening? "Yes."

His inhale was sharp, like I'd just slapped him. "Why?"

I didn't want to talk about Felix with him. I didn't want to talk to him at all. "For starters, he's not embarrassed to talk to me in public. And he's always been my friend."

"Brooklyn…"

"But you have nothing to worry about because he clearly hates me now." I wasn't even sure who I was more upset with. Matt or myself. This was the longest elevator ride of my life. Matt would never understand. He had tons of friends. He had a family. Everyone loved him. All I had were Kennedy and Felix. That was it. And now I only had Kennedy.

"That wasn't my intention."

"No?" I finally made eye contact with him. "It wasn't your intention to make him hate me when you were punching him in the face?"

"I hit him because he touched you."

The elevator doors finally opened with a happy little bell jingle that made me want to scream. "He's allowed to touch me. You and I broke up!" How many times did I have to tell him this? He was acting like he wasn't there when I told him it was over. I shoved my way past him.

I saw Miller standing in front of the Pruitts' door. How did he beat us here? God, I didn't want to go back inside that haunted prison. I also didn't want to stand here and listen to Matt. My brain was screaming at me to make a run for it. That was my plan all along…to flee. But I'd messed it all up. No, Matt had. He'd ruined everything. I swallowed down the lump in my throat. He'd ruined me.

Kennedy had told me I needed to be brave. But I wasn't brave. I took a step back and collided with Matt. His arms encircled me and I immediately felt more comforted. But thinking about how he had that effect on me just made me feel claustrophobic. I didn't need him. I didn't need anyone. I slipped out of his embrace and for a second I just stood there. I couldn't run for my freedom. No matter which way I turned there was someone there to stop me. And right now, anything seemed better than standing next to Matt.

"Please just go home," I said to him.

"Not until you talk to me."

God, why couldn't he just respect my decision? Couldn't he tell that I could barely think right now? Let alone talk to him. I took a deep breath. It didn't matter, he wouldn't have a choice once I told Miller to not let him in. I made my way over to Miller and he opened the door to let me in. I'd feel better once I was in my room. The rest of the apartment was too creepy to comfort me. "Take him off my list," I said to Miller. I didn't wait for a response. I hurried through the foyer and up the stairs. But still I heard the footsteps behind me. I wished it was a ghost. I'd take the place being haunted over having Matt alone with me in my room. Or Miller, if he was the one following me. I didn't want to speak to either of them. I didn't want to see anyone.

I tried to close the door to my bedroom, but two strong hands stopped it.

"Brooklyn, I just need five minutes."

Matt. "You've had plenty of my minutes. I don't have any more time to waste on you." I tried to close the door but he was too strong.

"I've never wasted a second with you," he said.

That was certainly poetic, but it was even more false. He didn't get it. He'd never understand. "Time is limited, Matt! And every time you don't have my back, that's time I can never get back." *I'm running out of time.* I pictured my mom unconscious on the kitchen floor. I pictured my uncle coughing at the kitchen table. I'd never have enough time.

He pushed the door open hard, knocking me backward. I fell back and landed on my butt.

"Shit," he said as he reached down to help me up.

I didn't need his help. I didn't need anything from him. I pushed his hands away from me.

"Just let me help you up." He grabbed my bicep when I wouldn't let him grab my hand.

I could smell the cinnamon on his breath. And feel his fingers digging into my skin. Suddenly all I could think about was being closer to him. I just wanted to feel something. Anything. I grabbed the front of his t-shirt and pulled him toward me.

His lips collided with mine in a frenzy as I pulled him onto the floor with me. He was pissed. I was furious. And for some reason, for a few heartbeats, this made it better. I was sick of feeling sad and angry and alone. Or worse, nothing at all. I needed this. I needed him.

His fingers slid ever so slightly underneath the bottom of my sweater, the pads of his fingertips warm against my skin. We'd been in this position dozens of times. And it always stopped here. But today I couldn't bear the thought of stopping. And his hands were higher than usual because my sweater was cropped short. I wanted his hand to slide up higher. I shifted beneath him. No, I wanted his hand to slide lower. So much lower. I needed more. I just needed something to make me feel like I wasn't drowning. And I knew he had the power to do that. I knew he could make me forget.

I ran my hand down the front of his shirt until I reached the waistline of his jeans. All I could think about was touching him. And him touching me. My fingers fumbled with the button on his jeans.

He grabbed my hands and lifted them above my head, pinning them to the carpet. "Not like this," he said.

"We can move to the bed…"

"You're high, Brooklyn." He was staring at me like I was lost. It didn't matter if I was. I just wanted him to stop looking at me like that.

"I know what I'm doing," I said. I tilted my hips and I could feel him pressed against me. I knew that he wanted this too. The evidence was clear enough.

He pushed himself off of me.

This felt like the one thing that would make me feel better. And him denying me? "You'll sleep with the whole cheerleading team but you won't sleep with me?" My voice sounded so small. I slid away from him and stood up.

"Who told you that?"

It wasn't a denial. "Screw you, Matt." I pulled my sweater back down.

"I didn't sleep with the whole cheerleading team."

"Just most of them then?" I thought about Isabella and I felt like I was going to be sick.

"I can't undo my past. But I told you I'd wait for you now. And I have. I'm not the one letting someone else touch…"

"We broke up!"

"I never agreed to that."

"You don't have to agree with it. It still happened. It's done."

He just stared at me. "I'm not done with you."

That's not how this works! "Let me make this easier for you to comprehend, because clearly you're struggling. I hate you." I wasn't sure I really meant it, but I certainly meant it right then. I freaking hated him for barging in here uninvited. For making me feel unwanted when he'd already been with everyone else. For not listening to me.

He had the audacity to smile. "Tough luck. Because I love you."

I opened my mouth and then closed it again. What the hell was I supposed to say to that?

He took a step toward me and I didn't retreat. His words were swirling around in my head and I didn't know how to process them.

"You really want your first time to be like this?" he said. "With you mad at me?" He put his hand on the side of my face.

Obviously, or I wouldn't have tried to unbutton your pants. I swallowed down the words. I didn't want him to remove his hand.

"Do you know how badly I want you all the time? How many times I pictured you saying you were ready for more? But not like this. Not when all you need is for me to be here for you. Not today." He swiped his thumbs under my eyes to remove the tears I didn't even realize I shed.

I knew that he thought he loved me. And I could forgive him for a lot of things. I could love him in spite of his flaws. But not this. "If you loved me, you would have stood up for me."

"We've already talked about all of this. Isabella…"

"I know. You did something and Isabella is holding it against you. But you don't even trust me enough to tell me what it is. Or what she's threatening." I removed his hands from my face. "All you said is that it would hurt James, but don't you see that I'm hurting? All I've been doing for the past few months is hurting. And *you* hurt me, Matt."

"I'm sorry. But that's why I'm here. Because I know you're hurting. I know you need me."

"If you're that sorry, you can fix it. Just tell me the truth."

He pressed his lips together.

His silence was the problem. Didn't he see that? "Get out." Maybe I was high, but I was damn sure about this.

"Brooklyn…"

"Get the hell out!"

"You don't understand. James…"

"He's one of your best friends. I know. I get that. What I don't get is why I don't matter. You make me feel like I'm nothing."

"Of course you matter. I'm standing here telling you I love you. You mean everything to me."

"It's not enough. Love isn't ignoring someone when they get milk thrown on them during lunch. Love isn't not acknowledging me in public…"

"You know I can't. You know what will happen if Isabella tells James…"

"That's the thing, Matt. I don't. What will happen to James if you come clean? What secret do you have that will hurt him? What could possibly be worse than this?"

"I can't…"

"Tell me! What is worse than not being there for your girlfriend when she just lost everything? What is worse than that?"

"Losing him!"

It felt like his words echoed around me. "You're scared he won't be your friend anymore? I'm pretty sure friendship has built-in forgiveness." At least, I hoped so. Because I needed a lot of forgiveness from Kennedy if she really was in love with Felix. But my stomach was twisted into knots. Because shouldn't all relationships have built-in forgiveness? And I wasn't forgiving Matt. *What is wrong with me?*

He sat down on the edge of my bed. "No, I don't mean he'd stop being my friend. But yeah, I'm sure that would happen too."

"Then what did you mean?"

"I think he might kill himself, Brooklyn." It looked like he was going to cry. Like the confession was breaking him in two. But instead he just put his elbows on his knees and looked down at the ground.

I didn't know what to say. All I could think about was that James looked…sad. If there was one word I could have chosen to describe him, that probably would have been it. He drank too much. He was addicted to some kind of drug to the point where he'd blackmailed me. He was even more lost than me. "Do you really think James would do…that?"

"Yes. No. I don't know. Maybe." He looked so sad. "His parents gave him some bullshit ultimatum about having to break up with Rachel or they'll cut him off."

I'd heard the rumors about how Isabella and James were supposed to end up together. I thought it was just…rumors. But his parents cutting him off for dating someone else? All rumors were based on the truth. "What is he going to do?" I asked.

"I don't know. But he's already depressed. Did you know that he used to play football with Mason and me? And then suddenly his parents decided sports were a waste of time, so they pulled him from the team. He started drinking first. I don't even know what the hell he's taking anymore. He's drowning and I feel like I'm the only one that can tell it's getting worse every day. And I don't know what to do."

"Matt." I knelt down in front of him so that I could see his face. "If you're worried that he might try to kill himself, we need to tell someone."

"You don't think I've tried that?" He finally made eye contact with me. "Rob just thinks I'm being paranoid because of what happened last year. He says he has it all under control. But he doesn't. He can't watch James 24/7."

"What happened last year?"

He looked up at me with a frown, as if he was realizing he let too much slip. "Nothing."

But I wasn't going to let him out of this conversation so easily. "Did James already try this?"

"No."

"So what happened?"

He shook his head.

"We need to tell James' parents about this." *No, they were the worst.* They were part of the reason all this was happening. "Or maybe the school counselor. Or some other adult. What about your parents? They could help."

"They wouldn't listen either."

"Why? I believe you. I've seen James out of control. We can't get him the help he needs. I wouldn't even know where to start. But an adult would. And they'll believe you too."

"They won't actually."

"Why not?"

"Because they all know the truth." He looked down at his hands.

I slipped my hand between his.

"I'm not supposed to tell anyone about what really happened," he said, as if that was the end of it.

"I think I've proven that I know how to keep a secret. Please, Matt." *Let me in.*

For a few moments, he didn't say anything at all. I wasn't even sure if he was breathing. "My parents paid someone off to change the autopsy report, but the Hunters know. They were there that night." He cleared his throat. "And I guess now you'll know too." He still didn't look up at me.

I squeezed his hand.

"I found my aunt hanging from the chandelier in my house last Christmas Eve. And I...I don't want to find someone I love like that ever again."

Oh, Matt. Tears welled in my eyes. I thought about the rumor about how his great great grandmother or something like that had hung herself from the chandelier in their foyer. Rumors always started with a grain of the truth. I'd just thought that about James and Isabella. And it was true in both cases.

Matt was always so put together. He was the only Untouchable that I thought was truly happy. But that was just the front he put on. He was as broken as me. That was why he always knew the right thing to say to me. That was why he knew all I needed was for him to hold me. He just...knew. He knew what it felt like to lose someone.

I climbed up on his lap and straddled him on the bed. I understood all of it. The pain he carried around. The fear too. I placed my head on his shoulder and wrapped my arms around his back. "My heart hurts for you," I whispered into the side of his neck.

For a few minutes we just sat there holding each other in silence. It always felt like he took away some of my pain when he held me. I hoped I was doing the same for him.

"I can't stand the thought of you hating me," he said into my hair. "I can't lose you too."

It didn't matter how mad I was. I loved him. I loved him so much that it hurt. That's why I was hurting right now. That's why he was hurting. I didn't want to cause him any more pain. "Of course I don't hate you, Matt. I just didn't very much like you for a couple days there."

"I'm sorry."

I shook my head. He didn't have to apologize. I got it. I really did. He was scared of losing someone else. Maybe he was projecting his fears of suicide onto James. Maybe he wasn't. But either way, I could see his fears becoming reality. And I would never do something to jeopardize James' health.

"Can you tell me about your aunt?" I asked. And then my stomach growled embarrassingly loud. I laughed because I didn't know what else to do.

He leaned back with a smile on his face. But I saw it now. The sadness in his eyes. How had I not seen it before?

"I don't even know if you're going to remember any of this tomorrow," he said. "But yeah, I'd like that." His smile grew. "You have the munchies, though, so let me go grab us some food from downstairs and then I'll tell you all about her."

I moved off his lap and watched him leave. And I tried not to think about the fact that he knew where the kitchen was because of his visits with Isabella. Or the fact that I might forget all of this in the morning. I touched the side of my head. *Stupid Cupcake.*

I shook away the thought. Our fight from a few minutes ago had changed everything. Matt had lost someone too. He was just like me. I didn't feel nearly as alone anymore. And at least I understood now why he couldn't just come clean. But I was very aware of the fact that nothing had really changed. He hadn't told me what Isabella was blackmailing him for. And I'd still be a secret.

CHAPTER 16

Saturday

It was hard to picture Matt as a little kid. He was just so big and intimidating now. I couldn't imagine him small. But I'm sure his hair was just as golden back then. And his smile was probably equally contagious. He was smiling now, reminiscing about moments with his aunt from when he was younger. They used to paint together. I had the same reaction to the idea of his hands being little and holding a delicate brush. They seemed much too big to hold a paintbrush. But they were probably a lot smaller back then.

"Do you miss that?" I asked.

"Spending time with her or painting?"

I stared into his eyes. "Both."

He nodded. "Both," he agreed.

"You could still paint, you know. Maybe it'll make you feel closer to her?" Like how I felt close to my mom when I looked at the stars on the fire escape. Or saw the color yellow. Or wore the sneakers she gave me. I swallowed down the lump in my throat.

He reached out and pushed a strand of hair behind my ear. "I don't have that much free time."

Because of football practice? Because of me? Because of worrying about James? He didn't offer an explanation. And I didn't know if I should push anymore. He'd already told me his fears. He'd told me a secret he was keeping. He was finally letting me in. "She sounded like a wonderful person."

"I didn't even know she was depressed. How self-consumed was I that I never noticed?"

"It's not your fault, Matt."

"I should have seen it."

"You're just a teenager. It wasn't your job to see it. Or fix it." I saw the irony in my words. Because James was a teenager. And if his closest friends didn't see his behavior as worrisome, who else was going to take the time to? The way Rob had described their parents was chilling. All James had were his friends. And his girlfriend, but his parents were pressuring him to break up with her. I didn't know what to say.

We were stretched out on my bed. Close, but not touching except for our intertwined fingers. I wanted to pull him in closer, but I wasn't sure if he was still mad at me. The empty Pringles can Matt had pilfered from down-stairs was lying between us, like an impenetrable wall. And thinking about Pringles made me hungry all over again. I was never going to eat pot sugarcakes again. *Focus.* "What are we going to do about James?"

"You're going to forget I said anything. And let me handle it."

"But…there has to be something I can do to help. Or maybe if we can figure out a way to get Isabella to stop blackmailing you? What happened to the private investigator you hired?"

"He didn't find anything. I'm pretty sure she got to him and paid him off."

"She paid off a PI that was hired to find dirt on her?" What kind of tangled mess was Matt caught in?

The door to my bedroom flew open and Matt and I both sat up.

Mr. Pruitt was standing there with a frown on his face. He cleared his throat.

Matt practically fell out of the bed as he moved away from me. His hair was sticking up funny in the back and I'm sure I looked equally unpresentable.

"Matthew, could you please give me a moment alone with my daughter?" Mr. Pruitt's voice was even icier than usual.

Matt smoothed his shirt as he stood up, just making the scene look even worse. We'd barely touched, let alone whatever it looked like now. "We were only talking," Matt said.

"Mhm. Downstairs. Now."

Matt turned around, giving me a reassuring smile. "I swear we didn't do anything. But I'll wait downstairs so she can tell you herself." He walked past Mr. Pruitt.

I busied myself sweeping some of the crumbs from my bedspread back into the Pringles can and looking anywhere but at him.

"There are rules in this house," Mr. Pruitt said as he made his way over to me. Before I could climb off the bed, he sat down on it next to me. "Each designed to make sure you're behaving like the lady you now need to be."

The lady that I wasn't? I think normally I'd be offended by the comment. But instead I wanted to laugh. I bit down on the inside of my lip to prevent myself from even smiling. I was definitely still high. And I had a feeling that was probably against one of Mr. Pruitt's rules.

"We follow a very strict no-processed foods diet, for starters." He lifted the Pringles can out of my hand.

"I don't usually eat like that either." *Only when Cupcake drugs me.*

"Good, good." He tossed it into the trash, landing a perfect shot.

"Nice!" I said. Every ounce of me wanted to lift my hand for a high-five, but it was better not to risk it. Instead, I slid my hands underneath my legs to keep them still.

A small smile spread across his face.

God, he knows I'm high.

"I used to play basketball in my youth."

I breathed a sigh of relief. He was smiling from the compliment on his shot. Not the fact that he was about to call me out on my drug usage. "It shows," I said. "You played in high school?"

He laced his fingers together. "You're just like your sister when you're in trouble. Trying to change the topic to anything but your conduct."

I swore I threw up a little in my mouth at the comparison.

"Another rule is that you are not under any circumstances allowed to have gentleman suitors in your room."

Who talks like that?

"Unless they've asked me for your hand, of course. But clearly you're too young for such talk. So...no boys upstairs."

I nodded. "No boys in my room. Got it."

"Are you two being sexually responsible?"

I made a choking sound and he stared over at me as I gasped for air. "No."

He lowered his eyebrows. "Brooklyn, it's very important that you're responsible when it comes to protection and…"

"No! I mean…no, we aren't doing that. But I'd be safe if we were." Who was he to tell me about safe sex? I was literally a walking example of why he wasn't a reliable source. It was hilarious that he thought he could tell me any of this. *Don't laugh. Brooklyn, don't you dare laugh.*

He nodded. "All your tests came back clean. A clean bill of health is better kept than tainted. A sexually transmitted disease could jeopardize your health."

"I'm not having sex." My voice came out squeaky and high-pitched.

He cleared his throat. "Do you have any questions about sexual relations? Or the aforementioned diseases?"

This isn't happening. It was like the awkward conversation with my uncle about condoms. Only worse because I didn't even know this man. And at least my uncle didn't use weird big words when talking about STDs. "My mom already taught me about the birds and the bees. The public school system covered that topic pretty thoroughly too. And I've had this conversation with my uncle. I'm all up to date, I promise."

"Very well." He stood up and brushed off his pants like sitting on my bedspread had been a dirty thing. "But there probably are a few more options for you in regards to birth control now that you're living with me. You can get on the pill, or there's even a shot. Please come to me first before you put anything like that into your system though. We'll want to take a thorough read-through of all the side effects, yes?"

"Sure." Did anyone ever read those things? They were pages long.

"And I'd be happy to accompany you to any such appointments to discuss these things with Dr. Wilson."

This conversation was so invasive even for a normal father, let alone one I just met. "Sure," I said again, even though I wouldn't be going to any such appointment. Especially with him or Dr. Wilson.

"Will Matthew be joining us for dinner?" The air of concern about my sexual activity had vanished. Mr. Pruitt seemed to be in a good mood.

"Oh. I don't know. I didn't ask him."

"I'll extend the invitation. How about you freshen up and meet us downstairs in the dining room?"

I nodded.

He disappeared as quickly as he'd come.

What the hell was that? I buried my face in my hands. I didn't know whether to be mortified or pissed or just plain confused. The last option won by a landslide. Mr. Pruitt was so weird. He went from terse to overly caring in two seconds flat. Why did he even think I was having sex? Matt had clearly been dressed. *Matt.* I couldn't leave him down there alone with Mr. Pruitt. That would just be asking for trouble. I didn't want to walk in on them talking about sex either.

I ran toward my door but then remembered that Mr. Pruitt had basically told me I needed time to freshen up.

When I reached the bathroom I was horrified to see my hair in a tangled mess. *No wonder he thought we were banging.*

I grabbed a brush that was lying there and pulled it through the mess. My hair detangled in one stroke. *Huh.* I looked down at the brush. It must have been some magic, rich person brush. I put it down gently, afraid that I might break it. And then I went to go save Matt from what was surely an awkward conversation.

But when I walked into the dining room, it was only Matt sitting there.

"Hey," I said. "Where's Mr. Pruitt?"

"He said he needed a few minutes in his office. But that we could start without him. You want me to stay, right?"

"Of course." I sat down next to him at the table, avoiding the chairs Mrs. Pruitt and Isabella had sat at the other night. "If it was up to me, you'd never leave." I opened my mouth to say something else, but one of the staff members I hadn't met yet bustled in carrying a tray of salads.

She didn't question the unannounced guest, the absence of Mr. Pruitt, or the fact that Mrs. Pruitt and Isabella were missing.

"Thank you," I said when she placed a bowl down in front of me. "This looks great."

She seemed surprised that I was talking to her. "You're welcome, miss."

"I'm sorry I didn't meet you the other day on my tour. I'm Brooklyn. What's your name?"

She glanced at Matt nervously. "Tiffany," she said. Her skin was so pale that I thought she might faint. But then I thought that maybe she was just never allowed to leave the apartment. *Like me.* Besides, the rest of her looked healthy enough. She couldn't be much older than me, and her mousey brown hair was shining and I wondered if she had one of those magical hairbrushes too. "It's nice to meet you," I said.

Tiffany smiled, but it faltered when there was a noise from somewhere in the hall. It almost sounded like the heat had just kicked on, even though it wasn't quite chilly enough for it. She scurried away as quickly as she had come.

"Why does everyone always look so shocked when I talk to them?" Justin had acted the same way earlier. I shoved a huge forkful of lettuce in my mouth.

Matt laughed.

I looked up at him and tried to swallow my food as fast as I could.

"You don't see it, do you?" he asked.

"See what?" It took every ounce of restraint I had not to shovel more food into my mouth. I was so freaking hungry.

"They react that way because people usually ignore them. And you...you're so nice. And kind. And sincere. It's refreshing."

I felt my cheeks blush.

"And beautiful," he added.

I laughed. "I don't think that's why they're shocked when I talk to them."

"I was shocked when you talked to me."

"No you weren't." But I was smiling so hard that my objection didn't sound like much of one at all. He thought

I was beautiful. He was acting like he was the lucky one in this relationship, not me. "Are we still…I know I said I wanted to break up, but…"

"Are you asking me out, Brooklyn?"

"Yes?"

He smiled. "As far as I'm concerned, we never broke up." He reached out and grabbed my hand. "And I don't care about what happened with Felix. I deserved it for not sticking up for you."

"Nothing happened." Minus the fact that I'd told him I loved him. But I was freaking high. I had no idea what I wanted. Except Matt. I knew I wanted him back. I squeezed his hand. "But nothing has really changed. You still won't be able to stick up for me in public."

"What if we have a secret code?"

"A code?"

"So that you'll know I'm on your side even if I can't say anything."

"I'm not sure that will really help."

"Or a signal so I know to help get you out of a situation?"

It should have been pretty clear when I needed help. But maybe a signal would assist him. And it would allow us to communicate without anyone knowing. "What about sticking out our tongues?"

He laughed. "People will think we're sick. How about you bite your lip."

"Like this?" I bit my bottom lip and I swore he groaned.

"Yeah. Like that." He did the same and I realized why he groaned.

Something about the way his teeth dug into his lip made me wish he was doing it to me. My lips. My skin. Anything. He could bite me anywhere he wanted. "You don't think it's too suggestive?"

He smiled. "You might be right. How about we rub the tip of our nose with our index finger?"

"That works for me."

Matt ran his thumb along my palm, sending shivers down my spine. His touch was a lot better than a signal. But the signal would have to do in public.

"Stop the hand holding for a moment," Mr. Pruitt said as he walked into the room with a huge pile of papers.

I pulled my hand out of Matt's and stared at the papers as Mr. Pruitt plopped two stacks down in front of me. So the noise that scared Tiffany away earlier wasn't the heat coming on. It was the printer whirring to life. "What are these?"

Mr. Pruitt snapped his fingers and Tiffany rushed out with his salad. "These," he said as he placed his napkin on his lap, "are a relationship agreement for the two of you. As well as the list of rules for the household for you, Brooklyn. Matt already signed the guest rules years ago. But I'll need his signature on the relationship agreement. And your signature on both of them."

"A relationship agreement?" Why did Mr. Pruitt have any say in my relationships?

"The two of you are in a relationship, are you not?" Mr. Pruitt asked and started to eat his salad.

Matt looked at me and then back at the document. He looked so uncomfortable.

What could we possibly say here? Mr. Pruitt had already seen us together. He might let something slip to Isabella. Signing a freaking document seemed like a bad idea. And I knew Matt loved me. I didn't need his signature on some kind of weird relationship document. "Actually, Matt and I are taking it slow. We'd rather not let anyone know about our relationship just yet."

Mr. Pruitt wiped at the corner of his mouth. "Is that true?" he asked and turned his head to Matt. "You'd rather keep your relationship a secret?"

Matt looked up from the document. "We're just not ready to share it yet." Something about the way he said it made me sad. I was ready to share it.

"Are you embarrassed about dating someone from the wrong side of the tracks?" Mr. Pruitt asked.

"No. That's not…"

"Brooklyn is a Pruitt now. And I expect you to treat her like a Pruitt. Sign the papers or you can leave."

I didn't even know if Mr. Pruitt realized he was standing up for me. It was all I tried to say on Friday when Matt and I broke up. I just wanted Matt to acknowledge that I wasn't invisible at school. But none of this was his fault. I don't know if it was Kennedy's pep-talk about being brave, or the weed in my system, but I was suddenly tired of all the secrets. "Matt and I have to be a secret because Isabella is blackmailing him."

"Brooklyn…" Matt started, but I kept talking.

"She's trying to make both of our lives a living hell."

Mr. Pruitt nodded like he wasn't at all surprised by my words. But his eyes were focused on Matt. "And what is she blackmailing you over?"

"I can't say," he said. "It doesn't just involve me."

Mr. Pruitt clasped his hands together and sighed. "But you can confirm that my other daughter is doing what Brooklyn said? Blackmailing you? Trying to ruin both your lives?"

"She's certainly not making my life any easier," Matt said.

Mr. Pruitt sighed. "Interesting. Well, I will have to look into that for you as discretely as possible. I'm assuming she threatened you with my assets?"

Assets? What is he talking about?

"Yes," Matt said. "But I wasn't worried about that. I've only ever been concerned about Brooklyn's safety."

Mr. Pruitt sighed. "I'm sorry. I've had this conversation with Isabella before and I guess I need to have it again. Go ahead and sign the papers and Isabella won't know. And I'll make sure to look into this inconvenience without putting either of you in danger. Isabella knows better."

"What are you talking about?" I asked. "My safety? Danger? What else did Isabella threaten you with, Matt?" I asked.

Matt didn't respond.

"Oh, she threatened to have him killed," Mr. Pruitt said like it was nothing. "You too I presume. But she knows the rules. She's not allowed to escalate anything to homicide. It's actually in that document there," he said and nodded toward one of the stacks of papers. "I expect you to have that signed and back to me by the morning," he said and started to eat again.

"She was going to kill me?" I asked. I remembered her friend Charlotte saying how easy it would be for them to make me disappear. She'd been freaking serious.

"No. She's not allowed to use my assets like that. Another thing in the rules. An amendment specifically added for her."

"So not murdering people is in the house rules? Why the hell does that have to be in the rules? And why did it have to be added because of Isabella? Has she already killed someone?"

"Mind your language at the table." Mr. Pruitt seemed so calm as he took a sip of his wine. "Keeping family secrets is one of the rules. And I can't discuss anything further with you until you sign the papers."

"I'm not signing this." I shoved the stack of papers away.

"If you want my protection, you'll sign the rules," he said.

"I don't want your protection. I've told you, I don't want anything from you. I…"

"It doesn't matter what you do or don't want from me. You need my protection."

"Why? I was perfectly safe before."

"But you aren't now," he said firmly. "So please sign the papers and don't disobey me again."

"I need to know why I'm not safe now. What am I not safe from?" I thought about Miller checking everything so thoroughly in Felix's apartment. What exactly had he been looking for?

"Because you're a Pruitt," Matt said, like that was explanation enough.

I just stared at him. "I don't know why that changes anything."

Mr. Pruitt looked exhausted as he pushed his salad to the side. "Because there are a lot more people that want you dead besides Isabella now. Let's have the main course, shall we?" He snapped his fingers.

I wasn't sure if it was to signal the server or to show that it was the end of the conversation. But I was too stunned to speak anyway.

CHAPTER 17

Monday

I walked up the steps of Empire High in my new uniform. It didn't feel like students were staring at me anymore. Whatever rumors had been circulating had died down, probably thanks to some other rich-person scandal. I made my way through the big wooden doors and down the crowded hallway.

The rest of my weekend passed in an awkward blur. Mr. Pruitt wasn't how I'd imagined him. He was protective of me, despite the fact that he swore he only just found out about me. He treated me like I belonged. And he was trying hard to get to know me. But when he presented me with a contract bigger than any of my textbooks, it made me wary.

I'd signed the relationship agreement as soon as Matt had. I didn't even really get a chance to look at it. If Matt trusted it, so did I. But as for the house rules? I hadn't signed those yet. Mr. Pruitt had given me a stern look when I didn't have it signed and ready yesterday morning like he'd requested. But instead of chastising me, he handed me a section of the Sunday paper to read. Instead of reading anything, I just stared at the crossword puzzle and missed my uncle.

I spotted Kennedy by her locker and hurried over to her. She hadn't answered any of my calls yesterday. Or the night before. And I was dying to talk to her. "Hey, are you okay?" I asked.

"Hm?" She looked up at me. "Shouldn't I be asking you that?"

I just stared at her. There were dark circles under her eyes. One of the times I'd called, her mom had said she was taking a nap. If that were true, wouldn't she look a little more rested? "I'm fine. I was worried about you after you ran off."

"That was nothing."

It wasn't nothing. She'd confessed that she loves Felix. Well, kind of. She hadn't actually said his name. But I knew. She knew that I knew, right?

Kennedy started playing with her camera instead of looking back up at me. "How was the rest of your weekend?" she asked.

Should I push this? I stared at the way her bangs hid her face when she was fidgeting with her camera display. If she wanted to talk about it, she would. I couldn't force it. "Um. It was okay. Mr. Pruitt gave me some weird house rules document to sign. I've only read about half of it, but it's all pretty insane."

She finally looked back up and she was smiling. "Did you expect anything less than crazy from him?"

I laughed. "Not really."

"I'm sure it only gets weirder. I'd just sign it and get it over with."

"Fair point." She was probably right. I couldn't memorize all the rules anyway. I thought about the contract sitting on my bed. Signing it would make Mr. Pruitt happy. And he was significantly more pleasant when he was in a good mood. "Oh, and Matt and I made up."

"Well that's good. How did Felix take it?"

Oh balls. I'd been so happy that Matt and I had gotten back together that I hadn't even thought to tell Felix. "Um…I haven't told him. Felix and I got into a pretty bad argument after you left." It wasn't much of an argument. He'd pretty much just said I was the worst and walked away. And I was. I'd treated him awfully. I hadn't even meant to.

"So you and Felix are done?" she asked.

It was a weird question. I'd just told her I was back with Matt. But it was less weird if she was secretly in love with Felix. "Mhm. I'll try to talk to him today though. I really want to be friends."

"Do you think he'll still sit with us at lunch?"

"I don't know." Kennedy and Felix were my only friends at Empire High. I didn't even want to think about the fact that there was a chance I'd lost that. He'd forgive me, right? I hadn't intentionally led him on like he believed. I was trying to protect Matt. I was dealing with other things. But it didn't matter what I told myself. I still felt guilty. "At least I won't have to sit with Isabella at lunch today."

"Are you sure about that?" Kennedy asked.

"Yeah. She didn't come home. I guess she's still in the Hamptons."

"Are you sure about that?" Kennedy asked again and looked over my shoulder.

Isabella and her minions were walking down the hall, their high heels clicking on the linoleum.

"What are the odds that she'll just ignore me?" I whispered.

"Based on the fact that she's coming this way? Slim to none." Kennedy slammed her locker shut. "Come on." She grabbed my arm. "Let's just get out of her way."

But before I even took two steps, Isabella called my name.

Kennedy and I both froze.

"Sissy, whatever are you doing?" Isabella said and stopped beside me. "It's like you're trying to avoid me."

That's exactly what I'm doing. "Of course not," I said. God, when had she gotten back? Just seeing her made my stomach roll. Her fake smile made me nervous. And the nickname Sissy? *Come on.* She wasn't fooling anyone.

Isabella flipped her hair over her shoulder. "You'll sit with me at lunch again today, yes?"

I couldn't even fake being nice this time. "No. Absolutely not."

She looked surprised by my answer. "But I talked to Daddy."

Ew, stop calling Mr. Pruitt that. "Great."

"And I know I messed up and I'm…sorry." It was like the apology pained her because her fake smile faltered for just a moment.

Apology not accepted. "Okay. But I'm still not eating lunch with you."

"Please, Brooklyn," she said, her voice lowered. "I said I was sorry. Truly I am. And if Daddy thinks we're not getting along, he'll send me away again."

She was acting like a trip to the Hamptons was a punishment. It sounded pretty glamorous to me. Especially if that house wasn't haunted too. "I'll just tell him I sat with you. He doesn't have to know."

"But, Brooky, we're sisters now. It's okay if I call you Brooky, right?"

I just stared at her. "I prefer Brooklyn."

"Okay, great, I'll just call you Sissy then. So we're on for lunch then?"

How were either of those things the conclusions that she came to? But just then Matt walked past us. Our eyes locked for a second and he ran his index finger against his nose and then winked. I was pretty sure I melted right there. It wouldn't be as bad now that we had a signal, right? Maybe it would be nice to sit with him this time. I quickly looked away before Isabella could notice. "I'll think about it," I said.

Her smile grew, and for the first time I wasn't sure if it was fake. She actually looked relieved. "Daddy will be so pleased with this news. I know it's his wish for us to become close. And now I can tell him we're doing just that. See you later, Sissy." She blew me a kiss and her and her posse clicked off, everyone in the hallway parting for them to pass.

"Sissy?" Kennedy said under her breath. "Could she be any more manipulative?"

"It's fine," I said. "I'm not actually going to sit with her. But I don't think she's planning anything sinister today."

"Oh yeah?" Kennedy raised her eyebrows. "What makes you say that?"

"Because Mr. Pruitt has my back." He'd kicked her out of the house after the milk incident. And he was keeping my relationship with Matt a secret. He wasn't even going to let Isabella kill me anymore. Although, I still wasn't sure of the specifics on that. Mr. Pruitt refused to elaborate and I hadn't seen the amendment in the document yet. Either way, Isabella was scared. I could tell. She wouldn't pull anything like that again at lunch.

"So you're coming around to him?" Kennedy asked. "Is it the new clothes?" She looked down at the blue tights I was wearing. There wasn't a single hole in them.

"You know my love can't be bought," I said.

"It certainly can't hurt." She stopped outside her homeroom. "I'll see you later."

"Kennedy, wait," I said. "Did I do something wrong?"

She hugged her books to her chest. "No. Nothing. I just didn't feel well yesterday, and I think I still have whatever bug it was."

I could tell she was lying, but I didn't know what to say. I'd already told her I was worried about her. But she just brushed it off. "Are you sure that's all?"

"Yeah. I gotta go. The bell's gonna ring." She turned around and hurried into the classroom.

I just stood there for a moment. Felix hated me. And now I was pretty sure Kennedy was mad at me too. In the course of one weekend I'd gone from two best friends to none. It didn't matter if I had Matt back. I wasn't going to survive going to Empire High without my friends. I needed to find a way to fix it.

"Everything okay, Sissy?"

I almost screamed. I hadn't seen Isabella sneak up behind me. "What? Yeah."

"I rushed over because it looked like you were distressed."

"I'm not distressed."

"Oh. I think I know what's going on. Let me give you a piece of sisterly advice. It's better to cut off ties from your lesser associates sooner rather than later, don't you think? Your little friend will never belong in our world. And she's clearly bitter about your new status. You don't need that kind of resentment and negative energy in your life. It'll just give you worry lines. And Daddy won't allow us to get Botox until we're 18. See you at lunch." She turned on her heel and left as quickly as she'd come.

Isabella was the negative energy in my life, not Kennedy. And I didn't care about worry lines, I was just worried that I was losing my best friend. The bell rang and I hurried toward homeroom. But what if Isabella was right? It did seem like Kennedy was bitter about my new clothes. I tried to dismiss the thought. Anything Isabella said was toxic. But I couldn't shake it. Did Kennedy really resent me?

CHAPTER 18

Monday

All I wanted to do was talk to Felix. But when he chose to play basketball with Cupcake instead of heading outside to run, I knew he wasn't going to give me a chance to explain. He was ghosting me. A part of me knew I deserved it, but it still stung. No, students weren't staring at me and whispering behind my back today. But I still felt isolated. I thought running would clear my mind. But I was no closer to figuring out why Kennedy was mad at me, and I had no plan on how to make Felix stop hating me.

I sighed as I headed toward lunch. I just wanted things to go back to normal. *Normal.* I tried to push the thought aside. I didn't even know what normal was anymore. And I certainly didn't want today to be my new normal. The only person that had been nice to me all day was Isabella. What twisted reality was I living in?

"Not sitting with Isabella?" Kennedy asked but didn't look up from her chicken sandwich.

"No, I'm sitting with you. Like always. Where's Cupcake?"

She shrugged.

I tried to spot Felix and Cupcake in one of the lines for food. But I didn't see either of them. I knew Cupcake would sit with us whenever he got here. And that should draw Felix over too, right? I just needed five minutes to explain what happened. He'd listen about the blackmail. He'd understand that I just didn't want anyone to get hurt. *Except I hurt him.*

I swallowed hard. I needed to focus on fixing one relationship at a time. And since Felix wasn't here…I needed to figure out why Kennedy was giving me the cold shoulder.

"Do you want to come over after school?" I asked. I hadn't gotten Kennedy on Mr. Pruitt's list yet, but I had a feeling Miller would let me sneak her in. Maybe I could force her to take half the clothes that the stylist had given to me. Kennedy was taller than me, but we'd swapped clothes before. Besides, she liked her skirts and dresses shorter than I did.

"I'm still not really feeling that well. I think I'll just head straight home after school."

"Could I come over to your place then?" I asked.

She pushed around some applesauce with her spoon and didn't look up.

"What are you doing, Sissy?" Isabella said from behind me.

Couldn't she see that my best friend was distressed? Of course she couldn't. Isabella only cared about herself. "Eating lunch," I said.

"But you promised to eat with me and my friends, sillykins. I saved a seat for your bffl too this time. Come, ladies." She turned on her heel and walked over to the Untouchables' table. I saw the two seats beside Matt were empty. I could finally sit right next to him at lunch for the first time since Isabella had started blackmailing him. Or threatening to kill me. Or whatever the hell she was doing.

I pressed my lips together. But I couldn't go over there. Not when Kennedy was mad at me. God, why had I even considered it? Isabella was a monster. I could hang out with Matt some other time. Today I was solely focused on making sure Kennedy was alright. "We don't have to," I said, but Kennedy was already grabbing her tray.

"No, I want to," she said.

"You do? But there isn't a seat for Cupcake."

She laughed. "It's fine, I can't pass up the opportunity to watch Isabella in her natural habitat."

At least she'd laughed. "If you're sure it's alright?" I said and stood up too.

"Absolutely. Plus, you'll get to sit with Matt."

I couldn't even hide my smile as we walked over to their table. Matt looked up at me as I approached. He rubbed his nose and I'm pretty sure my smile grew. I sat down next to him and I realized I was holding my breath. I quickly exhaled and tried to pretend this wasn't momentous.

"Hey," James said. He was the first person to acknowledge my presence and I was grateful. "How was your weekend?"

Awful. Wonderful. "Weird," I said.

He smiled.

"I heard you got into Harvard. Congrats."

His smile faltered. "Thanks."

"Congratulations are in order for me too," Mason said as he lightly punched James' shoulder. "He's not the only one that got his letter."

"Wow, that's awesome," I said.

Mason gave me his signature smile that had the whole female student body kneeling at his feet at parties. It didn't have the same effect on me. It just made me feel uncomfortable. And reminded me that Mason didn't know that I was dating his little brother.

"You seem surprised," Mason said. "What, you don't think I'm as smart as this guy?" He pointed to James.

"What? No. I…"

"He's just messing with you," Rob said. He leaned forward so he could see me from his seat on the other side of Matt. "What's it like living with Isabella?" he asked.

"It's so fun," Isabella said, before I had a chance to say I didn't really know because she'd been banished to the Hamptons. "Brooky's the long-lost sister I've always wanted."

Barf.

Rob laughed. "What's it really like, Sanders?"

Matt shifted in his seat, making his thigh brush against mine and distracting me from Rob's question.

"Interesting," I said. It came out as more of a question than anything and Rob laughed.

"You're hilarious, Sissy," Isabella said. "I'm always telling her that."

What the hell kind of game was she playing here? I realized that in all the awkwardness, I'd forgotten to introduce Kennedy. "Oh and guys, this is Kennedy," I said.

"You're dating Cupcake, right?" Rob asked.

"Mhm." Kennedy's voice had never sounded so small before. I wondered if she truly was sick.

"Speaking of dating," Isabella said and batted her eyelashes at James. "How's your girlfriend handling the Harvard news?"

Matt had told me the other night that James' parents were giving him an ultimatum. His girlfriend or Harvard. It was like Isabella had been waiting for the perfect time to make this jab at him. What was her problem?

James ran his fingers through his hair, looking more distressed than he had after I brought up Harvard in the first place.

I studied his face. Or did he just look…sad? I tried to view him like Matt did. The drinking. The drugs. His behavior was sporadic. But his general mood wasn't. James Hunter was always sad. It was one of the first things I ever noticed about him.

"You have told her, haven't you?" Isabella asked when James didn't respond.

"Isabella, stop it," Matt said.

"Oh no," she said. "You have to tell her the truth about this. Secrets are so toxic in relationships. Isn't that right, Matthew?" she said and turned to him.

I was pretty sure I stopped breathing. *No. No, no, no.*

"I know you guys were thinking that I'd never let Brooklyn sit with us again after that milk spilled on her the other day. Let alone that I'd extend the invitation to her little friend. But that was before I realized that she actually is one of us. Isn't that right, Sissy?"

"I don't know what you're talking about," I said. But I was scared I did. She had to be talking about me dating Matt. What else could it possibly be? Mr. Pruitt said he'd talk to her. Had he really told her everything? He'd said he'd fix it. Not make it a million times worse. *Damn it, Mr. Pruitt!* This was why Isabella invited me over here. To torture me again. She'd even let me sit right next to Matt so she could publicly shame both of us.

Isabella frowned. "Of course you do. You're dating Matthew. And by extension, you're one of us now."

Everyone at the table was eerily quiet.

James raised his left eyebrow and stared at Matt like he was trying to figure out why he'd been left out of the loop.

I didn't know what to say. And clearly Matt didn't know what to say. Did this mean that we were in the clear? That she was done blackmailing him? Maybe Mr. Pruitt had actually fixed it.

"You ruined the surprise," Kennedy said, finally breaking the silence. "They were planning on telling everyone later this week." She kicked me under the table. "Right, Brooklyn?"

I bit the inside of my lip so I wouldn't yelp. "Yeah."

Matt seemed to relax next to me.

"It's about time you asked her out," Mason said. "He's been crushing on you since the beginning of the semester."

I could feel my cheeks turning red.

"You're awfully quiet," Mason said to Rob. "Did you know?"

Rob shrugged. "Yeah, I have a class with them. They're kind of ridiculous. Always making me feel like I'm third-wheeling on our group project." He winked at me.

"Why didn't you tell us, Matt?" James asked.

"Dating someone our parents don't approve of isn't exactly working out so well for you," Rob said.

I felt myself sinking in my chair. I knew that's what Rob thought. That I was from the wrong part of town. That Matt's parents wouldn't accept me. Matt had just let Rob assume he was embarrassed of me. It stung.

"That's not it," Matt said. "I don't care what Mom or Dad think. They'll probably love her." He looked over at me, the first time really acknowledging me in front of all his friends. "But none of that matters. Because I love her."

For a second, everyone drifted away. All I saw was him. And he slid his hand into mine, showing our solidarity. It was the first public display of affection we were ever allowed to have at Empire High. And I was smiling so hard it hurt.

"So why didn't you tell everyone right away then?" Isabella asked. "If it wasn't the very reasonable idea that you were embarrassed of her upbringing and where she lived and how she, you know…carries herself." She waved her hand at me like that explained everything.

"Secret relationships are fun," Kennedy said, trying her best to stand up for me. "The forbidden aspect and all that? They were just having fun sneaking around."

"We both know that's not it, sweetie," Isabella said. "Matt, I think it's about time you told James the truth, don't you? Come clean. The truth shall set you free."

She was a murderous psychopath. And now she was quoting scripture? This girl was completely nuts.

"What is she talking about?" James asked.

"Nothing." Matt was glaring at Isabella. "Can I talk to you in private? Now?" He pulled his hand out of mine.

"Why? I think it's time we put it all out there. I mean, you finally came clean about your charity case of a girl-friend. Why not admit to the rest of it?"

I wanted to know what Isabella had on Matt. Desperately. But not like this. Not right in front of James when Matt swore it was going to hurt him.

"Isabella…" I started.

"Shut your Daddy-stealing mouth. I wasn't talking to you. I was talking to your whore of a boyfriend who owes my future hubby an apology."

I didn't close my mouth because she'd told me to. I closed it because I wanted to know why she'd described Matt as a whore. And how it had anything to do with James.

"James, can I talk to you for a second?" Matt said.

"No, Matthew. Here. Now. You have five seconds to tell him the truth or I'll tell him for you."

"This is going to sound bad," Matt started. "But I swear James, if you give me a chance to explain, it's not what you think…"

"Oh, it's exactly what he's going to think. When I was referring to secrets, I didn't actually mean your secret rela-tionship. I was referring to the fact that you're a liar. And manipulative. And a pretty terrible friend." She reached out and grabbed James' arm. "Remember that party over the summer where you and Rachel had that huge fight? Matt was there to console her." She paused and a sinister smile crept over her face. "Sexually that is. I caught them in the act in the pool house."

"What the fuck, Isabella?" Matt yelled. "That's not even close to what happened."

"Did you have sex with Rachel?" James asked. His voice was calm. Cold. Calculated.

Everything about the way James spoke made me want to hide under the table. But I was glued to my seat. Matt had slept with James' girlfriend? That was what Isabella was blackmailing him for? He wasn't allowed to speak to me in public because he'd slept with someone else? It didn't even feel like he wanted to keep it from James. It felt a lot more like he was just keeping it from me. My whole body went cold.

"You know I wouldn't do that," Matt said. "It was all Rachel. She was upset and she…"

James lunged across the table, his hands making perfect contact with Matt's throat.

Kennedy screamed and more students joined in.

Mason grabbed James by the back of his blazer, pulling him off. "Stop it! Both of you!"

"I'm gonna fucking kill you," James said.

"I didn't do anything! Rachel kissed me and…"

"Get her name out of your mouth!" James shoved Mason off of him. "Fucking asshole." Instead of trying to attack Matt again he stormed out of the cafeteria. But not before his fist collided with one of the windows. The sound of glass shattering echoed all around us.

For just a second, no one moved. Or spoke. All I could hear was my own breathing.

But then Matt went to follow James.

"Don't," Rob said and stopped him in his tracks. "What the fuck, man? How could you do that to him? You of all people?"

"I didn't. Rachel…"

"Nice, take the high road and blame his girlfriend? Screw you."

Matt shoved his way past him, beelining toward the doors James had just gone through. I felt myself shrinking all over again. He hadn't looked at me once. Not once since the truth had come out. But it was better that he hadn't. Because Rob was right. It took two people to kiss. Matt had gone on and on about not wanting James to get hurt. When really? He'd already hurt him. Matt didn't care about anyone but himself.

"Daddy said I shouldn't tell," Isabella said. "But I decided not to listen. Because I think everything is better out in the open. Don't you agree?"

"You're a nasty bitch, Isabella," Rob said.

I'm pretty sure everyone was thinking it. But she still looked shocked that someone had actually said it out loud.

She rolled her eyes. "And you're a little twerp who uses humor to hide from the fact that he's living in his brother's shadow. I was hoping we could all discuss this like adults, but clearly I've overlooked the fact that you're all so juvenile. Ladies," she said and turned to her friends who were sitting in silence watching their horrid ringleader. "Let's go."

All her minions stood as one and followed her from the table.

"Did you know?" Rob asked me. He sounded hurt. I wasn't sure if it was because of what Isabella said or if he was somehow channeling James' pain. Maybe it was both.

"No. He said we had to keep our relationship a secret because Isabella was blackmailing him. He never told me what she had on him. He'd hinted that if it came out it might hurt James." I shook my head. I was such an idiot. What else would have hurt James?

Rob sighed like the weight of the world had just been put on his shoulders. If Matt was right about James, maybe it had. What if James tried to hurt himself? What if I was the only one besides Matt who realized he might?

"I should go stop them before they try to kill each other again," Rob said.

Mason stood up. "I'll come with you. Kennedy, do you mind telling your boyfriend I need to talk to him?"

She nodded.

"Thanks. He's probably the only one that has something to smooth this over." Mason followed Rob out of the cafeteria.

"Are you okay?" Kennedy asked.

I nodded, even though I wasn't.

"I guess I should go find Cupcake. I'll see you later." She dumped her tray of uneaten food in the garbage and hurried off.

I didn't know if she was sick. Or if she hated me. All I could think about was how many times I had dreamed of sitting at the Untouchables' table. The first time I'd been here, Isabella poured milk on me. And this second time? I was sitting all alone at their table. Isabella had tricked me with her fake niceness again. I was so naive.

I stared at the empty table. I'd been right all along. I didn't belong in their world. I didn't want to be an Untouchable. And I didn't want to be with someone like Matt.

CHAPTER 19

Monday

"Please, Miller," I said from the back seat. I tried to hide my tears from him. Matt and Rob hadn't shown up to our entrepreneurship class. I hadn't seen any of the Untouchables the rest of the day. Even Isabella had left me all alone. Felix was ghosting me. And Kennedy hadn't shown up with a smile and her camera at my locker to walk me out of school. It was like the whole school was hushed. And being alone with my thoughts? I felt like I was being swallowed whole. I needed my best friend. I had to go see Kennedy. I needed to fix whatever was broken between us before I lost everything.

"She's not on the list," Miller said.

"Please." My voice cracked.

He didn't respond. He just kept driving in the opposite direction of my old neighborhood. "Only if you tell me what's wrong," he said.

I lifted my face out of my hands. "It doesn't matter." Blabbing on Isabella the first time just made everything worse. I wouldn't be making the same mistake twice like I had at lunch. As far as I was concerned, around Mr. Pruitt and his staff, Isabella's name would never fall from my lips again.

"It matters. Tell me and I'll turn the car around."

For the first time since James had lunged across the table at Matt, I felt a teensy bit of hope. Miller was going to let me see Kennedy. "There was a fight at school…"

"Are you okay? Did you get hurt?"

"No. Nothing like that." How could I say this without incriminating my devil sister? "Everything just blew up between some of my friends. Matt…he…lied." I know he technically just hadn't told me the truth. But the truth was momentous enough that his omission felt even worse than a lie.

Miller kept driving in the wrong direction, so I figured he needed more than that.

"James is upset with him. They're all upset with each other. And I just need to talk to Kennedy."

He still didn't turn around.

"I think she's upset about what happened at Felix's this weekend. I haven't had a chance to clear the air with her."

No response.

"And Felix is mad at me too. I'm pretty sure you already knew that. Can you please, please just take me to Kennedy's? She's the only person still speaking to me and I'm worried that she's going to pull the plug on our friendship too. And I don't know what I'd do without her."

Miller put on his blinker and I breathed a sigh of relief.

I didn't say anything else in fear that he'd change his mind. When we pulled up to the curb of my old apartment building, I practically flew out of the car.

I pressed the call button. "Mrs. Alcaraz, it's me…"

The door buzzed before I even had a chance to explain why I was there. I didn't even realize that Miller was following me until I heard his heavy footsteps behind me on the rickety old stairs.

Mrs. Alcaraz was standing in her doorway, an apron around her waist and the smell of delicious food hanging in the air around her. "Mi amor." She pulled me into her embrace and I felt calmer than I had in days. The familiar smell of spices in the air and the soft fabric of her worn clothes almost made me want to start crying again, but this time from joy. It was so good to be home. She squeezed me so tight, like she was happy I was home too. I didn't ever want to let go.

"I'm so glad you're here. She won't talk to me," Mrs. Alcaraz said. "I'm worried sick."

I pulled myself out of her arms. I guess I wasn't the only one worried about Kennedy. But Kennedy and her mom talked about everything. I was surprised Mrs. Alcaraz wasn't shaking her head at me for being a terrible friend.

"No," she said before I could respond. "You are not allowed in my home. Be gone."

I turned around to see Miller standing there awkward-ly. "It's okay, Mrs. Alcaraz. He's one of the good ones."

She'd reserved all her head shaking for Miller. "Nunca. Not in mi casa." She untied her apron like she was going to whack him with it.

"Please, Mrs. Alcaraz." I grabbed her hand to prevent her from whatever she was about to do. "I'm not allowed to come in unless he comes too."

She sighed and lowered her slapping hand. "Mi amor, do not trust a rat."

It was probably one of the rudest things I had ever heard her say. But I didn't have the energy to diffuse the tension. I needed to see Kennedy.

"Please just don't touch anything," I said to Miller as I stepped past Mrs. Alcaraz. The last thing I needed was for him to turn over every lamp and couch cushion in their small apartment. There wasn't anything dangerous here. Especially since it seemed like the only person who wanted me dead was Isabella. And she'd never be caught dead in a place like this.

I knocked on Kennedy's bedroom door but there was no response. Less than a week ago, this had been my room too. As far as I was concerned, she couldn't kick me out of our room. I opened the door.

Kennedy was curled up in a ball on her bed, staring at the wall. Staring at nothing at all.

"Kennedy?"

She didn't turn her head, but I heard the distinct sound of her sniffling.

"Kennedy?"

She still didn't acknowledge me.

And that was fine. Because I knew what she needed, and right now that wasn't words. I kicked off my shoes and climbed in bed beside her. I wrapped my arms around her and her body shuddered as her tears started anew. I just held her tighter. And the longer she let me hold her like this, the more sure I was that I wasn't the one she was mad at.

"Tell me what's wrong," I whispered.

"I can't."

"You can tell me anything. You know that."

She wiped at her eyes and turned to face me. "I lied at lunch. I'm not dating Cupcake anymore."

"What happened?"

She sniffed. "He dumped me."

So maybe I wasn't the only one that understood her confession of falling for drug dealers, plural. "Well, he's an idiot," I said. "Screw him."

She didn't say anything. "I told him I loved him. The day before we all hung out. And he said it back. How could he just change his mind?" She pulled her knees up to her chest.

"Like I said, he's an idiot. Hey," I said and grabbed her knee. "Don't waste any more time thinking about him."

"How can I not? I gave him everything. He tricked me."

My stomach dropped. "What do you mean by that?"

"That wasn't the first time he drugged me without me knowing, Brooklyn. I didn't even have any idea he was selling. God, I'm such an idiot. Apparently I was high when I told him I loved him the other night. And when I let him have sex with me." Her voice was so quiet, I barely even heard her.

"What?"

"I barely even remember my first time, Brooklyn. He used me. And I let him." She started crying again.

I pulled her into my chest. A million thoughts were running through my head. Wasn't that rape? She needed to tell someone. She needed to get tested. She needed to...I looked down at the top of her head. Right now, she need-ed to cry. And she needed someone to hold her. I cried too. For everything she lost. For how much she was hurting. I cried because she'd been alone in this secret for days. I was so acutely aware of my own pain, how had I not seen hers?

"I really liked him, Brooklyn," she sobbed. "And I thought he liked me back. Why does no one ever like me back?" Her body shuddered as she cried.

I held her until she ran out of tears.

"You need to tell your mom about this, Kennedy."

"How? She'd be so ashamed of me."

"No, she'll hurt for you. She'll be mad for you. But she won't be ashamed. He took advantage of you, Kennedy. He can't just do that and get away with it."

"Of course he can." She finally looked up at me. "You really think our lawyer - the one who couldn't even get you away from the Pruitts - is going to get some kind of justice against the Dicksons? Everyone at Empire High can get away with anything they want. Except for us." She sat up and wiped the remaining tears from her eyes. "I just feel so dumb."

"You're not dumb, Kennedy." I sat up too.

"Everyone else knew he was selling except me."

"I didn't. Hey." I grabbed her hand. "You're one of the smartest kids at Empire High. Everyone else goes there because their parents pay the exorbitant tuition. You're there because you're smarter than everyone else. And you're going to go farther than everyone else too. We both are."

She sighed. "Well, I might be book-smart. But not relationship-smart. I asked Cupcake to stop selling. That's why he dumped me. Apparently money and cocaine are more important to him than I am." She shook her head, but the sadness was gone from her voice. The fiery Kennedy I knew was back. "Puta mierda."

"What does that mean?"

"Nothing worth repeating. I'm sorry I didn't tell you sooner. I was just so mad. And then embarrassed. And then I couldn't even think about it without crying." She looked determined not to cry again.

"Can I tell you something if you promise not to get mad?" I asked.

She nodded.

"I've always hated Cupcake."

She laughed. "Yeah, I kinda figured you hadn't forgiven him for nailing you in the face with a dodgeball."

"I mean…who does something like that?"

"Cupcake. Ugh. And what a gross nickname."

"Right?! Seriously, if that kid went to my school back home, he would have been made fun of so hard."

"I'm just pissed that I already wasted money on a homecoming dress."

I looked over at the beautiful purple dress hanging in her closet. "I don't think that should go to waste," I said.

"Homecoming is this Saturday. I won't find a date before then."

"Me either. Which is why we're going together. We'll make everyone there so jealous that they didn't think to go with a friend instead."

She suddenly looked sad again. "I'm sorry, I didn't even ask you about what's going on with Matt. Did you talk to him after lunch?"

"No. All the Untouchables kind of disappeared from school after that." I tried not to think about the fact that it bothered me that Matt hadn't reached out. I didn't blame him for running after James. But it was like he'd completely forgotten that the news would affect me too. "But I'm definitely not going to homecoming with him after that. And Felix isn't talking to me. So…will you go with me?" I'd gone from two dates to none. And I was actually a little relieved. A girls' night sounded so much better.

"It's a date," she said with a laugh. "Do you know what you're going to wear?"

I had dozens of appropriate dresses now. But they weren't me. There was only one dress that I wanted to wear. The blue one my mom used to wear on special occasions when I was growing up. I just hoped it would fit me as well as it had fit my mom. I'd never tried it on before. "Mhm. I already have the perfect dress picked out."

"I should probably get some homework done. I've gotten a little behind over the weekend."

I climbed off her bed. "Will you tell your mom?" I asked before I could stop myself.

Mrs. Alcaraz would know what to do. And I knew Kennedy would feel better once it was off her chest.

She nodded. "But don't tell anyone else, okay?"

"I won't." Even though all I wanted to do was storm over to Cupcake's and kick him right in the nuts. Or ask Mr. Pruitt to sic his lawyers on him. But what good would that do? Kennedy couldn't get her virginity back. She couldn't undo that night. And Cupcake would always be an asshole. I'd stay silent because she asked me to. But I really hoped she wouldn't stay silent.

I closed the door behind me. Matt had stopped me from trying to have sex with him when I'd accidentally eaten tons of pot sugarcakes. He promised to be all my firsts. But I was so grateful that he hadn't taken that one too. I was done with him. Done with the Untouchables. Done with all the boys at Empire High.

CHAPTER 20

Monday

"Princess, how was school today?" Mr. Pruitt asked Isabella.

Of course he calls her princess.

"Superb, Daddy. Is it okay if I go out on the town after dinner? I need to pick up my homecoming dress."

I ignored the rest of their conversation when I felt my phone vibrate in my pocket. I wasn't sure why, but I'd been carrying around the stupid thing all afternoon. Hoping Matt would call. Hoping he wouldn't. Hoping Felix would call. Hoping he wouldn't either. I wasn't sure anymore. But as soon as I felt the vibration, I couldn't lie to myself. I wanted it to be from Matt. Even if I wasn't sure I'd ever be able to forgive him. I pulled my phone out of my pocket and hid it under the tablecloth so that no one would see.

It was from him. I held my breath as I read the words. "Meet me outside after you're done with dinner." I read them again as if a second glance would make them make any more sense. No apology. No explanation for what he'd done with James' girlfriend. Nothing. *Meet me outside after you're done with dinner my ass.*

"Daddy, she's definitely on her phone," Isabella said. "I heard it buzz."

I looked up. I'd been doing a great job of avoiding Isabella and Mrs. Pruitt's evil glares all night. But now I was locked in Isabella's.

"We don't allow phones at the table," Mr. Pruitt said. "I'm guessing you haven't finished going through the rules?"

"I'm almost done." I wasn't. And I was leaning toward just signing them like Kennedy had suggested. I quickly slid the phone back into my pocket.

"Did you hear what I asked you?" he said.

I shook my head. I hadn't realized that their conversation had turned to me.

"Would you like to go with Isabella to pick up her homecoming dress? Maybe you can try on a few yourself?"

"Oh. No. That's okay." Even if I hadn't already decided to wear my mom's dress, I wouldn't have taken him up on the offer. I'd stopped tattling on Isabella at dinner because there was no point to it. She'd always win. But I wasn't going to go out of my way to do things with her. I wasn't insane.

"Do you already have one or something?" Isabella asked.

"Mhm."

"Oh. Is it one of the ones in your closet upstairs?" she asked.

"Yes." It came out as more of a question. This felt like some kind of trap, but I didn't know how.

"What color is it? What style?"

This was definitely some kind of trick. Because everything with her was a trick. "Why do you want to know?"

She laughed. "Because I don't want to accidentally get something similar, Sissy. How embarrassing would that be? So describe it to me."

"It's green." The lie came easily to my lips. I knew this was one of her games, even though I couldn't figure out what exactly her motive was. It was easier to just go along with it. I tried to picture one of the new dresses hanging in my closet. "A deep emerald green. It's tight all the way through except for the bottom that flairs out."

"Sounds pretty," Isabella said.

"It is." Just not as pretty as my mom's dress, which I'd actually be wearing. I was happy that I'd lied when Isabella got a smug smile on her face. *What are you up to?*

"May I be excused, Daddy? The girls are waiting for me outside."

How did she know that unless she was also hiding her phone under the table?

"Sure thing, princess. Don't be home too late."

"I won't." She gave him a kiss on the cheek and practically skipped off in evil joy.

"I take it the two of you are getting along better now?" Mr. Pruitt asked.

No. You told her everything you promised you wouldn't. She made another scene at school and dragged all the Untouchables into it. She's worse than ever. But there was no point in the truth with the Pruitts. "Mhm," I said. It was alarming how quickly I'd grown used to lying. My stomach twisted in knots with guilt. What would my mom think of that?

"May I be excused as well, Richard?" Mrs. Pruitt asked.

"Of course."

Mrs. Pruitt placed her napkin down on the table and stood up. Without looking at me, she said, "Thank you for wearing shoes to the table." And then she walked off. It was like Mr. Pruitt had asked her to give me a compliment and that was the only thing she could think of to say.

I'd never come to the table without shoes again if I knew she was going to be here. A shoeless home was just that. A home. This wasn't a home. I'd learned that just as quickly as I'd learned to lie. Because I was living in a haunted mansion full of crazies. As if the ghosts could hear my thoughts, there was a loud crash in the foyer.

Mr. Pruitt and I both rushed out to see what happened. One of the large vases had toppled over. Glass was all over the floor. Mrs. Pruitt was nowhere to be seen. Had she knocked it over? Had it been something else? *Someone* else? A chill ran down my spine.

It didn't matter who or what had done it. Someone needed to clean it up. I got down on my knees to start to help pick up the pieces.

"Get up." Mr. Pruitt's voice was stern.

I looked over my shoulder.

"It's not your job to clean." His voice softened when he saw my expression. "Not anymore." He grabbed my arm and helped me to my feet. And for a second his hand just stayed there. "You look so much like her."

"My mom?"

His smile was so sad. "I loved her. But she never would have fit into this world. I know you don't want to be here. I know all this isn't you. But please try. Please be patient with my wife and Isabella. I don't want to lose you too. You're all I have left of her." He dropped his hand

and walked into his study, slamming the door behind him. I was left all alone surrounded by the glass.

What the hell was that? I took a step forward and my shoes crunched on the shards. He loved my mom? Had he loved her all this time? I wanted to knock on his door. I wanted more information. But if he wanted to share, he would have stayed out here. I retreated up the stairs, trying not to think about the mess I was leaving behind.

I couldn't handle today. I didn't understand Mr. Pruitt. Or his horrid daughter or wife. All I knew was that I could feel the hole in my heart. Just him mentioning my mom made me want to cry. I'd been filling up my thoughts with Felix and Matt and even Miller. Like I'd been trying to latch on to someone to fill the void.

I walked as quickly as I could to my room, but my feet froze when I reached the room I wasn't supposed to ever go in. There was a new lock on the door. A keypad like the one on the front door. It definitely hadn't been there before when I'd tried to open it. *Right?*

The same chill I felt in the foyer ran down my spine. I spun around. Someone was watching me again. I knew it. I could feel it in my bones. I spun around again. But no one was there. I ran the rest of the way to my room, closed the door, and locked it behind me. Not that it would help. I'd locked the door before, and Justin had just magically appeared inside my room the next morning with tons of clothes I didn't want.

Before I could reach my bed, my phone buzzed again, this time repeatedly. I pulled it out and saw that Matt was calling instead of texting this time. I answered it before I could chicken out. "I can't do this with you, Matt."

"Do what? I need to talk to you. Come outside."

"I can't." And it wasn't just because I didn't have the code to get out. "I told you not to break my heart. I've told you a million times. I'm not okay. I haven't been okay in a really long time, and you're making it worse. Everything you do just makes it worse."

"Just give me a chance to explain."

"No one person should ever need to give this many explanations."

"Brooklyn…"

"I can't."

"I didn't sleep with Rachel. I would never do something like that to James. You have to believe me…"

"Believe you? I did believe you. That's the whole problem. I believed that you cared about your friends. I believed that I was special. I believed a lot of things. And I don't anymore. I don't believe in you."

"I do care about my friends. And you are special. You're so fucking special."

I closed my eyes. I could hear the emotion in his voice. He needed me. He'd held me when I needed him. But the circumstances couldn't be more different. I thought about what Mr. Pruitt had just said to me. That my mom didn't belong in this world. That he wanted me to. But I didn't. I never would. "It wasn't going to work out anyway, Matt."

"What are you talking about? We're forever, Brooklyn."

Forever was too long for someone with his privilege to understand. But me? I understood that forever could be cut short far too soon. That forever felt endless when you were alone. I needed someone from my own world. "I'll never fit in with the Pruitts and Hunters and Caldwells of the world. I'm a Sanders. I'll always be a Sanders." I hung up the phone.

It immediately started buzzing again.

God, why did anyone think cell phones were a good idea? I turned it off so that the grating buzzing noise would finally stop. And then I shoved it in a drawer for good measure.

I'd broken up with Matt once. You'd think it would hurt less the second time. But if anything, it hurt more. Because I didn't love him any less. I hated him. I hated him so much. But God, I still loved him too. And it was infuriating. Why couldn't I just stop?

I went over to my closet, pushed past the green dress I'd described to Isabella, and grabbed my mother's dress. *I'm a Sanders.* If my mom had lived longer, she would have warned me about the kind of boys that went to Empire High. She'd have made sure I didn't make her same mistakes. Matthew Caldwell was a mistake in all capital letters. I needed to be with someone like me. Someone who wanted to pick up glass when it shattered. Someone that knew what it was like to not be elite.

I held my mother's dress in my hands as I retraced my steps past the locked room and down the stairs. Miller had shown me where the staff resided. Left, right. Left, left. This door wasn't locked. I made my way down the second set of stairs and through the empty hallway.

There were nameplates outside each door I passed, but I didn't recognize any of the names. The only two people I knew besides Miller were Tiffany and the chef

Barbara, but I didn't know their last names. And the nameplates were all last names. I passed door after door. So many people I hadn't even met yet. And then finally, at the end of the hall, much like my room, was a nameplate that read Miller.

I knocked before I could chicken out. I didn't know what I was doing down here. This was probably a mistake, but my feet stood firmly rooted in place. I needed a friendly face right now. I needed him.

Miller answered the door. He was wearing a pair of gray sweatpants and no shirt. I wasn't sure which was sexier. The outline the gray sweatpants gave the muscles in his legs or the exposed muscles of his very defined six-pack. I swallowed hard and my throat made a weird squeaking noise.

"You shouldn't be down here," he said.

I held up my mom's dress. "I need to hide this from Isabella. Can I keep it down here with you?" I knew that Isabella was up to something devious. But I didn't know what. And I'd be devastated if my mother's dress got caught in the crossfire.

He leaned out of the doorway, looked both ways, and then grabbed my hand to pull me inside.

The room felt small as soon as I entered it. Or maybe it was just because Miller was so massive.

His hand fell from mine. He grabbed my dress and hung it in his closet amongst a sea of crisply pressed suits. He cleared his throat. "Was there anything else?"

I just want to be with someone like me. Even if only for a minute. I shook my head, but I didn't move to leave.

"You're going to get me fired." He didn't sound mad.

"You'd be fired if someone found me down here?"

"I'd be fired for a lot of things when it came to you. Letting you get high. Letting you go to the Alcaraz's. But this? Yeah, this is probably the worst."

"Why? I'm just standing here."

I watched as his Adam's apple slowly rose and fell.

Was he thinking it too? That he wanted to do more than stand? My eyes wandered to his bed behind him. It wasn't made, and something about that felt so homey to me. I wanted to crawl under his sheets and never leave.

"You need to go," he said.

"You're the only one here that makes me feel like I'm not alone."

"I can't be that person for you."

"Why?" I hated how small my voice sounded.

"Because I work for your father."

"He's not my father. A father is someone who's there for you when you fall off your bike and skin your knee. A father is someone who hugs you when you're crying. A father is someone that didn't pay off your mother just to get rid of you. He isn't my father. He's a monster. No matter how hard he tries, he'll always be a monster. Because that was how my mother remembered him. And I'll never dishonor her memory."

I didn't even realize that he'd drawn closer to me. He reached out and ran his index finger and thumb down a loose strand of my hair. "It doesn't matter how you think of him. He's still going to take care of you. And I'll never be able to. Not the way he can."

"Are you talking about money? I don't care about money…"

"You date guys like Felix Green and Matthew Caldwell."

"I *hate* guys like Felix Green and Matthew Caldwell."

"Hate and love are a fine line, kid."

I wasn't a kid. I was barely younger than him. "You were right, I shouldn't have come down here." I stepped around him but he moved to block my path.

"What did you want when you came down here?"

"For you to hide my dress."

"That's it?"

I shook my head. "I wanted you to make me feel less alone. Like when we ate ice cream together."

"I'm not a cure for loneliness."

I took a step toward him. "I know. But you also said a guy who doesn't stick up for me isn't someone who's worth my time. And I have a feeling you'd always stick up for me."

His eyes dropped to my lips. "I'll never belong in your world," he said.

My world? What world? The Pruitt's? I didn't belong there. I stared at him. But he was saying that I didn't belong in his either. But his world was the same as my old one. How could I not belong in my new world or my old one? Where the hell was I supposed to be?

Before I even realized what was happening, his lips were on mine. His words said leave, but his grip on my hips and his tongue in my mouth begged me to stay. And I was more confused than ever as his kiss made my head spin.

He pulled away far too soon, his forehead pressed against mine. "I'll make you feel less alone whenever you want. I'll let you see your friends. I'll stop checking every room you walk into if that's what you want. I'll let you eat my ice cream and borrow my phone. I'll give you the code so you can sneak out whenever you want. But don't ask me to let you spend the night when I know you're in love with someone else."

I wanted to tell him that I wasn't in love with someone else. That I wanted to stay. But I couldn't do that. "You could get fired for all those things," I said, trying to lighten the mood.

"They're worth it if they make you smile." He pulled back from me.

"So you're offering me kisses but not…" my voice trailed off as I looked at his bed "…snuggles."

He shook his head and laughed. "You're definitely too young for me." He walked over to his door and opened it.

"But you want to kiss me again?" I really was being juvenile right now.

He smiled. "I'm finding it hard to say no to you, Brooklyn. Which is why I'm leaving right now. Because I'm finding it increasingly hard to control myself. I've clearly lost all reason." He walked away before I could respond.

I wasn't sure where he was going. Because I was in his room.

CHAPTER 21

Saturday

I snuck down to Miller's room every night after that. Eventually he stopped turning me away. One of the only house rules I knew was that boys weren't allowed in my room. What would Mr. Pruitt say if he knew I spent every night in Miller's? Technically it wasn't breaking the rules. Just the spirit of them. And honestly I didn't care about Mr. Pruitt's endless rules. That's why I'd signed the papers without reading any further. Isabella didn't follow half the ones I'd read. And I had no intention of following them either. But for some reason, I hadn't given the signed papers back to Mr. Pruitt. It was almost like if I gave them to him, I'd officially be one of Pruitts. And I didn't want that at all.

Miller and I both knew he could get in trouble. But I wasn't sure either of us cared. Sometimes we'd kiss. Mostly we just talked. He was always a complete gentleman. I was pretty sure he viewed my late night knocking as temporary. Even though I viewed it as necessary. I think we were both just lonely in a house that neither of us belonged in.

I opened my eyes and stared at the wall of Miller's small room. I didn't want to move. There was nothing more comforting than being wrapped up in someone else's arms. Miller's breath was light on the back of my neck, but his arm was heavy around my waist. It was hard to feel alone like that.

But each morning, just like this one, I still woke up feeling lost, if not alone. Nothing made sense anymore. Kennedy was suddenly as scared of the other students at Empire High as I was. We started eating lunch every day in the library instead of the cafeteria, tucked away from prying eyes. But I wasn't sure anyone was even looking. Cupcake never came close to her, which was good, because I could strangle him for what he'd done to Kennedy. He broke her. And I think not having Kennedy act like Kennedy broke me too.

My phone was still sitting turned off in my drawer. And Matt hadn't come to school for the rest of the week. I didn't know if he was okay. I didn't know if any of his friends were even talking to him. And even though I was mad at him, I was worried too. Because there was one thing I did believe that he'd said. James did seem capable of hurting himself. He'd shown up drunk to school at least twice. His eyes were bloodshot. His tie was always a little askew. He had stubble on his face when he was usually clean shaven. He was a mess. So I watched him whenever I could. Because even though I was still mad at Matt, I didn't want his fears to become a reality. Besides, if Matt wasn't at school watching James, who was?

"What are you thinking about?" Miller's voice was groggy.

"That I should probably get back to my room before anyone else wakes up."

"You weren't daydreaming about homecoming tonight?"

I turned to look at him. I'd studied his face a lot over the last several days. But I'd never seen that expression before. He looked wary of me. "No." What was there to daydream about? I was supposed to go with Matt, but we were no longer an us. I was supposed to go with Felix, but he'd stopped speaking to me. I was looking forward to going with Kennedy, but it wouldn't be the same. It would be the first homecoming dance I'd ever gone to. I'd been looking forward to it for weeks. I just thought it would be more magical than this.

"Not even a little bit?" asked Miller.

"I wish you could come with me," I said.

"I'll be there."

I propped myself up on an elbow. "What?"

"Mr. Pruitt doesn't want me to let you out of my sight. I have to be there."

I wanted to make some joke about how he didn't even let me out of his sight when I was sleeping. But it didn't feel right. "Why is he watching me so closely?" It was the one question I couldn't get a straight answer about.

There was that look again. Maybe he was just wary of the awkward situation. "You know I can't talk to you until you sign the papers."

"I signed them." I bit the inside of my lip. "I just need to give them back to Mr. Pruitt."

He sighed and sat up, his ab muscles tightening in a delicious way. "We'll talk about it again after you give them back." He stared at me, searching my face. "You read all of it then?"

"Yeah," I lied. I'd had homework to do, Cupcake revenges to plot, texts from Matt to ignore, plans to go over to avoid Isabella whenever possible, and of course my daily fifteen-minute cry session after school. When would I have had time to read that monster of an agreement?

"You're sure about that?" he asked.

I hated when he treated me like a child. "Of course."

He nodded and then turned away. "We should head out a little early so we can swing by and grab Kennedy before the football game."

I almost forgot about the homecoming game. I could feel the smile stretch across my face. "Really? Can she get ready here too?"

"I'll see what I can do."

"Thank you." I leaned over and kissed him.

He caught my hipbone in his hand and pulled me closer. "You should go. Before you get caught." He reluctantly let go of my waist.

I climbed out of his bed. "Maybe if I get caught, they'll throw me out." I pulled on my white puffy robe over my pajamas.

"And where would you go if that happened?" asked Miller.

"I don't know." I looked at my mother's dress hanging in the closet. "Somewhere far away from all this." *Home.* I turned back to him and he was frowning. "What?"

"I assumed you were no longer planning on running away." He grabbed his watch off the nightstand and strapped it in place on his wrist. "They'll be up soon."

He was right. I didn't have time for this conversation right now. But I didn't want to leave it like this either. "You're right. I'm not leaving. This place is finally starting to feel like home." And by this place, I meant specifically Miller's room.

He smiled.

"I'll see you in a bit." I looked both ways before leaving his room and then hurried off to my bedroom. I thought I was in the clear, but as I rounded the corner to the staircase, I saw the whole family sitting at the dining room table.

"There you are," Mr. Pruitt said. "Where have you been? We were all worried."

I saw Isabella roll her eyes.

Think of something to say. Think. "I was just exploring."

Mr. Pruitt raised both eyes. "Exploring? Haven't you been given a proper tour? I'll have to talk to Miller about that."

"No, it's not his fault." It felt like I was digging my own grave. Or maybe Miller's. "I just get so easily turned around."

"It's fine, darling. Come eat with us."

Isabella looked shocked by his term of endearment. She used to call me that when we first met. But not in a nice way. The way Mr. Pruitt said it reminded me of how my mom used to say it to me. There wasn't a hint of evil behind it. He sounded almost loving. And I had a weird feeling that maybe he used to call my mom that too. And that maybe she called me that because it reminded her of him.

"Are you deaf?" Isabella said. "Don't just stand there when Daddy tells you to join us."

Mr. Pruitt shot her a harsh stare.

I hurried over to my seat, trying to ignore the fact that I was in a robe and slippers and they were all fully dressed. I was sure Mrs. Pruitt was displeased, but I made sure not to look at her. "This looks great," I said as I stared at the normal breakfast buffet. It was too much food. What did they always do with the leftovers?

"So are we allowed to eat breakfast in our pajamas now, Daddy?" Isabella asked.

"No," her mother said. "We're not troglodytes."

At least as I sunk lower in my seat I was comfortable because my robe was so lush.

"Have you even given her the rules to sign yet?" Mrs. Pruitt asked. "Or will homeless-casual be the new dress code for all of our meals? We have to raise both of them with the same rules, Richard."

"She'll sign them once she's read over them," he said, seemingly oblivious to her hateful tone.

"It's okay, I actually did sign them," I said. "I'll go get them now." I doubted anyone protested, but I wouldn't have known because I practically ran out of the room. Once I got upstairs, I quickly changed into clothes that would be suitable for the homecoming game. I opened up one of my boxes that I hadn't unpacked yet so I could find my Keds. But the first thing I saw on top was Matt's varsity jacket. I tried to swallow down the lump in my throat, but it wouldn't go away. I'd never even gotten a chance to wear it.

In a different world, I'd be wearing it today. I'd be cheering him on from the crowd. But I wasn't even sure if he'd show up to play. And I wasn't exactly in a cheering mood. For him or anyone else at Empire High. Honestly, I was surprised that Kennedy still wanted to go.

I tried to shove the thoughts aside, along with the jacket, as I pulled out my Keds. Mrs. Pruitt would hate them as much as Isabella did. And for some reason I found that wonderfully pleasing. I laced them up, grabbed the signed stack of papers, and headed back downstairs.

"Here you go," I said and handed Mr. Pruitt the papers, trying my best to ignore the evil ladies of the house staring at my shoes.

"Splendid. I'll update the will immediately." He snapped his fingers and a staff member I hadn't met before appeared. "Have this sent over to my lawyer at once," he said.

"Your will, Daddy?"

"Yes." He took a sip of his coffee. He was so calm when all I felt in the room was building tension.

"You have to be joking," Mrs. Pruitt said.

"I'm not. I have two daughters now, and I'm splitting my will accordingly."

"Without discussing it with me first?"

"If either of you say another word I'll alter the will a third time, and I promise you that you won't be pleased."

Mrs. Pruitt's jaw actually dropped. I would have reached across the table and pushed it back into place, but that was probably against the rules. Besides, I was a little shocked myself. "It's okay," I said. "You don't have to update it at all. I don't want anything."

"Which is exactly why I'm updating it. You haven't used your Amex card once since I've given it to you. Do you have any idea how much these two spend in a week?"

"Richard…"

"I've already made up my mind," he snapped. Instead of throwing his coffee mug against the wall like I expected him to do, he just drank another sip calmly. "I'm going to call the lawyer in my study. Please do not disturb me." He stood up and grabbed the newspaper. But before he walked off, he peeled away the page with the crossword puzzle and handed it to me.

He must have seen me staring at it last weekend. He noticed. He cared. He was changing his freaking will. What if I was entirely wrong about him? Some beasts had a Belle. Maybe my mom was his. And maybe he didn't resent my existence. Maybe I really was all that he had left of the woman he truly loved. Maybe he was telling the truth when he said he didn't know I existed. It was a whole lot of maybes. But even if a single one of them was true? He wasn't such a monster after all.

Isabella's chair squeaked across the wooden floor as she stood up. "You'll never replace me, Brooklyn. Hell, your name says it all. Go back to the borough you belong in. Because Daddy only has one daughter. Me. And I'm not sharing him with you. And I'm certainly not sharing my inheritance with trash." She turned on her heel and walked out of the room.

I knew her sweet act was in fact an act. But the way she could flip the switch so easily was terrifying. I never found the part in the rules about not murdering people. But I hoped there weren't any loopholes to that rule. Because if there were, I was seriously worried for my wellbeing.

"Your mother was a slut," said Mrs. Pruitt. She was so quietly sinister that I had practically forgotten she was still at the table.

"Excuse me?"

"As I'm sure you are too. You'll slip up soon. And when you do, I'll see it. And I'll be the one to tell Richard. I'll strip you of everything you thought you could gain. Because mark my words, you are temporary in this house. My husband had one weak moment in his life and it resulted in you. And I'm going to protect his legacy even if he has decided not to. Even if I have to make you disappear myself." She didn't storm off like her daughter. Instead she left with a sigh, like my presence was exhausting her.

Her words echoed in my head. There was a lot that should have made my knees shake. But there were two sentences that had me literally trembling. *Even if I have to make you disappear myself.* Maybe the murder rule was for Mrs. Pruitt too. I knew it was a threat. But it was the other thing that stuck out even more. *When you do, I'll see it.* I felt the familiar chill run down my spine and turned around to see no one at all. She was watching me. I knew she was. And I'd already slipped up every night when I went to Miller's room. Did she know? God, she had to know. I heard the clock ticking down in my head that I always heard when something bad was about to happen. I'd never been wrong before. I'd always been good at knowing when my time was running out.

Tiffany came out to clear the dishes. "Are you alright?" she asked. "You look a little pale."

Because I just found my ghost. "I'm fine."

"You barely touched your food. Do you want me to send a plate up for you?"

"No, that's okay. Thank you though." Tiffany seemed nice enough, but I suddenly saw everything differently. I could think of a million loopholes to a murdering rule. One being that she could pay someone else to do it for her. A little drop of something in my food.

Tiffany smiled at me.

I needed to get out of this house before I wound up dead.

CHAPTER 22

Saturday

I could feel the stands rumbling as Kennedy, Miller, and I searched for three seats together. Music blared through the speakers, pumping up the crowd for the upcoming game. The stadium was a blur of Empire High blue and orange, except for a small section of the stands where our rivals Bernstein Prep were sitting.

"Go ahead and grab those seats," Miller said and gestured toward a section of the bleachers where he most definitely wouldn't fit.

Maybe I'd misunderstood. I could barely hear him over the music. "Aren't you going to sit with us?" I asked.

He tilted his head to the side and I followed the direction with my eyes. Mr. and Mrs. Pruitt were seated across the aisle a few rows ahead. They were here to see Isabella cheer I guessed. I didn't know whether or not either of them were alumni of Empire High. But they were sitting with a group of other adults, right next to Mr. and Mrs. Caldwell. I quickly turned away. Matt had said he'd told his mother about me. Did he tell her we broke up too? Did she know everything?

I swallowed hard and turned back to Miller. "Well, this sucks."

"It's fine. I'll just be a few rows back keeping an eye on you. Grab the seats before someone else does."

Kennedy grabbed my hand and pulled me past a few familiar faces from school. Familiar as in I'd seen them, not that they'd ever spoken to me. Kennedy and I sat huddled together, bracing ourselves from the chilly fall breeze. For just a second I let myself think how nice it would be if I could have worn Matt's varsity jacket.

"Go Eagles!" Kennedy shouted at the top of her lungs and jumped to her feet with the rest of the crowd.

What the hell? I didn't realize she was so school spirited. And why was everyone standing? There were perfectly good bleachers to sit on.

She pulled me to my feet. "They're coming out!" she screamed over the cheers.

I turned in the direction she was pointing just in time to see the football team burst through a homecoming sign that the cheerleaders were holding. I wanted to think it was corny. The kind of scene you'd see in slow motion in a movie. But I'd be lying if I said I wasn't cheering along too. It was easy to get swept up in the excitement. The stands shook even more as people stomped their feet and cheered.

I tried my best not to stare at Matt as he jogged onto the field in his football gear. *God, how did he look even better in that than he did in a suit? Stop it.* I'd been avoiding looking over at the cheerleaders, but my eyes wandered in their direction. Isabella was bopping around, waving her pom-poms in the air. I wasn't sure if it was just the angle I was sitting at, but I swore her skirt was significantly shorter than the other cheerleaders.

"Let's go, Eagles!" Kennedy yelled again as part of some cheer I didn't know that the cheerleaders were chanting.

How did she know it? She worked weekends just like I did. She must have gone to a few games last year. But I didn't even question her, because she was jumping up and down with a smile on her face. I hadn't seen her smile in a week. It was like I finally had my friend back. It had been so hard seeing her walk around like a shadow of her former self.

"You're in a good mood again," I shouted to her over the crowd.

"That's because I got revenge," she said.

"Revenge? What do you mean?" I was yelling at the top of my lungs so she could hear me.

"I started a rumor that Cupcake has a little dick!"

I didn't know when it happened, but the crowd had definitely hushed right before she said, "Cupcake has a little dick." A gasp fell out of my mouth. I couldn't even help it.

A few students turned their heads to look at us.

"Joe Dickson has a small dick!" she yelled, just in case someone in the stadium hadn't heard. "It's the size of a peanut!"

"Kennedy!" I grabbed her arm to pull her back down to her seat as we had both exploded in a fit of giggles. A few other kids snickered. "Oh my God, that was amazing."

Her smile grew even wider. "If he's going to tell the whole school I was an easy lay, I can at least prevent him from doing it to someone else with that tidbit of information."

I wanted to ask her if it was true. If Cupcake really did have a mini-dick. But I didn't want her smile to disappear. If she'd wanted to tell me any more details, she would have. And it made me sick to my stomach to know that she might not remember any more details. Because that asshole had drugged her. He deserved this. Hopefully no one at this school would ever fall for his games now.

I pulled her into my side, keeping us both warm. "You're amazing," I said.

"I know. Let's hope our team is as good as they were last year. Because I seriously hate Bernstein Prep."

I didn't mind the change of subject. This was my first homecoming game. My first high school football game ever, actually. And it didn't matter that I was in love with one of the players. *Used to be in love.* I was going to try to enjoy this. If Kennedy was smiling, I could smile too.

Besides, this was the first time where I was able to stare at Matt without Isabella giving me shit. Or someone else being suspicious. I could stare at two of the Untouchables unabashedly. And they were both freaking amazing, totally lost in their element. It seemed like every pass Mason made went straight into Matt's arms.

"Go Matt!" I yelled and jumped to my feet as he rushed toward the endzone.

His head turned like he could hear me. And maybe he had, because I swore for just a second we locked eyes. Right before some asshole from Bernstein Prep completely decked him. I threw my hand over my mouth.

"Stop distracting them," Kennedy said and pulled me back down into my seat.

"Is he okay?" I wanted to run down there and make sure. But a piece of me hated myself for it. He'd never run after me in public.

"Of course. He's used to being tackled. See."

Matt was already standing up, straightening his jersey over his pads. He looked back up at me in the stands and my heart started racing. He ran his index finger across the tip of his nose. My heart melted. *Our secret signal.*

But then he turned his head as if he was looking for someone else. My heart started beating faster. Who else was he looking for? Was I even allowed to be jealous? I'd spent every night the past week in Miller's arms. But I still found myself following Matt's gaze, my heart beating faster.

My eyes landed on his mother. Mrs. Caldwell was staring right at me, a smile on her face. I quickly looked away. I didn't know what that meant. Matt said she'd seen me at my uncle's funeral. Did she recognize me now? Did she know I was responsible for breaking her son's heart? And if so, why was she smiling?

"I really hope they go for a two-point conversion if they score," Kennedy said. "Prescott is shitty at converting the PAT."

"How do you know so much about football?" I asked. I needed her to distract me from Mrs. Caldwell's prying eyes. But when I looked at Matt's mom out of the corner of my eye, her attention was back on the field.

"I used to watch it with my Dad every Sunday."

I pressed my lips together. Neither one of us talked much about what we'd lost. But whenever she did share something about her father, I felt that much closer to her.

I'd gotten close to Matt, Miller, and Felix. But only Kennedy knew what it was like to lose a parent. *Matt lost his aunt. Stop.* I couldn't think about that. I didn't know if anything he said to me was true. Ever. He was a liar. He was just playing me. *Like I played Felix?* God, my head was going to explode.

Kennedy jumped to her feet and starting cheering like crazy when we scored. And I cheered right along with her. Mostly because it just felt good to scream at the top of my lungs. And maybe a little bit because it was easy to get caught up in the excitement.

By halftime we were up 19 to 7. It should have been 21, but Kennedy was right. Prescott was shitty at kicking the PAT. He'd missed two. The stands started emptying out.

"Where is everyone going?" I asked.

"Probably to grab something from the concession stand. Or to use the bathroom."

I felt silly. I thought there was some weird homecoming congregation or something. But food and using the toilet was the logical conclusion. "Are you hungry?"

"No. You?"

I shook my head.

"So what's going on with you and Miller?" Kennedy asked.

I was glad it had quieted down enough for us to not have to yell. "Is it that obvious?"

She smiled. "No. I was kinda joking because it's literally his job to stare at you." She turned around and waved at him. "But now I know it's more than that."

I grabbed her arm to make her face forward again. "He's the only one at the Pruitts' apartment that isn't a monster."

"I thought you were getting along better with Satan?" Satan was Kennedy's new affectionate term for Mr. Pruitt.

"I don't know. Sometimes he's nice. Sometimes he's rude. I don't know if he means to be. But I don't fit in with any of them."

"And you fit in with Miller?"

"Yes." It came out as more of a question than a statement.

Kennedy laughed and adjusted her thin fall jacket. I made a mental note to give her one of my new ones. "Doesn't he remind you of someone?" she asked.

"What?"

"Brooklyn, he's just an older-looking version of Matt."

"He is not."

"Um...yes he is. Matt a few years in the future with brown hair."

I turned and looked at him. His broad shoulders. His easy smile. Not that Matt's smile came easy anymore. I quickly turned back around. "I don't see it." But it was a lie. I did see it. Is that why I climbed into his bed each night and let him hold me?

The marching band had come onto the field, making it a little harder for us to talk. But that didn't deter Kennedy.

"I bet Miller played football when he was in high school," she said.

I shook my head. Yes, maybe Miller looked a little like Matt. But the resemblance ended there. Miller couldn't be more different. And he was definitely no jock. I knew for a fact that his muscles were from a moving company he used to work for before Mr. Pruitt hired him. He'd told me so. Miller wasn't cocky. He wasn't privileged. He was real. He was like me.

"Are you two serious?" she asked.

I shrugged. "He knows I still like Matt."

"You're still in love with Matt after everything he did?"

"I didn't say that."

"Yeah. But it doesn't mean it isn't true. Brooklyn, he kept you a secret for weeks because he didn't want James to know he'd screwed Rachel. He lied to you. He…"

"Technically he didn't lie. He just didn't tell me."

She shook her head. "Same difference."

"Is this the part of the lecture where you tell me you warned me about the Untouchables? That guys like that don't end up with girls like us?"

"What? No. It's not a lecture at all. I'm just worried about you. It's not like you to tell Felix you love him, then Matt within the same day, and now you're with Miller a few days later? I'm worried about you."

I bit the inside of my lip.

"What's going on with you?" she asked.

I wanted to tell her she barely knew me better than any of those guys. But that wasn't true. She knew me. Which was why it didn't feel like I could filter myself. "I think maybe I just miss the feeling of being loved by someone. Unconditionally. And I know that there's conditions with all of them. But for a few seconds when Miller holds me, I feel like someone's on my side. Like I'm not alone."

She kicked my shin lightly. "Girl, you have me. I love you. My mom loves you."

"But I'm not allowed to live with you guys. Do you have any idea what it's like for me to go back to the Pruitts' after school every day? To live down the freaking hall from Isabella? I'm terrified all the time. I'm scared of her and her mom. I'm even scared of Mr. Pruitt. I don't trust any of them. Some mornings my bedroom door is open. Did you know that? And I lock it, Kennedy. I swear I lock it."

She pressed her lips together. "I'm not judging you. I'm just worried about you. If you still like Matt, you should tell him. Or if you like Felix more..." her voice trailed off. "You should tell him that then."

I stared at her. She didn't get what it was like in my shoes. Yes, she'd lost a parent. But she didn't lose her *only* parent. And she didn't lose Uncle Jim the same way I had. We both loved him, but I needed him. He was all I'd had left. And now I felt starved for love. Just thinking about it made me feel cheap. I owed Felix an apology. I owed Miller an apology. I even owed Matt an apology, but I wouldn't give it to him because he owed me a lot more. But the worst part was, I was worried I loved a piece of each of them. I was too confused to know better. I just liked the way they made me feel.

"I'll talk to them," I said. "As soon as I figure out which one I like the most."

She laughed. "We both know it's Matt."

I didn't contradict her. We did both know it. And we also both knew he was an asshole. It was one trait I wasn't sure how to overlook. Everything else I thought I'd known about him had just turned out to be a lie.

"You're eventually going to need to talk to him," she said.

"I don't want to think about it today. It's homecoming. Shouldn't we be having fun?"

She laughed. "I am having fun. I'm watching my favorite sport with my bestie. And now everyone knows that Cupcake has a mini-dong. What's more fun than that?"

I laughed. But in the back of my head, I was thinking that a swift kick in the nuts would be more satisfying than a rumor. Cupcake deserved worse for what he did to her.

"Oh the floats are starting." Kennedy pointed to the field. Several convertibles led the way, each with two members of the homecoming court sitting in them. I hadn't been paying attention to homecoming details at all. But I wasn't surprised to see that James, Mason, Isabella, and a few of Isabella's minions had all been nominated for homecoming king and queen.

The stands started to fill up again so that everyone could watch who would be crowned. Not that I cared in the slightest. Although I really wished Isabella wouldn't win. If she did it was probably because she'd threatened the student body. *Stupid Pruitt rules that she doesn't follow.*

Behind the convertibles were floats that each grade had been assigned to decorate. Neither Kennedy nor I had been asked to participate. I watched the senior float go by. It was a 007 theme, which was pretty clever for their graduating year. The junior float didn't look nearly as good. There was an Eagle made of crepe paper that was practically falling off the float. Apparently the juniors were a bunch of slackers.

Then the sophomore float started to go by and I could barely breathe. Matt was standing in the middle of it, still in his football gear but without the helmet. A few of his teammates were on either side of him. He was holding a microphone in his hand and staring right at me.

Music started blaring through the speakers of the stadium. It was a *You're An American Reject* song that I knew pretty well called *My Dirty Little Secret*.

"What is happening?" Kennedy asked right before Matt lifted the mic to his mouth. She gasped. "Oh my God he's going to sing to you."

"No he's not."

"This one's for all the beautiful ladies out there!" Matt yelled into the microphone.

"See," I said, but my voice was so weak I doubted Kennedy heard it. Had he really moved on that quickly? Hadn't I? I swallowed hard. I hadn't. That was the whole problem.

"Just kidding," Matt said. "This one's for my girl. Brooklyn Sanders in the house!"

Oh my God. He really is going to sing to me.

Kennedy nudged me with her elbow.

"This isn't happening," I said as students had already started looking back and forth between me and the float.

"Oh, it's happening," Kennedy said with a laugh as the music got louder.

"I know what I've done wrong," Matt sung. If you could even call it singing, because it was way off key. "I've known it all along. I've tried to come clean a time or two. But I won't steal any more time from you."

I stared at him in horror. He was changing the lyrics to be about…us. *I think?* "What the hell is he doing?"

Kennedy grabbed my hand. "It's a grand romantic gesture. He's winning you back!"

I could feel my face turning bright red.

"What am I doing?" Kennedy said and pulled her hand out of mine. "I need pictures of this." She lifted up her camera and started snapping away.

"Tell me you haven't thrown me away," Matt sung. "Because I'm done playing games with you, babe."

His football friends leaned into the mic and added an out of tune, "Done playing games, babe."

I wanted to run away from all the prying eyes. But my ass was firmly glued to the cold metal bench. Had he lost his freaking mind?

"Everyone needs to know about us," Matt sung. "Brooklyn you're not a dirty little secret."

"No dirty little secret," his football friends sang.

"I'll tell everyone because you are not a regret." Matt and his backup football dancers did a weird little spin maneuver. "Not a regret, hope you can believe that. You are not a dirty little secret, everyone needs to know." He pointed up at me and did a weird hip thrust.

"We all know," the football chorus sang and did matching hip thrusts.

It felt like everyone left in the stadium was turning my direction. Except for someone in a suit who looked beyond pissed who was running up to the float. *Oh my God, it's the principal.* Coach Carter, my gym teacher and the football coach, ran up to the float too. He was waving his hands in the air in clear agitation.

Matt ignored both of them. "Apart we live fragile lives. But together is the best way to survive."

"Best way to survive," the other boys sang.

"Get off the float!" Coach Carter yelled. "Right now."

"I've been around a time or two." Matt winked at me, not seeming to care at all about the fact that he was in serious trouble.

I laughed because I didn't know what else to do. At least he wasn't lying anymore. He'd definitely been around a time or two.

"Stop this right now!" hissed the principal.

"I've never wasted a second on you!" Matt sang as Coach Carter lunged for one of his legs. "Shit," Matt said as he ran into one of his backup dancers.

I was pretty sure he mumbled it, but it was into a microphone so it was really freaking loud.

I started laughing harder than I had in a really long time. This was freaking amazing.

The principal climbed onto the float and demanded for Matt to hand over the mic. Instead of complying, Matt jumped off the float. Coach Carter and the principal started chasing him.

"Tell me you haven't thrown me away!" Matt sang as he ran across the field, picking up his pace. "You're not a game and I'm sorry. You are the only one. I love you, Brooklyn." He chucked the mic on the field and sprinted toward the gym, Coach Carter hot on his trail. The principal had stopped at the 30 yard line, panting hard, his hands on his knees.

The stadium erupted in cheers that were just as loud as when the Eagles had scored a touchdown.

"If that's not an apology I don't know what is," Kennedy said.

It was a grand gesture, just like she'd said. Matt was not a good singer. Or dancer. And he'd just done both in front of the biggest crowd I could imagine, despite the fact that the principal was pissed. What was more public than that? I wasn't his dirty little secret anymore. He wanted me back. I wasn't sure if he had up until this point, but it was pretty clear now.

I felt Miller's eyes on the back of my neck, pricking my skin. The question was…did I want Matt back? The smile on my face screamed yes. My heart that was still in pieces? That was a different story.

"That was seriously the most amazing thing ever," Kennedy said. She snapped a picture of me and pulled the camera away from her face. "I haven't seen you this happy in forever. This is going to be the best homecoming ever. Do you think he has anything else planned for the dance? Can you even imagine how he'd top that?"

I nodded, but I wasn't really listening. I was doing my best not to look over to see if Mrs. Caldwell was staring at me. Or the Pruitts for that matter.

I watched as things calmed down on the field and the homecoming king and queen were crowned. James Hunter and Isabella Pruitt. *Figures.* I stared at the two of them. James looked so drunk I doubted he'd remember a minute of this. Did no one else notice? And then there was Isabella, who looked…furious. We locked eyes for a second and

I felt myself sinking. She was definitely upset. And it was directed fully on me. Why was she mad at me?

Her anger slowly shifted to a smile as pictures started to snap. She flipped her hair over her shoulder and jutted out her hip like she hadn't just given me a death stare. She even leaned over and kissed James on the cheek, much to his dismay. He looked like he was going to be sick. I would have maxed out my untouched credit card to see him throw up on her cheerleading outfit. But he didn't. He just looked so freaking sad. Like his heart had been stomped on too.

I didn't want their life. I wanted a little house in Delaware with a yellow kitchen. I didn't want to be Untouchable. I just wanted to be loved. And Matt had just sung about loving me. I pictured him and his friends thrusting again and I laughed out loud. What the hell had he been thinking?

CHAPTER 23

Saturday

We were stuck in traffic in the small parking lot at Empire High for what seemed like centuries. And sitting in the car with Miller after Matt's performance wasn't exactly fun. I breathed a sigh of relief when Miller was finally able to pull the car out of the parking lot.

Kennedy was busy going through pictures on her camera. I turned to look out the window and could still see the team celebrating in the distance. They'd sat Matt for the third quarter, but let him play again in the fourth. Empire High had lost the lead while he was benched. I was pretty sure that was the only reason they let Matt back on the field. But we'd ended up winning by a landslide.

The game was a great distraction. It was easy to get caught up in the cheers, which were surprisingly easy to learn. And Kennedy filled me in about some things I didn't know about the game, like being offsides. Starting too soon…maybe that's what I'd done with Matt. I started something with him too soon after I lost my mom. I needed more time to heal. That's why my heart was so confused. Because it was still broken.

"Check this one out," Kennedy said and showed me the display on her camera. It was an image of Matt thrusting.

I couldn't help but laugh. It was ridiculous. The smile on Matt's face was contagious and my cheeks hurt from all the pictures she kept showing me. But I could feel Miller's eyes on me in the rearview mirror. And the awkward tension in the air seemed to grow with each laugh.

Miller had been so professional since walking us down the stands. Not one personal comment even though the three of us had talked the whole car ride to the game. I knew Kennedy felt the awkwardness too. But she was trying to drown it out with funny pictures. It was homecoming. We were supposed to be laughing and having fun. The twisted feeling in my stomach seemed like all I ever felt anymore. And I was so tired of it.

"I'm really sorry, Miller," I said. "That was so awkward. Can we just pretend that didn't happen?"

He let his eyes travel to the rearview mirror for a second before looking back at the road. "You don't have anything to be sorry for. Consider it forgotten if that's what you want."

"Are you planning on serenading Brooklyn now?" Kennedy asked. "To level the playing field?"

"Brooklyn knows how I feel," he said and hit the turn signal.

I absolutely did not know how he felt. Most nights when he held me he'd just let me talk about my awful day. He was really good at listening. Not so much at sharing. He was literally my shoulder to cry on. And I hadn't been very good at returning the favor. If I really thought about it, I barely knew him at all. How had that happened? I was pretty sure he knew everything about me.

"And how *do* you feel, Miller?" Kennedy asked, as if she could read my mind.

"Right this second?" He focused on the road. "I feel like my patience is wearing thin."

Kennedy laughed.

I didn't. It had to have been hard to watch Matt sing to me.

"I really think a grand romantic gesture would do you well after that performance," Kennedy said. "Maybe you could choreograph a dance with the other security guards! That would be so much fun."

"Actually bothering to show up is the best gesture," Miller said.

I jumped in, hoping to end the awkwardness. "Agreed."

"Sick burn on Matt," Kennedy said.

I saw a hint of a smile on Miller's face at my agreement. He was right. Matt dancing was wonderfully public and hilarious. But it didn't really change anything. He had still slept with his best friend's girlfriend. And yes, he still tried to call and text me, but he stopped showing up to school. He stopped showing up for me. He'd never shown up for me before that either. I was a dirty little secret, despite what he sang. Miller, on the other hand, was always there. He was solid like a rock. Literally. I stared at the way his muscles bulged beneath his suit jacket. He'd never let anything bad ever happen to me again. All Matt did was make bad things happen to me, sprinkled with moments that tricked my mind into forgetting. But I wasn't an idiot.

"Well, if you can really sneak me into the Pruitt's apartment, that's a pretty grand gesture all by itself," Kennedy said. "This is going to be so much fun." She elbowed me in the ribcage.

This really was going to be fun. I took a deep breath. Tonight was going to be the best night ever.

***

Sneaking in turned out to not be hard. At all. Despite the traffic, we'd beaten Mr. and Mrs. Pruitt back in record time. All we had to do now was get safely to my room. Sneaking back out would be harder, but we'd deal with that little hiccup later.

I tried to pull Kennedy through the foyer but her feet had frozen in place.

"This place is…" her voice trailed off as she turned in a circle.

"Cold? Over the top? Massive? Vulgar?"

She laughed. "No. It's…haunting," she finally said as she eyed a portrait of the Pruitt family above a vase Mrs. Pruitt hadn't gotten a chance to smash yet.

Her words sent a chill down my spine. Or maybe it was just the dead look in Isabella's eyes when they were so blown up. Or maybe it was because it felt like someone was watching me.

"You two should get up to Brooklyn's room before they come back," Miller said. He handed Kennedy her homecoming dress.

Kennedy folded her dress over her arm. "Yeah, I really don't want to run into Isabella outside of school if I can help it."

Welcome to my new life. "Her bedroom is on the other wing upstairs. I actually run into her less here than at school." Now that I thought about it, that was pretty weird. It was like she avoided me here but sought me out in public. A game she played for her father, I guessed. *Our father.* You'd think she'd pretend to like me here right in front of him. And the more I thought about it, the less any of it made sense. I'd never understand Isabella. And I never wanted to, because if I did I was worried it meant I was truly becoming one of them.

"But you see her at family dinners," Kennedy said. "I love those stories. I can't believe your life now."

"Oh God, don't get me started on family dinners," I said with a laugh.

"Can I see the dining room real quick? I want to be able to picture your epic stories of the upper class better."

"The Pruitts just pulled up," Miller said as he looked down at something on his phone. "You have about three and a half minutes until they come in. Make it fast and I'll go get your dress from my room." He walked away without waiting for a response, suddenly all business.

I wasn't sure if he was upset with me or not. Maybe he was just tense because he was putting his neck on the line by letting me sneak Kennedy in.

"The dining room is this way." I grabbed Kennedy's hand so she wouldn't keep stopping and staring at everything along the way.

"Why is your dress in Miller's room?" she asked as we stopped outside the dining room.

"It's silly. I thought maybe Isabella was trying to sabotage me or something. But maybe she really was worried we'd be wearing the same color." The feeling of being watched all the time was getting to me. I was even making up evil moves by Isabella. She was horrible. But it didn't mean she was out to get me all the time. Surely she had other people she had to harass. Her list of enemies was probably quite long.

"The same color dress for homecoming? Oh the horror," Kennedy said with a laugh. "Which wall did Satan throw the wine on when he got mad?"

I laughed and pointed to the far wall. Kennedy loved hearing stories about Mr. Pruitt, and I loved reenacting all of it for her. I'm pretty sure hearing about my horrid living situation was the highlight of her day. And I was happy to give her all the dirty details because they distracted her from Cupcake. And his assholery.

"He seems legit crazy," she said.

"Yeah, and you legit don't want to run into him. I have no idea what his reaction would be. He pretty much banned me from seeing you. And I signed all these papers agreeing to it." *I think. I really should have read that contract.*

She rolled her eyes. "How can I hate someone that I don't even know?"

"Easily when it's a Pruitt," I said with a laugh. "But come on, let's get upstairs. The last thing I need is to get Miller fired."

She followed me up the ornate staircase. "This place is seriously insane. I can't believe you live around all this gold." She ran her index finger along the gold trim of the railing.

"Isn't that just paint?"

She leaned down and tapped it with her finger. "I don't think so."

The sound of locks clicking open echoed around us.

"Hurry," I whispered and sprinted up the stairs with Kennedy hot on my trail. But when I reached my room I realized that Kennedy wasn't with me. She had stopped in front of the door down the hall with the new security system.

"What the hell is in there?" she asked as she stared at the keypad.

"I have no idea."

"You haven't asked? It's right by your room."

"Miller said not to go in. Which I promptly ignored," I said with a laugh. "But it was locked when I tried to open it. And the next thing I knew there was all this," I said and pointed to the display.

"That's really freaking creepy, Brooklyn. What do you think is in there that they don't want you to see?"

I shrugged. "I'm sure Miller would warn me if it was something *really* bad."

"Yeah. You're probably right." But she didn't look that convinced.

I didn't have time to think about what was behind that door right now. All I could think about was the fact that I couldn't get Miller fired. I'd never be able to forgive myself. Especially because my heart was still so stupidly confused.

This time when I pulled Kennedy to my room she didn't protest. I practically pushed her in when I heard the sound of footsteps on the stairs. I was about to close and lock my door, but I heard her gasp.

I turned around to see what she was upset about. My heart dropped to the floor.

"What the hell happened in here?" asked Kennedy.

My clothes. All the beautiful clothes that Justin had organized for me were on the floor in shreds. Thousands and thousands of dollars worth of clothes that were so nice that I hadn't even touched them. I swallowed hard. It wasn't just all my new clothes. *No.* I took a few steps into my room and I felt like I was about to burst into tears. The few outfits that I'd owned were ruined too. The sundress my mom had always complimented. Her old riding boots. My favorite pajamas. Even my black dress shoes that hurt my feet. Everything. It was all torn to pieces.

All I could think about was how lucky I was to have been wearing my Keds. I was never going to take them off again.

"Seriously, what the hell happened?" Kennedy asked as she wandered toward the mess. She lifted up a pair of designer jeans. "They look like they were cut with scissors."

"What?" I walked up and looked down at the mess. The rips were precise. Perfect. Planned.

"Oh no, Sissy," Isabella said from behind us with zero shock in her voice.

Kennedy and I both spun around to look at her.

She was holding a tiny, fluffy white dog in her arms. The smile on her face was eerily calm. She slowly stroked the fluffy dog like a psychopath as her smile grew. "Sir Wilfred must have accidentally gotten into your room."

"Sir Wilfred?" I asked. Had she had a secret dog this whole time? I hadn't heard a single bark.

"Yes, isn't he such a cutie pie?" She scratched behind his ears.

"When did you get a dog?"

"I got him this morning as a reward for my good behavior. Daddy always lets me get whatever I want when I'm good. Because he loves me the most."

I was going to be sick.

Isabella walked farther into my room. Just her standing here made the room feel less safe. She was invading my space. And I knew for a fact it wasn't the first time. A dog didn't do this. Like Kennedy had said, it looked like my clothes had been cut into perfect pieces with scissors. They hadn't been shredded by dog claws and teeth. I'd been right. Isabella was trying to sabotage me. But why'd she even bother asking what dress I was wearing when she was planning on ruining everything and blaming it on an innocent dog?

Isabella lifted up what was left of the emerald green dress I'd described to her the other day at dinner. "Sissy, your homecoming dress is ruined. And all your other dresses too." She dropped the dress on top of my other shredded clothes. "I guess you can't go to homecoming after all." She shook her head like she was actually upset. The smile on her face was proof that she wasn't. "What. A. Shame. Oh well." She turned to walk away.

"You're such a bitch," Kennedy said. "These clothes were cut with scissors. Obviously." She picked up a shirt that was cut in half. "You did this."

"Are you calling me a liar?"

"If the shoe fits."

Isabella continued to pet her dog. "At least I have shoes. It looks like Sir Wilfred got to all of Brooklyn's." She stifled a laugh. "Such a shame. Wait, what are you even doing here, Kennedy?" A vicious smile spread across her face. "Daddy!" she screamed at the top of her lungs. "Daddy there's an intruder!"

"Stop yelling," I hissed. I could handle all my clothes being destroyed by a monster. What I couldn't handle was getting Kennedy kicked out and Miller fired. What the hell had I been thinking bringing Kennedy here? Of course we'd be caught. "Please, Isabella, I'll do whatever you want. Go tell your dad that everything's fine. Tell him not to come up."

"Whatever I want?" she asked.

"Anything. Please."

But it was too late.

Mr. Pruitt was standing at the door with a frown on his face.

CHAPTER 24

Saturday

"Sorry, Daddy," Isabella said with a smile. "Everything's fine. It's just Brooklyn's friend. I was mistaken."

He didn't seem to care what she said. "Where is Miller?" he asked.

"I don't know," I said. "I snuck Kennedy in on my own though. It wasn't his fault." I stepped in front of Kennedy as if that would save her from his wrath.

"Not his fault? It's his job to watch you 24/7."

Miller was watching me 24/7? What? I tried to shake away his comment. That wasn't important right now. "I'm sorry I snuck her in," I said. "But…"

"Did your little friend do this?" he asked and gestured to my destroyed clothes.

"What? Of course Kennedy didn't do this. It was like this when we got here. It was…"

"It was Sir Wilfred," Isabella said, cutting me off. She gave me a death stare. I didn't dare contradict her when she was staring at me like that. I'd heard Mr. Pruitt loud and clear the other day. Isabella had murdered people before. *I think.* And I just wanted to go to homecoming, not land six feet under.

"Yeah, I'm pretty sure it was Sir Wilfred," I said.

Mr. Pruitt shook his head. "Isabella, I told you that you had to keep him in your room while he's being trained. We talked about this."

"I'm sorry, Daddy. He must have slipped out when Anderson came in to clean. I told you we should fire her. She's horrid help. This is all her fault. Not mine. And not poor Sir Wilfred's. He didn't know any better. But Anderson did."

Anderson. I didn't know any of the staff's last names besides Miller. I wondered who was going to take the blame for Isabella's cruel prank. I bit down on the inside of my cheek. I didn't want to start World War 3.

"Very well," Mr. Pruitt said. "I'll take care of Anderson. As for this…" he shook his head. "Will you be a dear and let Brooklyn borrow one of your dresses for homecoming? I'm sure the two of you can find something that fits her."

"But, Daddy…"

"No buts. Your dog did this. So you will share with your sister." He turned to me, his expression void of the anger that had been there moments before. "Brooklyn," he said and cleared his throat. "I wasn't sure if you had hired someone to help get you ready, so I arranged for Justin to assist you. He'll be here shortly. And I'll have him order another of everything that was ruined." He sighed like Isabella was as exhausting to him as she was to me. "Your friend can stay, of course. It's the least I can do after this disaster." He stepped forward and put out his hand. "I'm Richard Pruitt. You must be Kennedy Alcaraz. I'll add you to Brooklyn's list of approved visitors."

For a second Kennedy just stared at his hand. "It's a pleasure to meet you," she finally said and shook it. I swore she curtseyed, and the corners of Mr. Pruitt's mouth ticked up ever so slightly.

"The pleasure is all mine. You two have fun getting ready. And if there is anything you need, please don't hesitate to ask. I'll be in my study." He turned back around. "Apologize before you leave, princess," he said as he walked past Isabella and out the door.

It looked like Isabella was going to explode.

The three of us just stood there awkwardly for a moment as Mr. Pruitt's shoes echoed in the hallway.

"If you think I'm loaning you one of my dresses, you're out of your damned mind," Isabella said. "And I can't wait to cash in on that favor you owe me."

"What favor? Your dad came up here anyway. I don't owe you anything."

"Yeah, but I told him I made a mistake. That everything was fine. That's what you asked me to do. And I did."

What the hell was wrong with her? "You were supposed to do that before he came up here. I don't owe you a thing."

She shrugged. "Too bad. We had a verbal agreement, Sissy. Now you owe me whatever I want. I believe your exact words were...*anything*."

"You should be thanking me," I said. "I went along with your Sir Wilfred lie."

She kissed the side of her dog's head and put him down on the ground. "Which was your choice. I can't help it if you're a little slow. Make, Sir Wilfred."

I was about to ask her what she was talking about when Sir Wilfred pranced over and proceeded to pee all over the pile of ruined clothes.

"What is wrong with you?" Kennedy said and held her nose closed.

"Me?" asked Isabella. "Absolutely nothing. I'm perfect if you haven't noticed. Come, Sir Wilfred. I need to get ready for the dance."

The fluffy dog lowered his leg and ran after his evil master.

"Stupid dog," Kennedy said when Isabella left.

"Stupid Isabella."

"Why'd you go along with her?" Kennedy asked. "The clothes clearly weren't destroyed by that dog."

I didn't want to admit that I was scared of Isabella. That I was worried she'd actually kill me. I was pretty sure it was all in my head. And I needed to learn how to stand up to her if I was going to live here. "I've learned to pick my battles with her."

Kennedy flopped down on my bed. "What do you think she's going to do when she realizes your homecoming dress is in Miller's room?"

I had completely forgotten. I breathed a sigh of relief. *Thank God.* I couldn't care less about homecoming. But I would have cried if something had happened to my mom's dress. "She's going to lose her mind. Well, she'd lose it if she hadn't already."

We both looked at each other and laughed.

"This is actually great," Kennedy said. "We got Isabella's shot at sabotage out of the way early. Now we can just relax and have fun."

That was a good point. "Unless she's planning more." I sat down next to Kennedy on the bed.

"Why would she? She thought her first trick would prevent you from going at all."

I nodded. "You're right," I said with a smile. But I was thinking about Anderson. And if there was a way to make sure whoever she was didn't get fired for something she absolutely didn't do.

"Your dad actually seems kinda nice."

"Mr. Pruitt is not my dad."

"Technically…"

"I never saw the results of the tests," I said with a laugh.

"Fair enough. But he took your side over Isabella's. No one ever takes anyone's side over Isabella's. Maybe he's not so bad. He's letting me visit now. And he's going to replace all the clothes. He's at least trying. He seems kinda nice."

Nice? He'd immediately blamed her for destroying my clothes. But I bit my tongue. Mr. Pruitt was trying. I knew that. And yet…I was still uncertain about him. But maybe if I could convince him not to fire Anderson. If he took my side on that, then maybe I could finally let my walls down. Because he was trying. He did care. He was acting like the father I never had. And I was pretty sure that was a good thing. Maybe I'd just been fighting it off because Uncle Jim had felt like a father to me too. And as soon as I'd let him in, I'd lost him.

Tiffany, the timid server, rushed into the room carrying some black trash bags. "Mr. Pruitt said I needed to clean up…" her voice trailed off as she looked at the mess. "Oh my. I'll get right to it." She hurried over.

"I can help," I said and started putting clothes in the plastic bags before Tiffany could stop me.

"This was probably cute," Kennedy said as she started helping us too. She was holding a pink dress that would have looked amazing on her. I made a mental note that when Justin replaced it, I'd give it to her.

"It smells so gross." I shoved another jacket into the trash.

Tiffany laughed.

"What the hell happened in here?" Miller said. My mother's dress was clutched in his hands.

"Isabella," I said as I grabbed a pair of pants by the leg where there was no pee.

He shook his head as he stared at the now stinky ruined clothes. He looked beyond pissed.

"Oh, you're so lucky that you had a dress at the dry cleaners," Tiffany said.

I guess she didn't realize that the dry cleaner's bag was years old and not from New York. Which was good. Because there was no other excuse for Miller to have my dress.

"Let me grab that so I can steam it for you," she said and pulled it out of Miller's tight grip. "You're wrinkling it." She laughed.

"Sorry," he said.

I stood up as I put one of the torn pairs of leggings in the trash bag. "Who's Anderson?" I asked.

Tiffany pulled my dress out of the dry-cleaning bag and turned around. "That's me."

What? My face fell. She was so sweet. And polite. But up here she'd laughed at our jokes. She didn't complain about the dog pee. She was wonderful.

"Why?" she asked.

I swallowed hard. Why did Mr. Pruitt send her up here to help with this mess if he was just going to fire her? "No reason," I said. "I actually need to run to the bathroom real quick. I'll be right back." Mr. Pruitt wasn't a nice man. He was a monster just like his legitimate daughter. And I was going to give him a piece of my mind.

I practically ran into Justin as I beelined for the door.

"Careful, darling," he said as he adjusted two large plastic containers in his dainty arms.

"Sorry, I need to…"

"What in tarnation happened here?" Justin asked. "All my clothes! And is that urine I smell?"

"Miller will fill you in," I said. "I'll be right back."

"Well I certainly have no problem with Miller filling me wherever he pleases," Justin said and handed off the plastic containers to him. He winked at Miller. "But we don't have much time to get ready for the dance. And it's my understanding that I need to give *two* makeovers in the time I'd allotted for one." He looked over at Kennedy.

"Great," I said. "You can get started on Kennedy and I'll be right back. It's a bathroom emergency." It seemed like no one had any intention of letting me get away. But adding that it was an emergency silenced the room. *Awesome.*

Yes, it was nice that Mr. Pruitt had asked Justin to help Kennedy get ready too. But that didn't take away the fact that he sent Tiffany up to clean up a mess she hadn't made. Right before he was going to fire her for that very same mess. He had some explaining to do. I hurried out the door before anyone else could stop me.

CHAPTER 25

Saturday

Miller caught my wrist right after I made it into the hall-way. "There's a bathroom attached to your room, Brooklyn."

God. Stupid rich people with fancy bathrooms in their bedrooms. I'll never get used to this stuff. "Oh. Right. Well, I'll just use the downstairs one now since I'm already on my way." I actually didn't even know where the downstairs bathroom was. But there were probably several. I'd eventually find one.

He looked down the hall to see if the coast was clear and then pulled me to his chest. "You can tell me the truth. You know that."

I breathed in his familiar scent. "Isabella said it was Tiffany's fault for not watching Sir Wilfred better. Mr. Pruitt is going to fire her."

"Who is Sir Wilfred?"

"Isabella's stupid new dog. But that's not even the point. Isabella did it. The clothes weren't ripped by a dog. They were cut with scissors."

Miller shook his head.

"But I'm going to go fix it. I'm going to go talk to Mr. Pruitt now."

Miller tilted his head down to mine. "You're amazing, you know." It looked like he wanted to kiss me.

I smiled up at him. "I'm not amazing. But I am going to try to save her job." I looked down the hall to see if anyone was looking, but Miller grabbed my jaw and kissed me. Every now and then when I'd climb in his bed and talk his ear off, he'd kiss me. Maybe to make me stop talking so he could sleep. Maybe because sometimes he just wanted to be closer to me. I didn't know why sometimes he did and sometimes he didn't. Maybe it depended on what I was talking about. But this kiss didn't feel sleepy. Or convenient. It felt a lot more real than all the others. He pulled away far too soon.

"I want to make sure you know how I feel," he said. "I'm not a grand gestures kind of guy. But I'm here for you. I know you're confused right now. But I'm not."

"You're not?"

He smiled. "Not even a little."

"You're going to get yourself fired," I said with a laugh.

"Maybe so. But I don't care as long as you come with me wherever I go afterwards." He pushed a loose strand of hair behind my ear.

"I thought you didn't want me to run away from here anymore?"

"The unselfish part of me. But the selfish part? I want to get you as far away from these people as possible."

Something about the way he said it made me remember what Mr. Pruitt had said. "Do you watch me 24/7?"

His eyebrows pulled together. "What?"

"Mr. Pruitt said that it was your job to watch me 24/7."

"Yeah, technically that is my job."

I stared up at him. "What does that mean? Like…are you…are there…" I looked up at the ceiling. "Are there cameras somewhere?"

"There are cameras everywhere, Brooklyn. Their locations were listed in detail in the contract you signed. Remember?"

"Oh. Right. Yeah." I definitely didn't remember. Since I hadn't actually read the contract. "Wait. So you watch me when I…change?"

He shifted away from me. "It's not like that. I'm not staring at the screens nonstop. I don't watch you undress. I'm not a creep."

It felt a little creepy to me. Suddenly the feeling of being watched made so much more sense. "Who else is watching me?"

"Each of the security detail is assigned one person."

"Then don't they see me coming downstairs to you at night?" My heart was racing. And I wasn't sure if it was because I was mad that he was watching me. Or I was worried that someone else was.

"There aren't any cameras around the staff floor. Or anywhere near the door to our floor for that matter. There's no reason for them."

I nodded, not feeling all that convinced. "Is someone watching us right now?"

"You're the only one living in this wing." He pulled out his phone and brought up a screen filled with different shots and angles of the apartment. "So I'm the only one that needs access to the cameras in this wing." He showed an image of us on his screen. I could also see a few angles of my bedroom. Kennedy and Tiffany were laughing about something and Justin's hands were on his hips. At least there wasn't a shot of my bathroom.

But still. It all felt wrong. Why hadn't Miller told me he was watching me? "I...I should really go talk to Mr. Pruitt."

"You're not mad at me, are you?"

I looked up at him as he shoved the phone back in his pocket. I wasn't mad. I knew he was doing his job. And if I'd read that stupid contract, I would have known about the cameras. It was weird, though. I'd had no idea he was watching me. "You swear you don't watch me change?" I asked.

He smiled. "I swear."

"Well, that's good." I laughed awkwardly.

"I wouldn't look at all if it wasn't necessary. But I have to make sure you're safe."

Safe from what? And that was the whole problem. It was another thing I wanted to talk to Mr. Pruitt about. Why was any of this necessary? He said if I signed his contract he could fill me in on what he did for a living. "I'll be back up in a minute, okay?"

He smiled, even though he still looked tense.

"I'm not mad. I promise." I stood on my tiptoes and kissed his cheek.

***

I knocked on the big wooden door of Mr. Pruitt's study.

"Come in," said a muffled voice from the other side.

The door was heavy and it slammed closed with a loud thud behind me. I'd never seen Mr. Pruitt with glasses on before. It made him look even more sophisticated.

"How can I help you?" he asked as he pulled his glasses off.

Reading glasses. That was even more peculiar. Wouldn't he need them when he read the morning paper? Did Mrs. Pruitt even know he needed glasses? Did anyone?

He set his glasses down, shaking me out of my thoughts. "You can't fire Tiffany," I said. "It wasn't her fault. Isabella…"

"I know," he said. "Isabella and her friends cut up all your clothes after you left for the homecoming game."

"How…how do you know that?" Miller had just told me that only he had access to the cameras in my room.

Mr. Pruitt closed the lid of his laptop. "I have my ways."

A chill ran down my spine. He had pretty much just admitted that he was watching me too. Who the hell else was watching me? First it seemed like Mrs. Pruitt was. Then Miller. Now Mr. Pruitt too? Was my bedroom on full display for everyone?

Mr. Pruitt stood up from his chair and walked around his desk. "I'm not a fool, Brooklyn." He leaned against the side of his desk. It was the most casual I'd ever seen him. "Isabella seemed to be in a rather great mood this afternoon, even for homecoming. She and her friends giggled during the whole car ride to the game. And the scissors from my desk were missing. She didn't even bother to cover her tracks. She's testing me."

"Testing you?"

"To make sure I love her more, I assume." He sighed. "But you're as much of me as she is. More maybe. Because you haven't been hardened by my wife. I see so much of me in you from when I was your age. And so much of your mother."

I felt a lump forming in my throat. Maybe his heart was hardened by his wife. Maybe he was kind to my mother. Maybe he wasn't always like this. I'd seen glimpses of his kind heart. He was nice to me too.

"My wife will never approve of you." He tilted his head to the side as if he was inspecting me. "But I do. I don't want you to change. I want you to come to me when you think something is unjust. I want you to tell me if I'm doing something wrong. And I don't want you to be scared of standing up for what you believe in, even if it goes against Isabella or my wife."

"Is that why you liked my mom? Because she told you when things were unjust?"

"I loved your mom because she was everything I could never have. She didn't care what people thought of her. She was beautiful inside and out. She was honest. She was…happy."

She was beautiful. And always honest. But I held on to his last description the most. Because knowing that my mom was always happy was what I needed to fall asleep at night. The memory that even in her last days, I was the reason she smiled. "She was happy." Even during the hard times. She had always been quick to make me laugh. I wiped beneath my eyes, trying to hide my tears. She never spoke about Mr. Pruitt. But she also never dated anyone. I was pretty sure he had broken her heart. And that she'd always loved him.

He nodded. "She wouldn't have been happy with me. It was good that she left." He cleared his throat and stood up straight. "You have my word, Anderson's job is secure."

"Good."

He walked back around his desk, seemingly dismissing me. But I had one more thing to discuss.

"I signed the papers," I said. "So you can tell me what you do now."

He smiled. "I'm a businessman."

"Right." I'd gathered that much. "But what kind of business?"

"You can think of me as a CEO of sorts. Of a lot of different businesses." He opened up his laptop again.

"Of what businesses?"

"Family run businesses. Well, a few families really."

"Can't you be more specific than that? We're not in public right now."

He looked up from his screen. "We're always in public. Even when you think we're not."

"What does that mean?"

"That I never discuss business outside this room."

I nodded even though I didn't know what he was talking about. "Are you a hitman?" I blurted the words out before I could stop myself.

He laughed. "A hitman?" He laughed again. "Heavens no. And they prefer to be called wet workers."

What? I'd certainly never heard that term before. And I had a sinking feeling in my stomach about why he knew that random fact. If he wasn't a hitman, did he hire them? I thought about how he'd asked if Isabella had threatened me with his assets. "Do you have wet workers on your payroll?"

He steepled his fingers above his desk. "Brooklyn, my line of work is dangerous. And by association, my family's lives are also in danger. And our extended family of business owners. I take every precaution to keep what's mine safe."

"So that's all you can tell me? That it's a dangerous family business?"

He leaned back in his chair. "Trust me, that's all you need to know. Don't you have a dance to get ready for?"

"Was my mom scared of you? Is that why she left?" I needed to know everything. There were missing pieces in my story. I wanted him to fill them in.

"I was married when I got your mother pregnant. I was trying to do the right thing by my family." He looked back at his laptop. I thought he was going to tell me to leave, but then he added, "If I could go back, I wish that I could say I'd do it differently. But my obligations are hard to break ties from. I had to let your mother go. For her own safety. She wasn't scared of me, but she should have been."

I swallowed hard. "Should I be scared of you?"

"Are you?"

Honestly? "A little."

He smiled. "A little fear is always a good thing in my book. It means you're precautious. It'll do you well."

"That was not in any way an answer."

He laughed. "You have no reason to fear me, Brooklyn. You're my daughter. I couldn't make your mother mine. But I already made you mine. You're Brooklyn Pruitt. You're protected under my name. You're untouchable."

Untouchable. The nickname for the Hunter and Caldwell brothers wasn't lost on me. Officially I was now one of them. Unofficially? I'd never be.

Mr. Pruitt had said something about my last name being Pruitt before. Had he actually changed my last name without my permission? Legally? That seemed like a discussion for a different day. Because he still hadn't answered my other questions. "If I'm untouchable, then why do you have Miller watch me 24/7?"

"Because sometimes people like to touch what isn't theirs, now don't they?"

"What is that supposed to mean?" It felt like I was in trouble. And I'd come here to get Tiffany out of it, not push myself into a hole.

"Matthew Caldwell signed your relationship contract and had a different date than you did. He said your relationship started several weeks before you did. Which means that you were already seeing him before you came here. You're just like me. Always trying to reach for more."

"That's not why I like Matt." Mr. Pruitt was basically insinuating that I was a gold digger.

"Then why do you like him?"

"Because he liked me even when I was invisible."

"Invisible?" Mr. Pruitt shook his head. "No one like you could possibly be invisible. And if you ask me, you should be dating Mason. He's going to inherit MAC International, not Matt. Mason's the better choice."

"Maybe for someone else. Not for me."

"So you're choosing Matthew then?"

"Yes." My voice was a little more firm than my heart. I loved Matt. I did. But he...God, I didn't even know anymore. He didn't love me enough.

"Very well. I'll need you to change the date on that document then. So it matches Matt's."

He pulled open a drawer and rifled through a few folders. "Here we go." He handed me Matt's copy and then mine.

Matt had put in an earlier date. He'd put in the date of his father's birthday party. Where Matt had followed me into the restroom after I cut my hand. The real start of us. It was as sweet as it was arrogant. Because I wasn't his then. Hell, I was barely his now.

"And maybe take a lesson from me and stop sneaking off to the staff floor between midnight and 6 am every day. If it continues I'll have no choice but to figure out who it is you're seeing and fire him. Do we understand each other?"

Oh my God. Of course he knew. But it seemed like he didn't know it was Miller. And at least that was a relief. "That's nothing. I..."

"Do we understand each other?" he asked again.

There was no backtracking. He knew. "Yes."

"Wonderful. I need to get back to work. But please knock again before you leave. I'd love to take a picture with you in your dress. I need one of you for my desk." He gave me a kind smile that didn't at all match his latest threat.

CHAPTER 26

Saturday

It was easy to push the conversation with Mr. Pruitt to the back of my mind when I went back to my room. Kennedy was sitting on my bed getting her nails painted, laughing with Justin. Her hair was piled on top of her head in big rollers. I wasn't sure I'd ever seen her with such a big smile. I just wanted to focus on the dance and having fun for one night.

Besides, Miller wasn't here. So I couldn't talk to him right now anyway. Going down to the staff floor was absolutely not the right move. Mr. Pruitt was clearly watching me. And I wasn't going to give him a reason to fire Miller.

"Don't you love this color?" Kennedy asked as she showed me her purple nails. The hue matched her dress perfectly.

"It's great." I sat down next to her on the bed. "So let me get this straight, Justin. You're an assistant, a stylist, and a…"

"Self-proclaimed makeover artist!" He put the brush back into the nail polish. "Your father called and asked if I had any recommendations, so I recommended myself right into this gig. I knew you'd be a valuable client. Now pick a color. We don't have much time." He opened up one of the plastic containers he'd come in with. It was filled with a whole rainbow of nail polishes, a blow dryer, more bobby pins than I could imagine, and so much freaking hairspray. More hairspray than should ever be in anyone's hair. I suddenly understood how Justin always kept his hair just so.

"If we're running low on time, I can skip doing my nails," I said. "I never really bother to paint my nails."

"Nonsense. There's always time to be fabulous." He rifled through the colors and lifted up a silver one with sparkles. "How about this?"

Kennedy gave me an encouraging nod.

The silver sparkles looked fun. I felt a smile spreading across my face. "Okay."

"I could get used to this," Kennedy said as she blew on her nails. "Oh, our drinks are here!"

I looked up to see Tiffany coming in with a tray of glasses filled to the brim with something clear and bubbly.

I remembered when I'd gone over to The Hunters' house for help with my project. They'd had someone serve alcohol even though we were all underage. Why were adults agreeing to this?

"You asked her to bring us drinks?" I asked.

"No. She offered," Kennedy said and lifted one off the tray. "Don't worry. It's just sparkling water. Not punch."

I laughed. I couldn't be mad about sparkling water. I grabbed one too. "Thank you so much, Tiffany."

She smiled. "Anything else I can grab for you? I know Barbara just pulled some chocolate scones out of the oven."

Kennedy and I both looked at each other.

"We would love some scones," Kennedy said in a ditsy voice that sounded a lot like Isabella.

Tiffany laughed.

For a few minutes there, I thought Kennedy was getting more used to this lifestyle than I was. But she was just having fun. And Tiffany was enjoying it too.

"Right away, ma'am," she said and we all giggled.

"I swear to God, if you girls smudge your nails I'm not redoing them," Justin said as he snagged the sparkling water out of my hand for himself. "Be still."

"Yes, sir."

He laughed too. But then slapped the back of my hand when I fidgeted again.

"This room isn't nearly as bad as the rest of the house," Kennedy said. "I love the color. Everything is so light and airy now that the smell of pee is gone. It reminds me of this beach house I went to when I was a kid."

"Mr. Pruitt picked out the color," I said.

"No."

"Yes."

"Interesting. I guess his wife decorated the rest of the apartment? Who knew he was such a bright and cheery guy?"

Justin laughed and then silently scolded himself for some imperfection I couldn't see on my nails.

"My mom loved yellow," I said. "And he remembered."

"That's sweet." Kennedy reached up to touch one of her rollers.

"Don't you dare touch that," Justin said. "It needs time to set." He screwed the cap back on the silver nail polish. "Now what to do with your hair," he said to me and shoved the sparkling water back into my hand.

I didn't really have any suggestions for him. I'd never had my hair done before.

He continued to stare at me for a few more seconds before he snapped his fingers. "I've got it. It's going to be fantabulous. You're going to *love it*." His voice went up about 12 octaves and his eyes rolled back into his head when he said *love it*.

He seemed to be selling it pretty hard. But I trusted his judgment. The clothes he'd helped pick out had looked good on me. He knew what he was doing. He was going to plan weddings one day. So he could surely handle a hairdo.

Kennedy lifted her camera, being careful not to mess up her nails, and snapped a picture of me. "This is seriously the best day ever. I don't want to ever forget it. Can you get one of us together?" she asked Justin and handed him the camera.

"Promise you won't touch your hair again?" he asked.

She nodded.

He took the camera from her. "Say cheese," he said.

I smiled as big as I could. Kennedy was right. I didn't want to forget today either. We'd basically gotten a spa day without leaving my room. Plus Kennedy was allowed to visit whenever she wanted now.

"What happened to your new cell phone?" she asked as she took the camera back from Justin.

"It's in my dresser."

"Why?"

"Because it was annoying."

She laughed and walked over to the dresser. "Why was it annoying? It has so many new features that mine doesn't." She pulled it out and turned it back on. It immediately started buzzing in her hand. "Whoa."

"What?"

"You have so many missed calls and text from Matt." She squealed and started reading the texts to me:

"Brooklyn please just let me explain," she said in a deep voice.

"I never slept with Rachel. I swear to God."

"You can't shut me out too."

I swallowed down the lump in my throat. None of the Untouchables had been seen together all week. I was pretty sure their friendship had burst into flames just like Matt and my relationship. Probably around the same time that James put his fist through a window. Matt had lost everything. And I knew what that felt like.

Kennedy scrolled down. "There's like a bajillion messages here, Brooklyn. How could you ignore all of these? Oh my God, they get even better." She continued reading:

"I'll do anything to get you back. Just say the word."

"Meet me downstairs. Please."

"Mr. Pruitt won't let me up anymore because our relationship contract has a discrepancy. What the hell is he even talking about?"

"I'm sorry I made you look like a fool at lunch by not telling you the truth. I should have told you. But nothing happened between me and Rachel. Isabella jumped to a wild conclusion. And she was holding it over my head. You know that I'm worried about James. You know that this would hurt him. I don't understand why you don't believe me."

"I'd never lie to you, Brooklyn. Never."

"Will it help if I make a fool of myself?"

Kennedy looked up from the phone. "He made a fool of himself for you, Brooklyn. Even though he didn't know if it would work because you were ghosting him. It's so romantic." She pressed the phone against her chest with a sigh.

"What did he do?" Justin asked as he started messing with my hair.

"To make me mad? Or to try to win me back?"

"I got the gist of the mad part. He hooked up with someone else while you were together."

"No, not while we were together. Before we were together."

Justin lowered his round brush. "So why are you mad at him exactly? He can't undo his past."

"Because he didn't tell me about it." And he hurt his friend who he swore he was trying to protect. The only thing Matt had been protecting was himself.

"Did you tell him about all of your past relationships?" He propped the brush on his hip like he was going to hit me with it.

"No. But I've never been in a relationship before. There was nothing to tell."

"Oh, honey. You have a boy blowing up your inbox. And another hunk of a man staring at you with googly eyes." He waved his hand in the direction of the door, and I assumed he was talking about Miller. "I don't see the problem."

I wasn't really sure if I did anymore either.

"I'd kill to be in your shoes. All the good men are straight." He started working on my hair again.

Maybe he was right. Not the straight thing. I honestly had no idea if that was true. But my shoes seemed pretty great right about now. I looked down at my Keds. What the hell was I doing?

Kennedy put the phone down on my lap, with another text message opened on it:

"Brooklyn, I love you. I wouldn't have said it if I didn't mean it. I've never told anyone else that. I've never felt like this about anyone else. I don't want to give up on us. Please talk to me. I need you."

I pressed my lips together.

"You have to text him back," Kennedy said. "What if he's telling the truth? What if he didn't sleep with Rachel? What if it's all just a crazy big misunderstanding?"

I stared at the phone. I needed to hear Matt out. I owed him that much.

"Before you text him back," Justin said. "What in the name of Judy Garland is a relationship contract? Is that some kind of kinky sex thing? Because if it is, I need a copy ASAP."

"No." I laughed. "It's because my dad's a crazy person and needs to know all my business."

Kennedy gasped.

But I'd already heard what I said. It was the first time I'd ever referred to Mr. Pruitt as *my dad*. It made me feel all warm and fuzzy. I had a dad. And he acted like it too.

"Well, your father tips well," Justin said. "So how bad could he really be?"

If good versus evil was so easily defined by a tip, my life would be so much better. But Justin did have a good point. A monster wouldn't leave a tip at all. My dad wasn't a monster. I looked down at the texts. Maybe the monster was me.

I quickly typed out a response to Matt. "Are you still going to homecoming?"

Matt's response came almost immediately. "Yes, I'll pick you up in an hour."

Of course he jumped to that conclusion. I wasn't going to give in to him taking me. I already had my date. Kennedy and I were going to have a fun, drama free evening. "I'll just see you there."

The phone buzzed. "Save a dance for me?"

"Always." I clicked send before I could change my mind. I'd give Matt the length of one dance to explain himself.

CHAPTER 27

Saturday

"Wow," Kennedy said when Justin finished my makeup and hair. "You look so amazing, Brooklyn."

I smiled and looked over at her. "No, you look amazing." Justin had finished her makeup first and she was flawless. The eyeliner and mascara made her eyes pop even more than usual. The hair rollers that Justin had taken out had given her updo more volume. Cupcake was going to eat his heart out.

"Thank you," she said with a smile. "But I'm serious." She grabbed the handheld mirror and lifted it in front of me.

I looked just like my mom. I swallowed hard. My loose curls cascaded down past my shoulders. I wasn't used to wearing much makeup. I looked all grown up. I blinked fast, making sure my tears wouldn't fall. Everyone always said I looked like my mom. But it was almost like I was staring at her reflection.

Justin was the most talented person I had ever met. I wanted him to do my makeup every day. I felt closer to my mom than I had in months. I didn't know whether to cry or try to hug the mirror. But then my eyes settled on the crown on top of my head that sparkled with crystals.

"I...I can't wear this," I said.

"What do you mean?" Kennedy pulled the mirror back. "You look just like that picture of your mom that you had on your nightstand back at Uncle Jim's. You look beautiful. You're going to make Matt lose his mind."

"It's not that." I shook my head and turned to Justin. "You did a fantastic job, but you have to take the crown out of my hair."

"Why? Honey, you look fabulous. When you step into the room everyone will be looking at you."

"Isabella's homecoming queen," I said. "She's supposed to be the only one wearing a crown. She'll kill me if I go like this."

Justin laughed. "Well, maybe you should have won," he said. "That'll show that nasty bitch. Maybe it'll teach her some manners."

He almost made me laugh. Not because it was super hilarious, but because Rob had said something so similar about Isabella before. Was it possible that Rob was gay? *What am I even thinking about? I need this crown off my head!* "I'm a sophomore, I couldn't have won. Please just take it out." I lifted up my hand but Justin smacked it away.

"You're a masterpiece," he said. "A vision. And you will not ruin my work. Now let's get you girls in your dresses before you give me a coronary." He sashayed off toward our dresses. It seemed like the angrier I made him, the more his hips swayed.

"Really, Brooklyn," Kennedy said. "Screw Isabella. She literally destroyed every piece of clothing you've ever owned. And then had her demon dog pee on everything. And then tried to blame it on me. She deserves to be knocked down a level."

"I know that. But I'm just scared of what she'll do when it happens."

"Nothing to be scared of. I'll be with you the whole time."

"Not when I come home." *God, did I just refer to this horror house as my home?*

"Maybe we can convince your dad to let us have a sleepover. Come on, don't worry. Tonight is supposed to be fun," she added before standing and walking over to Justin.

Isabella was going to kill me. I didn't dare glance in the mirror again. Maybe if I pretended the crown wasn't there, it would magically disappear. Just like Justin had magically made me look exactly like my mom.

Kennedy and I both changed. She didn't seem at all concerned that Justin didn't leave the room. I covered my chest awkwardly as I pulled on my dress. He walked over as I tried to reach around my back to pull the zipper up myself.

"I've got it," he said and pulled it into place. "It fits you perfectly. And vintage is all the rage. You're absolutely slaying this look."

I looked down at my mother's dress. Maybe it wasn't magic that had made me look like her. Maybe I was just growing up.

"Twirl for me," Justin said.

I pictured my mom twirling me around as we danced in the kitchen together and smiled. I turned in a circle and the dress flared up around me. It really was perfect. I felt like Cinderella.

"What in the hell?" Justin asked. "Oh my God, no. Just. No."

"What?" I asked.

"Your shoes." He lifted up the hem of my dress and stared at my Keds in horror. "You need to change them this instant."

"But I can't leave them here unattended. Isabella's trying to ruin everything I own. Besides, I think they look kinda cool with the dress."

"No," he said with zero sass. He was all business.

"But, Justin…"

"No. Absolutely not. No one wears a crown with sneakers."

"Isabella destroyed all her shoes," Kennedy said. "She doesn't have any other ones to wear."

"Don't you have like millions of dollars?" Justin asked. "I'm already late for my next appointment but I'll literally go buy you a pair right now if the tip is right. And any tip is right because this is literally a fashion emergency."

Kennedy grabbed his arm. "Her mom got her those. I think they're cute, Brooklyn. It's very rockstar of you."

"You think?" I lifted the skirt of my dress and looked down at my Keds.

Justin looked horrified but then he pinched his face and looked away. "Very rockstar," he agreed.

I knew he was just saying it to be polite, but I appreciated it none the less.

He clapped his hands to end the discussion. "No matter how sweaty you get dancing, don't wipe your face. Blot it. It's all about the blotting, ladies. Your makeup and hair should have no problem lasting through midnight."

Midnight? It was the last Cinderella coincidence I could take. "Justin, you're like my fairy godmother."

"Did you just call me a fairy?" He put his hand on his hip. "Do you have any idea how offensive that is?"

"Oh…I…I didn't mean…"

He laughed and leaned in to hug me. "I'm just kidding. Knock 'em dead tonight. And call me before your next event. I'll bring an even bigger tiara." He winked at me as he let me out of his embrace. "I gotta run. I can't believe you two made me late! I'm never late!" He grabbed his boxes of beauty products and hurried out the door.

"I freaking love him," Kennedy said.

I laughed. "I'm 99% sure he's gay."

"Why only 99%? Girl, he's definitely gay. There's not a doubt in my mind. Trust me, I don't want to date him. I don't want to date anyone for a long time. I just meant that he's the coolest person ever."

"He really is."

"But if he was straight, I'd marry him in a heartbeat. I love being pampered like this. That was so much fun. When can we do it again?"

I laughed. "Hopefully soon. I feel like we're in one of those makeover shows."

"Queer Eye for the Straight Teenager," Kennedy said.

"We should pitch that idea to Justin."

"We really should. I'm going to run to the bathroom real quick and then we can go?"

I nodded and she went over to the bathroom. Even she knew it was attached to my room. I bit the inside of my lip. Every ounce of me wanted to ask her about Felix. I'd heard her the other day when she said she always fell in love with drug dealers. Plural. And Felix and Cupcake were the only two drug dealers we knew. I wanted her to open up to me about it. But I couldn't yank the information out of her.

Regardless of whether she wanted to tell me or not, I had a plan for tonight to fix everything. First I had to talk to Felix and apologize. He'd been avoiding me at gym ever since the fight at his house. The longer I had to think of it, the more I realized how much I was in the wrong. I needed to tell him I was sorry for leading him on. And then I needed to somehow get Kennedy and him to dance together. If she wouldn't admit that she had feelings for him to me, maybe she'd admit it to him. *Operation Felix*. It had a name now, so I had to go through with it.

"You all ready?" Kennedy asked. She emerged from the bathroom fidgeting with one of the loose locks that fell from her updo.

"Mhm. You better stop touching your hair, or you'll give Justin a heart attack from miles away."

She let her hand fall. "You're right. Now we just need to remember to blot and not wipe and we'll have a fabulous evening." She looped her arm through mine as we made our way down the hall.

We froze at the top of the steps. We hadn't planned this out at all. I just assumed that Isabella would have been long gone with weird homecoming queen duties or something. But she was standing at the bottom of the stairs with her minions. They were all giggling as they took photos in the foyer. Their generic dates all looked the same in their black tuxes, except for Mason Caldwell. He was dressed the same, but he filled out his tux differently than the rest.

I had no idea how much he knew about me and his brother. But I wasn't about to find out. Or let Isabella notice me.

"We should go back…" I whispered just as Isabella turned.

The look on her face could only be described as vicious. I took a step back even though we were a whole staircase apart.

"Sissy, what on earth are you wearing?" Isabella said with a laugh. "It looks like it's straight out of the 80s."

I probably would have tried to cover my dress if Kennedy's arm wasn't still looped in mine. Kennedy tugged on that arm.

I knew what she wanted me to do. I needed to stand up to Isabella if this was ever going to stop. I tried to hold my head up high even though her jabs stung. "It was my mom's." They weren't fighting words. And I had no idea why I thought something personal could work against a monster.

Isabella laughed. "You're wearing a hand-me-down? Good God, you're so pathetic."

I looked down at my dress. It was beautiful, even if it was old. And Justin had said that vintage was in.

"And I bet those aren't even real diamonds on your tiara?"

It seemed to be a rhetorical question, so I didn't say a word.

"My dear sweet, ugly half-sister. Take off the crown you don't deserve. And then do the world a favor and stay locked in your room tonight like the hideous ogre you are. No one wants you at the dance."

"Isabella," Mason said. "Isn't that enough?"

"No, I'm not nearly done…"

"You look fucking hot, Brooklyn," he said. "And I know my brother is excited to see you at the dance."

My cheeks flushed.

Isabella's mouth was hanging open. Apparently she wasn't used to being cut off mid-sentence. She was used to doing the cutting. "Who even invited you here, Mason?" Isabella spat.

"My date. Laci." He pointed to one of Isabella's minions.

"Freaking Laci," Isabella said under her breath, but loud enough for everyone to hear.

I swore a few of Isabella's other minions inched slightly away from the girl in question. *Poor Laci.*

"Well you can both get the hell out," she said to Mason and Laci. "Talking to an ogre makes you an ogre."

Mason leaned against one of the tables displaying a vase. Somehow his bulky frame didn't knock it over. "You were literally just talking to her, Isabella. So doesn't that make you an ogre too?"

Laci had the audacity to laugh.

Isabella took a deep breath, but it looked like her head was about to explode. "Semantics. None of this matters. Sissy, you aren't going to the dance. Now be a dear and go back to your room. Now."

"She's not a dog," Kennedy said.

"Right." Isabella glared at her. "She's not dirty and living in a cesspool. That's you."

"I'm gonna kill her…"

I grabbed Kennedy's hand to stop her from storming down the stairs and doing God knows what to Isabella. Even though Isabella most certainly deserved it.

Isabella put her hand over her mouth, stifling a laugh. "You're literally on a leash, Kennedy."

Kennedy tried to lunge for her again, but I didn't let go of her arm.

"It's fine," I said. "We're just going to go back to my room. And we'll leave after you're done taking pictures down here."

"No. You're not going to the dance at all. Get it through your thick skull."

"Why don't you want me to come?"

"Because I said so."

"That's not a reason, Isabella. Why are you so hellbent on torturing me? Why do you hate me so much? What did I ever do to you? Can't we please just start over? Or at least be civil?"

Her lips were pressed in a thin line so hard that I could barely see them.

"Is everything alright out here, princess?" Mr. Pruitt asked as he emerged from his study. "Or should I say queen?"

Isabella spun around. "Yes, Daddy. We were just having a bit of fun." Her voice was laced with sugary sweetness.

"You look beautiful," he said.

Isabella beamed and adjusted the crown on top of her head. "Sissy was just telling me she felt ill. I'm worried about her. I think we should make her stay home."

What the hell? She couldn't lie her way into preventing me from going to homecoming. Could she?

CHAPTER 28

Saturday

Mr. Pruitt's eyes traveled up the stairs to me. For a second, I thought he looked horrified. I was wearing a dress from the 80s. It wasn't vintage. It was just old. I could practically feel his embarrassment. I just wasn't sure if he was embarrassed of me or for me. But then he smiled. A real one. Way more genuine than I'd ever seen. "You're breathtaking, Brooklyn."

My dad thought I was beautiful. I wasn't an ogre. I didn't deserve to be locked in my room. He'd let me go to the dance.

Mr. Pruitt walked up the stairs, stopping one step below me. "She kept it all these years?" He reached out and touched the fabric. It barely seemed like he was looking at me. It was more like he was looking through me.

"You knew my mom used to wear this?"

He smiled. "I bought it for her." His hand fell from my shoulder strap.

She kept it all these years.

"You look just as gorgeous as she did."

"Thank you." I almost tacked on a *dad* at the end of my sentence. I wasn't even sure why. Maybe because he was looking at me like he loved me. Like he loved my mom too. Like I wasn't a mistake.

"Are you really not feeling well?" He gently put the back of his hand against my forehead. "You don't feel warm. But I should probably call Dr. Wilson just in case." He was already pulling out his cellphone.

"I'm fine," I whispered. "Isabella just didn't want me to go."

His eyebrows drew together. "But you're sure you're alright?" he whispered back.

"Positive."

"Then I can handle this." His smile was back. "I'm so glad you're feeling better," he said loudly enough for everyone to hear. "Come on, I want that picture with you." He put his arm out for me. "You too, Miss Alcaraz," he said and offered her his other arm.

Kennedy laughed and took it.

I couldn't help but glance at Isabella as her father escorted Kennedy and me down the stairs. Pure venom. And so priceless.

"Do you mind if I get a shot?" Kennedy asked and pulled her camera out of her back.

"That would be delightful, thank you," Mr. Pruitt said. "The tiara suits you," he added right before Kennedy snapped a photo.

He didn't actually call me princess like he called Isabella. But it was pretty much the same thing. I smiled harder when Kennedy took another shot.

"Would you be able to send me copies?" Mr. Pruitt asked.

"As long as I can sleep over tonight," Kennedy said.

He laughed. "You strike a hard bargain. Very well." He turned to Mason. "Mason, why don't you come over and get a picture with Brooklyn too?"

Oh my God. I thought about my conversation with Mr. Pruitt earlier. About how he thought Mason was the better choice. Was he seriously trying to push us together? I just wanted to laugh. Because it was such a protective father thing to do. I was even a little embarrassed. *My dad's so embarrassing.*

Mason shrugged and walked over to me. "You okay?" he asked. He didn't even have to do the head nod toward Isabella for me to know what he was talking about.

"I'm used to it."

"You shouldn't have to be used to it." He smiled for the camera.

I looked up at him. "It's kind of the new normal, right?"

"You could always crash at our place. James and Rob are there half the time anyway."

I didn't know that.

"Well. They used to be." He shoved his hands in his pockets.

Used to be. They didn't come over anymore since the fight? I'd expected as much. I hadn't seen any of the Untouchables together in days. But it still made me sad. The four of them were best friends. How could everything crumble with one secret? Weren't the elite propped up with secrets and silicone?

"I can't," I said. "Mr. Pruitt is really strict. And I don't even know what's going on with me and Matt."

"Well, I do. Matt's never been this into someone before." Mason looked down at me. "You gotta give him another chance. He's a mess without you."

Mason was a playboy. Everyone at Empire High knew it. So it was shocking to hear him talk like this. First being open about the riff between the Hunters and Caldwells. And now about his little brother missing me? I could have been wrong, but it seemed like Mason Caldwell had a soft side.

"Time to go," Isabella said.

"Make sure to let Brooklyn and Miss Alcaraz ride in the limo with you," Mr. Pruitt said to Isabella.

"But Daddy. She can't come. She's wearing a crown and she wasn't voted queen. It isn't fair."

"You will be nice to your sister or you'll be the one staying home."

Isabella's eyes grew wide. "But…"

"No buts." He turned to me. "And Brooklyn, if you do feel ill, please call me right away. I'll come get you."

It was silly and overprotective. But I was smiling so hard.

Mr. Pruitt walked back to his study and closed the doors.

For a few seconds the foyer was eerily silent.

"When hell burns over we'll take the same limo," Isabella said. "Come on, ladies. We're leaving."

"Do you want me to call a ride for you?" Mason asked me.

"It's okay," Miller said.

I hadn't even seen Miller approach.

He stopped beside me, sizing up Mason. "I'll be taking them."

"Cool." Mason lifted up his hands like he was innocent. Which he was. "See you at the dance, Brooklyn," Mason said. "You too, Kennedy," he added before joining his date.

"Well that wasn't the best start," Kennedy said as Isabella and her friends left. "But at least we get to have a sleepover!"

I laughed. "I can't believe you want to spend the night here."

"Both of you can't fit in my bed," Miller said with a smile.

I shoved his arm. And then immediately pulled back. Mr. Pruitt was probably watching us right now. But I didn't want to have this conversation with Miller right in front of Kennedy.

"Obviously I'm sleeping in Brooklyn's bed, perv," Kennedy said.

Miller laughed. "Let's get you girls to homecoming."

"While we're at the dance, would it be possible to have all of Isabella's clothes cut up?" Kennedy asked.

That was a great question. We all laughed, even though I actually wanted to know the answer. How was I going to get through living with Isabella until she went off to college next fall?

I looked over my shoulder at Mr. Pruitt's study door. I was only safe from Isabella when he was in the same room as us. And for the first time, I felt a chill run down my spine when I left the apartment instead of when I entered.

CHAPTER 29

Saturday

Back home, all the dances had been held in the high school cafeteria. But Empire High had rented out the same ballroom where I'd first talked to Matt. Miller's sedan stuck out like a sore thumb amongst all the limos when we pulled up to the front. It was like a show of wealth that I didn't understand. If they all showed up in limos, it didn't exactly make it special. I looked down at my Keds sticking out from underneath my mother's dress.

I smiled over to Kennedy when she snapped a picture of me. She was rocking a much more modern dress, but it was second-hand too. I was pretty sure we'd be the only two here not wearing new dresses, and for some reason that made me happy. Kennedy and I were showing up in style. Not the same designer's dresses and cookie cutter limousines as everyone else.

Kennedy took a deep breath. "You ready for this?"

I wasn't really sure if I was. Operation Felix was in the back of my head. The fact that my dad knew I'd been running down to the staff floor every night was making my stomach twist in knots. But most of all? I knew Matt would be through those doors. And I didn't know what any of it meant. All I knew was that my broken heart felt like it was being tugged in three different directions.

I glanced out the windows at the other students laughing and taking pictures. The last time I'd been here, I'd had to go around to the staff entrance on the side. But tonight? I'd get to walk through the front doors. *Or…* "You know we could just ditch the dance and go see a movie or something."

Kennedy laughed. "Oh, come on. This is going to be amazing. I've only ever waited tables here." She unbuckled her seatbelt.

"Yeah." It was kind of amazing. We weren't servers tonight, we were part of the elite. I unbuckled my seatbelt but didn't move to follow her out the door. "Do you mind giving me just a second to talk to Miller?" I asked.

"No problem. But don't take too long, it's getting cold." Kennedy slipped out of the car and slammed the door behind her. She didn't go up toward the ornate hotel doors. She waited for me right on the sidewalk, just like I would have done for her. I wasn't sure either of us would have wanted to venture into the dance alone. Kennedy was braver than me. But neither of us were dumb. Walking into that hotel alone was just asking for trouble.

Miller turned in his seat so he could look at me. "You look really beautiful, Brooklyn." There was something sad in his eyes that I didn't understand. Apparently I looked sad too, because he added, "is everything alright?"

"No, not really." I took a deep breath. I'd lost both my mom and my uncle in the span of several weeks. I was a mess. And I'd been pulling so many people into my mess with me. Just because I needed comfort, it didn't mean I was allowed to just take love wherever it came from. I needed to make up my mind. But it was so hard when

Miller was staring at me like that. It was him. He was the right choice. He was always there for me. He'd always stand up for me. He'd be my rock. Why was life so cruel?

"What's wrong?" He reached out and took my hand.

I squeezed it tight, because I didn't want to let go. I hated myself for being so indecisive. But this decision was out of my hands. "Mr. Pruitt knows I'm seeing a member of the staff."

He shook his head. "That's not possible."

"Trust me, he does. He just told me. He's been watching me, I think. He knows I sneak out of my room each night and come back around 6 in the morning."

Miller shook his head. "I'm the only one who has access to those cameras."

"I don't know what to tell you. He must have access to them too. He said he didn't know who I was visiting downstairs though. He doesn't know it was you. And I don't think he suspects you."

Miller exhaled slowly.

"But he said I had to stop. Or he'd take the time to figure out who it was."

"So we'll need to be more careful."

"Do you have any idea how scared I was that you'd lose your job today for sneaking Kennedy into the apartment? I can't ask you to do me any more favors. I have nothing to give you in return."

"I'm not asking for anything in return. I just like spending time with you."

I pulled my hand out of his grip. "We have to stop."

He lowered his eyebrows. "Is this about Matt? Or what's his name...Mason?"

"No. And absolutely not." I didn't even know if I was going to forgive Matt. But regardless, I needed to do this. I owed Miller so much. I clasped my hands together so I wouldn't reach out for him again. "I appreciate you being there for me. I don't know how I would have survived the past week without you. But I won't keep putting your job in jeopardy." I could feel my tears threatening to spill. This hurt. I wanted to choose him. My heart was screaming at me to.

"I don't care about my job."

"Of course you care. You said you needed the money for college."

"You think I would seriously leave you alone in that house with them and go off to college? I already mentally pushed it back two years."

My heart skipped a beat. "Miller, you can't do that."

"And you can't tell me what to do, kid."

Kid. He used that nickname when he was annoyed with me. And every time I heard it was like a punch in the gut, reminding me of my uncle calling me kiddo. What was I doing? Why was I trying to push him away when he made me happy? Why did I have to choose right this second? Why couldn't I just catch a break? "I really like you." It was the opposite of what I was supposed to be saying. But it was the first thing I said to him tonight that felt right.

"I really like you too."

I pressed my lips together. "I'm still confused."

"I've got time." He smiled out of the corner of his mouth. "And I never asked you to make a decision tonight."

"I know, I just…" I ran my hands down my dress. Felix's harsh words were in the back of my head. "I don't want to lead you on."

"You haven't. I knew full well what I was getting myself into when I let you climb into my bed."

I laughed. "You make it sound so much more salacious than it is." Just saying the words out loud reminded me that there was more to the reason why we couldn't be together. "But it's not just Mr. Pruitt knowing," I said. "I signed a contract that said I was with Matt. A relationship agreement or something like that. And I didn't read through it. I don't even know what will happen if I break it."

"Why would you sign something you didn't read?"

I shook my head. "I don't know, Matt signed it without looking at it and I just…"

"You read all the house rules and signed that contract. That was like a freaking book. It took you days but you took the time to go over all those details. You could have taken a few minutes to read the relationship one too."

I didn't have the heart to tell him I never finished reading the first contract Mr. Pruitt gave me either. Not when he was looking at me like I was crazy. "I'm sure whatever it is isn't that bad."

He sighed. "I'll try to get a copy without raising suspicion. Next time don't sign something without reading it. You know how detailed those contracts are. You're practically signing over your life. For all we know you're freaking betrothed to the guy."

I swallowed hard. What did he mean by that? Signing over my life? It didn't matter if he was disappointed in me for not reading the contracts. I needed to know what was in them. "Miller, I…"

A car honked behind us.

"You should get in there," Miller said. "You're already late."

I glanced out the window at Kennedy. She was standing there shivering. *Crap.* I hadn't meant to make her wait in the cold. "Okay." I'd confess that I hadn't read the first contract after the dance. There wasn't a rush. Besides, I was pretty much stuck in this world. So what if I'd signed a few papers agreeing to that fact? As soon as I graduated, I'd still be able to move out. "I'll see you after?" I asked as I grabbed the door handle.

"I'm not going anywhere. I have to watch you 24/7, remember? I'm going to go park and then I'll be right in."

I nodded. Right, 24/7. Because Mr. Pruitt did dangerous work. I stared at Miller for another beat. That meant Miller was dangerous too. I knew that and yet…he didn't seem dangerous to me. Not even a little. But neither did Mr. Pruitt. And I knew for a fact that Mr. Pruitt was dangerous. He'd even told me as much. *And I'd freaking signed his contract without reading it. I'm a complete fool.* My heart wasn't just confused anymore. My head was too. What kind of man said he was dangerous and then put his hand to my forehead to check my temperature? It didn't make any sense.

"Don't make me too jealous tonight," Miller said with a wink, trying his best to lighten the mood.

He didn't have to worry about being jealous. I'd probably only dance with one boy tonight. Matt had one dance to tell me his side of the story. That was it. Everyone else would just treat me like the social pariah I was. It would be Kennedy by my side, no one else. I'd gotten a small taste of what it felt like to fit in. But it would only ever be a taste. I was back to being invisible. Which was actually fortunate because I was an awful dancer.

"Trust me," I said. "You have nothing to worry about. Kennedy is my dance partner tonight." I climbed out of the car to join her.

She grabbed my arm before I had a chance to wave goodbye to Miller. "It's freaking freezing!" She pulled me toward the entrance. "What were you guys talking about?"

"I'm sorry. My head and my heart are really confused and I just needed to talk to him."

"Because of Matt or Mr. Pruitt?"

"What?"

"Your dad isn't exactly the evil monster you described. He's kind of sweet. Or are you talking about the fact that you still have feelings for Matt?"

God. "All of it."

"You know what you need?" She looked so excited and for some reason it made me wary.

"No…what?"

"Your favorite." Her voice was weirdly high-pitched.

I just stared at her confused.

"Punch!"

I groaned. "I will never ever drink punch again in my life." Numbing the pain wasn't worth it. It was one of the few lessons I'd learned with my uncle by my side. I'd made a promise to him that I wouldn't get drunk again. My promise was one of the only things I had left of him. "Never," I added when she was still smiling. "I mean it,

Kennedy. Being hungover was not something I ever want to experience again. Punch is the freaking worst."

"I'm pretty sure you said the exact opposite the last time you had it. If I recall correctly you said you loved it. Like really loudly. You screamed it at the top of your lungs."

"Yeah…because I was drunk."

"Well, we're at a school dance this time. I'm sure this punch isn't even spiked." She winked at me and I didn't believe her at all.

CHAPTER 30

Saturday

"Wow," I said when we entered the ballroom. It looked completely different than the last time I'd served here. There weren't any tables, just a huge dance floor. There weren't even any adults in sight. Well, maybe a few. I spotted Mr. Hill yelling at some kids about dancing too close, but I quickly looked away. The last thing I needed was for him to yell at me instead.

I looked around the ballroom. There were gold balloons everywhere. I wouldn't have even been surprised if they were somehow made from actual gold. "Do you think we could pop one?" I asked.

Kennedy didn't respond. She was just staring at the dance floor where tons of students had stopped dancing.

It was like someone had lit up a big neon sign saying to quiet down. Heads turned toward me. Everything was hushed. I swore the music volume even lowered. And then the whispering started.

"What is happening?" I said to Kennedy out of the corner of my mouth.

"They're probably staring at you because of that song Matt sung on the float. Just ignore them. Who cares what they think?"

I wish I didn't.

"Come on. Let's get some drinks." She grabbed my hand and pulled me through the crowd like the whispers didn't bother her at all.

I wanted to be like Kennedy when I grew up. She was so good at brushing things off. I tried to stand up a little straighter.

I swore I heard someone whisper the word *slut*. And I had a feeling that some of the whispers weren't about me. Kennedy gripped my hand a little tighter. She'd heard the word thrown at her too. But the smile remained on her face.

For some reason I found it easier to be strong for her even though it was hard to be strong for myself. I squeezed her hand back. "You're right," I said. "Who cares what they think?"

We stopped in front of the bar that was usually decked out with alcoholic beverages for adult events. Tonight it was filled with juices and sodas galore.

James was standing there, drumming his fingers along the wooden bar top. His crown was lopsided on his head, but otherwise he looked more sober than I'd seen him all week. Maybe being the king to Isabella's queen had finally sobered him up.

But when the bartender wasn't looking, James unscrewed the cap off a flask. He looked over his shoulder to make sure no one was looking and proceeded to dump the whole flask into the punch bowl. He shoved the flask back in his pocket just before the bartender turned around.

"Can I get you ladies anything?" the bartender asked, completely oblivious to what James had just done.

"I'll have some punch," Kennedy said and stepped forward.

I opened my mouth but then closed it. Kennedy could drink one glass and I could still keep my promise to Uncle Jim. Honestly, if people were whispering about me being a slut, I'd want a drink too. I'd keep an eye on her.

"What about you?" James asked me. "Don't you want some too?" He tried to straighten his crown but it just made it more lopsided.

"Um…no thanks."

For some reason that made him smile. Smiles from James were few and far between. Especially real ones.

I wasn't sure why he was even talking to me, let alone smiling at me. Aside from Matt's performance today and his texts, all the Untouchables had been avoiding me like the plague ever since the truth had come out. Well, except for Mason tonight. He'd been weirdly kind. And he'd hinted that the Caldwells and Hunters weren't really speaking anymore. Which broke my heart.

"So no drink," he said as Kennedy joined me by my side. "How about a dance then?"

I forced myself not to look over my shoulder, even though I couldn't believe James was asking me for a dance. Wait…why was he asking me? "Actually, Kennedy and I…"

"Kennedy is just going to drink this real quick and join you two on the dance floor in a bit," Kennedy said. She raised her eyebrows and stared at me like I was insane.

Which was weird because she was the one that was acting insane. James and I weren't friends. He was nice sometimes. Other times he was just plain cruel. And I didn't feel like playing whatever game he was currently making up in his head. "Um…"

"Come on, Brooklyn," he said and put his arm out for me. "I promise I won't bite."

I glanced at Kennedy who was shooing me away. This felt like some kind of weird trap. But I wasn't exactly sure how to get out of it without looking like an ass. And after what Matt had done to James? The least I could do was cheer him up with a dance. I looped my arm through his and the smile came back to his face.

A slow song cut in as soon as we walked onto the dance floor. He pulled me in a little closer. Too close. I could smell his cologne and the mint on his breath. Why was he so close?

"Is Rachel here?" I asked.

James' hands settled on my waist. "What do you think?"

"Well…if you're anything like me…you haven't spoken to her all week."

He laughed. "Yeah, that sounds about right."

I looked up at him. There was nothing I could say. If Matt was telling the truth, Rachel had come on to him. Not the other way around. And I didn't want to ask James about what he thought actually happened. It would just make everything worse. "So you aren't speaking to her. Or Matt?"

"Or Mason."

I nodded. "Or Mason. Aren't they your best friends?"

"Best friends don't fuck their said best friends' girl-friends."

Fair enough. "Congrats on being homecoming king." It was a terrible segue, and we both knew it.

He laughed again.

It was so strange hearing him laugh. I liked the sound. I wished he'd do it more.

"It was rigged," he said. "The homecoming king. I'm sure Mason won. Everyone actually likes him. Well, except for all those girls he screwed and dumped."

"I think they make up enough of the student body that he wouldn't have won." But now that I thought about it, Mason was the one always high-fiving people in the hallway. He was usually smiling. He wasn't nearly as silent and brooding as James.

James shrugged. His expensive tux felt like silk against my forearm. "It was still rigged, trust me. Isabella found out she was going to win queen, by threatening someone I'm sure. And then she manipulated it for me to be king."

"I'm sure she didn't." Although, I wasn't so sure. That sounded a lot like something Isabella would do. Threats and manipulation were her first language.

"No, she told me as much."

Oh. "I'm sorry."

"Why? I'm the freaking king." He didn't look so happy anymore.

"Well, it looks good on you." I reached up and straightened his crown for him.

"It looks better on you. The tiara I mean."

I wasn't so sure about that. But I could feel my cheeks blushing. And I realized my hand was still on his crown. I moved it back to his shoulder.

His eyes traveled to my flushing cheeks and he smiled.

For some reason it just made me blush more.

"You know…" he said, his voice trailing off as his eyes drifted to mine. "I was thinking. Maybe there is a way I could get over Matt being an ass."

"Yeah? And how would you do that?" I wanted James to be happier. I didn't want to have to worry about him. And he had such a nice laugh. It would be nice if the world could hear it more often.

"For starters, we could fuck."

I stopped swaying back and forth. It took every ounce of restraint not to slap him. I knew he was up to no good. Asking me to dance so he could prove some kind of point to Matt? Screw him. "I don't think that would fix anything, James."

"Really? I think it would fix everything."

I stared back at him. "How would that fix anything? You're dating Rachel. And I'm dating…" Who the hell was I dating? Felix? Miller? Matt? God, was I kind of dating all of them? I'd had zero punch and my head was still spinning.

"You know, this summer I told Rachel I'd give everything up for her. All this shit I don't care about. That I'd pass on Harvard. That I'd renounce my inheritance. I'd give up all my responsibilities. That we could run away together. And she got mad at me. Furious, actually. That was the night Matt screwed her. And all I keep thinking about is that my mother was right. That Rachel just likes me for my money. Rachel thought I was going to give it all up so she hopped in bed with someone else. I don't want to believe that. But…" his voice trailed off and he shook his head.

"I'm sorry that you're hurting." I truly was. This was one of James' nicer moments. And all I could wonder was if Matt was right. If he was hurting so much that he might do something to himself. He wouldn't, right? He couldn't.

He smiled. "Then how about you make me feel better?"

Just when I thought he was being nice. "I'm not sleeping with you, James. I don't do…that."

"Don't do what? Have revenge sex? Let me tell you, you're seriously missing out." His hands slid slightly lower on my waist.

I looked away from him, searching for Kennedy in the sea of other students. She said she'd join us on the dance floor. Where was she?

"Oh my God," James said.

"What?" I didn't look back at him. *Kennedy, please magically appear and save me from this awkward conversation.*

"Are you a virgin?"

I forced myself to look back at him. "That's none of your business." I was done being polite. I didn't have to dance with him. He wasn't my responsibility to look after. "I'm going to go find Kennedy."

"Wait." He caught my arm as I tried to flee. "I'm sorry, I just…it would make Matt so fucking mad. How could you not want that? He kept you his dirty little secret for weeks. He didn't tell any of us about you. Doesn't that piss you off? That he was that embarrassed of you?"

"He wasn't embarrassed of me. Isabella was threatening him. She…"

"Isabella threatens everyone. He's a pansy if he was scared of her. It's her father he should be worried about."

I tried to ignore his last statement. Mostly because I was worried it was true. The thought of that unread contract made my stomach twist into knots. But if I thought about that now I was pretty sure my head would explode. "Matt said Isabella threatened to kill him. And me."

"And you believe him? After everything he put you through? It wouldn't be the first time Matt lied just to get into some chick's bed. You're allowed to be mad at him, Brooklyn. Freaking let it out."

"You know what? I am mad. I'm mad that you're trying to use me to get back at him. I'm not a pawn."

"I didn't say you were. I just thought we might feel the same way. Rachel used me. Matt used you. Why can't we make each other feel better by making them feel like shit?"

"Because you don't even like me."

"Why do you think I don't like you?"

"Because you're being an ass."

He laughed. "Well, my offer stands. I rented a room for the night. 315. Take a key." He pulled out a keycard from the same pocket he was hiding a flask in.

"No thanks."

"I do like you, Brooklyn. You're everything I thought Rachel was."

"And what did you think Rachel was?"

"My way out of this hell." He slid the keycard down the front of my dress.

This time I was going to slap him. Because his hand had frozen on my left breast. James Hunter was not a very nice boy.

Just as I was about to lift up my hand, I realized he was staring at something behind me. And he looked even more pissed off than I was. I turned around to see Matt walking into the ballroom. With Rachel on his arm. If I thought the room had shushed when I walked in, this was a whole other level. It was freaking silent.

Matt's tux fit him perfectly. And Rachel looked beautiful on his arm. They were both smiling and it felt like a punch in the gut. Maybe James was right. Maybe I did hate Matt. Maybe I did want to get back at him.

Matt's eyes locked with mine. His gaze traveled down to where James' hand had just dropped the keycard in the front of my dress. Matt's smile faltered, despite the fact that he was literally walking into the dance with another girl.

"I'm going to fucking kill him," James said.

"Not if I do it first."

"Better idea," James said. Before I even realized what was happening, James had pulled me back into his arms. And his lips were on mine. Revenge tasted bitter even though his lips were sweet.

CHAPTER 31

Saturday

I would have blamed the kiss on the fact that James was drunk. A lot of things James did could be blamed on that. But he didn't taste like alcohol as his tongue traced my lips. And I didn't smell any smoke on him either. He was sober. He knew what he was doing. He knew exactly the reaction he would get.

I heard the gasps around us.

Part of me wanted to open my mouth to James. How could Matt walk in here with James' girlfriend on his arm? How could Matt pretend he was still interested in me, making me promise him a dance? How could he be so cruel? I didn't even recognize this version of him.

James' hand tightened on my waist.

But I recognized this feeling. The want. It's how Matt used to kiss me. And I knew I'd kind of dated Felix. And I was kind of seeing Miller too. But I never did any of it intentionally hurt Matt. I did it because all he ever did was hurt me.

Maybe James was right. Maybe revenge would make us both feel better. After all, he was an expert in this area, not me. But I couldn't do it. I couldn't kiss him back. It felt wrong. This wasn't me.

James moved his free hand to the back of my head, locking me in place.

"Kiss me back, Brooklyn," he whispered against my lips. "Hurt him back. Let him know how much it fucking hurts."

It was wrong. All of it was wrong. It was like I was literally staring sin in the face. And hatred. And sadness. James was in pain. I knew it, because I felt it too. I was freaking drowning in it.

"Please," he whispered. "Do it for me."

I put my hand on his chest like I was going to shove him away. But instead my hand froze there. When I first saw James, all I could see was the sadness behind his eyes. I wasn't attracted to him because we were both drowning. But maybe he understood me better than anyone else here.

James looked down at my hand and then back at my face. It was like the permission he needed. This time when he lowered his mouth back to mine, I parted my lips for him. I let him use me just this once. Because Matt fucking deserved it. He was a terrible friend. It was as if Matt's favorite pastime was ripping out people's hearts and stomping on them for fun. And I was so tired of all the games. I was just so freaking tired. So for just a second, I wasn't drowning alone. I was drowning with the saddest boy at Empire High. And maybe doing this favor for him would make him feel better. Even it was for just a few seconds.

"What the fuck, James?" Matt was pulling James off of me. He shoved James hard in the chest and James' crown toppled off his head.

"What?" James said with a smile. "I thought you liked to share."

Matt took a swing but James ducked.

I realized that maybe James was sober for the first time in weeks because he had been hoping for this fight. Planning it. Using me. I'd already known it, but I still felt cheap.

"Enjoying my sloppy seconds?" James asked. "You can keep Rachel. I'm pretty sure I like Brooklyn better anyway. Finders keepers, if you know what I mean."

"James, stop," Rachel said. "Please just talk to me for five seconds so I can explain. You owe me at least that."

"I don't owe you anything," James said. "Besides, I'm busy. I was just about to take Brooklyn to my suite. Right, babe?" he said to me with a wink. "She promised I could be her first."

God. It was the absolute worst thing he could possibly say. Not just because it was horribly embarrassing. And untrue. But because Matt was convinced that he'd be all my firsts. My whole body felt hot as everyone's eyes turned to me. Couldn't James see that he was making everything a thousand times worse? I shouldn't have listened to him. Revenge didn't make anything better. And I didn't realize that James had a death wish.

This time Matt's fist collided hard with the side of James' jaw.

It was like James wanted to be hit. Like he was craving the taste of blood. Because all he did was laugh and wipe the blood off his mouth with the back of his hand. "That's all you got, Caldwell?" he asked. "You hit like a little bitch."

Matt took another swing, hitting James' jaw in the same spot.

James spat blood out on the dance floor and laughed again. "I gave you two shots because you're two years younger." He tilted his head to the side and cracked his neck. "But now you fucking die." He lowered his shoulder and rammed into Matt.

The two of them fell to the floor.

"Stop it!" Rachel screamed. "We didn't do anything! I didn't sleep with him! James, I swear I didn't!"

I heard the sickening crunch of bone on bone.

Rachel started sobbing, but all I could focus on was the fact that James' hands were wrapped around Matt's throat. Matt was bigger than James. But apparently James had a lot of pent up rage and a perfect target to unleash it on.

"James!" I grabbed his arm but he didn't let go. "James!" I yelled louder.

Matt pulled up his knee, slamming it hard into James' groin.

"Fuck," James said and toppled over, grabbing his junk.

I moved out of the way just in time so that I didn't end up falling to the floor too. Everyone around us stepped back, creating a circle around us. It was like they'd created a little fighting ring.

"Someone do something," I said. There were plenty of guys just watching. Why weren't they breaking this up? But no one listened to me. Apparently I was back to being invisible at the worst possible time. I looked around to see if I could find Miller in the crowd. Oh God, if he was here then he'd seen the kiss. What the hell had I been thinking? But I shoved the thought aside. Miller could stop this. He'd broken up a fight that Matt was in before. But everyone was towering over us. I couldn't see a single chaperone.

"Of course you'd take a cheap shot," James said, pulling my attention back down to them.

"I didn't sleep with your girlfriend, you idiot." Matt stood up. "And if you'd get your head out of your ass and listen to me, you'd know the truth. I was trying to fix your relationship, not ruin it. Why don't you believe me?"

James' face was still twisted with pain, but he grabbed Matt's ankle, knocking him to the floor again. "Because you're a liar," James said with a wince as he continued to hold his injured bits.

"What the hell?" Rob said and kicked Matt's ankle out of James' hand. "Can't you go two minutes without trying to ruin my brother's life?" Rob helped James to his feet.

"Me?" Matt said. "I'm trying to fix it." He grabbed his wrist like it had hurt to take so many swings at his friend's face.

"Like you were fixed on having your dick in my brother's girlfriend?" Rob said.

Matt lunged at Rob, knocking him to the floor too. "Why the hell won't either of you listen to me?!" yelled Matt.

"Stop it!" I screamed. "All of you, stop it!" God, where were all the grown-ups? For the first time in my life I actually wanted Mr. Hill to appear. I needed someone, anyone to help me break this up. I reached out again, this time to grab Matt's arm, hoping I could pull him away. But he was as solid as rock.

"James, if you'd just..." Matt started.

Rob slammed his elbow into Matt's throat like he was literally trying to silence him. Matt's arm fell out of my grip. James seemed to finally be able to breathe again after being hit in the nuts and he had the audacity to wink at me like he thought everything was going according to plan.

And then Mason came out of nowhere and rammed into Rob's side, knocking him to the floor. They rolled over, running into James who fell back down on the ground too.

Mason punched Rob. Rob hit Matt. James kicked Mason. And Matt kneed James.

Rachel was sobbing uncontrollably. Someone screamed at the top of their lungs. I would have sworn it was Justin from how high-pitched it was, but I was pretty sure he wasn't here.

"Stop it!" I yelled. I tried to step in to pull Rob away and had to dodge an elbow. "All of you stop it!"

The music came to an abrupt stop, as if the DJ thought I was begging him to stop. Someone started chanting "fight." Soon everyone was chanting it. And all I could see were fists flying and blood. There was so much freaking blood.

What the hell had I done?

"I didn't sleep with Rachel!" Matt yelled. "She kissed me and I pushed her..."

His words were drowned out when James punched him in the side of the mouth.

"You pushed her right onto your lap?" James said. He somehow got free of Mason's grip on his legs, stood up, and did what I could only describe as a body slam on top of Matt.

Matt grunted like all the wind had left his lungs.

"Brooklyn's a great kisser," James said with a smile, blood dribbling down the side of his mouth. "I bet the rest of her tastes just as sweet."

Mason grabbed the back of James' tux, tearing the fancy fabric as he shoved him off of Matt.

"That's enough," Mr. Hill said as he walked in between the flying fists. I was wrong before, it wasn't James with a death wish. It was Mr. Hill.

But all four of them froze.

"Rob, James…why don't you cool off outside for a minute. Matt and Mason, go get a drink and clear your heads. This is a dance not a street fight."

"James, I'm sorry, I…" Matt started.

"Don't even try to explain it again," Mason said and helped his younger brother up. "Clearly the Hunters' ears are too clogged to hear."

"Fuck off, Mason," James said. "Don't you have some stupid blonde you need to give an STD to?"

"I don't have any STDs." It looked like that was the most insulting thing Mason had ever heard in his life. Mason took a step forward, but Matt grabbed his arm.

Rob laughed and elbowed James in the side like that was the funniest thing he'd ever heard.

"We're done," Mason said. "With both of you."

"Great," Rob said. "Because we're done with both of you. Why'd the music stop?" he yelled and turned to the

DJ. "Turn it the fuck up. This is a party." He threw his hands into the air.

"Rob," Mr. Hill said. "Language." As if that was the worst thing that had happened here tonight.

The DJ was standing there completely stunned. But it was like Rob's words had pulled him out of a trance. He turned the volume up even louder than before so I couldn't hear what else Mr. Hill yelled at the Hunters and Caldwells.

Rachel was sobbing harder, making it even more impossible to hear Mr. Hill. I would have tried to console her...but I didn't know who was telling the truth and who was lying.

So I just stood there completely stunned.

The Untouchables slowly separated. James and Rob went for the doors. And Mason and Matt made their way to the bar.

I didn't understand why they weren't being kicked out of the dance. But then I remembered how Isabella hadn't gotten detention even though I had. They were all allowed to do whatever they wanted, including beating each other up in the middle of homecoming. They could get away with anything.

Kennedy appeared at my side. "I think you just broke the Untouchables," she said.

But I barely heard her because Isabella had just stepped into the circle where the Untouchables had been fighting. She leaned down and lifted James' crown off the floor. She wiped off some of the blood that had splattered on the crown. Her eyes locked with mine and I felt more hatred than the Hunters had for the Caldwells. Or vice versa. I wasn't sure who hated who more right now. But none of it compared to how much Isabella hated me.

James had kissed me. If all those rumors were true about her being betrothed to James, I'd just touched what was hers. I'd crossed the line.

She's going to kill me.

CHAPTER 32

Saturday

Isabella and I both just stared at each other for a second. She was holding James' crown so tightly in her hand that I thought it might snap.

I could barely breathe. Maybe she was planning on snapping the crown in half and then slicing my throat with it. I gulped.

But then Isabella just turned away and disappeared into the crowd. And for some reason that felt even worse than her just getting it over with right here. She was going to plot out something awful, which made it that much more terrifying.

"Did you just see Isabella's face?" Kennedy asked.

"Yes." My voice came out weird and squeaky.

"She's going to do something awful." She turned to me. "I know you're mad at Matt, but why the hell did you kiss James of all people? Couldn't you have just made Matt jealous by making out with Miller?"

"I…I don't know. Because he asked. I…" I shook my head. I felt like an idiot.

She laughed. "It'll be fine. Isabella can't try to pull anything on you tonight because I'm sleeping over. So you're at least safe for one more day. And we can tell your dad about it when we get back to your place. He'll make sure she doesn't do anything."

"Mhm."

"Come on," she said and hiccupped. "Let's dance."

How much had she had to drink while I was making terrible choices? "Kennedy," I said and looked down at the empty cup in her hand as she started shimmying her hips. "Haven't you had enough?"

She laughed and threw her hands up in the air. "Nunca!" She threw the glass in the air along with her hands and it shattered on the floor. But the noise was drowned out by the music blaring all around us.

She looked so happy and carefree that all I could do was laugh along with her. I couldn't be mad at her. And she wouldn't let me be mad at myself, because she grabbed my hands and we started spinning in a dizzying circle. At least, I couldn't be mad until she let go of my hands.

I stumbled backward and right into someone's strong arms. No, not just someone. I looked up and saw a very familiar looking clean-shaven chin. "Hi Felix."

"I was just about to tap you on the shoulder, but you literally fell into my arms," he said.

I turned around, easing out of his grip. "Thanks for catching me."

He gave me a small smile.

I knew he was right in front of me. But this didn't feel like the perfect time to go forth with Operation Felix. This felt like the perfect time to dance with my best friend and not think about the fact that I'd kissed James or that the Hunters and Caldwells had gotten into a fist fight. Or that Miller was somewhere here watching all of this. And I'd told him I'd just be dancing with Kennedy all night. *Screw me.*

"May I have this dance?" Felix asked and gave me an adorable bow like we were in some old-time movie.

"Felix…"

"It's fine," Kennedy said with a huge smile on her face. "You two dance. I'm going to go get another drink. I saw Rob spike it too so it's extra strong now."

"No. Kennedy." I reached out for her but she literally bolted in the other direction and disappeared into the other dancers. *Shit.*

"I heard there was a fight," Felix said. "I wish I could have seen Matt get the shit beat out of him, but I got here kind of late."

He hadn't been here for the fight? He hadn't seen any of it? "There was a fight. But do you mind if we catch up in just a second? I really need to go check on Kennedy."

"Sorry that was not the way I planned to start this conversation." He roughly put his fingers through his hair. "The last thing I wanted to do was bring up Matt. Let me just rewind for a sec." He put his hand out for me. "May I have this dance?"

"I…actually, Kennedy…" my voice trailed off. "I need to go make sure Kennedy's okay."

"I'm trying to apologize here, newb. Just give me a minute."

How many more cups of punch could Kennedy consume in a minute? Probably not that many. I'd been waiting for Felix to talk to me again all week. And here he was wanting to talk. Not that he needed to say anything to me. I was the one that needed to apologize. And instead of manning up to it, I was trying to run in the opposite direction. What was wrong with me?

I took a deep breath. Instead of taking his hand, I just started talking. "Felix, I'm so so sorry. I never meant to lead you on, I swear. It's just that Matt made me promise I wouldn't tell anyone we were seeing each other. And we weren't exclusive. Him and I. Or you and I." This was all coming out in a jumbled mess. And Felix was just staring at me. I wasn't even sure he could hear me, so I started talking louder over the music. "Felix, you're one of my best friends. I hate fighting with you. I hate you being mad at me. Please don't shut me out. I know I was a jerk, but I didn't mean to be. In the moment I just really really needed a shoulder to cry on. Literally. And you were there. And you're so handsome." My gaze had locked on to his ocean blue eyes. *What am I even saying right now?* I was supposed to be setting him up with Kennedy, not telling him he was dreamy.

Finally a smile spread over his face. "Newb, I came over to apologize to you. Not the other way around." He stopped asking for a dance and just grabbed my hand and pulled me into his chest.

The way he was staring at me made my heart race. I needed to focus. And not on the way his body felt pressed against mine. "I like being friends with you," I said.

"You're not looking at me like a friend," he said.

"Yes I am."

"No…you're not." He tilted his head a little lower to mine.

I closed my eyes to drown out the image of him in front of me. "Felix Green, it's true, I am attracted to you.

And I love talking to you. You have no idea how much I missed our conversations this week. But none of that matters because I'm so confused that my head literally hurts. I'm a freaking mess."

"You're not a mess. You're beautiful."

My stupid stomach betrayed me by feeling butterflies. "You weren't here a few minutes ago, but I freaking kissed James Hunter because he made me feel like I owed him. And that Matt deserved it. Or something. I don't even know why I did it. That's how big of a mess I am. That's what caused the huge fight. Me. All of it's my fault."

"Don't you see what's happening? Those boys are messing with your head, newb. They don't care about anyone but themselves. They don't care about you. But I do. I'm not one of them. You and I aren't like them."

I opened my eyes again. "I'm a Pruitt." The name felt gross on my tongue.

"No." He tucked a loose strand of hair behind my ear. "You're a Sanders. Always and forever."

Always and forever. "I also sleep in my bodyguard's bed most nights because I'm terrified of the Pruitts' apartment and he's kind and lets me cry in his arms."

"That Miller guy?" Felix laughed. "Isn't he a little old for you?"

That Miller guy. Oh God, I didn't even know Miller's first name. And I didn't know how old he was either. I pressed my lips together.

"So you ran into another man's bed because I wasn't talking to you all week," Felix said. "That's kind of on me."

Or did I do it because I'd iced out Matt all week? My head was spinning. What was Operation Felix again? "Do you know who's not a mess? Kennedy. She's not a mess at all."

"You sure about that? I mean…aren't all three of us a mess? We're all going to a school we don't really belong at."

"Kennedy belongs at Empire High. She's so smart. And you belong here too. It doesn't matter that you're not old money. You belong here, Felix. With Kennedy."

"With Kennedy? Are you dropping out or something?"

Why wasn't he getting this? "No. I mean you should be with Kennedy."

He looked at me like I was crazy. "Kennedy hates me."

"No she doesn't."

"Are we talking about the same Kennedy? Kennedy Alcaraz? She's literally told me she hates me on several occasions. Sometimes she yells at me in Spanish and I don't know what she's saying, but I can tell from her tone that it's not very nice."

"Well you should read between the lines."

"There's probably knives between the lines."

"She doesn't hate you." But it was true, usually the things Kennedy said in Spanish were not the kindest. I was still wondering what a *puta mierda* was. But I figured it wasn't good because of the tone she'd used.

"Well, we can agree to disagree on that one," Felix said. "Besides, it doesn't matter. Because I'm pretty sure I'm addicted to you. I tried to stay away, yet here I am. Do you think I'd ever be caught dead at a freaking homecoming dance if it wasn't for you? This isn't exactly my scene, newb."

Like participating in gym class wasn't his scene. I'd known that when I fell into his arms. He wouldn't have ever come to this dance if it wasn't for me. It was sweet and...*damn it!* I wasn't supposed to be confused about this.

"And if you're still up for kissing people to make Matt jealous, he's watching right now."

Oh no. I looked over my shoulder to follow Felix's gaze. Matt was staring at us like he was about to internally combust. I was surprised I didn't see steam coming out of his ears. He downed a cup of punch in one gulp. Did he not know that it was double spiked?

"I don't think that's a good idea," I said and turned back to Felix.

"Yeah, you're probably right. I only just got rid of my last black eye."

"I'm so so sorry about..."

"You already apologized. And I already told you, I'm the one that needed to apologize. Which, I still need to do. And no, I'm not going to sing about it and get chased by Coach Carter."

I laughed.

"But I am sorry. You told me you were confused. You told me you needed time. And I took it personally that you were spending some of that time with Matt. When I never made it clear that I still want us to be official." He cleared his throat. "So, newb. That's what I want. When you're ready. I want you to be my girlfriend."

"But I just told you about Miller. And James. And you know about freaking Matt."

"Well, I'd want you to stop sleeping in Miller's bed every night. And definitely stop kissing James Hunter. Nothing good could ever come from that. And as for Matt? Do you really want to be with someone who kept you a secret so that he wouldn't have to confess to sleeping with his best friend's girl?"

No. No, I didn't.

"I'm asking you to choose me. Like I chose you over my company. Brooklyn, I gave up everything for you."

My stomach twisted into knots. But not just because of the fact that his words were true. He had given up his drug business for me. He'd stopped selling, just like I'd begged him to do. But it had just made everything worse. "Well I didn't know that giving up your business would leave room for Cupcake to start one of his own."

"Well…I mean…we're partners. Fifty-fifty. But I'm not selling anymore, so you don't have to worry about anything. Cupcake handles the distribution now."

"By putting it into cupcakes."

"Right. Pretty clever, huh?"

I took a step back from him. "No, not clever. Felix, he gave those cupcakes to all of us without even telling us what was in them."

"He was testing the recipe…"

"He'd already tested it on Kennedy!"

"What?"

"You know that rumor going around? Kennedy's not a slut."

"I didn't say that she was…"

"Cupcake drugged her. And took advantage of her. And you let it happen."

"Whoa." Felix put up his hands. "Yes, I told him to put the pot in cupcakes. But we were supposed to work on the recipe together. I had no idea he'd already done it. I found out about it the same time you did. And I definitely didn't tell him to hide the fact that there was pot in the cupcakes. The whole point is that people do know. That's how we make money."

I didn't care about how he made money. I cared about my friend. "He raped her, Felix."

His Adam's apple rose and fell.

"I wanted you to stop selling altogether," I said. "Not pass the business off to a monster."

"And you asked me to give up my business when you won't even commit to being my girlfriend. You don't know how much you keep asking for. And I'm trying my best to give you everything you want. I'm sorry about Cupcake. I'll talk to him. I'll fix it."

"You can't fix it. You can't undo what he did to her."

He pushed his hair off his forehead. "I'm sorry. I know you hate those words, but what else can I say right now? I'm really fucking sorry that happened. I'll talk to Cupcake. And I'll talk to Kennedy. I'll try to stop the rumors."

"Don't talk to Kennedy." I put my face in my hands for a second. She didn't want me to tell anyone about this. God, I was supposed to be pushing them together, not telling Felix not to speak to her. I pulled my face out of my hands. "I promised not to tell anyone."

"Okay. I won't talk to her."

Operation Felix was a complete bust. All I'd accomplished was remembering how easy it was to get lost in his eyes. And forbidding him to speak to Kennedy. This was a total mess. And suddenly everything just felt so heavy. I was used to carrying the weight of the world on my shoulders. When I'd been worried about my mom every day. And now I'd messed up this fresh start in New York. Everything just felt even heavier. It was like I was stuck in quicksand and I couldn't get out.

"Hey, come here." He pulled me into his arms. "I won't let him do anything like that ever again. I promise."

Since Kennedy wouldn't tell anyone else about it, his words did make me feel better. He'd make sure it didn't happen to someone else. That was the best that could be done. "Thank you." I rested the side of my head on his chest.

The music had changed to an upbeat song, but neither one of us seemed to care.

"You can't deny that this feels right," he said.

No, I really couldn't. I held on to him a little tighter. Him cutting me out of his life had felt terrible. I never wanted that to happen again. I breathed a sigh of relief. I forgot how much the weight on my shoulders seemed to transfer off when I was in his arms.

"I know Cupcake is here somewhere," Felix said. "I better go find him."

I leaned back so I could look up at him. "Thank you. For believing me." I knew that was part of the reason Kennedy wasn't saying anything. She was worried no one would believe her. Especially with the rumors going around.

"Save me another dance?"

I nodded as his hands fell from my waist. "Thanks, Felix. For being understanding. And patient. And…you're just…thank you."

He smiled. "I'd wait a lifetime for you, newb."

CHAPTER 33

Saturday

My heart was more confused than ever as I turned in a circle looking for Kennedy. Tonight was officially a disaster. I knew that I'd just promised another dance to Felix. And I still owed one to Matt. But I needed to get the hell out of here before I did anything else crazy.

I didn't see Kennedy anywhere. It seemed darker in here than before. The music was louder. The students rowdier. If the dancing was an indicator, it wasn't just Matt and Kennedy drinking the spiked punch. I looked over at the bar.

Matt was downing another glass of punch. He slammed it down on the bar as we made eye contact. I was surprised the glass didn't shatter.

And then he started to make his way over here.

Shit. I couldn't talk to him right now. Not after what I'd done with James. Not after that conversation with Felix. I needed a second to breathe. The kiss with James meant nothing. But Felix didn't mean nothing to me. I'd always really liked him.

Matt was taller than a lot of the other students, and I could see him clearly beelining right for me. He was only a few seconds away. And I had no idea what to say to him. I had no idea if I could trust him. James had seemed pretty adamant that Matt was a liar. And I'd had my fair share of Matt's lies to add to the list.

Rob stepped in front of me. "Wanna dance?" His lip was cut from the fight. And he'd lost his bowtie somewhere. It was probably trampled on the floor.

"Um…" It was tempting, just to give me a few minutes before I had to talk to Matt. But the last thing I wanted to do was give anyone else the wrong idea. I'd kissed James. Fallen for Matt. Mr. Pruitt apparently wanted me to be with Mason. The last thing I needed was another Untouchable on my radar.

It was like Rob could see my hesitancy. So he made the decision for me. He grabbed my hand and pulled me into his chest without waiting for a response. "Trust me, Sanders," he said. "You don't want to talk to Matt right now. He's kind of an angry drunk."

So he'd seen Matt coming over here too. Rob's words slowly registered in my brain. Matt was an angry drunk? I tried to see him over Rob's shoulder, but Matt had disappeared somewhere. I'd seen Matt angry. But I'd never seen it directed at me. "So you're rescuing me from an awkward conversation?"

"No. I'm trying to get on his nerves because he's an asshole."

"Rob…"

"He is. I know it. And you know it too. What are you doing wasting your time with him?"

I shook my head. "How could you say that? Even with everything that's happened, he's one of your best friends. I don't get why you basically just turned homecoming into a fighting ring."

"We *were* best friends. Past tense."

"So punching him in the face was your solution?"

"No." Rob looked at me like I just wasn't getting it. "He punched James in the face. Twice. I was defending my brother."

James asked for it. He was itching for a fight. But I kept my mouth shut. "You don't know the whole story."

"I know enough."

"Are you really not going to hear Matt out?" I asked. Not that I could really judge. I'd pushed that conversation with Matt off all week.

Rob lifted his chin a little. "Brothers before bros."

"Is that really a thing?"

He pulled me a little closer. "I didn't realize it had to be a thing. But yeah, it is. Matt crossed a line."

"Friends are supposed to forgive friends."

Rob smiled. "That's why I've forgiven you for dating a Caldwell."

I laughed. "Rob, you and I aren't really friends."

He put one of his hands on his chest. "Sanders, I don't just go around giving nicknames to anyone."

"That's hardly a nickname. It's my last name."

"Rumor has it that it's actually not your last name anymore."

I pressed my lips together.

"But I promise I won't start calling you Pruitt instead." He put his hand back on my waist.

"I appreciate that." I tried to peer over his shoulder again, this time looking for Kennedy. "Have you seen Kennedy? I really need to go see if she's okay."

"Yeah, I saw her at the punch bowl a few minutes ago."

Damn it. "I should probably…"

"You still owe me a favor you know," Rob said.

"Hmm?" I asked, even though I knew exactly what he was referring to.

A smile spread over his face. "Don't play dumb with me, Sanders. You screamed my name, remember?"

"As you locked me in Matt's room. Yeah, I remember. But you tricked me. I don't owe you anything."

"Actually, you do."

"I swear to God, Rob, if you ask me for a kiss I'm going to lose my mind."

He laughed. "Sanders, I don't need to win a bet to kiss you. If I wanted a kiss from you, I'd just take it. And then you'd beg me for another."

I laughed. "No."

He smiled. "Maybe."

"Definitely not."

He laughed again. "You're the one who immediately thought I'd ask for a kiss. Clearly you were the one thinking about it."

"I most certainly was not."

"Keep telling yourself that, Sanders. But since you don't want a kiss…I was thinking…" his voice trailed off. He stared down at me like he was deciding how to torture me.

"Rob, I already did this dance with James. If you're trying to make Matt jealous, I don't want anything to do with it."

"Oh, this favor would have a lot more to do with screwing over Isabella."

He'd officially piqued my interest. "You want me to help you screw over Isabella?"

"Yes. Unless sisters before bros is your new motto."

"Not a chance."

He laughed. "Do you have access to her bedroom? Because I've been over to the Pruitts' place countless times and I've never been allowed upstairs."

"Well, I think I do. Maybe. I sleep in the opposite wing. I've never really been down the hallway that leads to her bedroom. But I'm sure I could find it." Isabella had been in my room. Certainly I could go into hers.

"What are your feelings about frogs? Like…lots of them?"

"You want to put frogs in her bed?"

"Well…yeah. Wouldn't that be kind of amazing?"

I could already picture Isabella's face. And her screaming. But for some reason the scene made me feel bad for the frogs. "Couldn't we do something where it wasn't possible for her to hurt an innocent animal?"

"You're worried she'd kill the frogs?"

"First the frogs. Then me." I laughed even though I was very serious.

"She's not going to kill you. Do you have any idea how many times she threatens to kill me on a weekly basis? It's a lot. And she's never gone through with it. Rumor has it that she had to sign some contract with her dad promising not to ever do it again."

Again. That was the same kind of thing Mr. Pruitt had said. That Isabella was no longer allowed to use his assets to freaking kill people. "What do you mean *again*? She's killed someone before?"

"Yeah, I used to have a little brother."

"Oh my God, what?!"

Rob started laughing. He was laughing so hard, the muscles in his arms tightened, pulling me closer.

"Miss Sanders," Mr. Hill said in that same tone he scolded me in class. "Mr. Hunter. One foot between dancers at all times." He shoved a ruler between Rob and me.

My face had to be bright red.

"Sorry, Mr. Hill," Rob said when he was finally able to catch his breath. "I'll make sure she keeps her hands off me."

"Rob." I shoved his shoulder.

"See what I mean?" he said. "So handsy."

Was he trying to kill me from embarrassment?

Mr. Hill shook his head and went to go measure some other couples' distance.

"What is wrong with you?" I shoved Rob's arm again.

"Absolutely nothing is wrong with me. You're the one all over everyone tonight. Kissing my brother. Dancing with Felix. I even heard you took some cute homecoming pictures with Mason tonight. And now you're all up on me."

Yeah, my face was bright red. "All of those instances are taken out of context." But I could see how it looked. I wasn't an idiot, I knew I'd freaking lost my mind tonight.

He laughed.

I needed to change the subject or he'd find a way to torture me all night long. "You were saying something about Isabella?" I asked.

He shrugged. "Oh, right. Her murderous ways? It's all just based on a rumor. But in elementary school, Isabella didn't have a whole posse. She just had one best friend. Stephanie. At recess, Stephanie kissed some boy that Isabella liked. And then none of us ever saw her again."

I swallowed hard. I'd kissed James. Isabella really was going to kill me. "Elementary school? So when she was just a kid?"

"Yeah, she's always been a nightmare."

A murderous nightmare. Fuck me. I felt like there wasn't enough air reaching my lungs.

"You okay?" Rob asked.

"I kissed James. She's going to kill me just like she killed Stephanie."

Rob laughed. "Don't you think Rachel wouldn't be breathing if she killed everyone James kissed?"

That was a good point. But it didn't really calm me down. "Oh my God, maybe that's what this whole thing with Matt is about. Maybe Isabella wasn't trying to ruin Matt's life with the blackmail. Maybe she was trying to torture Rachel." And Matt had just gotten stuck in the crossfire. How had I not seen this before?

"Huh." Rob lowered his eyebrows like he was thinking it over.

If that was true then… I swallowed hard. Isabella tormented everyone that got close to James. She was going to kill me. Or make my life more hellish than she was already making it. I pictured her cold stare as she'd picked up James' homecoming crown. She was plotting something awful. It could happen at any moment. "I need to get out of here."

The smile that was permanently on Rob's face faltered. "You're shaking."

"I'm not shaking."

He gripped my waist a little tighter. "Yes you are."

"I need to find Kennedy and get out of here." Kennedy was going to spend the night. She'd be with me. I'd be safe back at home. *Home? God.* Was I safe there? Isabella had snuck into my room earlier and cut up all my clothes. What if she was going to slice my neck next?

"Are you okay?"

"No, I'm not okay. I kissed your brother because he convinced me it was a good idea somehow. And I still have feelings for Felix and Matt." *And Miller.* Damn it, where was Miller? I needed him to get me out of here.

"Hey, take a deep breath," Rob said.

It felt like the air I breathed in wasn't reaching my lungs. "Everyone's so mad at me."

"No one's mad at you."

That was a lie. I gasped for air.

"Take a deep breath, Brooklyn. I think you're having a panic attack."

"Isabella's going to kill me."

Rob pulled me against his chest. "She's not going to kill you."

"She is…"

"She's not. Breathe, Brooklyn."

I tried to.

"Just breathe. In and out. Just breathe."

"I want to take it all back," I said. "I want to un-kiss James. And unlike Felix. And unlove Matt. I want to undo all of it."

"Breathe in," Rob said. "And breath out. Just breathe."

There was something calming about his voice in my ear with all the chaos around us.

"Breathe."

I tried to focus on taking deep breaths.

And I wasn't sure how long we stood like that in the middle of the dance floor. Just breathing. I knew there were a few changes of songs. I knew they weren't slow ones and I knew we looked ridiculous. I was surprised Mr. Hill wasn't back measuring us apart.

I pulled away from him. "How did you know how to fix that?"

He shrugged. "I'm used to taking care of people."

I knew he was used to taking care of James. Did James get panic attacks? Or was Rob just used to picking up the pieces after James' drunk and high escapades? "I'm sorry."

"Why? You didn't pull me into your hot mess," he said with a laugh. "I'm practically the only person here that you haven't kissed."

I laughed, even though it still felt like my lungs weren't quite working right.

"Will you help me find Kennedy?" I still needed to leave. The sooner the better.

He raised both eyebrows. "Thinking about kissing her next? If so, I'll definitely help you find her."

"No," I said with a laugh. "I just think maybe I've had enough homecoming for the rest of my life."

He smiled. "Luckily for you, she's right behind you. And if you do decide that you want tonight to get even crazier…kissing her really would do the trick. You might even get people to forget about that fight you caused."

"I'm not kissing Kennedy."

"I don't know…you still owe me that favor…"

"Rob. You need to reserve that favor for the prank we're going to pull on Isabella."

"Nah. Pretty sure you're down for that prank anyway. I'll hold on to my favor for now. I'm sad you're bouncing though. Things were just getting fun." He gave me a wink and dropped his hands from my waist just as Kennedy threw her arms around me.

"Best. Homecoming. Ever!" she screamed at the top of her lungs.

I heard Rob laugh. And a few other students cheered around us.

"Are you going to hook up with Robert Hunter too?" she asked. Her words were slightly slurred. "I can't believe you just came into town and you're already going to hook up with every single one of the Untouchables. What is your life? A fairytale?"

Hardly. Unless it was one of those real fairytales where everyone died terrible, gruesome deaths. Maybe I was living one of those. "I promise I'm not going to hook up with all of them," I said. "Do you mind if we leave early? I have a really bad feeling. Isabella's planning something, I know she is."

"What can she do here? We're in the middle of a dance! Back to the topic of Rob real quick."

"Kennedy, I really think we should get going…"

"Can I have Rob then if you don't want him?" She removed herself from my embrace. "I'm going to go ask him for a kiss. Wish me luck."

Oh my God, Kennedy, no! I'd made plenty of bad decisions tonight. But it didn't mean she had to too. I tried to grab her wrist but she was already twirling over to him.

"Kennedy!" I hissed as I ran after her.

But she didn't listen. And her long legs were faster than mine even when she was twirling instead of running. She twirled between a couple, preventing Mr. Hill from having to put a ruler between them. She zig-zagged away from me and started twirling in the opposite direction.

"Kennedy get back here!"

But she was like a freaking dancing ninja. I couldn't catch up with her. Twirling, ducking, and…jumping? Did she just jump over that girl that was bent over in front of that guy? Why wasn't Kennedy on the track and field team?

"Kennedy!" But she'd already reached Rob on the dance floor. I pushed past a couple dancing very inappropriately, just in time to witness the horror that was this moment.

Kennedy tapped her hip into Rob's in some weird dance move I'd never seen in my life. "Hey, tiger," she said. And then she made a rawring noise.

Oh God, no.

CHAPTER 34

Saturday

"Kennedy, do you want to go get a glass of water?" I asked.

She ignored me and clasped her hands behind Rob's neck. "Hey," she said and smiled up at him.

I waited for her to rawr again, but luckily she didn't.

"Hey yourself," Rob said with a smile. He didn't seem as phased by the whole tiger thing as I was.

"Do you want to go make out in Mr. Hill's classroom?" she asked.

Oh no. This was bad. Really bad. I wasn't going to let her put herself in a position to be taken advantage of again. And how was she even planning on breaking into Empire High to make this happen? Before I could protest, Rob started laughing.

"That depends on three things," he said. "Exactly how many cups of punch have you had? Are you actually broken up with Cupcake? And are you still in love with Felix?"

Kennedy gasped. "Well, I do not know how many cups I've had. Less than tweleven. But I know for a fact that I will never, ever let Cupcake near me again. Nunca," she said and poked Rob in the middle of the chest. "That means never, in case you don't know. It's me and Brooklyn's favorite word."

"Nunca. Got it." Rob smiled. "And what about the third thing?"

"I don't remember you mentioning a third thing."

"Are you still in love with Felix?" Rob asked.

"I do not know what you're referring to regarding Mr. Green."

He laughed. "I'm referring to the fact that you look at him with stars in your eyes. And that I'm pretty sure you should be asking him to go to Mr. Hill's classroom instead of me."

"Nunca."

"Is that all you can say?" he said with a laugh.

"Nunca." Kennedy started laughing too.

"I should probably steal her back," I said.

Rob whispered something in her ear before I stole her from his embrace. Just because I'd done a lot of crazy stuff tonight didn't mean Kennedy had to too.

"If you two need a ride home, let me know," Rob said. "You can take my limo."

"That's okay. We have a ride." I just needed to find Miller so we could get the hell out of here.

"Later Kennedy," he said and disappeared into the crowd.

Kennedy was smiling so hard. "Brooklyn!" She turned to me. "He whispered in my ear." She pointed to the ear that Rob had whispered in. "He said he didn't believe the rumors. He said I looked beautiful in my dress. And that he owes me a kiss whenever I'm in a state to remember it. Whatever that means. Isn't he the best?"

"He really is." I ducked my arm under hers to walk her toward the bar for some water.

"What do you think he means by me not being in a state to remember a kiss?"

"That might have to do with how much you've had to drink."

"Oh, he means that I'm drunk!" She giggled. "I might be drunk. But I have the best idea!" She started twirling in a circle, dragging me with her. "Let's dance off the booze!"

Tonight, couldn't be saved. Even by sweating out whatever her punch had been spiked with. "After some water," I said and grabbed her hand.

"Water!" she yelled and threw her hands up in the air, almost knocking me over.

"Yup. Water." I pulled her off the dance floor. *Oh, no.* Matt was still standing at the bar. Staring at me. Although he didn't look as mad anymore. He just looked...intense. My feet froze as he lifted his finger and ran it across the tip of his nose. His lips even turned up in a smile.

Why was he smiling at me and giving me our signal? Hadn't he seen all the terrible things I'd just done? I knew I'd promised him a dance. But not right this second. I needed a moment to just breathe.

I turned us in a circle and Kennedy yelled.

"Yay, we're dancing!"

I spotted Miller standing along the wall. His arms were folded across his chest. And he was also staring right at me. Matt no longer looked that pissed, but Miller sure did. Despite that, it still seemed easier to walk toward Miller. I pulled Kennedy with me.

Miller raised his eyebrow at us as we stopped in front of him.

"So I'm guessing you saw that?" I asked.

His arms remained folded across his chest. "Which thing?"

That was a fair blow. "I'm really sorry…"

"You said you were only going to dance with Kennedy. Yet…Kennedy's been hanging out at the punch bowl all night. Which now that I'm paying attention to her instead of staring at you dancing with literally every guy in the place…I realize that the punch bowl is spiked. Fuck."

"I'm sorry."

"You've already said that." He ran a hand through his hair. "I need to go tell them to dump the punch before anyone else drinks it."

"Miller." I reached out and grabbed his arm. "Please, can you just take us home?"

"There aren't any other guys you want to make out with first?"

I winced. I deserved that. "Miller…"

"I think I need a minute, Brooklyn." He walked past me. But instead of going over to the bar to warn the bartender of the spiked punch, he pushed out the doors of the ballroom.

Shit.

Kennedy pulled on my arm. "Come on. This is supposed to be the best night ever. I don't want to go home yet. Dance with me."

"Kennedy, I messed everything up." I felt like curling up in a ball and crying. This wasn't the best night ever. It was the worst.

"What happens at homecoming stays at homecoming!"

"I don't think that's a thing."

"Sure it is. Please." She stuck out her bottom lip. "Dance with me?"

I'd already let her down tonight. And Miller said he needed a minute to cool off. It wouldn't kill me to dance while I waited for him to come back. "Okay."

Kennedy dragged me onto the dance floor. But I kept my eyes on the ballroom doors. Song after song passed, but Miller didn't come back.

I started to look around for Rob. He'd said we could borrow his limo. Or maybe Felix could get us home. He was still here somewhere. Right?

The later it got, the more my stomach twisted into knots. I had that same feeling in my gut that I did the day my mom had passed away. The same feeling I did when the ambulance had come to Empire High. It was like a ticking time bomb. I needed to get us out of here.

The music died away and Mr. Hill tapped on the microphone. "Let's give a hand to our homecoming king and queen, James Hunter and Isabella Pruitt." He clapped his hands together as Isabella and James walked up to the stage where the band was set up. "It's tradition for the king and queen to have a dance," Mr. Hill said and stepped to the side of the stage as Isabella and James walked on.

Isabella grabbed the mic from him. "And it's tradition for the queen to make a speech," she said into the microphone.

"No, that's not..." started Mr. Hill.

Isabella directed one of those glares I thought was reserved for me right at Mr. Hill. He shut his mouth.

Isabella cleared her throat. "Who's having a fun night?!"

Tons of students cheered.

James stood there with his hands shoved in his pockets. He must have tossed his torn tux jacket. There was what looked like a footprint on his white dress shirt. And he was sporting a black eye. He looked like he'd rather be anywhere in the world than on that stage with Isabella. And I didn't blame him.

"James, come here," Isabella said. "You lost your crown earlier in that silly bit of argy-bargy."

James didn't move. So Isabella walked over to him and put his crown back on.

"Perfect," she said as she placed her hand on the side of his face.

He grimaced.

"Speaking of perfection," Isabella said into the mic. "I recently discovered that I have a baby sister. It was the most unexpected but brilliant news. I've always wanted a sibling. Sissy! Sissy, where are you? I want to officially introduce you to everyone."

My traitorous fellow classmates parted like the red sea.

Kennedy and I were just standing there with everyone staring at us. The ticking in my head stopped. This was the explosion I was expecting. God, what was she going to do?

"Oh splendid," Isabella said. "Don't you all love her tiara? I thought it would be perfect for her to wear one tonight. The princess to my queen. Do we have a spotlight? Can we put a spotlight on my sister?" She looked over at the DJ.

He just shrugged.

"Fine. Be unhelpful." She turned back to me. "Brooky, I've been having so much fun getting to know you." She put her hand to her chest. "You're the sister I've always dreamed of. And it's so nice that my friends are your friends. And your friends are my friends. Isn't that right, Kennedy?"

I turned to Kennedy. "What is she talking about?"

"What?" whispered Kennedy. "Isabella's actually super cool. We've been hanging out all night. She kept telling me how pretty I looked. And she made sure I never ran out of punch shots."

What the hell is happening right now?

"So I just wanted everyone to know that there's a new girl in town," Isabella said. "My little sis. She'll be unforgettable at Empire High. Just like me. And just like tonight! Cheers, Sissy." She realized she didn't have a glass so she just lifted the mic in the air. "Love you!" she shouted.

Everyone started clapping and cheering. When had everyone lost their minds?

"And now I shall dance with my king. Future hubby," she said and put out her hand to James.

He slowly pulled one hand out of his pocket and put it into hers.

"Smile for the pictures," she hissed at him before Mr. Hill took the mic back.

"Your homecoming king and queen," Mr. Hill said and everyone cheered as the music started up again.

I watched James in what looked like the most miserable dance of his life. When the song finally ended, he pulled off his crown and practically ran away from Isabella. And right into Rachel's arms. Rachel laughed, stood up on her tiptoes and kissed him. He put his crown on top of her head and kissed her back as another song started.

Well, at least the whole revenge thing had worked out for him. Me? Not so much.

What did it mean that they were back together? That James believed Matt? Or that he just forgave Rachel? Or that he was just too drunk to have any idea what was happening? It felt like my head was spinning when Isabella appeared right in front of me with a huge smile on her face.

"I came over to dance with my new besties!" she said.

"The elephants are coming!" Kennedy and Isabella both laughed like it was some kind of inside joke. And if it was, I definitely wasn't getting it.

Had Kennedy forgotten about the fact that Isabella had destroyed all of my clothes just a few hours ago? Or the fact that she made it her mission to torture us at school?

As if Isabella could read my mind, she shouted, "I'm so sorry about your clothes, Sissy. It was a moment of weakness. I'll replace every single thing that Sir Wilfred destroyed."

So we were going back to the dog lie?

"He's just a baby! He doesn't know any better."

Mr. Pruitt told me it was Isabella and her friends. Why did she keep being fake nice to me?

"Besides," said Isabella as she danced with Kennedy. "You look amazing in vintage. I'm sorry I ever said otherwise."

That actually kind of felt genuine. Maybe because she was smiling at me like she wasn't internally screaming at me.

"Thanks?"

"And blue really suits you."

All the words were nice. But I couldn't trust her. She was hateful.

"Come on," Isabella said. "What can I do to make you forgive me? I want us to start over. To be real sisters."

My first instinct was to tell her to bite me. But I was worried she actually would. Or that she'd get Sir Wilfred to bite me. "I'm just going to need some time," I said.

"Time. Well, we all have plenty of that." She started hopping up and down with Kennedy.

No we don't. We never had enough time. I blinked fast, trying not to think about my mom and my uncle. Someone like Isabella didn't understand how precious time was.

It was too hot in here. Too loud. Too fake. God, where was Miller? I turned toward the doors and practically ran straight into Matt.

CHAPTER 35

Saturday

For just a second, when I saw Matt I was relieved. He'd been there for me after my uncle died. He'd literally been my shoulder to cry on. He was the only reason I didn't fall apart. But it was just as easy to remember all the bad. And I'd had to cry on someone else's shoulder because of him.

I took a step back before I did something else stupid. Miller was already mad at me. I'd already made enough mistakes for one night. I was exhausted mentally and physically. And I knew if I danced with Matt, he'd be wonderful and sweet and as irresistible as always. I knew my heart couldn't take it.

"You promised me a dance," he said and put out his hand.

I looked at his face. I didn't think Rob was telling the truth. Yes, it did look like Matt was a little drunk. But he didn't look angry at all. He looked...goofy. There was a big grin on his face. And his eyes looked so eager.

Don't look at his puppy dog eyes. "Matt, I think it would be better if we talked tomorrow. Kennedy and I were just leaving."

"It looks like Kennedy's still dancing. And so are you. With me." He looked confused about what he just said. "Yeah. That made sense." He put his hand out again. "I've been waiting all night. I haven't interrupted you. I just...we're running out of time. It's almost midnight." He looked so hopeful.

I did tell him I'd save him a dance. And could tonight really get any worse? It was better to have this conversation and get it over with. I'd hear him out. And then I'd finally have all the facts about everything and maybe I could make a freaking decision so my mind didn't explode.

I took a deep breath. "Okay. One dance."

"That's all that you need. I mean, all that I need." He shook his head, then grabbed my hand and pulled me into his chest. "All that we need."

God, I forgot how good he smelled.

He rested his chin on top of my head. "I forgot how nice your hairs smell. Hairs? Or is it hair? It's hairs because there's lots of them. They're so pretty. I love all of them."

I laughed. "Matt?"

"Yes?"

"Are you drunk?"

"No. Yes. I don't know. I think someone may have spiked the punch. And I drank a lot of it while I waited for you. Why'd you make me wait all night while you danced with everyone else?"

Because I'm worried I'll hate your explanation. Or that I'll understand it and fall for you even harder. I didn't know how to answer him when my thoughts were at war.

He dropped his head lower, nuzzling his nose into my hair. "I've missed you," he said, forgetting his question.

I've missed you too.

"Did you like my song?" He pulled back so he could look down at me. "It was for you. I was singing just for…" He lifted his hand and booped me on the nose. "…you."

Yup, Matt was wasted. "Your song was perfect." And hilarious. Almost as hilarious as he was being right now. His finger was still on my nose so I grabbed it and pulled his hand down. Now we were awkwardly slow dancing on one side and holding hands on the other.

"I'm not a good singer," Matt said, his goofy grin spreading. "But I'll sing it again if it'll make you forgive me. I'll sing it forever. Oh, let me sing it again right now. I need to find my backup dancers." He tried to take a step back from me.

I held on tight to his hand so he wouldn't leave. "Once was enough, Matt. You don't have to sing it again." I tried not to think about the fact that I was clinging to him. Or about the fact that out of everyone I'd danced with tonight, it was easiest to breathe in his arms.

The grin on his face grew. "So we're good? You forgive me?"

"Matt, I don't even know what you did."

"Oh yeah, that. That's so…James wasn't listening. I was trying to explain. But no one's listening to me. Why didn't you listen?" He shook his head like there was a fly buzzing around him.

"I turned off my phone, so I didn't see your texts. You never tried to explain it to me in person. You ran after James at lunch and just left me sitting there. You didn't come to school for days."

He stopped shaking his head. "But I told you. I told you I was worried about him." He dropped his forehead to mine. "You're strong. You're so fucking strong. I knew you'd be okay. But I didn't know that James would be okay. He needed me."

I swallowed hard. "I'm not strong."

"Yes you are. You're the strongest person I know. You lost your mom. And your uncle. And you freaking live with Isabella and that horrible family. You're strong, baby. And you smell so good." He dipped his nose into my hair again.

I blinked fast so I wouldn't cry. I wasn't strong. I was lonely and scared and I'd run straight into Miller's arms. What had I done?

"James needed me," he said again. "I didn't want him to hurt himself. I couldn't leave him alone, even though he wouldn't even let me in his stupid house. I'm sorry. I'm so sorry." He pulled me closer like he was scared I'd disappear.

Part of me just wanted to forget everything. Drunk Matt was somehow even more endearing than sober Matt was. And clearly I wasn't strong. Because I was seriously considering dropping the whole subject without questioning him more. I tried to stop smelling his cologne so I could think straight. "What did you do with Rachel?"

"That's what I've been trying to tell everyone. She and James got in a fight at some dumb party this summer. And she came to me crying. I went to give her a hug because I hate when people cry. Baby, I hate when you cry." He pulled back and stared into my eyes. "I hate that I make you cry. I just want to make you happy." He reached out and ran his thumb beneath my eyes even though I wasn't crying.

"Matt, focus." I grabbed his hand. "What happened with Rachel after you hugged her?"

"She freaking kissed me. She kissed me and I pushed her away. But Wizzy must have seen. And she thought something else had happened. But I swear, Brooklyn. I didn't kiss Rachel back. I didn't sleep with her. I don't want anything to do with her. I love you. I've only ever loved you."

"Matt." My voice cracked.

"James hates me. He won't listen. And Rob believes him over me. I lost my best friends. I don't want to lose you too." He hiccupped. "I should have tried to explain it to you before I ran after James. But he's like a brother to me. And I didn't want to lose him. But I lost him anyway." He hiccupped again.

"I'm sure if you explained…"

"Explained what? That I didn't kiss his girl? Fuck that, he kissed mine. You're mine. He's not allowed to kiss you." Matt ran his thumb along my lower lip. "Mine."

My heart didn't stand a chance with him. "You swear you didn't sleep with Rachel?"

"Mine," he said again. It was like he was entranced by my lips.

"Matt, focus. You didn't sleep with James' girlfriend?"

He lowered his eyebrows. "No. Why does everyone keep saying that? Why does everyone think I'm a monster?"

"I don't think you're a monster."

"Yes you do. You don't answer my texts. I'm a monstrositor. Monstrocitini. No. That's not it." He snapped his fingers. "Monstrosity."

I didn't know whether to laugh or cry. He wasn't a monster. He'd gotten caught in Isabella's path just like I had. I didn't know how to explain the last week. I should have looked at my phone. But I was angry and hurt. "I was terrified living at the Pruitts'. And you disappeared on me. You didn't explain to me what happened. You just let me sit there thinking the worst. I thought you hadn't been keeping the secret to protect James. I thought you'd been keeping the secret to protect yourself. And you didn't care that you had to keep me a dirty little secret in the process."

"No. No." He grabbed both sides of my face. "Didn't you hear my song? You're not a dirty little secret. That was what the song was about. I should really sing it again…"

"Matt. You made me feel like one."

"No. No, that's not how you were supposed to feel. You're supposed to feel loved. Because I love you."

"I didn't feel loved. You acted like you loved me in private. But then whenever we were in public you treated me like nothing. Like I was invisible. No one should be treated the way you treated me. That wasn't love."

He breathed in and out slowly, tickling my skin with his breath. "I'll love you out loud then. I'll tell you all the things I love about you right now. I love how soft your hair is. And I love that you put me in my place when I'm an idiot. I love that you laugh at my jokes even if they're not funny." He laughed like his own comment was funny and then looked serious again. "I love playing football. And barbeques are great because of all the burgers. Wait, I'm supposed to be talking about you."

He took a deep breath. "I love the way you look at me. I love the way you look when you look at me…like your whole face lights up." He put his hand on my face, covering my eyes. "Oops." He removed his hand. "I think I probably look like that when I look at you too. And I love your skin." He ran the tip of his nose across my cheek. "It's even softer than your hair. And you always smell like fresh air. Even when it's hard to breathe in the city. I love that you don't care about money like everyone else in my life does. I love that you haven't asked me once what I want to be when I grow up. For the record, I want to take over my dad's company but he's going to give it to Mason. Which isn't really fair because I think I'd be really good at it. But I won't even get a chance. A few months ago I even did a SWOT analysis for why he should be doing more digital advertising than traditional print advertising. I made a stupid slide show and everything. And he told me he didn't have time to even see it. Digital advertising is the future and he doesn't believe in me enough to even hear me out."

God, Matt. He was rambling, but I didn't want him to stop. I wanted to know every confession he had. Drunk Matt was honest and talkative. Not angry.

"I love that you don't care about what other people think of you. Not even me. Especially not me when you're mad. I kinda even love when you're mad. Because you stare at me with all this heat in your eyes and it makes me hard. It's so hard to control myself around you because you're so beautiful. I love talking to you. And I love that you're wearing sneakers with your dress. It's cute but somehow fucking hot too. You look amazing."

I looked down at my Keds. He was the only one that noticed them all night. He was drunk. I knew that. But he still noticed things about me that no one else did. He saw me. He knew me. And he wasn't embarrassed of me. He was just worried about his friend. Ex-friend. He'd made a few mistakes, but I certainly had too.

"Does that answer your question?" he asked. "I don't remember what you asked. Did you even ask a question?" He laughed and put his chin on top of my head again. "Your hair smells so good."

"You've mentioned that."

He leaned forward, putting more of his weight on me. "I didn't like it when you kissed James. Can you please not do that again?"

"I promise I won't do it again."

"And you won't sleep with him, right? Because I've been waiting really impatiently to be your first. Do you know how often I have to take cold showers because of you?"

I laughed. "No, I don't."

"A lot. But I jerk off thinking about you more than that."

I swallowed hard. Drunk Matt was definitely honest. "A lot, huh?"

"Mhm." He moved his lips to my ear. "I need to tell you a secret. I don't think I mentioned this yet, but I'm a little drunk tonight."

"Oh you've mentioned it."

"Well that's not the secret. The secret is that it's okay if you want to take advantage of me. I won't press charges."

I laughed. "Maybe a different night. When you'll remember."

"Okay. I'll just dream of you again then. I dream of you a lot too. It's better than sheep." He laughed.

Did he mean counting sheep? He wasn't making any sense.

He leaned forward, putting more of his weight on me. *Oh my God, he's so heavy.* "Matt, I can't hold you."

"Just for a second."

"You're too heavy."

He giggled. "Oh no." He moved back and looked down at his perfect torso. "Is that why you don't want me? You think I'm fat?"

"What?" I couldn't help but laugh. "No. You're perfect."

"Then why are you torturing me?"

"I'm not trying to."

"Then why'd you dance with Felix right in front of me?"

That was a good point for a drunk person to make. "I'm sorry."

"I made one mistake, Brooklyn. I should have told James right away, but I was being stupid. Isabella got under my skin. But that doesn't mean I'm not allowed to be happy. That doesn't mean you aren't my forever. You are my forever. I know you are."

Of course he was allowed to be happy. And of course he was allowed to make mistakes. I'd certainly made a ton of them.

"I want to make a deal." He stuck out his hand for me. "No more secrets between us. Ask me anything," he said. "And I'll answer it." He grabbed my hand and shook it before I could decide.

"Okay, Matt."

"You didn't ask a question."

I'd already asked him all the questions I needed to. And I believed him. Rachel was clearly a mess, not that I was one to talk. Her relationship with James had to be toxic because James was toxic. And who knows. Maybe James was right. Maybe Rachel had thrown herself at Matt because all she cared about was money. And she was scared James was going to renounce his inheritance.

"Ask me anything," Matt said again.

"Why do you call Isabella Wizzy? What does it mean?"

He started laughing. "Wizzy?" He laughed even harder. "Oh you're going to like this. And she'd probably kill me for telling anyone. Actually, I think Mr. Pruitt's telling the truth. I don't think she can actually kill us."

"I hope so."

"Yeah, me too." He went to go put all his weight on me again, but I pressed my hand against his chest to stop him. He was going to knock me over.

"So what does Wizzy mean?"

He giggled. "Isabella peed in our pool during Mason's 12th birthday party." He put his hand over his mouth to help stifle the laughter. It didn't help and now I was laughing too.

"But how would you even know that she did? It's not like she pooped in the pool."

"We have that urine-indicator dye. It turned bright purple all around her. You should have seen her face. She tried to swim away and the purple followed her."

"Is that seriously a thing?"

"Yes!" He giggled. "Wizzy didn't know it existed either." He looked at me so seriously. "But now she does."

Wizzy because she whizzed in the pool. That was amazing. And maybe that information would somehow be useful whenever Isabella decided to torture me next. I looked over my shoulder at Kennedy and Isabella dancing.

"Hey." Matt turned my face back toward him. "Are we okay? I swear I don't have any other secrets."

I swallowed hard. Maybe he didn't. But I did. I stared into his eyes. He was drunk. He might not remember this. But I needed to tell him anyway. "When we weren't talking...I kind of started hanging out with someone else."

"Felix is dumb. Don't date him." He stuck out his tongue.

I laughed. "Not Felix."

"James is dumb too. He's the worst. He's not my friend anymore."

"Yeah." Matt was breaking my heart. He looked so sad when he said James wasn't his friend. "But it wasn't him either."

Matt made a farting noise with his mouth.

"Put that away, I'm trying to talk to you." I tapped on his tongue, which just made him lick my hand. "Matt!"

"Brooklyn!" he said in a high-pitched voice that probably matched my own.

I couldn't help it. I burst out laughing. Which just made him laugh too. Which somehow ended up with him pressing his lips to mine. For just a second we stood like that. Remembering what it felt like to be us. But then he proceeded to make the farting noise again against my mouth.

"Hey." Mason wrapped his arms around Matt's shoulders, pulling him away from me. "I think I should get you home before you start doing something embarrassing like making farting noises against your girlfriend's mouth." He winked at me.

"But I was just talking to Brooklyn. I need another minute."

"Trust me," Mason said. "You've probably done enough talking. Let's get you home."

Matt nodded. "Okay. I'll see you tomorrow, Brooklyn. Don't sleep with someone dumb tonight. I love you."

I laughed. "I love you too." The words fell out of me. I meant them. I did. I just wasn't sure why my chest ached when I said them.

Matt smiled at me over his shoulder as Mason walked him toward the ballroom doors. "You are not my dirty little secret!" he sang as Mason opened the door. Mason elbowed him in the ribs to make him stop which just made both of them laugh.

I wanted to go after them. I wanted to go to sleep in Matt's arms and tell him everything I'd done wrong. All the mistakes I'd made. I wanted a fresh start.

But Kennedy bumped into me, almost toppling us both over. I grabbed her to steady her on her feet. Mason would take care of Matt. And I needed to get Kennedy home. But where the hell was Miller?

CHAPTER 36

Saturday

"I'm sleepy," Kennedy said with a huge yawn. But she continued twirling in a circle. It looked like she was going to fall over.

"I know." I grabbed her around the waist to try to support her. "I think we should call it a night. Let's go find Miller so he can take us back to the Pruitts'." I looked over toward the doors. Seriously, had he gone on a walk or something? I thought he'd be right back.

"You can catch a ride with me, chicas," Isabella said. "Kennedy taught me that fun word."

Kennedy laughed. "The elephants are coming!"

"The elephants are coming!" Isabella yelled back.

What the hell do they keep going on about elephants for? It didn't make any sense. The elephants weren't even our mascot. I hated that Kennedy had an inside joke with Isabella. The thought of the two of them being friends made me feel sick to my stomach.

"I was just heading out anyway," Isabella said. "I pronounce this dance officially dead. Let's all go home and hang out there instead."

Hang out? As in the three of us? That sounded like my worst nightmare. Isabella had her own friends. Why was she trying to steal mine?

"Yes!" Kennedy said and stumbled forward.

Isabella grabbed the other side of her to keep her up straight.

"It's okay, Isabella," I said. "I got her. We're gonna go find Miller."

"Don't worry about Miller. Donnelley will drive us home. And I'll have him text Miller and let him know you're safe with me."

Safe and *Isabella* weren't two words that made sense in the same sentence. "I don't know…"

"Come on, it'll be fun," Isabella said and started walking toward the doors, dragging Kennedy and me with her. "We can stop for milkshakes. I know how much Kennedy loves milkshakes."

"Oh, I do love milkshakes!" Kennedy said. "They bring all the boys to the yard."

"That's one of my favorite songs!" Isabella said.

"Me too!" Kennedy squealed. "Kelis is a lyrical genius. I bet she's going to have a million more hits."

"Absolutely," Isabella said.

I hated this. I hated tonight. I hated the fact that I didn't know Kennedy loved milkshakes or Kelis songs. And that I didn't know what *the elephants are coming* meant. "Really," I said as we pushed through the ballroom doors. "We're just going to look for Miller. I'm sure he's here somewhere." I looked both ways down the hall, hoping Miller would just be leaning against one of the walls, but he was nowhere in sight.

"But milkshakes," Isabella said.

Kennedy turned toward me. "Please, Brooklyn. I really want a milkshake." She stuck out her bottom lip.

"And we rented a limo."

"A limo!" Kennedy looked so excited. "I've never been in a limo. Please, Brooklyn."

I'd been a terrible friend all night. The least I could do was let her get a milkshake. And maybe then she'd sober up and remember that Isabella was the worst. "Okay…"

"Yay!" She threw her arms up and almost fell over.

Isabella and I caught her before she could face plant on the marble floor. The three of us walked out into the chilly autumn night. Isabella's driver, Donnelley, had already pulled up to the front of the hotel. He was smoking a cigarette and it took a second for the puff of smoke to drift away from his face. He looked so sinister.

I really didn't want to do this. I looked around once more for Miller, but he wasn't out here either.

"This is so exciting," Kennedy said.

Exciting for her. Torture for me.

Donnelley tossed his cigarette on the ground and rubbed the heel of his shoe against it before opening the back door of the limo for us. Kennedy practically jumped through the door with a squeal of delight. Isabella followed her with a laugh.

"Will you text Miller and let him know I got a ride home with you instead?"

He didn't even bother to look at me. "Mhm." His voice sounded weirdly high-pitched like he was nervous.

"Are you okay?" I asked.

"What? Yeah, of course." He wiped a bead of sweat off his forehead, even though it was freezing out here.

"Are you sure? You seem nervous about something."

He laughed. "You try driving a huge limo in this city. It's a nightmare. I had to circle around the hotel like 5 times because I couldn't merge."

Oh, that made sense. "Yeah, I wouldn't want to drive it around either. I'm sorry about that."

He lowered his eyebrows as he looked at me. "Thanks."

I knew that look. It was the same one Justin gave me when I asked him what his goals were. And the same one Tiffany gave me when I thanked her for the food. Donnelley was underappreciated. The Pruitts didn't treat him like a human. I'd never be like them. "I'll try my best to keep them quiet back there. So we don't distract you."

"Thanks, I really appreciate that."

"No problem. Thanks for driving us home." I followed Kennedy into the back of the limo and Donnelley closed the door behind us.

Wow. I'd never been in a limo before either, and it was pretty awesome. There were lights along the roof of the limo and everything was glowing. There were even glasses of what looked like champagne sitting there ready for us. And strawberries. *Yum.*

Isabella's little demon dog, Sir Wilfred, jumped up on the seat beside me. He wagged his tail and looked up at me like he hoped I had treats. Had he been sitting in this limo all night? I reached out to pet him and was relieved when he didn't bite my hand off.

"We're going for milkshakes," Isabella said as Donnelley climbed into the front seat. The little separator between the front and back of the limo was down.

"I think I should just take you girls home," Donnelley said.

"No. We want milkshakes."

"But…"

"Milkshakes, Donnelley!" Isabella screamed.

"Isabella," I said. "Maybe we should just go home."

She stared at me like she was going to rip my face off when I said the word *home*. But it was just for a second. Her face morphed into a fake smile right away. "We can go home after we get milkshakes," she said loud enough for Donnelley to hear. "Give me one second, chicas." She went to the separator and started whispering at Donnelley. But it seemed a lot more like she was hissing at him.

"Mmm," Kennedy said as she lifted up a glass of champagne.

"I think that's enough alcohol for one night," I said and grabbed the glass out of her hand.

"You're no fun. Isabella's fun."

Ouch.

"We're all set," Isabella said as she sat down between me and Kennedy. "Milkshakes then home."

Great. They started talking about elephants again. I looked out the window at the busy city streets. Sir Wilfred nestled into my side. He actually looked kinda cute when he wasn't being a menace.

"Where are we getting milkshakes from?" I asked. The buildings were starting to get more spread out and more rundown. Surely there was a fast food place closer to our apartment.

"Oh there's a little local joint that I think you'll appreciate. I think it'll remind you of your real home."

Okay. She was being even weirder than usual. Kennedy snored.

I reached out to shake her awake. "Kennedy." It didn't seem like a good idea for her to be asleep without drinking gallons of water first.

"Don't bother," Isabella said. "She won't be waking up for roughly…five hours."

"What?" I climbed out of my seat. "Kennedy." I grabbed her shoulders. "Wake up." I shook her. *What the fuck is happening?* "Kennedy!"

Isabella laughed. "Tragic, isn't it? That someone like her could possibly ever believe that I would be friends with them? Like I'd ever be friends with a mutt."

God, you hateful bitch. I turned to face her. "What did you do?" I tried to keep my voice even, but I'm pretty sure it betrayed me.

She just laughed.

For a few minutes, I thought that she and Kennedy were actually friends. But Isabella wasn't capable of having real friendships. She was demonic. "What did you do to her?!"

Isabella brushed some unseen piece of lint off her shoulder. "I slipped something in her drink. And then learned just enough about her to manipulate her into getting you both in my limo with me tonight. You know…the usual."

Oh God. "Wh…why?" I hated how much my voice shook.

"You're about to find out, sillykins. That's half the fun, don't you think?"

The limo pulled to a stop.

I looked out the window. We were definitely in some kind of parking lot. I squinted and saw what looked like a rundown warehouse in the darkness. *Shit.*

"Now get the hell out of my car," Isabella said.

"What are you talking about? I'm not getting out here." I turned back to Kennedy. "Kennedy, wake up." I shook her harder, but her head just lolled forward. *Please, Kennedy. You're not a mutt. You're perfect. I'm sorry I was a bad friend tonight. But I love you. Wake up.*

"Get out of my limo, peasant."

Then I heard a noise that I'd only ever heard in movies. The sound of a gun being cocked.

It felt like my heart was beating in my throat. I turned to see a pink pistol pointed right at my forehead. *Oh my God, she really is going to kill me.* And it wasn't like she just picked up a random gun. It was pink. She owned the thing. Mr. Pruitt had to know she owned a gun. He knew what she was capable of and he still let her have a weapon?

I dropped Kennedy's shoulders. "Isabella…"

"Get out. Now."

I didn't want to leave Kennedy like this. But my brains getting blown out wouldn't exactly help anything. And it would be better if I got Isabella and her gun away from Kennedy. I backed up, my butt hitting the door. I felt behind me for the handle and pushed the door open.

Sir Wilfred whimpered as I climbed out of the limo, followed by Isabella. She slammed the door so her dog couldn't follow us.

"Just like home sweet home, yes?" Isabella said.

I didn't take my eyes off her. I got the point. We were standing in an abandoned lot surrounded by decaying buildings. But this was nothing like my home back in Delaware. Our house had been small, but it was beautiful and full of beautiful memories that a person like Isabella would never get to experience.

I looked at the limo. Why wasn't Donnelley doing something? He was supposed to be protecting both of us. Why was he letting this happen?

"Answer me," Isabella said. She lifted the gun a little higher.

"Yes, this is just like home." That was the answer she wanted right? "Because I'm garbage." I didn't believe the words I was speaking, but saying them out loud made me feel so small.

"Rotten. Disgusting. Hideous. Pathetic. Oh my God, are you crying?" She laughed.

I reached up to touch my cheek. I didn't realize I was crying. But the moisture on my cheeks proved otherwise.

"This is even better than I imagined. Now take it off."

I stared at her. "Take off what?"

"This isn't the time for sass, Sissy. Take it off."

I was pretty sure she was staring at the top of my head. The tiara. Of course that's what she wanted me to take off. My hands shook as I reached up to unpin it from my hair.

"Now!" she screamed, her voice echoing around the empty parking lot.

My fingers were still shaking, making it impossible to unpin fast enough. So I pulled the tiara, and did my best to stifle my scream as it tore out some hair with it.

"So much better. But I mean all of it."

I was clutching the crown in my hand. "What?"

"The dress. Take it off."

"Isabella…"

"It's as hideous as you. I'm doing you a favor." She took a step forward. "Or would you rather I kill you?"

I pushed the straps off my shoulders. And when she kept the gun pointed at my face, I reached around and tugged at the zipper. The dress fell to the ground, pooling at my ankles. I was standing there in my underwear, bra, and sneakers. The cold fall air bit at my exposed skin.

"Oh my God. Get rid of the shoes too."

My body was shaking. I wasn't sure if it was because of the cold or because I was terrified. Maybe it was both. But I couldn't take off my Keds. I couldn't let her take the last thing my mom had gifted me. "Please, Isabella."

"Take them off and maybe I'll let you live."

I swallowed hard. Isabella could destroy physical things. But she'd never be able to take away my memories. Unless she killed me. I slowly kicked my shoes off.

"Much better. Now do you want the good news or the bad news?"

I didn't want anything from her. I just stared at her.

"You're no fun." She backed up and tapped on the limo window.

Donnelley slowly climbed out of the car. He was holding a large cardboard box in his hands.

"Donnelley!" I said and took a step toward him.

"Don't even think about it," Isabella said. "Donnelley is on my side. Not yours. Isn't that right Donnelly?"

He didn't say a word. But he looked miserable. And so freaking guilty. I could tell he wasn't coming to my rescue tonight. Especially since he was looking at the ground instead of at me.

"So which is it, Sissy? The good news or the bad news?"

CHAPTER 37

Saturday

The good news or the bad news. This felt like a trick question. There was no way anything she was about to say was good. Maybe I could make her evil head explode. "The good news," I said.

"Splendid," Isabella said. "The good news is…I'm probably not going to kill you tonight. Even though I don't understand why, killing you would make Daddy very mad. And I don't want to make Daddy mad. So if you follow my instructions precisely, I suppose I'll allow you to live." She lowered the gun to her side and I felt like my lungs inflated with air for the first time in ages.

It was good news. Maybe. It kind of depended on what she was going to make me do.

"But the bad news is that you're leaving town." She grabbed something out of the box and walked over to me. "Here's a map." She tossed it onto the ground in front of me. "It's about 10 blocks to the nearest bus station. You can use the walk to clear your head. Sound good?"

I was literally in my underwear. She didn't even let me keep my shoes. And I didn't have any money. Not that they were going to allow my half-naked self into the terminal anyway. "Isabella…"

"I don't even care where you go. Just so that you're out of the city. Gone. Poof." She snapped her fingers.

"You can't just make me disappear."

"Of course I can."

Her ridiculous pink gun was still lowered to her side. She loved her dad. She didn't want to disappoint him. Which meant...she wasn't going to kill me. If she was, she already would have done it. Right? I took a deep breath. "No."

"Excuse me?"

"I'm not leaving."

A smile broke over her face. "Oh, I was actually hoping you'd say no." She took a few steps toward me. "Do you want to know why I'm doing this?"

"Because you're insane?"

"Oh Sissy, you're hilarious." She tapped the gun against her thigh. "You know the actual funny part of all of this? I did want a sibling when I was younger. We could have been friends. I could have at least tolerated you. But no. You sunk your claws into everyone and everything that's mine! You've been ruining everything!

"First you took Daddy. I don't know what you did to wrap your poor fingers around him, but you can't have him. I'm Daddy's princess. Not you. Daddy is mine."

Gross.

She took a deep breath. "And then with James..."

"Isabella, I'm sorry about kissing James. It didn't mean anything. We were just..."

"James is just another minuscule blip, you imbecile. You're not letting me finish!" She stared at me like I was the insane one. "I don't love James. You think I want to be someone's second choice? He doesn't love me. And I don't love him. His parents were in Daddy's debt. And James is smart and has a good future ahead of him. So they paid off the debt by offering me James' hand.

Whoa. What?

"And I'm going to marry him because Daddy says I have to. And I like making Daddy happy. But I still have four years until I'm supposed to do that. Four years to do whatever I want with whoever I want, as long as it's not in the public eye. Only four years to be free. And then you came in. And you ruined all my plans."

"Isabella, I have no idea what you're talking about."

"Matt."

"What about him?"

"I love him."

Oh my God. I remembered when she first started torturing me in school. I thought it was because I was staring at the Untouchables' table at lunch. But it was because I was staring at one Untouchable in particular. Matt. I thought about how she was blackmailing him with that made up sex scandal between him and Rachel. She used it as leverage so Matt couldn't hang out with me. She made her minions watch him in class. I thought about her death stare when Matt sang to me at the homecoming game. It was all about Matt the whole time.

"I love him," she said again. "So you need to leave."

But he doesn't love you back. Love doesn't work that way.

"I get him for the next four years because he's the one thing in my life I get to choose, and I choose him. Once you're gone, everything will be perfect. Matt will be mine.

And then once I have to marry James, I'll keep Matt as my house boy."

What the hell is a house boy? I didn't even want to know. "You don't get him for the next four years. You can't just say something and it becomes real."

"Yes I can. I'm a Pruitt."

"No you can't. Matt doesn't love you. He loves me. And I love him back." Apparently a conversation with a psychopath was all I needed to see everything clearly. Or maybe it was getting a gun pointed at my head. Or the freezing air against my exposed skin. But I saw it. I saw my future with Matt. And she couldn't have him for the next four years. Because he was mine forever.

"He's infatuated with you because you're new in town. It'll fade. Now grab your map and get lost."

"No."

"Are you sure you don't want to leave? Maybe this will help you decide." She walked over to the cardboard box and lifted out some kind of black device with wires and a timer on it. Another thing I'd only seen in movies. I was pretty sure it was a bomb.

I waited for her to throw it at me or something, but she just walked over to the limo and placed it on top. She pressed something on the side and the timer started ticking down from three minutes.

No. Kennedy!

Isabella turned back around. "If you don't leave in two minutes and 58 seconds, Kennedy will go boom."

"You can't. You're not allowed to kill people, Isabella. Your father told me the rules." I wanted to believe it. For some reason I did believe that she wouldn't kill me. But

Kennedy? I had no freaking idea what Isabella was capable of.

"There are ways around rules, Sissy. Accidental limo explosions are one of those ways. Besides, no one's going to miss her. For some reason it's so much more fun now that I got to know her first, you know what I mean?"

No, you crazy bitch! "Sir Wilfred is in there! You can't blow up your dog."

"Hmmm. Good point. But moot. I saw you pet him. Sir Wilfred is officially tainted. Besides, he's hardly trained. I'll just buy another."

"Donnelley, do something. Please."

Isabella laughed. "Oh, darling. You're crying again. Such a hot mess. And don't speak to Donnelley. He can't help you."

"Of course he can. Donnelley, please!"

"No, he can't," Isabella said a little sterner. "Donnelley here is from a very religious family. And do you know what I caught him doing a week ago? Making out with your new friend Justin in a closet." She laughed. "How fitting right? Since Donnelley is in the closet. And what on earth would his dear mother think if she found out he was batting for the wrong team?"

You horrible witch. All she knew was blackmail and hatred. I looked over at Donnelley. He was crying too. I could see it in his eyes. How sorry he was. But this wasn't his fault. None of this was his fault.

"Tick tock," Isabella said. "Only one minute left. What are you going to do?"

It wasn't a choice. I couldn't let Isabella kill my best friend. I couldn't let her out Donnelley. I couldn't even let her blow up her evil dog.

I picked up the map.

"Good girl. And don't worry. I'll take great care of Matt. Now disappear, trash goblin."

I pulled the map to my chest. I wanted something to come to me that would help me out of this mess. Something clever. But all I could think about was that I had to run. I had to save them.

A gust of wind made goosebumps rise all over my skin. The map blew out of my hands. I tried to grab it, but my feet slipped in a puddle. I fell to my knees, the water splashing all over me.

Isabella laughed.

I looked down at myself sitting in the puddle and I hated that I saw what Isabella saw. Trash. I couldn't think of a clever way out of this because I wasn't a scholarship student at Empire High. I was the janitor's niece. I never belonged here. All I'd done was broken the Caldwells and Hunters lifelong friendship, put my best friend's life in jeopardy, and ruined the last few months of my uncle's life. I'd been trying not to think about the last few months, but as soon as I did, it hit me like a ton of bricks. It didn't matter that Uncle Jim had reassured me otherwise. He still could have been doing anything in the world, but he gave up everything for me. And why? I stared at my hands in the muddy puddle. I was trash.

"Oh, and Sissy?"

I didn't turn to look at her. I didn't want her to see the tears streaming down my face. I didn't want her to know exactly how much she had won.

"If you ever come back to NYC, I'll shoot you in the face."

How had it come to this? Yes, I'd made mistakes, but I wasn't trash. It was just like Matt had said. Even people who made mistakes were allowed to be happy. I didn't want to have to leave without telling him that he was right. Right about that. Right about us. A sob escaped my throat.

Isabella's laughter pierced the autumn night.

And it was like the sound of it shook me out of my trance. Isabella was a monster. But I was half Pruitt. That meant that I was half monster too. It was in me some-where. I knew it was.

I took a deep breath and stood up. I tried to hide the fact that my body was shaking from the cold. I put one foot in front of the other, ignoring the pavement tearing at the soles of my feet. And I tried to keep my head held high even though her laughter tried it's best to cut me down.

I'd make it look like I was leaving NYC. But Isabella wasn't the queen. And I refused to bow down to her. As soon as I was sure Kennedy was safe, I'd be back. I would never let Isabella win. I would never let her break my spir-it. I would never let her hurt me like this again. I would never let her torture Matt. *Nunca.*

WHAT'S NEXT?

Betrayal (Empire High Book 3) is now available.

But before you read it...find out what Matt was thinking when he first met Brooklyn!

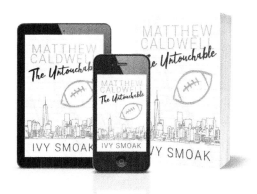

To get your free copy of Matt's point-of-view, go to:

www.ivysmoak.com/ehe-pb

A NOTE FROM IVY

I know what everyone's wondering - why is Brooklyn never mentioned again in The Hunted universe? And why is Matt single? Is this the answer? Maybe? You'll have to keep reading to find out!

I know, I know...I'm pure evil. And another cliffhanger? Seriously, Ivy? But I promise all will become clear soon. Afterall...this is Matt's story. I'm not sure I ever said it was Brooklyn's...

But I have another quick story for you right here right now. It's about my dedication for this book. Growing up I was terribly shy. I always tell my husband that I had an awkward stage between kindergarten and 12th grade. 100% accurate. And with a voice too shy to speak up for myself...it wasn't a great combination. So it was easy for me to write Brooklyn's character because as a little girl, I'd been through some of her struggles. Yes, Empire High is all about love, friendship, and betrayal. But it's also a story about bullying.

And the ironic part? While advertising book one of this series, I posted some pictures and videos of myself. Do you know what happened? Tons of comments telling me my hair looked terrible, that color looked bad on me, I should stick to writing and not be put in front of a camera. People laughing. Calling me names. Pointing at me. Hateful comments about my body to hateful comments about me as a person.

But guess what? I'm not that same little girl anymore. I've spent the years since school focusing on believing in myself. Several years ago, if I'd read one of those comments I would have burst into tears. But seeing them now?

I refuse to let people like that affect how I feel about myself. I will not let others shame me into silence. Even if their voices are louder than my own.

For all those people out there that have had to endure comments like that: Ignore the haters. Shake it off. Other peoples' opinions do not reflect who you are. There's no room for people like that in our lives. You are loved. You are brave. You are better than the trolls of this world.

And to all those hateful people out there like Isabella: I hope you one day find peace in a world that is too forgiving for you. Later, Wizzy.

P.S. Thank you to all the people that defended me. The Smoaksters will always bring each other up instead of tearing each other down.

Ivy Smoak
Wilmington, DE
www.ivysmoak.com

ABOUT THE AUTHOR

Ivy Smoak is the USA Today and Wall Street Journal best-selling author of *The Hunted Series*. Her books have sold over 3 million copies worldwide.

When she's not writing, you can find Ivy binge watching too many TV shows, taking long walks, playing outside, and generally refusing to act like an adult. She lives with her husband in Delaware.

Facebook: IvySmoakAuthor
Instagram: @IvySmoakAuthor
Goodreads: IvySmoak

Recommend *Elite* for your next book club!

Book club questions available at:
www.ivysmoak.com/bookclub

Printed in Great Britain
by Amazon